Stanley Brambles
and the Pirate's Treasure

Stanley Brambles
and the Pirate's Treasure

Owen Spendlove

iUniverse, Inc.

New York Lincoln Shanghai

Stanley Brambles and the Pirate's Treasure

Copyright © 2007 by Owen Spendlove

iUniverse books may be ordered through booksellers or by contacting:

iUniverse
2021 Pine Lake Road, Suite 100
Lincoln, NE 68512
www.iuniverse.com
1-800-Authors (1-800-288-4677)

This is a work of fiction. All of the characters, names, incidents, organizations, and dialogue in this novel are either the products of the author's imagination or are used fictitiously.

ISBN: 978-0-595-43792-4 (pbk)
ISBN: 978-0-595-88122-2 (ebk)

Printed in the United States of America

CHAPTER ONE:
THE LAST DAY OF SCHOOL

Stanley Brambles awoke one fine morning to the sun blazing in through his bedroom window. The birds were singing in the trees outside, announcing the start of a new day. Stanley yawned hugely and rubbed his eyes, before dragging himself out of bed. Looking out the window, he could see all the way down Bubbletree Lane. He always looked out of his window in the morning, and he always half hoped that he might see something new beyond the glass—maybe a jungle, or a volcano, or an alien spaceship landing in Mr. Jones's front yard two doors down.

But the view from Stanley's bedroom window was always the same. The same old street with the same old houses, the same old trees, and the same old playground down on the corner. "Bubbletree Lane," Stanley murmured to himself. "The most boring street in the most boring neighbourhood of the most boring town in the whole entire world."

It wasn't that East Stodgerton (the town in which Stanley lived) was a bad town, or a nasty town, or even a dreary town; it was just so *ordinary*. People just got up and did the same old thing, day after day! They went to work, or school, or *whatever*, and then they went home for a while, just so they could get ready to do it all over again the next day. There seemed to be no end to the monotony, and Stanley was getting tired of it.

His mood improved substantially, though, as he remembered what day it was—*it was the last day of school before the summer holidays*. The summer holidays were one of his favourite things, even if he did have to spend them in boring old East Stodgerton.

Stanley went into the bathroom across the hall to do his morning business. As he washed his hands, he regarded himself in the mirror. He was an ordinary-looking kid, which, he supposed, was to be expected when one lived in an ordinary town like East Stodgerton. Kids in big cities had cool clothes, and wild hair with crazy colours, and weird piercings—like in their *noses!*

But no, none of that for Stanley Brambles. He was an ordinary kid; twelve years old (going on thirteen in July), with brown hair and blue eyes. He was fairly thin, of average height for his age, and possessed no remarkable features of any kind. Just one more kid from East Stodgerton.

As was his custom, Stanley stumbled downstairs skipping every second step, and thundered into the kitchen where Mrs. Brambles was bustling around trying to eat her breakfast, make Stanley's lunch, and stuff a stack of essays into a bulging briefcase. Mrs. Brambles was a professor at the local university. Stanley sometimes wondered how a rinky-dink little town like East Stodgerton had gotten itself a university; but then again, maybe universities were just extremely common.

"Morning, Stanley dear," said Mrs. Brambles with a smile as Stanley plunked himself down at the table. She shoved a plate of toast and an empty cereal bowl under his nose.

"Morning, Mom," said Stanley, pouring himself some Rice Krispies.

"All ready for the end of school?" Mrs. Brambles asked, tousling his hair.

"Um-hum" said Stanley, his mouth full of cereal. Mrs. Brambles smiled, then looked at her watch.

"Well, I've got to run, have a good day, love," she said, leaning over and kissing Stanley on the cheek.

"'Bye Mom," he called as she swept out of the room and down the hall, shoes clunk-clunk-clunking all the while. The door slammed shut and a moment later there was an "EGAD, LOOK AT THE TIME!" from the upper floor, followed by the sound of Stanley's father falling down the stairs in a mad rush. He poked his head into the kitchen and looked around uneasily.

"Morning, Stanley," he said breathlessly. "Was that Mom leaving just now?"

Stanley nodded. "Yeah, Dad, she just—"

"Can't talk now, son!" said Mr. Brambles as he ran down the hall and flung the front door open.

Stanley listened to his father shouting out the door.

"*Rose! Wait!*" Cried Mr. Brambles, and the next instant he was out the door. Stanley got up and hurried to the front window. The family car was halfway down the street, with Mr. Brambles running after it. He was still in his pyjamas. The car screeched to a halt, then sped back towards the house in reverse. Mrs. Brambles hadn't stopped to let Mr. Brambles in. He was now sprinting back up the street, arms flailing wildly. He stopped beside the now stationary vehicle, apparently listening to Mrs. Brambles shouting at him, then nodded vigorously and ran up the driveway. The door swung open and in bounded Mr. Brambles, followed closely by Mrs. Brambles' shouts.

"… HAVE TIME TO GET DRESSED!" she shrieked. "IMAGINE, RUNNING DOWN THE STREET IN YOUR BEST PYJAMAS! GET DRESSED, YOU RIDICULOUS MAN!"

"Everything all right, Dad?" said Stanley as his father leaped for the stairs. Mr. Brambles gave him the 'thumbs up', but he looked slightly shaken. Three minutes later, he was downstairs again, buttoning his shirt.

"I'll have to put this on in the car," he said sheepishly, holding up a hideous green and orange striped tie. "Well, g'bye again, Stanley," he said as he headed for the door.

"Dad, wait!" said Stanley.

"Sorry son, no time! See you tonight!"

And the door slammed shut. Stanley groaned; Mr. Brambles was still wearing his pyjama pants.

The ordeal finally ended when Stanley fetched his father's pants for him and flung them out the door as he came back to get them. Mr. Brambles barely had time to get back in the car before Mrs. Brambles hit the gas pedal and sped off down the street. Stanley saw his father's leg sticking out the window as the car turned the corner at an alarming angle.

"Whew," breathed Stanley as he sat back down to his breakfast. Bruno, the family dog padded into the kitchen and put his head on his lap. "That's the most excitement I've had all month." Bruno rolled his eyes.

Mr. Brambles was the curator of the East Stodgerton Museum of Natural History, and he hadn't been on time for work for the past twelve years. Luckily, all the other museum workers arrived an hour later than he did. Mr. Brambles blamed the buses for his lateness, saying that they never left at an appropriate time. He didn't seem to notice that having Mrs. Brambles drive him to work didn't help much, and if she suggested that he get up earlier, he would quickly change the subject.

Stanley finished his breakfast and took a quick look at the morning paper (mostly the comics), then picked up his backpack, said goodbye to Bruno, and headed out the door and down the street. He stopped on the corner and waited. Several minutes later, someone rounded a corner two blocks away, and, upon seeing Stanley, began to jog towards him. The someone was a tall, thin boy with dark hair and pale skin.

"Hey, Stanley," the pale boy said brightly as he skidded to a halt.

"Hey, Alabaster," Stanley replied.

"How's it going?" said the pale boy named Alabaster.

"Good," said Stanley. "You?"

"Good," said Alabaster. "Well, shall we go?" And with that, the two of them turned and began to walk down the street.

Alabaster Lancaster (for so the pale boy was named) was Stanley's best friend, and had been for as long as either of them could remember. Alabaster was probably the least ordinary person Stanley knew. He was always doing and saying funny things, and, frankly, he seemed a bit out of place in East Stodgerton. Mr. and Mrs. Lancaster were both archaeologists, and sometimes had to go away for a long time on a dig. During these times, Alabaster would stay with the Brambleses and cause Stanley's mother no end of grief. Mr. Brambles didn't seem to have a problem with Stanley's and Alabaster's hijinx; he said (out of their earshot, of course) that he found them very entertaining, and would reminisce about his boyhood days any time Mrs. Brambles scolded them.

*   *   *   *

The last day of school before summer is often a fun and relaxing day for students. *Often*, but not always. Every teacher at Babblebrook Public School threw an end-of-the-year party for their class … every teacher, that is, except for Mrs. Drabdale, the meanest teacher in the entire school, if not the world. *She* made her class write essays about their summer plans. As the report card marks had already been put into writing, nobody took this assignment very seriously. Alabaster, in fact, wrote something rather rude in his essay, concerning what he was going to leave on Mrs. Drabdale's front doorstep one night. When she read his essay, she flew into a fantastic rage, but Alabaster had already escaped by way of an open window. Mrs. Drabdale turned a violent shade of red, and stormed out of the classroom in a futile attempt to catch Alabaster before he got off school property. The rest of the students took this as an early dismissal, and minutes later had burst through the front doors of Babblebrook Public School, and into the waiting arms of summer.

Many of them simply threw their book bags aside and sprawled full-length on the front lawn. Stanley found Alabaster hiding in a bush, and congratulated him on his command of the written word. Alabaster laughed, and the two boys looked back at the school building, raised their arms to the heavens, and loudly recited that timeless end-of-school rhyme:

"NO MORE PENCILS, NO MORE BOOKS! NO MORE TEACHERS' DIRTY LOOKS! WHEN THE PRINCIPAL RINGS THE BELL, DROP YOUR BOOKS AND RUN LIKE—"

"*Hello, boys,*" said a familiar voice, as a menacing shadow fell across the sidewalk.

It was Mrs. Drabdale, and a look of cold triumph burned in her eyes.

"Leaving so soon?" she inquired, smiling wickedly as she loomed over them like a gnarled old willow tree. Stanley and Alabaster took an uncertain step backward.

"Thought you'd make a nice joke out of my end-of-year assignment, hmm?" she said, her smile swiftly changing into a grimace, "Couldn't resist one last bit of tomfoolery?

"Well," she said, rolling up her sleeves, "Forgive me for saying so, but you two will *not* be leaving now. You will remain in class until the three o'clock dismissal bell, as you were *meant* to do. Come with me."

The situation was looking very bad to Stanley, and he could think of only one way out. He elbowed Alabaster, and said,

"On three?"

"On three!" said Alabaster.

"What?" said Mrs. Drabdale, her monstrous grimace faltering slightly.

"One," said Stanley.

"Two," said Alabaster.

"Enough foolishness!" is what Mrs. Drabdale *would* have said, but she was interrupted as both boys yelled, "THREE!" and ran off as fast as their legs could carry them.

Mrs. Drabdale made a noise of shock and disgust before bellowing, "COME BACK HERE, YOU HOODLUMS! I'M NOT AFRAID TO GIVE YOU A DETENTION—NOT EVEN TODAY!"

Then she did something most astonishing: she ran after them. The two boys were just starting to slow, when Alabaster glanced over his shoulder and gave a cry of dismay. Stanley looked back, too, only to see a red-faced Mrs. Drabdale bearing down on them like a bull.

"Faster!" Stanley shouted.

"Is she allowed to do this?" gasped Alabaster.

"Just keep running!"

They were almost to the fence that encircled the school grounds, but it was dishearteningly low. Stanley feared that at the pace Mrs. Drabdale was going, she would clear it in a single bound. The boys vaulted flawlessly over the fence and made a beeline for the ravine that lay beyond the school property.

There was a loud *rip* and thud, and Stanley risked a quick glance over his shoulder. His heart sank. Mrs. Drabdale had indeed cleared the fence, but she had ripped her skirt in the process. She was, however, not deterred. If anything, her fury over her ripped skirt gave her new vigor; she was catching up.

Stanley's chest was starting to hurt, his lungs begging him to stop. "Just a little further," he kept muttering. All of a sudden, Alabaster shouted "RIGHT!" and ran off into the shadowy ravine. Stanley followed unthinkingly. Alabaster leapt across the stream and ran alongside it. Stanley followed suit, and was very surprised when a thundering crash and splash rang out behind him. Mrs. Drabdale, who had been inches away from catching him, had slipped on the muddy bank at the last possible second, and was now writhing and spluttering in the shallow stream. Stanley might have laughed had he not been so terrified.

Finally he came to the stream's mouth, a smallish culvert which ran under Butter Street. He paused to catch his breath, wondering what had become of Alabaster. Suddenly, he was aware of a sound like a bear crashing through the trees. This was no bear, however. This was much worse. It was Mrs. Drabdale. She was soggy, she was muddy, and she was furious. With a howl of rage and triumph, she charged at Stanley, who backed up against the culvert and closed his eyes.

Just then, a hand reached out of the culvert mouth and dragged Stanley inside, just as Mrs. Drabdale reached the spot where he'd been standing. The hand, of course, belonged to Alabaster.

"You alright, Stanley?" he puffed.

"Yeah," said Stanley, giving Alabaster a high five.

Mrs. Drabdale, whose rage had exceeded all known human limits, was trying frantically to get at them, but she was just too large to squeeze in.

"Let's get out of here," said Stanley, casting a slightly fearful look at Mrs. Drabdale.

"Yes, let's!" wheezed Alabaster.

They crawled to the other end of the culvert, listening to Mrs. Drabdale's shouts and threats all the while.

"*You just wait till next year!*" She shrieked. "*You two will rue the day you ever crossed* my *path!*" And then she was gone.

Stanley and Alabaster hopped out of the culvert and looked around. They were behind the local supermarket, and the sounds of people walking and talking were very reassuring to both of them. Stanley flopped down on the ground, breathing heavily. Alabaster did the same.

"That," gasped Alabaster, "was the most frightening thing I've ever experienced."

Stanley nodded.

The two boys lay there for a time, panting like dogs, until Stanley sat up and noted that they were both exceedingly filthy. He turned to Alabaster and said,

"Uh, maybe we should go home and get cleaned up."

Alabaster sat up and examined his white T-shirt, which was now brown. "I think I'm going to have to agree."

CHAPTER TWO:
THE PROPOSAL

When Stanley's mother and father came home that evening, they gave him a stern talking-to about his escapades of earlier on.

"Imagine!" said Mrs. Brambles, "Crawling through a culvert! I don't know *what* you were thinking … and your clothes! Ruined!"

Stanley had been very careful not to mention *why* he and Alabaster had crawled through the culvert.

"Now now, Rose," said Mr. Brambles, "I'm sure he had a perfectly good reason for climbing through that filthy hole. It could have been worse!"

"Oh, I know, it's alright," said Mrs. Brambles in a softer tone. "At least you weren't hurt, Stanley, dear … I do wish you'd be more careful though."

"I'll try, Mom," said Stanley, giving her a big hug.

"That's my boy," said Mr. Brambles, clapping him on the shoulder. "Now let's get dinner on, shall we?"

✻   ✻   ✻   ✻

Stanley was just digging into his mashed potatoes and roast beef, when Mr. Brambles said,

"Son, there's something your mother and I have been meaning to talk to you about."

Stanley froze. Had Mrs. Drabdale called and told his parents what had happened earlier? She wouldn't ... not on the last day of school ... *would she?*

"Er, uh, what about, Dad?" said Stanley, trying to conceal the cold sweat which had broken out on his forehead.

"Well," said Mr. Brambles, not noticing Stanley's perspiration, "It's about the summer holidays."

Stanley's eyes widened as a horrible thought entered his mind. Mrs. Drabdale had told them everything, and now his parents were canceling his summer vacation. He would have to go back to school for the rest of the summer, to be taught by Mrs. Drabdale in a dark, dank, windowless classroom.

Stanley gripped the edge of the table, his fingernails digging into the polished wood surface. "Wh-what about the summer holidays?" he asked nervously.

"How would you like to spend a couple weeks at Uncle Jack's place?" said Mr. Brambles with a big smile.

Stanley, who had closed his eyes to prepare for the worst, was stunned for a moment and couldn't speak. Mr. Brambles' smile faltered.

"It'd only be for two weeks now, son, and besides—"

Stanley came back to his senses. "Uncle Jack?"

"Well, he's actually your great uncle, of course," said Mrs. Brambles. "You remember him, don't you?"

Stanley remembered him, alright. It had been a few years since he'd come to visit, but it wasn't easy to forget someone like Uncle Jack. He was a loud, jolly old fellow, full life and energy, and great fun to be around. Stanley's earliest memory of Uncle Jack, was being curled up beside him in the big easy chair in the living room, while the old man read to him from a huge and ancient-looking volume of *Treasure Island.*

Uncle Jack was a fanatic about all things nautical, pirates in particular. When Stanley got a bit older, Uncle Jack would take him to the East Stodgerton Old Time Theatre to see old black-and-white pirate movies like *Captain Blood.*

Some time ago, Stanley's family had gone on a trip to Disney World. Uncle Jack had come along, too, and to this day, Stanley's mother insists that between herself, Mr. Brambles, Stanley, and Uncle Jack, she had been the only adult there. They had all had a wonderful time, but Uncle Jack kept insisting that they go on the *Pirates of the Caribbean* ride. They ended up going on the ride eleven times, and Mrs. Brambles was getting *very* tired of it. Stanley remembered looking around and noting, with no small amount of surprise, that Uncle Jack was no longer with them in the boat. He pointed this out to his parents, and there was a brief period of confusion, but they soon found the old man sitting serenely at a table in one of the tavern scenes, surrounded by animatronic pirates.

That little stunt had nearly gotten them thrown out of the park, but it was easily the funniest thing Stanley had ever seen.

"You're remembering that time at Disney World, aren't you?" said Mrs. Brambles, noticing the big grin on Stanley's face.

Stanley and his father laughed out loud at this.

"Now *that* was a good trip," said Mr. Brambles, wiping a tear from his eye. "And Jack, sitting there with a pipe in his teeth, waving at everyone as they went by—"

"Ugh," said Mrs. Brambles, "I've never been so embarrassed."

"And then they turned around and offered him a job!" laughed Mr. Brambles. "I still say he should've taken it. He would've been fantastic! I mean, who better to *play* a pirate than the *real thing?*"

Mrs. Brambles rolled her eyes and sighed loudly. Stanley put a hand over his mouth to hide his grin. He knew what was coming.

"Robert," said Mrs. Brambles, gritting her teeth, "if I have to hear your theory about my dear, kind old *law-abiding* uncle one more time—"

"I'm not saying he was a villainous, pillaging buccaneer," said Mr. Brambles, gesturing with his palms up. "If anything, knowing Jack, I'd say he robbed from the rich and gave to the poor, and all that."

Mr. Brambles was convinced that Uncle Jack was, in fact, a real pirate, and he'd shared his theory with Mrs. Brambles many times before, much to her aggravation. For his part, Stanley had always thought there was something a little out of the ordinary about his great uncle, but didn't really know him well enough to agree or disagree with his father. He did know, however, that there hadn't been any swashbuckling, treasure-burying cutlass-wielding pirates in the world for a long, long time. To him, the idea of Uncle Jack being a pirate was little more than an interesting fantasy. Mr. Brambles thought otherwise.

"But it would all make such perfect sense," Mr. Brambles was saying.

"I don't want to hear it!" said Mrs. Brambles.

"But there's so much evidence!" Mr. Brambles countered, ignoring her. "I don't know where he got the money to buy that house of his—"

"It was probably cheap," said Mrs. Brambles sensibly. "No one in their right mind would spend heaven knows how many hundreds of thousands of dollars to live alone in a huge old place like that."

Mr. Brambles was still not paying attention. "And he had that parrot, the peg-leg, that old ship's wheel mounted on the wall …"

Mrs. Brambles had had more than enough of this conversation, and showed it by snapping, "*That will do, Robert!* He lost the leg in the war, bought the parrot at a pet shop, and the wheel at a flea market, and that goes for any other bits of nautical junk he's accumulated over the years! It's a hobby, and he's a sweet old man, not some filthy buccaneer!"

Mr. Brambles finally got the hint that that branch of conversation was closed. The three of them were silent for a time, and then Mrs. Brambles said,

"So, what do you think, Stanley dear? Would you like to visit Uncle Jack? He'd very much like to see you again."

"He would?"

"Oh yes, he phoned just a few days ago, in fact. He talked about taking you fishing, and sailing … he lives right by the sea, it'll be fun."

The idea did sound like fun, and Stanley reflected that he had never been to Uncle Jack's house; Uncle Jack had always been the one to come visit *them*. A thought suddenly popped in to his mind. "Wait," he said, "Er, what about you guys? You'll be coming too, right?"

Mr. and Mrs. Brambles exchanged a look that Stanley couldn't decipher.

"Well, about that, dear," Mrs. Brambles began.

"The thing is, son," interrupted Mr. Brambles, "Well, you see, the Lancasters are doing a joint project with the museum. They're supervising a dig down in Costa Rica, and they asked us to, ah, come along for part of it."

"Well why can't I come with you?" asked Stanley.

"We'll be working the entire time, dear," said Mrs. Brambles. "It'll be very difficult for us to look after you, and you'd be bored before the end of the first day." Mr. Brambles nodded in agreement.

To Stanley, an archaeological dig in Costa Rica suddenly sounded like much more fun than fishing with Uncle Jack. "I don't think I'd get bored," he said for lack of a more convincing argument.

"Trust me," whispered Mrs. Brambles, "If *I'd* get bored, *you'd* get bored."

"Did you say something, dear?" said Mr. Brambles.

"No, darling," said Mrs. Brambles, "I was just about to mention Alabaster—"

"Alabaster?" Stanley echoed.

"Oh, yes, of course," said Mr. Brambles. "Alabaster will accompany you to Uncle Jack's house. It'll be nice to have a friend along, won't it?"

"Alabaster's coming?" said Stanley. That certainly put a new spin on things. Having Alabaster along would definitely make the trip more fun. "Well," he said after a moment's thought, "I … suppose … yeah, sure, I'll go visit Uncle Jack."

"Splendid!" said Mr. Brambles.

"Make sure you spend time with Uncle Jack, though," said Mrs. Brambles, "Don't you two go running off without a word to him."

"Of course not, Mom," said Stanley, who was getting rather excited over the prospect of going sailing on a real boat, even if it *wasn't* a pirate ship.

*   *   *   *

Early the next morning, the Lancasters arrived on the Brambleses' doorstep, ready for the voyage ahead. Stanley, who was already up and packed, answered the door.

"Morning, Stanley, m'boy," said Mr. Lancaster.

Mr. Lancaster was tall and pale. He looked like Alabaster, only less gangly, and with glasses.

"Hi, Mr. Lancaster, Mrs. Lancaster," said Stanley, ushering them in.

"Hello, Stanley," said Mrs. Lancaster, who was a head shorter than Mr. Lancaster, dark-haired, and very pretty.

The Lancasters were dressed in khaki shirts and shorts. Mr. Lancaster was wearing an absurd pith helmet with a metal spike on top. Mrs. Lancaster had a much more reserved Tilly hat.

"Arthur! Guenevere! Good morning to you!" said Mr. Brambles heartily as he came down the stairs. He was dressed in much the same manner as the Lancasters, only he had navy blue socks pulled up to his knees, and no hat. His face fell when he caught sight of Mr. Lancaster's pith helmet. "Oh, Arthur, wouldn't you know it, I thought of everything but head gear!"

"Not to worry, Robert old boy, I came prepared!" Mr. Lancaster produced a pith helmet identical to his own from inside his voluminous backpack, and Mr. Brambles' face lit up when he saw it.

"Cheers!" he said, putting it on.

Mrs. Brambles had by now come downstairs as well, dressed in a navy blue shirt and shorts, with her own Tilly hat on her head. She exchanged an exasperated look with Mrs. Lancaster upon seeing the obnoxious pith helmets, then gave her own good mornings.

Stanley went outside to look for Alabaster, and found him kneeling on the lawn, apparently searching for something.

"Morning, Alabaster," said Stanley.

"Morning, Stanley," said Alabaster. "Aw, nuts, I've lost it! I—Oh, wait, here it is!"

"What have you got?" asked Stanley.

Alabaster held up an eyepatch. "It's for when we join your uncle's pirate crew. It'll be great! We can go sailing, dig for treasure, raid coastal villages ..."

Stanley laughed. "Er, sorry, Alabaster, but I don't think we're going to be engaging in any piracy while we're at Uncle Jack's place."

Alabaster looked confused. "But my Dad said *your* Dad said—"

"I'll explain in the car," said Stanley.

*   *   *   *

They all piled into the Lancasters' huge van and, after several trips back to both houses to pick up things that had been forgotten (Mr. Brambles' suitcase, for example), sped off down the road, waving goodbye to their neighbourhood.

The Lancasters had insisted on coming along to drop off Stanley and Alabaster, after which they and the Brambleses were to drive back to East Stodgerton, hop on a plane at the airport, and be off to Costa Rica, lickety-split.

The drive to Westport was a long one, and Stanley soon finished explaining to Alabaster that Uncle Jack wasn't really a pirate. Alabaster looked a bit put out by this, but was soon back to chattering about all the things they might do if *they* were pirates, and Stanley found that there was a lot to talk about.

They had just finished arguing over what the most disgusting sea creature was (they agreed on the giant squid), when the van rounded a hill and there, in all its glory, stood the sea. Stanley had never seen the sea before in real life (not that he could remember, at any rate), and the nature programs on television simply didn't do it justice.

Vast and blue it was, shimmering in the sunlight, stretching left and right as far as the eye could see. Stanley gaped at its crystalline beauty, and the power it exuded as the waves pounded the shore. Nothing could be seen in the distance; nothing but shining blue, all the way to the horizon. Stanley was still staring open-mouthed as they drove into the sleepy seaside town of Westport.

CHAPTER THREE: UNCLE JACK

The van wound its way through the streets of Westport, which looked as if they belonged in a different time. Ancient-looking buildings huddled closely together on either side of the cobbled streets, while old folks sat out front, enjoying the early afternoon sunshine.

"There sure are a lot of old people here," Stanley commented as they passed the *Shark's Head Inn*, which was crowded with codgers and gaffers of every description.

"Popular retirement community," said Mr. Brambles distractedly. He was looking at the street signs as they scrolled by. "Ah, here it is, turn here, Arthur."

Mr. Lancaster made a very sharp left turn onto a street called Hammerhead Drive. Unlike the main street, Hammerhead Drive was poorly maintained and terribly bumpy. The road continued all the way down to the town docks, where a great many boats were moored. The van was shaking so badly that Stanley feared it would fall to pieces. All of a sudden, Mr. Lancaster made another sharp turn, this time to the right, and the van immediately stopped shaking. They were now traveling up a long, long driveway of smooth asphalt, which went straight up a nearby hill. At the top of the hill stood a magnificent house, overlooking the sea.

"Wow!" exclaimed Stanley.

"What a house!" said Alabaster.

As the van pulled up in front of the palatial dwelling, the huge oak doors flew open and out came an old man with a shortish, scraggly beard. The top of the man's head was bald, and what hair he did have was wild and uncombed, giving him a wind-blown look. His face, which was wrinkled and leathery-looking, was drawn up in a wide and jolly grin. Stanley hadn't seen him for a few years, but there was no mistaking his Great Uncle Jack.

"Welcome, welcome!" he said in a gruff but friendly voice as his guests got out of the van, "How nice to see my relatives again, not to mention my relatives' distinguished friends!"

He shook hands with the Brambleses and the Lancasters, then approached Stanley and Alabaster. He walked with a pronounced limp.

"And here's Stanley!" the old man said, shaking his hand vigorously. "My, but you've grown! I hardly recognized you! It's good to see you again, m'boy. And *you* must be Stanley's friend," he said, turning to Alabaster. "What's your name, m'lad?"

"A-Alabaster, sir," stammered Alabaster, who seemed a tad frightened of Uncle Jack's loud voice.

"Alabaster, it's a pleasure to meet you," said Uncle Jack, now shaking Alabaster's hand. "We'll have a fine time, we will. Now, come in, come in!" he said, gesturing towards the open doors, "You're all just in time for a late lunch."

Stanley and Alabaster retrieved their suitcases from the van and followed everyone inside. The mansion's interior was ten times as magnificent as its exterior. The entrance hall was a vast, circular chamber with a red carpet. A marble staircase climbed up to the second and third floors, and a colossal chandelier hung from the domed roof high above. Beautiful paintings, all of which looked very old and expensive, decorated the walls, and Uncle Jack, noticing that his guests were gawking around with their mouths hanging open, said,

"Welcome, everyone, to my humble abode. You may find it a trifle gaudy, but it suits *my* taste just fine."

He folded his arms across his chest and stood silently watching them, as if expecting someone to say something.

Stanley paid no attention to what Uncle Jack had just said; he was staring, transfixed, at another decoration that no one else had noticed. It was at the top the stairs, on the second floor landing, mounted high on the wall: the stuffed head of a ghastly fish, although it was unlike any fish Stanley had ever seen. For one thing, it was much bigger. Its jaws, which were open in an endless hungry snarl and lined with razor-sharp teeth, could have easily bitten the Lancasters' van in two. Its head was rounded and shiny, as if protected by a thick armoured shell, and its bowling ball-sized eyes glared fiercely down upon the entrance hall. Stanley knew they had been replaced by fake glass eyes, but he couldn't help feeling slightly uneasy as he met the fish's lifeless gaze. He shivered, then glanced over at Uncle Jack, who gave him an odd look.

"Merciful heavens!" exclaimed Mr. Brambles, noticing the giant fish head, "That appears to be a specimen of a Dinichthys of the order Arthrodira, class Placodermi!"

Stanley had no idea what 'Dinichthys', 'Arthrodira', or 'Placodermi' meant, but they sounded like appropriate words for describing a monster like the one on the wall.

"You certainly know your fish, Robert," said Uncle Jack with a laugh, "Although I've always just called them *armour fish*."

Mr. Brambles was almost giddy with excitement. "Oh yes, I do, we have an excellent ancient seas exhibit at the museum … we have one of those, of course, but it's not nearly as big as … that wasn't there the last time we were here! Where on earth did you get it? The Dinichthyidae have been extinct for millions of …" he trailed off, and Uncle Jack spoke up as Mr. Brambles paused to draw breath.

"Oh, I've had it in storage for many years now … stumbled across it in the attic, and thought I'd put it back up on display. It's an excellent conversation piece."

"But is it … is it *real*?" asked Mr. Brambles breathlessly.

"Oh, very much so," said Uncle Jack.

"But where … where did you get … how could you possibly have … in such good condition … extinct!" Mr. Brambles looked as if he were about to faint. Mrs. Brambles was standing behind him, ready to catch him if he did.

"I procured it on one of my many trips," said Uncle Jack vaguely. "It was very costly, mind you, but sometimes you see something that just *grabs* your attention, and you simply *have* to have it." He was looking up at the fish triumphantly. Everyone was silent for a moment (except Mr. Brambles, who was still babbling about the fish), and then Uncle Jack said, "Well, who's for lunch?"

*   *   *   *

The mansion's dining room was almost as impressive as its entrance hall. The floor was a shiny black marble, and large white pillars ran up the walls to a vaulted ceiling, which was adorned with a beautiful painting depicting an armada of ships sailing on a choppy sea. Between each of the pillars on the west side of the room were tall windows which looked out over the ocean; on the opposite wall were paintings of distinguished gentlemen and pretty ladies, all in Victorian-style dress. Also decorating the walls here and there were more specimens of stuffed marine life, though none of these was as large or as ghastly as the one in the front hall.

"I don't keep the ugly ones in the dining room," said Uncle Jack, as Stanley admired a three-foot long fish with scales the colour of a night sky. "I find they take away people's appetite."

Stanley stared at Uncle Jack for a moment, unable to tell if he was joking or being serious. Were there more monster-fish heads elsewhere in this house? He gave a small, uncertain laugh, and was relieved to see Uncle Jack smile.

They were all seated at a long, polished mahogany table in high-backed chairs with red velvet padding. Stanley was surprised to see that words had been written underneath the table's flawless finish.

"The western wave was all aflame, The day was well nigh done! Almost upon the western wave, Rested the broad bright sun," Stanley read aloud. It seemed to be a poem, and it went all the way around the table.

"*Rime of the Ancient Mariner*," said Uncle Jack, before Stanley could ask, "A fine poem ... by Coleridge, I believe. You should read it sometime."

Just then a door towards the back of the room swung open and a tall, broad-shouldered man with deep brown skin and a shaved head swept into the room carrying a silver tray with a cover over it, like the kind you might see in a fancy restaurant. The large man beamed at the guests as he gently set the tray down on the table. Uncle Jack stood up and said,

"Thank you kindly, Benjamin," then faced the table and said, "I'd like you all to meet my dear friend of many, many years, Benjamin Stone."

Benjamin smiled warmly and shook everyone's hand. Stanley was surprised that although the big man's hands looked strong enough to crush rocks, his grip was very gentle. He didn't say anything, though, which seemed a bit odd.

Benjamin lifted the tray cover and a delicious smell wafted out. Around the outside of the tray were placed seven bowls of steaming, creamy soup, and in the middle, seven bright red lobsters were elegantly displayed. The guests gasped at the presentation. Uncle Jack was laughing, and said,

"Benjamin, I don't know why you go to all this trouble!"

Benjamin just grinned and shrugged.

"Really, my friend," said Uncle Jack, "Do stay and eat with us, won't you?"

Benjamin shook his head and tapped his watch thrice with his index finger.

"Oh, that's right," said Uncle Jack, looking at a nearby grandfather clock, "It's almost one-thirty. Well, I suppose you mustn't be late ... very well then, my friend, I'll see you soon."

Benjamin nodded once to Uncle Jack, then bowed low to the rest of the party, before exiting the room.

"Is Benjamin your cook, Mr. Lee?" asked Mr. Lancaster as they all reached for their bowls of soup, which turned out to be clam chowder.

"No, but you'd think that, with the way he acts—bowing and sweeping his way around! No, he's an old friend of mine … knew him when he was just a boy. We worked together for quite some time, then I moved here, and so did he. He lives in town, and works down at the docks—fixing boats, mending nets and the like. He's as strong as an ox, but he's smart as a whip, if not smarter. Just doesn't talk much, that's all … I keep telling him to use that brain of his and get a real job in the city. He could be an architect, or a doctor … people can get by without chatting all the time, anyway. You know what they say, sometimes the wisest man is the one who says nothing.

"Tells me he loves the sea, though … doesn't want to leave her, which I can understand …" He trailed off and stared out the window.

Mr. Brambles nudged Mrs. Brambles and raised his eyebrows at her. She ignored him completely.

"But Uncle Jack," she said, trying to change the subject, "why does Benjamin come up here? Does he cook all your meals?"

"No, no, of course not, Rosie," said Uncle Jack with a smile, "He visits often, though, and whenever he's here, he always makes a fuss over me—thinks I need looking after or something. Imagine, *me* needing looking after! No, I usually cook, clean and do all the housework, all by myself. Not that I don't appreciate Benjamin helping me out—he's the world's greatest cook, for one thing! Let's eat!"

✳   ✳   ✳   ✳

Lunch was delicious. Stanley, who had never had lobster before, thought that he had never had so much fun during a meal. There was something strangely satisfying about breaking apart the shells, not to mention the taste, which was like nothing else. Alabaster kept making his lobster dance, much to Mrs. Lancaster's embarrassment. Uncle Jack, however, found this most amusing, and so Mrs. Lancaster gave up trying to tell Alabaster to behave himself.

At length, the meal ended.

"You'll stay for supper, won't you?" said Uncle Jack, as he collected the plates.

"Oh, we'd love to," said Mrs. Brambles, "But we've really got to get home. We've got a flight to catch at seven o'clock tonight, and we'll have to leave before two if we want to make it."

"Ah yes," said Uncle Jack, "Oh well, I suppose it'll just be the three of us for supper, eh, lads?" He turned to Stanley and Alabaster, both of whom nodded uncertainly.

"Let us help you with the dishes, though," said Mrs. Lancaster, and the adults all filed out through the swinging door at the back of the dining room, leaving Stanley and Alabaster alone.

"Your Uncle Jack is pretty neat," said Alabaster

"He sure is," said Stanley, getting up from the table.

"I wonder where he hid it," Alabaster said thoughtfully as they made their way back to the entrance hall.

"Hid what?" said Stanley.

"What do you mean?" said Alabaster.

"What do *you* mean?" said Stanley.

"What do you mean, what do I mean?" said Alabaster.

Stanley held up his hands. "Okay, wait, let's start again."

"Okay," said Alabaster, holding out his right hand, "my name is Alabaster Lancaster. It's a pleasure to meet you."

"No!" said Stanley, "I mean let's go back to where you said 'I wonder where he hid it'."

"That's fine with me," said Alabaster, "but we *are* going to need a time machine."

"*Or*, you could just tell me what you were talking about."

Alabaster shrugged. "The treasure, of course."

"Treasure?" Stanley repeated.

"Sure," said Alabaster. "Being a pirate, your uncle must have a huge pile of gold and jewels, and doubloons and triploons, and pieces of eight, and—"

"Whoa, whoa!" said Stanley, raising his hands again, "Uncle Jack isn't ... isn't a ... a ..." He was, of course, about to say that Uncle Jack wasn't a pirate, but suddenly he wasn't so sure. He glanced up at the fish head on the wall. Where could the old man have possibly gotten something like that? Where had he gotten the money to pay for this massive house? Mrs. Brambles's supposition about it being 'cheap' didn't seem as plausible as it once did. Why did Stanley suddenly get the feeling that all the nautical decorations in the house had a deeper significance than he'd originally thought?

He was a bit surprised to find that now, here, in the entrance hall of this grand mansion at the edge of the sea, his father's theory no longer seemed like a silly flight of fancy.

Alabaster folded his arms. "I know what you're thinking," he said in a sing-song tone.

"You do?" said Stanley.

"Yep," said Alabaster. "You're thinking that there's something about this uncle of yours, something otherworldly, maybe—almost like he's wearing a disguise. But most importantly, you're thinking that he just might be—"

"A pirate?" said Stanley.

"Yessss!" said Alabaster, clenching his fists.

Stanley was, in truth, a little unnerved at how accurate Alabaster had been in guessing what he was thinking. He *did* get the feeling that there was something about Uncle Jack, a sense of something great and powerful lurking just beneath the surface. He reflected that though he had known him for years, he didn't really *know* him. Who was the *real* Uncle Jack? It was time to find out.

"Okay," said Stanley, "Here's the plan."

"Great!" said Alabaster.

"We wait till my Mom and Dad, and your Mom and Dad are gone."

"Right."

"Then, when Uncle Jack least suspects it …"

"Yeah? Yeah?"

"We yell YARRRR really loud, and see what he does."

Alabaster stared at him. "And?"

"And that's it," said Stanley.

Alabaster scratched his nose. "O-kaay, that's one idea …"

"What?" said Stanley, "What's wrong with it?"

"Well, the thing is," Alabaster said carefully, "It's just a *teensy* bit ridiculous."

Stanley made a face. If *Alabaster* thought it was ridiculous, it must have been pretty bad. "Okay, okay," he said, trying to come up with something else, "how about this: we wait till my Mom and Dad and your Mom and Dad are gone."

"This is the exact same plan as before!" Alabaster said excitedly.

"No, listen! We wait till they're gone, and then we *ask Uncle Jack if he was ever a pirate!*"

Alabaster stared. "It's so simple … direct, painless … it's beautiful!"

Stanley secretly thought that this plan was much lamer than the first one.

"Oop, no, wait wait wait," said Alabaster. "No good."

"No good?" said Stanley. "Why not?"

"There's a cardinal rule," said Alabaster, "which states that in this type of situation, the adult will never reveal his or her secrets if asked directly."

"I've never heard of that rule," said Stanley.

"Oh, it's there, trust me," said Alabaster. "*So*, if we want to confront your uncle about being a pirate, we're going to need some cold, hard evidence to back us up. And *that* means we have to—"

"Search the house from top to bottom for clues?" said Stanley.

"Exactly! Let's go!"

*   *   *   *

The very size of Uncle Jack's house meant that exploration would prove to be an arduous task.

"I want a closer look at that fish head, for starters," said Alabaster.

The head was even more frightening up close. Stanley and Alabaster stood on the second floor landing, gazing into the gaping maw. It wasn't actually lined with teeth, as Stanley had first thought; instead of teeth, the jaws were equipped with sharp, jagged shearing blades of bone, something like a snapping turtle's, only much more fearsome. Stanley reached up to touch the lower jaw, and cut himself on it.

"Ouch!" he muttered as a tiny trickle of blood issued from the wound.

"Gee whiz!" said Alabaster, "That thing's sharp enough to split hairs!" He stepped closer and tapped the side of the head. "Hard as rock! Look at those armour plates! This thing is incredible! I'll bet your uncle caught it himself. What do you think he did with the rest of it?"

Stanley tried to picture Uncle Jack hauling the fish out of the ocean with a giant fishing pole. The image failed.

"No, I think he really did buy it somewhere. It's got to be a reconstruction, anyway—Dad says those things have been extinct for millions of years."

Even as he finished speaking, though, he couldn't help but think how very real the head looked ... especially the eyes ...

Alabaster must have noticed the look of doubt in Stanley's eyes, for the next moment he said, "I think you think it's real."

"Well, I ... maybe, but ... oh, how should I know?"

Just then, the dining room doors opened and the adults poured through into the entrance hall.

"Stanley, Alabaster, we're leaving," called Mrs. Brambles.

The two boys hurried down the stairs and into the waiting arms of their mothers.

"Now be good to Uncle Jack," said Mrs. Brambles as she gave Stanley a big hug. "I'll miss you so much, my brave little Stanny."

Stanley went bright red with embarrassment, but was relieved to note that Alabaster was receiving a similar treatment from Mrs. Lancaster.

"Do behave yourself, dear," she said, not noticing that she was nearly smothering Alabaster, who mumbled, "Umph ill, um."

"Have a good time, son," said Mr. Brambles, clapping Stanley on the shoulder. Then he leaned forward and whispered, "Let me know if you find anything interesting!"

Stanley grinned and nodded.

"Well, I suppose we'd better be on our way," said Mr. Lancaster after saying goodbye to Alabaster.

"In that case," said Uncle Jack, "I'll thank you all for the visit, and invite you back any time you like! It was very nice to see you again, Bob and Rose, and especially nice to meet you, Arthur and Guenevere."

A round of 'thank yous' and pleasantries were exchanged, and then Mrs. Brambles was saying, "See you in two weeks," and Mrs. Lancaster was saying "See you in August, Alabaster, my darling! 'Bye Stanley!"

Minutes later the Lancasters' van was trundling down the long driveway. Stanley and Alabaster waved until it turned the corner and drove out of sight, leaving them alone on the doorstep.

"Well, that's that," said Stanley.

"Yep," said Alabaster. "… Hey, where's your Uncle Jack? He was right with us a minute ago."

They went back inside and found a door ajar on the east side of the entrance hall. The room beyond was filled with couches, chairs, bookshelves, and even a billiard table. Uncle Jack was seated in a big soft arm chair, head tilted back, mouth wide open, snoring loudly.

"He's fast asleep!" said Alabaster incredulously, "At a quarter to two in the afternoon!"

"Come on," sighed Stanley, "Leave him alone—we'll ask him about the fish head later."

✳   ✳   ✳   ✳

They spent the rest of the day exploring the mansion, while Uncle Jack snored away in the lounge. Starting on the ground floor of the west wing, they worked their way up, thoroughly searching every room they entered, which was a very impolite thing to do. There were sitting rooms, reading rooms, sun rooms, cloak rooms, storage rooms, bedrooms, bathrooms, and several rooms that didn't seem to have any purpose at all. There was a wide array of artwork throughout the house; paintings, statues, wood carvings, most of them nautically-themed, but that wasn't really enough to go on; plenty of old salts like Uncle Jack had houses full of souvenirs from their sailing days, and plenty more were collectors of nautical antiques. The massive fish head in the entrance hall was very unusual, of course, and there were a few other pieces that looked *really* old. One of these was an ancient-looking ship's wheel, mounted on the wall at the end of the east wing hallway. Stanley assumed it was the wheel his father had mentioned—the one Uncle Jack had supposedly 'bought at a flea market'. He was more impressed with what was *painted* on the wall: a scene depicting a stormy sea with white-capped waves and dark thunderheads in the sky above. Unfortunately, though, an old wheel mounted on a beautifully-painted wall was just a piece of art, and not irrefutable proof of piracy.

Stanley and Alabaster began to get discouraged. There was a blatant lack of pirate paraphernalia in the house, and their most interesting discovery to date had been a secret stairway that led from a pantry on the first floor to the inside of a closet on the third floor. The discovery of a secret passage had been very satisfying at first, but the boys found that after running up and down the stairway for two full hours, the novelty wore off.

"That was pretty neat though," said Stanley as they descended the stairs to the second floor.

"You're right about that," said Alabaster. "I think I'll make use of that stairway as often as possible … too bad we haven't found any pirate stuff, though."

"Well, we haven't explored everywhere yet … we've barely touched the third floor, and we haven't seen much of the east wing yet—"

"Ah, there you two are!"

Stanley and Alabaster looked down the stairs to see Uncle Jack limping into the entrance hall from the dining room.

"I was wondering where you two had gone," he said, smiling. "Giving yourselves the grand tour, I suppose?"

"Um, sort of," said Stanley.

"Of course, of course," said Uncle Jack with a chuckle, "I'd expect you to want to do a little exploring. Oh, but come on down to the dining room—I've got dinner on the table."

Stanley wasn't exactly starving after having a whole lobster and a big bowl of clam chowder for lunch, but he tucked into the roasted sea bass that Uncle Jack served, just the same.

Uncle Jack wanted to know what Stanley and Alabaster thought of his 'humble abode', and was delighted to hear that they had discovered the secret passage in the pantry.

"Ah yes," he said as they described it to him. "That one's a favourite of mine—it's the perfect route to take if one wants a midnight snack."

"Wait a sec," said Stanley, "You mean that's not the only secret passage?"

"Oh my, no!" said Uncle Jack. "There are, oh, about fifteen of them in this old house ... whoever built this place had them all put in, I suppose. Some of them are quite difficult to find—in fact, I've forgotten where most of them are."

"We'd be happy to find them for you, Uncle Jack," said Alabaster brightly; then his face went a bit red and he said, "I mean, uh, Mr. Lee ..."

Uncle Jack laughed. "That's quite alright, Alabaster—you can call me uncle! I'll make you my honourary nephew!"

"Alright!" said Alabaster.

The three of them sat talking long after dinner was over. Uncle Jack wanted to know about their lives in East Stodgerton, and laughed out loud when they told him about their many encounters with Mrs. Drabdale. By the time Stanley and Alabaster had finished their stories, it was a quarter past seven, and the sun was sinking low on the horizon.

Uncle Jack leaned back in his chair and yawned loudly. "Well, lads, thanks for the stories, but right now, I'm ready for bed."

"Bed?" said Alabaster, "At seven fifteen? The sun hasn't even gone down yet!"

"Ah yes ... but when you're my age, you tend to need a bit more sleep ... early to bed and early to rise, and all that."

"But Uncle Jack," said Stanley, "We were hoping that ... well, that maybe you'd tell *us* some stories?"

Uncle Jack, who had already gotten up from the table, smiled kindly and said, "Of course I'll tell you some stories. But they'll have to wait for another night, I really am quite weary.

"Your rooms are on the third floor, east wing," he added as he limped towards the door. "First doors you see on the right hand side." And then he was gone.

Stanley and Alabaster sat in silence for a moment.

"Well *I'm* certainly not tired," said Alabaster.

"Me neither," said Stanley. "Let's go to the games room."

The games room was full of board games, card tables, billiard tables, dart boards, and even a bowling lane. Stanley and Alabaster amused themselves until about ten o'clock, when, after nearly falling asleep over a game of Backgammon, Stanley said,

"Well, I think it's off to bed for me."

They went upstairs by way of the pantry stairway, which brought them to an unused bedroom on the third floor, which they exited quietly. They found their suitcases sitting outside two rooms near the staircase, and bade eachother good-night.

Stanley closed the door behind him, flicked on the light, and looked around his room. It was quite large, and very elegant. The walls and ceiling were painted royal blue, and an intricately-woven rug covered most of the polished hardwood floor. A door beside the cavernous wardrobe led to a private bathroom, and there was even a fireplace.

Stanley brushed his teeth, changed into his pyjamas, and climbed into the enormous four-poster bed. He left the bed curtains open so he could see the moonlight shining in through the window, and lay back listening to the sound of the waves lapping the shore far below. Moments later, he was asleep.

CHAPTER FOUR:
NELL

Stanley woke very early the next morning. Sunlight was streaming in through the window, and down in the village, the church bell was tolling. He groaned and squinted at the clock on the wall, which proclaimed the time to be six o'clock. Never an early riser, Stanley groaned again, closed the bed curtains, and tried to go back to sleep. He dozed fitfully for a while, but was soon brought back to full consciousness by an odd thumping sound. He sat up in bed and cocked his head, trying to discern where the sound was coming from. He heard nothing more, though, and decided he must have imagined it. Now fully awake, Stanley got out of bed and shuffled into the bathroom to do his morning business.

No sooner had he closed the door, when another loud thump made him start with surprise. It seemed to be coming from under the floor. He knelt down and pressed his ear to the tile. There came one more thump, then a loud click, and an entire section of the tile swung open like a trapdoor. Stanley stared wide-eyed as Alabaster's head appeared from the hole in the floor. Upon seeing Stanley, Alabaster said,

"Look, Stanley, I've discovered another secret passage! If you look behind the painting of the castle in the drawing room on the second floor, you find a ladder that leads—"

"Right into my bathroom," Stanley finished.

"Yeah, right into your—oh, sorry about that," said Alabaster. "Oh well, no harm done, eh? I'll make sure not to use this one again. I had a heck of a time opening this door, though—frightfully dark in there, and it took me forever to find the release switch. Are you just getting up? I've been up since five-thirty, looking for secret passages. I tried to wake you up, but you said you'd smother me with a pillow if I didn't leave you alone." He finally paused for breath.

"I'm sure I didn't mean what I said," said Stanley, who didn't remember anything before six o'clock.

"Oh well," said Alabaster, "I'm heading down for breakfast. See you in a bit." And with that, he disappeared into the dark hole. The trap door swung shut, and Stanley dragged a heavy statue of a mermaid over it. Just in case.

Not long after, a fully-dressed Stanley came striding into the dining room by way of the kitchen (he had once again used the pantry stairway). Uncle Jack and Alabaster were seated at the table, already halfway through their breakfasts.

"Morning, Stanley," said Uncle Jack heartily, pulling out a chair for him.

"Morning, Uncle Jack," said Stanley as he sat down.

"We saved you plenty of food," said Alabaster, nodding his head towards a plate covered with eggs, toast, sausages, ham, and hashbrowns.

Stanley helped himself to plenty of each; he hadn't realized it, but he was quite hungry.

Once they had all eaten their fill, Uncle Jack gathered the dishes and limped off to the kitchen. Stanley and Alabaster followed with the intention of helping with the washing up, but Uncle Jack had already begun loading the plates into an automatic dishwasher. He glanced over at them and said with a grin,

"Just because I'm old doesn't mean I like doing dishes by hand!"

Stanley and Alabaster laughed, and Uncle Jack led them out of the kitchen. Out in the entrance hall, Uncle Jack limped over to the front doors and picked up a small stack of envelopes that were piled beneath the mail slot.

"Ah, the morning post," he said happily. He opened the door and brought in a rolled-up newspaper. "And the news as well. Let's see, bills ... bills ... letter from Algernon, those are always interesting."

"Who's Algernon?" asked Stanley.

"Algernon Petrie. He's your great aunt Victoria's and great uncle Virgil's youngest son ... which makes him your cousin, I think. He's sort of an explorer, always off on some kind of adventure in foreign lands. Sends me letters from time to time."

"He should get acquainted with my Dad," said Alabaster.

"Or mine," said Stanley. "He's probably like Indiana Jones—always recovering lost artifacts. He could work for the museum!"

But Uncle Jack wasn't listening. He was staring at a large, brown, bat-tered-looking envelope. It was addressed in elegant black letters, and sealed shut with wax. The wax had the letters D and M imprinted in it.

"Who's that from?" asked Stanley, curious as to who had sent such a stylish envelope. Uncle Jack didn't answer, though. He just kept staring at the envelope, his hands shaking slightly.

Just as the silence began to get really uncomfortable, Uncle Jack looked up and said, "Er, boys, you'll have to excuse me. I've, er, really got to give this mail my full attention. Can't keep folks waiting too long for a reply! Why don't you go outside and enjoy the sunshine?"

And with that, he hobbled up the stairs to the second floor and disappeared down a corridor on the right. Stanley and Alabaster watched him go, not quite sure what had just happened.

*   *   *   *

"It was that big brown envelope that shook him up," Stanley said as he and Alabaster made their way across the mansion's front lawn soon after. "I wonder what kind of letter it is?"

"Got me," said Alabaster, "But I'll bet it's got something to do with pirates."

"What, do you think he stays in touch with all his pirate friends?"

"I dunno, it's just a theory."

"Well," said Stanley, "If it *is* from one of his former crew members, why would he look so upset over it? You'd think he'd be happy to hear from an old friend."

"Maybe it's from an *enemy*," Alabaster offered. "A pirate is bound to have lots of enemies. Maybe it's a threat letter!"

"I guess it *could* be …"

By now they had walked round to the west side of the house, the side that looked out over the sea. About a hundred yards away from the dining room win-dows stood a guardrail, and beyond that, a steep cliff dropped away to a stony beach a good distance below.

"Let's go down and look for crayfish," said Stanley.

They walked along the guardrail and gradually made their way down the slope of the hill, till the beach was a mere five foot drop below them.

Crayfish, though, turned out to be very scarce in this area, and after an hour and a half of fruitless searching, Stanley recalled that crayfish live in lakes, not oceans. He was just about to point this out to Alabaster when he became aware of an odd buzzing sound. It was coming from some distance away, but grew steadily louder as he looked around for its source. He was envisioning a massive swarm of enraged killer bees, when Alabaster cried,

"*Stanley, look out!*"

Stanley wheeled around just in time to see some kind of buzzing machine with a spinning blade flying right towards him. He dove aside as it buzzed by (narrowly avoiding a swift decapitation in the process), and fell *splash!* into the chilly water. He felt his hand hit something sharp as he landed, and the next instant he was being helped up by Alabaster.

"Sorry about that," said a voice that was not Alabaster's. Standing on the stony beach was a girl of about the same age as Stanley and Alabaster. Her long, chestnut hair was artfully braided and hung jauntily over her left shoulder. She was smiling a bit sheepishly, and Stanley would have noticed that she was quite pretty, had he not been so concerned about his own sogginess, not to mention his dignity.

"So that was *you*?" he asked crossly as he waded towards shore. "What the heck *was* it, some kind of flying killer robot?"

"No, it was my model airplane," said the girl, pointing upwards. Stanley looked where she was pointing, and saw the plane flying back towards him. He tensed involuntarily, but relaxed as the device came down and landed smoothly on the water, floating serenely on a pair of wooden pontoons.

"Neat!" said Alabaster. "Where'd you get it?"

"I built it," said the girl.

"You built it?" said Alabaster incredulously. "From scratch?"

"Well, I bought the engine, and the control." She held up a sophisticated-looking remote control. "And I just built the body out of wood."

"Cool!" said Alabaster.

"And I wasn't trying to kill you," she said to Stanley, "I just wanted to get your attention."

"Well, you could've just said—" Stanley began.

"Omigosh! You're bleeding!" cried the girl, interrupting him.

"Um, yeah, that would have worked, but 'hello' would have—"

"No, you're really bleeding! Look at your hand!"

Stanley looked down at his right hand, and stared wide-eyed at a nasty gash in his palm, from which a good deal of blood was flowing. He suddenly felt sick. The girl was watching him uneasily now, as if expecting him to throw up. Suddenly a great dizziness seized him, and the next thing he knew, he was lying on the beach, staring up into the anxious faces of Alabaster and the brown-haired girl.

Not having the slightest idea how he had come to be in this situation, Stanley said, "Uh, what's going on?"

Alabaster looked instantly relieved. "Boy, that was sort of scary, Stanley. You went all white, and then you fell backwards. Lucky I caught you!"

"I ... fell?"

"You fainted," said the girl. "We thought you might have gone into shock or something."

Stanley noticed that his legs had been elevated off the ground and were resting on a pile of rocks. The girl was holding his head steady and Alabaster was holding his injured hand in a tight grip.

"Ow!" said Stanley, "What are you doing, Alabaster?"

"Applying pressure to the wound," said Alabaster knowledgeably, showing him a wad of kleenex he was pressing into Stanley's palm. Stanley hoped they hadn't already been used.

"Do you think you can walk?" asked the girl. Stanley thought he could, so he got up, a little shakily at first, but found that he could walk on his own. The other two stayed close beside him, just in case.

The girl picked up her plane, and the three of them made their way slowly back up the hill towards Uncle Jack's house, with the intention of bandaging Stanley up properly.

"I'm really sorry about this," said the girl. "If I'd have known this was going to happen …"

"It's okay," said Stanley, who was more than a little embarrassed over the events of the past few minutes.

"I'm Nell, by the way," said the girl after a moment's silence. "It's short for Prunella, but nobody calls me that."

"Can we call you 'Nellie'?" said Alabaster enthusiastically.

"I'd rather you didn't."

"Okay then," said Alabaster. "My name's Alabaster."

"What an interesting name," said Nell.

"And I'm Stanley," said Stanley, not wanting to be left out of the conversation. "Thanks for helping me out after I, uh …" His face was feeling uncomfortably hot (which was probably a good sign after a faint).

"Oh, it was nothing," said Nell, going a bit red herself. She quickly looked down at her model plane, and Stanley became very interested in his shoes.

"Yeah, it was nothing," said Alabaster, clapping Stanley on the shoulder. "What are friends for?"

They had reached the mansion's front yard, and were walking towards the front doors when Nell stopped short and said,

"Wait a minute—you guys live *here?*"

"No, we're just visiting for a couple of weeks," said Alabaster. "The house belongs to Stanley's great-uncle, though."

Nell was thunderstruck. "Wow! I wondered who lived in this beautiful mansion. I've wanted to look around inside ever since I got here! ... Can you two take me on a tour?"

"Sure!" said Alabaster. "In fact, we're not even done exploring the place ourselves. You can help us! It'll be great, right, Stanley?"

Stanley, who wasn't feeling too well after his faint, muttered something about wanting to lie down for a while.

Uncle Jack was in the entrance hall, dusting one of the statues.

"Uncle Jack," said Alabaster, "Have you got a first aid kit around here somewhere?"

"Great Scott, Stanley!" said Uncle Jack, catching sight of Stanley, "What happened to you? You look like death warmed over!" He left the room and limped back a minute later with a wooden box in hand. "Here, let's take a look at that cut," he said gently.

Stanley held out his hand and Uncle Jack opened the box, drawing forth a bottle labeled 'Hydrogen Peroxide'. "Now, this'll sting a bit," Uncle Jack said as he unscrewed the cap and poured a bit of clear liquid into the wound. Stanley gave a loud yelp—it stung more than a bit. The liquid foamed unpleasantly, and Uncle Jack took out a large bandage and began to dress Stanley's injured hand.

"Well," he said as Stanley finished explaining what had happened, "That's about all I can do for you now. The cut's a bit deep, but I don't think you'll need stitches." He turned to Nell and said, "Don't worry, lass, these things happen. I'm sure Stanley's not mad at you." He smiled warmly, and Nell looked relieved. "Oh, but allow me to introduce myself. I'm Jack Lee, Stanley's great-uncle." He held out his hand.

"Prunella Hawthorne," said Nell, shaking Uncle Jack's hand. "Everyone calls me Nell, though."

"Well now," said Uncle Jack, "I imagine Stanley'll want to lie down for a bit. You can stick around here, if you want."

"Actually," said Nell, "I should probably get going. I've got a few chores to do for my aunt. Um, can I come back later though?"

"Of course!" said Uncle Jack. "You can stay for dinner, if you'd like, if your aunt doesn't mind."

"Oh, she won't mind," said Nell. "She'll probably be glad to have me out of the house. She and my uncle are always so busy running the inn."

"Well then we'll look forward to having you," said Uncle Jack. "Dinner's at six, usually."

"Alright, Stanley," said Uncle Jack, after Nell had left, "Let's get you upstairs. You look very pekid."

Stanley was happy to oblige. He still felt dizzy, and it was with great relief that he laid his head down on his pillow and went to sleep.

$$*\qquad *\qquad *\qquad *$$

Stanley woke up just before six, feeling quite a bit better. He went downstairs and found Uncle Jack waiting for him in the entrance hall.

"Ah, there you are," said Uncle Jack with a smile, "I was just about to come and wake you up. You certainly look livelier after a bit of rest. Come on, your friends are waiting in the dining room."

Before he knew it, Stanley was sitting in front of a plate of steaming pasta. Nell and Alabaster were very concerned about how he felt, but conversation soon became impossible, as they were all so busy stuffing themselves with Uncle Jack's 'shrimp alfredo'.

The meal ended, and soon everyone was talking again. Stanley, Alabaster, and Uncle Jack wanted to know all about Nell, and she was kept quite busy answering their questions.

Coincidentally, it turned out that Nell and her parents were actually moving to East Stodgerton at the end of the summer. She was staying with her aunt and uncle while her mother and father went house-hunting.

"That's awesome!" exclaimed Alabaster, "Stanley and I are *from* East Stodgerton! We can all hang out when you move!"

"Maybe you'll go to the same school as us," said Stanley. "It'll be good to have a cool girl there for a change—all the girls in our grade are prissy little teacher's pets."

Nell blushed slightly at the words *cool girl*, and so did Stanley, upon realizing what he'd said.

"Uh," he said, a tad embarrassed, "I mean …"

Uncle Jack interrupted, much to Stanley's relief. He went into a long story about how he knew Nell's aunt and uncle, who owned the Shark's Head Inn, and how it was one of his favourite haunts.

Nell explained that staying with her aunt and uncle was very boring, because they were always so busy running the inn, and that it was a rather noisy place to try and sleep.

"Why don't you stay here?" said Alabaster. "There's tonnes to do—there's the games room, and the library ... and a bunch of secret passages! You can come exploring with Stanley and me!" Alabaster, it seemed, had made himself right at home. "What do you think, Uncle Jack?"

"Well, I don't know," said Uncle Jack, scratching his chin. "It's alright by me, I suppose, but what about your aunt and uncle, Nell?"

Nell was looking quite pleased. "Oh, they'd be fine with it. Like I say, they'll probably be glad to have me out of the way. They don't *say* that, of course, but they always look like they're about to burst when I'm around."

"Well alright," said Uncle Jack, after a moment's consideration, "We'll put you up in the west wing—*away* from these lads, eh?" he jerked a thumb towards Stanley and Alabaster, who sat there with slightly confused looks on their faces.

Uncle Jack made a call to the Shark's Head Inn, and a surprisingly short time later, a big, rusty old pickup truck pulled up in front of the house, engine rumbling and horn blaring. Stanley, Alabaster, and Nell waited in the entrance hall while Uncle Jack went out to greet Nell's uncle. The man was big, burly, and hairy, and didn't pay any attention to the children as he tromped into the hall and dropped Nell's suitcase on the floor with a *thump*. Nell went out to the truck and came back a moment later holding her model airplane.

"Sure you don't mind takin' 'er off our hands, Jack?" said Nell's uncle, as if Nell weren't even there.

"Oh, er, not at all, Rupe, not at all," said Uncle Jack.

Nell's uncle grunted. "Well, I'd better get back. Bernice is probably being swamped by the dinner rush. See ya Jack ... and Nell," he said, pointing at Nell, "behave yourself."

Nell rolled her eyes as her uncle left the house and hopped into his truck.

"Alright!" said Alabaster, as the vehicle roared away, "Now it's official! C'mon, Nell, Stanley and I'll show you the secret passages we've found so far!"

Uncle Jack excused himself and limped off to bed, leaving the children to amuse themselves for the rest of the evening.

CHAPTER FIVE:
A REVELATION

Over the next few days, they saw very little of Uncle Jack. When they joined him at meal times, he always seemed preoccupied with something. He talked very little, and after the meal, he would disappear. Even the postcards and letters which Stanley and Alabaster had received from their parents failed to interest him. He did laugh appreciatively at one picture, in which the Lancasters and the Brambleses were posing in front of a ruined stone building and beaming, all except for Mr. Brambles, who was looking rather alarmed at having been set upon by a large and overly-friendly snake.

The three children had plenty to do, of course; they spent a good deal of time exploring the mansion, and they found eight new secret passages. One of these led from a secret door inside a stone pillar to the inside of Nell's wardrobe, much to Stanley's and Alabaster's embarrassment (they had discovered it on their own, and it took them a long time to convince Nell that their tumbling into her room while she was changing, had been an accident). Nell had switched rooms soon after.

Though the three of them were enjoying themselves immensely, their thoughts always returned to Uncle Jack. One evening after dinner, Stanley, Alabaster and Nell were sitting in the second floor lounge. Uncle Jack had excused himself and disappeared in his usual fashion, so the children were left to entertain themselves for the evening.

They sat looking at each other, each thinking the same thing, but not wanting to talk about it. Finally, Stanley spoke up.

"Guys, I don't know about you, but I want to find out what's going on with Uncle Jack."

Alabaster looked up and said, "Yeah, so do I, but how do we do it? Any time we ask him where he disappears to, he changes the subject and—"

"Disappears," finished Nell. "And then we don't see him again till the next morning."

"We've been all over the house, basement to attic," said Alabaster defeatedly. "It's obvious we're not going to get anything out of Uncle Jack, and we still haven't found any concrete evidence."

"Wait a minute," said Nell, leaning forward. "What kind of evidence are we talking about here?"

Stanley and Alabaster looked at eachother hesitantly. They hadn't told Nell about their theory.

"Nell," said Stanley, taking a deep breath, "we think that my Uncle Jack is a pirate, and we've been looking for clues to prove it."

Nell looked at Stanley, then at Alabaster, then back at Stanley, who looked down at his feet, expecting her to burst out laughing. An uncomfortable silence followed, and then Nell asked, quietly,

"So where do we go from here?"

Stanley gaped at her. "You mean you *believe* us?"

"Well, why not?" she asked, "It makes sense—the mansion by the sea, the painting on the dining room ceiling, the big fish head … your Uncle Jack even has an artificial leg."

Stanley was immensely relieved. "I never thought you'd take this seriously."

"Of course I would," said Nell. "But Alabaster's right, we haven't found any concrete evidence."

"What we need is a new plan," said Alabaster.

They sat and thought for a while. Finally, Nell said,

"Well, we could go to the town hall and get the house's blueprints out of the archives." Stanley and Alabaster stared.

"If they have them on file, that is," Nell went on. "Then, we can check every single room against the floor plans, and see if there are any rooms we haven't been in."

Stanley and Alabaster looked at each other. Stanley was certainly impressed.

Alabaster cleared his throat and said, "Why don't we jump out at Uncle Jack and yell YAAARRR really loudly?"

"That was *my* plan, and *you* said it was ridiculous," said Stanley.

"Desperate times call for ridiculous measures," said Alabaster.

"What about *my* plan?" said Nell.

"Darn," Alabaster muttered to Stanley, "I thought she would've forgotten about that by now."

"It was thirty seconds ago, and I can hear you," said Nell.

"I think it's a good plan," said Stanley.

"It has a fundamental flaw!" said Alabaster.

"*How is it flawed?*" Nell demanded.

"I didn't understand it," said Alabaster.

The look of disgust and annoyance on Nell's face, told Stanley that now was a good time to take a break. Quite frankly, he was just about ready to call it a night. He was tired, frustrated, and had to go to the bathroom. While Nell attempted to explain the basic concept of her plan to Alabaster, Stanley excused himself and left the room.

The east wing hallway was dark and silent. Stanley couldn't for the life of him remember where the light switch was, but there was more than enough moon-light shining in through the tall windows. As he made his way down the corridor towards the bathroom, he noticed something strange: At the very end of the hall, a door was slightly ajar, allowing a bit of light from the room beyond to spill out into the dark hallway. This wouldn't be a particularly odd thing to see, except that there was no door at the end of the east wing hallway.

Stanley checked his surroundings to make sure he hadn't gotten lost. He'd just come from the lounge, which meant that the bathroom was two doors down, with a painting of a waterfall across from it. Sure enough, the bathroom was there, as was the painting. At the end of this hallway there was supposed to be a wall with white-capped waves painted on it, and an old ship's wheel mounted halfway up.

Instead, there was a door. Alarmed though he was by the strangeness of the situation, Stanley couldn't help but wonder what was on the other side of that door. Eventually his curiosity overcame his trepidation, and he proceeded quietly down the hall. As he approached the door, he could see a tiled floor in the room beyond, but he suddenly froze at the sound of movement. His heart racing, he backed away from the door and slipped into a nearby closet, keeping the door open a crack so he could see what was going on outside. He heard footsteps, and then the sound of the mysterious door closing. Stanley held his breath as some-one passed by his hiding place.

It was Uncle Jack. Stanley could tell it was him before he saw him by the sound of his uneven footsteps. He watched the old man limp down the corridor, and turn towards the second floor landing. He didn't dare leave the closet till he heard his uncle's footsteps going up the stairs. Cautiously, Stanley crept back out into the hall. The mysterious door was gone, of course. There was the wall, painted with white-capped waves, and there was the wheel, in its usual place. He wanted to investigate further, but by now he had to go to the bathroom quite badly, and when he was done with that, he thought it would be a good idea to go and get Alabaster and Nell.

"So you're saying that they have blueprints for every building in town?" Alabaster was asking of Nell as Stanley came back into the lounge.

"*That's right*," said Nell slowly. "The important ones, at least."

"So then if you have a secret room in your house, everyone at city hall knows about it?"

"Guys," said Stanley, "come with me, I want to show you something."

"With pleasure" said Nell, sounding relieved.

"Wait," said Alabaster, "I'm still not clear on this blueprint thing."

"Oh, who cares," said Nell, "Just come on."

"Shh," said Stanley as he led them out into the hall. Alabaster nodded, then promptly fell over a large potted plant.

"*Be quiet!*" hissed Nell, dragging Alabaster to his feet while Stanley righted the plant. "Um, why *are* we being so quiet?" she asked of Stanley.

"I don't want Uncle Jack to know what we're doing," he answered. "I think he's got something hidden down here."

The three of them went silently to the end of the hall. "Okay, Stanley," said Nell, "What are we looking for?"

Stanley explained about seeing the door, and about Uncle Jack apparently coming out of it.

"I've got it!" said Alabaster. "It's another secret passage—and I bet this *wheel* is the key." He reached up, grabbed one of the wheel's handles, and hauled downward as hard as he could. There was a sharp *crack* as the wheel tore free of its mounting on the wall, and fell to the ground with a loud, clattering crash.

The three of them froze, listening intently for any sound from upstairs, but after a few tense moments, it seemed that Uncle Jack hadn't heard the noise.

"Uh, oops," said Alabaster, grinning sheepishly. Stanley and Nell glared at him.

"Next time don't go yanking on things you aren't sure about," said Nell, pushing Alabaster aside. "If there *is* some kind of secret door around here, we have to look for it *carefully*, not go tearing the place to pieces." She spent a few moments examining the wall, while Stanley tried to re-hang the wheel.

"I'm really surprised that wheel isn't a secret door mechanism," said Alabaster.

"We're going to need some tools to hang this back up," said Stanley, setting the wheel down on the ground. He felt bad about the damage, and wondered how they were going to explain it to Uncle Jack. Just then, Nell let out a heavy sigh.

"Would you two mind stepping over here for a second?" she said. Stanley and Alabaster came forward. "What does this look like to you?"

Nell was pointing at a spot roughly a third of the way up on the right-hand side of the wall. Stanley was about to ask what they were supposed to be looking at, but then, after taking a closer look, he saw it.

It was a door handle. Just a simple, old-fashioned door handle, but it had been painted just like the rest of the wall, making it difficult to see from a distance.

"Boy, how did we miss that?" said Alabaster.

"It *is* pretty hard to see," said Stanley.

Nell reached out and turned the handle. The camouflaged door swung open silently. "It's not even locked," she said.

"I guess that means it isn't a secret passage," said Stanley, tentatively stepping over the threshold and into the darkness beyond.

"It's sort of secret," said Alabaster, following him in. Nell came in last, closing the door behind her.

The room was dark, but moonlight shone in through a tall window at the far end. Stanley could see shapes in the gloom, but could not discern what they were. Suddenly, with an audible *click*, the lights came on; Nell had found the light switch. Stanley squinted at the sudden brightness, but let out a gasp of amazement as his eyes grew accustomed to the light. The room was filled with all sorts of things relating to the sea; paintings of sixteenth century sailing ships adorned one wall, while another was occupied by a glass case, inside of which many old and valuable-looking things were displayed. There were navigational instruments, gold and silver statuettes, maps and sea charts, and a host of other nautical knick-nacks. The wall on the right was covered with fish mounted on wooden plaques. They were either stuffed or models, and Stanley guessed the latter, because he had never heard of any fish like these before.

They looked like creatures from a sailor's worst nightmare. The image of the head in the entrance hall flashed into Stanley's mind and he shuddered. The fish displayed here were not huge, but they were certainly ugly. Most had gaping mouths filled with vicious-looking teeth. Their eyes were round and forever staring, lending a feeling of madness and hunger to the marine menagerie.

Alabaster cautiously examined one specimen that was little more than a mouth with a tail. The fish's jaws could have easily accommodated his head. Stanley was looking at an eel with particularly long fangs, when Nell said,

"Come look at this."

Stanley and Alabaster joined her at the far end of the room. She was pointing at one of the mounted fish, because it clearly did not belong as part of this display.

"That's just a regular rainbow trout," said Stanley. "My Dad catches them all the time up at the cottage." He glanced about at the other stuffed fish. "Kind of a funny place for a rainbow trout—it's pretty boring compared to all these other ones."

"Exactly," said Nell. "It seems out of place."

"The whole thing seems awfully *fishy* to me," Alabaster said loudly. Stanley and Nell rolled their eyes.

Stanley was examining the trout's head when he noticed something odd in the fish's mouth. It appeared to be a small, red button, and curious as he was, Stanley pressed it with barely a second thought. There was a loud *crunk*, and the three of them jumped back in surprise as the section of wall on which the trout was mounted swung open like a door.

"Cool!" said Alabaster, "Now *this* is a secret passage!"

"This isn't a passage," said Stanley, looking in. "It's a secret *room*!"

And it was. The newly-discovered room was round, and about fifteen feet across. By the light of a chandelier which hung down from the high ceiling, Stanley beheld what appeared to be a true pirate's room.

In the centre of the room, beneath the chandelier (which was made out of another old ship's steering wheel) was a massive wooden desk heaped with papers and rolled-up pieces of parchment. Most of these were maps or sea charts. Beside the desk was a great antique globe, which was almost as tall as Stanley. It looked very old and valuable, as did everything else in the room. On the other side of the desk was a large and sturdy-looking chest; Stanley wondered if there was treasure inside.

A low bookshelf ran all the way around the room, and above this, the walls were adorned with shiny cutlasses, old-fashioned guns, and black-and-white photographs of people who looked like real pirates. A full quarter of the wall was occupied by two maps. One was a map of the world, and the other was of a place Stanley did not recognise.

"What's that a map of?" said Alabaster, as he and Nell came over.

"Dunno," said Stanley. "It doesn't look like any map I've ever seen."

Nell was about to say something, when all of a sudden a voice shrieked,

"AVAST, YE MUTINOUS DOGS! WHAT BUSINESS HAVE YE HERE? YE'LL WALK THE PLANK FOR SURE!"

The children jumped with surprise, and looked about wildly for the owner of the voice, but no one could be found.

"Oh, great," said Alabaster, "The place is haunted!"

"No, look!" said Nell, pointing upwards.

Stanley followed her gaze up towards the ceiling. Perched on one of the rafters and eyeing the children suspiciously was a bright green parrot with blue tail feathers.

"STATE YER BUSINESS, LAND LUBBERS!" shrieked the parrot.

"Cool!" said Alabaster. "A pirate parrot! All real pirates have pet parrots." He motioned for the bird to come down, but that only started it into another round of inane babble.

"He's loud," said Nell. "He'll probably wake up your uncle if he keeps carrying on like that."

That reminded Stanley that they probably weren't supposed to be in here. "You're right, we should probably get out of here. C'mon, Alabaster."

Alabaster was still trying unsuccessfully to coax the parrot down from the roof. "Coming," he said, but he stopped by the desk and picked something up. "Hello, what's this?"

"Come on, Alabaster," said Stanley with a little more urgency in his voice.

"Wait," said Alabaster, "Look at this!" He held up an old-looking envelope with the address written in elegant black letters. "It's that letter Uncle Jack got a few days ago, remember?"

"Yeah, I remember," said Stanley, heading for the doorway. "Put it down and let's go!"

"Wait, it's open," said Alabaster, "Don't you want to read it? It's probably full of pirate stuff."

"Well, bring it if you want, 'cause we're not staying here."

"What? You can't bring it with you!" said Nell, "He'll notice that it's gone. Oh, this was a bad idea ..."

"Let's just read it now!" said Alabaster, shaking the envelope emphatically.

Stanley looked to Nell for help, but she simply folded her arms and shook her head. "Okay, okay, read it, and then let's go," he said to Alabaster.

Suddenly, with a swish and a snap, the parrot swooped down and snatched the envelope right out of Alabaster's hand.

"Hey!" said Alabaster.

The next few minutes were complete pandemonium. Alabaster dove after the parrot and knocked over the globe, which rolled out of its stand and bowled Stanley over as he rushed to help. A stabbing pain shot through his injured hand as he used it to save himself from falling flat on his face.

Nell hopped up onto the chest beside the desk and leapt into the air as the parrot swooped by. She caught the bird in mid air and tugged the envelope out of its beak as she landed lightly on the floor.

"Well that was fun," she said sarcastically, putting the parrot down on the desk. She sat down on the high-backed chair and held up the letter. Stanley and Alabaster came over and stood on either side of the chair, looking over her shoulders. As the three of them read, their mouths fell open with surprise.

This is what was written in the letter:

Thursday, 3rd April, Yr.512, Mi.4

To my friend and Captain, Jackson W. Lee, greetings.

Long has it been since we spoke last, my friend, and it is my prayer that the time at which we again stand face to face, is not far off. Alas, I know not even if this letter will reach you. Nonetheless, I must make at least one attempt.

The day you left, you told me that if I was ever in need of help and could find none, then I was to send a letter to the address you gave me.

Well, old friend, I am now in great peril. Much has changed since you have been gone. I have not the time to tell you all there is to tell, but I can tell you that I am, as of March 30th, a prisoner in the dungeons of the imperial palace. Yes, my friend, a prisoner, though I am ashamed to admit it.

'His Majesty', the King, passed away several years ago. Do not rejoice yet, my friend, for things are worse now than they were. Lacking a son to succeed him, His Majesty appointed our good friend, Lord Admiral Ezekiel Chamberlain as Regent Lord of the Empire. The King had given up searching for us, but as you know, Chamberlain is obsessed. Soon after he came

to power, he gave new strength to the imperial navy, and made it his personal mission to hunt down and capture each and every pirate to sail the seas.

Alas, my friend, he has finally captured me, and even now he roams the seas, accompanied by his force of elite soldiers, searching for the most feared pirate of all time, the legendary Black Jack Lee. Chamberlain seeks you, my friend, but that's not all. He also knows of the treasure. You know of what treasure I speak. My friend, we both know that in the wrong hands, certain pieces of that great hoard could prove extremely dangerous. I think we can both agree that Chamberlain possesses the wrongest set of hands in the empire.

Therefore, my friend, we must go in search of our treasure, and find it before Chamberlain does. He cannot be allowed to possess those relics, let alone the gold, which is rightfully ours!

I beg you to take great care. The Capitol is more heavily-guarded than ever before. Telling you not to come to my rescue is useless, I'm sure, but I must tell you this: if a rescue doesn't seem possible, don't try it. Things are different now, and Chamberlain is more powerful and ruthless than ever. Your priority is the treasure. I wish you luck.

Your friend and first mate,
~Diego Montigo

The three children were silent for a moment.

"Diego Montigo," said Stanley thoughtfully. He looked at the broken seal on the envelope. "D.M."

"What does it all mean?" said Nell.

"It means you've been snooping around in a place you're not supposed to be!"

Stanley, Nell and Alabaster looked up in surprise. There in the doorway stood Uncle Jack.

CHAPTER SIX:
JACK'S STORY

"Well? What have you got to say for yourselves?" Uncle Jack did not look pleased. There was a long and uncomfortable silence. The three children stared down at their feet, not wanting to meet Uncle Jack's gaze. At length, Stanley raised his head slowly and glanced up at his uncle. The old man's face was drawn up in a look of extreme disapproval, but his eyes showed something different, something that almost looked like fear.

"Don't have anything to say, eh?" said Uncle Jack, as Stanley quickly looked away.

"We're sorry, Mr. Lee," said Nell quietly.

"I *know* you're sorry!" said Uncle Jack, "But that doesn't change the fact that you've seen all … this! Why'd you want to go and snoop around here, anyway?" He looked intently at Stanley.

"We … we wanted to …" Stanley began.

"We wanted to find out if you were really a pirate," interrupted Alabaster. "We really wanted to know!"

Uncle Jack was silent for a moment. "A pirate, eh? Where'd you get *that* idea?"

"Well," said Stanley, "My Dad always had this theory about you being a pirate, and seeing all the decorations and stuff in your house made us want to find out for sure."

Uncle Jack folded his arms across his chest. "I see. So then, did your parents put you up to this? Did they want to find out if their *theory* is true?"

Stanley was about to respond, but Uncle Jack interrupted him. "Let me tell you something, you three." He took a few steps forward as he spoke. "I've lived here for some time, and even on this quiet little corner of the globe, I know how the world works. This's a world that's moved on from the old ways, and for the most part, forgotten what *wonder* and *magic* are all about. These days, if you saw some fellah walking down the street dressed up in ... oh, I dunno, a suit of armour, talking like something out of a Shakespeare play, you'd think he was off his rocker."

"That'd be awesome," said Alabaster. Nell elbowed him.

"That's not what most people would say," said Uncle Jack, "And the same goes for pirates. A pirate walking down the street would get some funny looks, wouldn't you say? And what if that pirate was a relative of yours, eh? You'd probably think he was crazier than an outhouse rat! And then, a few psychiatric exams later, I'd be locked up in a nice white room with padded walls."

The room fell silent.

"Look," said Uncle Jack, "I'm sorry for gettin' upset. I guess I can't blame you for being inquisitive. I just ..." Uncle Jack paused, as if searching for the right words. "I thought ..."

He sighed, and said, "I thought that if you found this room, you'd go and tell your parents about it, and, well, that'd be the end of me. They'd call the doc, an' he'd call the hospital and have me taken away in a straightjacket, to rot in some sanitarium somewhere."

"Mr. Lee," said Nell, "We didn't know, we just ... we didn't ..." she trailed off, not knowing what to say.

"Uncle Jack," said Stanley, "My Mom and Dad would never try to do any of that stuff to you. They don't think you're ... um ..."

"Mad?"

"R-right. You've got my parents all wrong, it was *our* idea to go looking for pirate stuff. No one else's."

"... Well, I must say, I'm relieved to hear that," said Uncle Jack, and he looked it. There was yet another uncomfortable silence, and then Alabaster said, in a quiet and defeated tone,

"So you're not *really* a pirate, Uncle Jack?"

They looked up at him, aware that their number one question was about to be answered. Uncle Jack didn't say anything at first. An odd look came over his face, and Stanley thought he noticed something like a twinkle in the old man's eye.

"Of course I was a pirate!" said Uncle Jack. They stared at him, mouths gaping. "In my youth, I was the most feared pirate to sail the seven seas! My crew and

I were the most infamous band of buccaneers that ever lived! I was never in any war, I was too busy battling against a tyrant king who cared nothing for his people. I didn't lose my leg to an explosive shell, it got bitten off by the very fish whose head is mounted in the entrance hall! My entire estate was paid for with pirate gold! I am the legendary Black Jack Lee!"

"I knew it!" cried Alabaster.

"It was true all along," said Nell wonderingly.

"But Uncle Jack, there's so much I don't understand," said Stanley. "How come we never heard of you and your crew? If you were so famous, why haven't we ever read about you in history class, or seen documentaries about you on T.V?"

Uncle Jack grinned. "Oh, you didn't hear about me 'cause you weren't in the right place. I'm not so well known around *these* waters."

"But Mr. Lee," said Nell, "You said that during the war you were fighting against a king. What king was it? And how did you keep from being noticed all throughout the war?"

"I was far, far away during that war," said Uncle Jack. "The ruling monarch at the time was King Tyrone the Fifteenth, ruler of Rhedland, and the entire Rheddish Empire."

"This is making absolutely no sense," said Nell. "Mr. Lee, I'm sorry, but I don't understand anything you're saying. Do you, Stanley?"

Stanley shook his head almost imperceptibly.

"Of course you don't understand," said Uncle Jack. "I didn't expect you to. No one ever did ..."

Just then, the parrot, who until now had been sitting quietly in the rafters, swooped down and landed on Uncle Jack's shoulder.

"Ah, there you are, Pericles," said the old man, turning his head slightly to look at the bird. "Where have you been all this time?"

"Listening to *you*, you old fool," said the parrot, in a voice quite unlike the one it had used to shriek at the children. "How do you expect people to understand what you're talking about, when you won't even answer their questions properly?"

The children gaped at the bird.

"Uncle Jack, your parrot can talk!" said Stanley.

"Well of *course* I can talk," said the parrot insolently. "What do you think I'm doing right now, breaking wind?"

"No, I mean you can speak and *understand words*. You can carry a conversation! I've never seen a parrot do that."

"Well, then you haven't seen many parrots, now, have you? Where *I* come from, all the parrots talk. Isn't that right, Jack?"

"Unfortunately, yes," muttered Uncle Jack. "Right now, however, I'd like to know what you meant by that 'old fool' remark."

The parrot scoffed. "I think that's plainly obvious! These children are asking questions of you, and the only answers you give them are the starts of even more questions! I think you'd better sit down and explain everything to them, top to bottom. It's the only way they'll understand."

"Rubbish," said Uncle Jack, brushing the parrot off his shoulder. "They think I'm an old nutter who likes playing at pirates. They don't believe me ..."

The parrot landed on the desk and opened his beak to say something, but Stanley stepped forward and said,

"We believe you, Uncle Jack."

The old man looked over at Stanley, a look of surprise on his face. "You ... believe me? *Really?*"

"Of course we do," Alabaster piped up, taking a step forward himself. "Stanley and I have believed in your pirate-ness ever since we first saw you, right, Stanley?" He looked over at Stanley, who nodded vigorously. "Nell believes, too," Alabaster continued. "Don't you, Nell?"

Nell looked at Uncle Jack and nodded. "I certainly do. Everything here proves it—your house, this room ... your letter." She held up the letter they had been reading.

"Me letter," Uncle Jack whispered as he took a step forward. Nell held the parchment out, and the old man took it with a trembling hand. Tears filled his eyes as he looked down at the elegant black letters, and he turned away.

There was a moment of silence, and then the parrot said, "I think it's time you told these children exactly what you're about, old friend."

Uncle Jack turned back to face them. His eyes were now dry, but they were red and puffy.

"Don't forget, you owe us a story," said Stanley quietly.

Uncle Jack smiled. "I most certainly do. C'mon," he said, motioning for them to follow. "To the lounge. Ye'll hear a story tonight, that's for sure."

*   *   *   *

Minutes later, they were all seated on comfy chairs in the second floor lounge. Uncle Jack had just finished building a roaring fire in the fireplace (despite the fact that it was high summer), and aside from the light cast by the flickering flames, the room was dark.

"First of all," said Uncle Jack as he settled into his own high-backed arm chair, "I'd better introduce you to Pericles, here." He motioned towards the parrot, who had a whole chair to himself. "Stanley, Alabaster and Nell, this is Pericles. Pericles, meet Stanley, Alabaster and Nell."

The children nodded and waved uncertainly. Pericles was, after all, a parrot.

"Charmed, I'm sure," said Pericles, making a comical little bow, which he obviously considered very elegant.

"Alright," said Uncle Jack, "I'm gonna tell you my story as best I can. Pericles can help me if need be. He was there for most of it." He was silent for a time, staring at the dancing light cast by the fire. When he looked up again, he had a distant look in his eyes.

"As I told you before, I used to be the most feared pirate in all the Rheddish Empire, maybe even in all the world. You've never heard of Rhedland, not many people 'round here have. It's very far away, but it seems much closer than it is. The Rheddish Empire spans two entire continents, and has colonies all over the world. The reason you've never heard of it, is that you simply don't know where to look. I'm afraid I can't explain it any better than that, not right now, anyway. You'll just have to trust me on it for now."

Stanley took the hint that now was not the time for questions. He guessed that Alabaster and Nell felt the same way.

"Your grandmother and I," said Uncle Jack, turning towards Stanley, "Are originally from Rhedland. Born in Ethelia, capital city of the Empire, we were, into a very well-to-do family. The Lee family had always had a proud naval tradition, a tradition that went back hundreds of years. As for me, I joined up as soon as I was old enough—not a whole lot older than you three, actually. Things were fine, at first. I did my job well, started to work my way up through the ranks, made loads of friends ...

"But there was one fellah who I just never got along with—a young officer named Ezekiel Chamberlain. We were just junior officers, but he was a rank or two above me—at first, anyway. I dunno what it was, but for some reason, him an' I, we just hated eachother from the moment we met."

"And with good cause!" put in Pericles, "He was rude, cruel, obnoxious ... it seemed like there was always someone being flogged when he was on duty."

"Aye, there's that," said Uncle Jack, "Very unpopular with the crew, he was, but feared by 'em, too. He was as ruthless and cold as anybody. I managed to stay out of 'is way at first, but ... well, a coupla promotions, an' he an' I were equal rank, an' I'll tell ya, he didn't like that one bit. From that point on, we were always at odds, always snipin' at eachother, one always tryin' to one-up the other … some people are just made to be enemies, I guess."

Uncle Jack sighed. "Then one day, somethin' happened that made my troubles with Chamberlain seem pretty small by comparison. Our ship had been assigned to deliver supplies, an' pick up goods from Sudona, one o' the Rheddish colonies down in Angoria. It was the first time I'd ever been to one o' the colonies … an' the first time I saw the true face of the Rheddish Empire. Sudona was little more'n a slave camp. The colonists had enslaved the native people, forcin' 'em to work in the mines, an' in the fields—workin' 'em to death, sometimes, an' all so the gold, an' jewels, an' spices could be sent back to Rhedland.

"I decided then an' there, after seein' the way my country treated the rest o' the world, that I wanted no more part in it. I was gonna resign my commission, but before I could, Chamberlain found out about my 'opinions'. He told the captain I was a traitor to the Empire, that I was plottin' mutiny, of all things! An' the captain believed 'im. I'd've been hanged if I hadn't managed to escape. An' escape I did, thanks to Benjamin Stone, an' Pericles, here. An', well, that's pretty much where my piratin' days began. I travelled all over the Empire for months, from Angoria to Verduria an' back, an' everywhere I went, things were the same: people bein' exploited by the Empire. It was enough to make a man sick! I decided that I didn't want to live in a world where such a corrupt system was in power. I decided that I would bring down the Empire.

"There were plenty o' folks who hated the Empire, o' course, so I didn't have trouble findin' help. I managed to scrape together a good number o' friends from me navy days, too, an' before I knew it, I was the leader o' the most feared band o' buccaneers to ever sail the seas! We spent many a year sailin' all over, takin' shots at the Imperials. Here we'd attack a treasure ship, laden with ill-gotten gold, there we'd seize an Imperial fort … an' as word spread, people from all over started joinin' our ranks, 'till we had a nice little fleet of our own. We went on like that for many years, an' had some great victories …" He trailed off and sat back in his chair.

"It sounds awesome," said Alabaster.

"Ah, but they weren't all good times, said Uncle Jack more gravely. "The sea can be harsh and cruel, and it's very dark and deep. It's not all sailboats an' sunshine; it's full of mystery. There are stranger and more frightening things than armour fish out on the ocean."

Stanley shivered.

"What about the treasure your friend Diego mentioned in his letter?" said Nell. "Where does that come into the story?"

"Ahh, right, the treasure," said Uncle Jack. "We spent many a year amassin' that great hoard. I'll tell ya one thing, though: when we were done collectin', every member of our crew got a cut—more than enough to set 'im up for life, with plenty to spare, but there was more treasure in that hoard than we could've spent in a lifetime. I'd say a good sixty percent of our treasure's still hidden."

"You couldn't spend it all, so you hid it?" said Stanley, "And now Chamberlain is looking for it?"

"Aye, that's right, Stanley," said Uncle Jack. "It's true we hid the treasure because we didn't know what to do with it, but there was another reason, as well. Our treasure wasn't all gold and jewels. Over the years, we found many strange artefacts—we're talkin' one of a kind, things that no one these days could ever hope to duplicate. Every one o' these relics was priceless, of course, but some of 'em were very mysterious—we didn't have a clue what they were—and some of 'em were downright dangerous. Weapons, and powerful magical devices, things that man was not meant to have."

"What kind of weapons?" asked Alabaster.

"Some of 'em were pretty scary. Things that could shoot lighting or fire, and swords that were alive, and sucked out your very soul if you used 'em too much. Some o' the things we found were like little prisons for monsters and evil spirits. Someone a long time ago took crystals and things like that, and magically sucked the creatures inside 'em. Sometimes you could see things inside the crystals."

Uncle Jack noticed the fearful looks on the children's faces, and smiled reassuringly. "Ah, don't be afraid—we found many wonderful and beautiful treasures, too: crystals that sang if you put 'em in the sun, suits of armour worn by kings, jewels of every description ..." He sighed. "It'll be good to see the treasure again."

"You're really going after it?" Stanley asked.

"That's the plan," replied Uncle Jack. "There's no tellin' how long it'll stay hidden, with Chamberlain on the trail. Even with all the precautions we took with hiding it, I have a bad feeling that it won't be safe for long. I've got to either find it myself, or keep Chamberlain away from it."

"But you hid it, right?" said Stanley. "You know where it is! Chamberlain has no idea—"

"No, Stanley, I don't know where it is. I hid it, true, but ... well, I think I should let Pericles tell this part of the story—the hiding of the treasure was his idea, after all."

Pericles, who had been silent until now, stood up straight and cleared his throat. "Thank you, Jack," he said graciously.

"Well, as Jack has told you already," began the parrot, "The *Blackjack Bonanza* (as our treasure became known) would be very dangerous in the wrong hands. We wrested many a deadly weapon from madmen of every description, and decided that parts of that hoard were not to be touched by human hands ever again.

"Thus, *I* came up with the idea to hide the treasure in a secret place, where no one would be able to find it. Well, that's what we *thought*, anyway." Pericles cleared his throat again.

"Ahem. The problem was, that no matter how secret, how clever, how fiendishly inaccessible a hiding place was, we, the crew, would still know about it. You can hide something from your enemies easily enough, but hiding it from *yourself* is another matter. We decided that no one could be trusted with the knowledge of the treasure's location—not Jack, not me, nobody, and that's why I decided that we would use the Memory Mirror."

Pericles paused, obviously expecting the children to gasp in amazement. When they didn't so much as twitch, he looked at Uncle Jack, who was smiling and shaking his head.

"Ahem, yes, well," said Pericles, "I suppose the Memory Mirror is not so famous around here. The Memory Mirror is an ancient and Magical device, which can store memories. If a person looks in the mirror, his memories are reflected. He can then cycle through them, and store them inside the mirror. The stored memories are no longer in the person's head, so he forgets them completely, until he retrieves them from the mirror."

"The Memory Mirror can be a dangerous tool, though," added Uncle Jack. "If you wanted, you could use it to completely erase a person's memory. They'd have no idea who they are, where they are … nothin'."

"Which is precisely why we liberated it from the clutches of Duke Norman," said Pericles. "He was using it as a brainwashing device, in order to gain control of—"

Uncle Jack interrupted him. "Pericles!" he said sharply, "we can tell 'em about Duke Norman later."

"Ah, yes of course. Well now, once we had hidden the treasure and returned to the mainland, every member of the crew used the mirror to store his memory of the treasure's hiding place. We then used the mirror's power to erase those memories, so that no one knew the treasure's location."

"But if you erased the memories, how will you ever find it again?" asked Nell.

"Well now this is the beauty part," said Uncle Jack. "Before we erased our memories, Diego an' I, we drew up a map that leads to the exact location of the treasure. We each memorised half of the map, and put that memory in the mirror. I memorised the left half, and Diego, the right. So, if I were to look in the mirror, I'd see my half o' the map, and Diego would see his."

"So that means you *have* to rescue Diego, right?" said Stanley.

"Not necessarily," said Pericles. "As a precaution, I memorised the locations of three landmarks. The treasure is within a certain distance of these landmarks, so, with my knowledge, and half the map, it *would* be possible to find the treasure … it would just require a lot of time and a bit of luck."

"Forget luck," said Uncle Jack. "I'm springin' Diego, and that's that. Even if I knew the treasure was just up the street, I'd be bustin' Diego outta jail before I touched a single coin of it!"

"I had a feeling you'd say that," said Pericles with a sigh.

"And rightly so!" said Uncle Jack. I'll not leave me first mate, not to mention me best friend in the world, to spend the rest of his days clapped in irons, rottin' in some slimy dungeon!"

"Yes, yes, I'm well aware of your feelings in the matter," said Pericles, "but if you'll recall, Diego himself said, in his letter, that you are not to attempt a rescue if a rescue seems impossible. I'm all for helping the man, but we have to consider the fact that there may be no way to—"

"There's always a way," said Uncle Jack. "An' if there ain't, we'll *make* one."

Pericles said nothing.

Uncle Jack took a deep breath as if to put his thoughts in order, then said, "We're leavin' tomorrow. Pericles, I want you to go tell Benjamin what's happening, and to be here and ready to go no later than six o'clock. I want to be under way well before eight."

Pericles nodded his understanding, and fluttered into the air and out the open window. Uncle Jack limped over to the window and stared out at the starry sky, hands clasped behind his back. The three children, who had been listening to the story with eyes as big as saucers, waited with stunned expectation to see what would happen next.

After several minutes of silence, Uncle Jack turned to face them, his face unusually set and grim.

"This is something I've got to do," he said quietly, meeting their wide-eyed gazes. "I know I invited you up for a holiday, but it'll have to be cut short. I wish this could've waited another week or so, but it can't. I don't expect ya to understand all o' this, but … there's a lot at stake here, and right now, I'm the only one who can do anything about it. It's a dangerous trip I'll be going on, and I can't bring you kids along, so—"

"We *have* to go!" said Stanley, standing up suddenly. As soon as he did, though, he wondered why he had.

Alabaster and Nell were staring at him.

"I, uh … don't know why I said that," Stanley muttered as he sat back down.

"Sorry, Stanley lad," said Uncle Jack, "Ya can't come."

"Aww, *pleeeease*, Uncle Jack?" whined Alabaster. "Can't we come with you? we'll be extra careful, honest!"

The old man shook his head. "No, Alabaster. This ain't some posh holiday cruise we're talkin' about here—it's a real sea voyage, with real danger, an' real enemies. If I run into Chamberlain an' his goons, I'm gonna hafta fight, an' a battle at sea is not fun, or cool, or whatever ya might be thinkin'. I refuse to bring you into a dangerous situation, not to mention what your parents would say. No, you three'll be stayin' here in Westport. I'll give Nell's aunt an' uncle a call in the mornin', an' make arrangements for you to stay at the inn."

Alabaster sighed and slumped back in his chair. Stanley glanced over at Nell, who didn't look pleased at the prospect of going back to the inn. He didn't blame her—he wasn't pleased about it, either; it looked as if his fun holiday at Uncle Jack's was coming to an end.

"I'm really sorry, mates," said Uncle Jack. "If there was any way around this, I'd gladly take it, but there's not. Maybe if ya were older, I could take ya along, but … as things are now, I can't. I promise I'll make it up to ya … assumin' I get back in one piece, that is." He sighed. "Well, let's go, off to bed—I wanna be up bright an' early tomorrow." He shooed the children out of the room, and guided them down the hall to the main staircase.

As he trudged up the stairs, Stanley glanced back at Uncle Jack. The old man's face was set as he watched the children for a moment, then turned and headed back towards the lounge. Stanley paused at the top of the stairs, wondering if, after tomorrow, he would ever see his Great Uncle again.

*   *   *   *

Back in his room, Stanley laid his head down on his pillow, but sleep would not come. He was worried about Uncle Jack, but what was keeping him awake was another feeling, a feeling which he could not place at first. Uncle Jack's story ran through his mind over and over again, and with it, images of great wooden sailing ships ploughing through mountainous waves, of strange, distant lands, of battles at sea, and of horrid sea monsters. He thought of what it must be like to sail away, to be alone on the wide ocean, to do some of the things that Uncle Jack had spoken of. He found himself wanting to run away, to taste a life of danger and adventure. Or, instead of running away, why not sail away? He wondered what it would have been like to be a real pirate, to travel with Uncle Jack, and spend the rest of his days on the open seas.

And then he realized what he'd been feeling: regret. He regretted not being allowed to join in on Uncle Jack's adventure, and it surprised him so much that he began to shiver.

"Stop it," he said aloud, "You're being stupid. You're just a kid from East Stodgerton, not some swashbuckling pirate."

This sobered him up nicely. He *was* being ridiculous. Him? Stanley Brambles, an average, normal, boring kid from an average, normal, boring town, embarking on a quest for buried treasure? Not to mention what his parents would say when they found out that he'd set sail for the ends of the earth with his Great Uncle and a talking parrot. No, he couldn't see that sort of thing happening to him. Best to leave the adventuring to the real adventurers.

Stanley rolled over and closed his eyes, and, his head once more filled with sensible thoughts, he went to sleep. His dreams, however, were anything but sensible.

CHAPTER SEVEN:
A SLIGHT CHANGE OF
PLANS

It felt to Stanley as if he'd just closed his eyes, when there came an urgent knocking at his bedroom door. It wasn't loud, but it was enough to wake him up. He sat up in bed and stared blearily at the door.

"Whoizzit?" he half mumbled. The door opened slowly, and Benjamin Stone's head appeared. "Benjamin?" said Stanley, "What are you doing back here?"

Benjamin put a finger to his lips, signaling for quiet. Stanley nodded his understanding.

"*What's going on*?" he whispered. Benjamin shook his head, and motioned for Stanley to come with him.

Stanley obeyed, and jumped as there came a tinkling crash of breaking glass from somewhere in the house. He was also aware of a deep, rhythmic booming sound that rang out every few seconds. Benjamin Stone stopped Stanley at the bedroom door and pointed to his suitcase.

"You want me to bring all my stuff?" said Stanley. Benjamin again signaled for quiet, then nodded once before leaving the room.

Had he been a little more alert, Stanley may have been overwhelmed by the strangeness of this situation, but, being not yet fully awake, he quickly threw his belongings into his suitcase, closed it, and heaved it out into the hall. The lights were off, but moonlight shining in through the bedroom window illuminated a small area outside the door. Benjamin Stone was standing there, and motioned for Stanley to follow him. Stanley stayed close behind, his slippered feet making hardly a sound as he padded along.

Benjamin stopped at the end of the corridor. Alabaster, Nell, Uncle Jack, and Pericles were already there, huddled at the edge of the entrance hall. What was going on here? Uncle Jack nodded to him, and signaled for quiet, as Benjamin had done. Stanley nodded back, and gave a small gasp as the booming noise resounded through the hall. It was coming from downstairs. He peered over the banister, and down to the main floor. The hall was awash in moonlight, and in the pale glow, he saw that the beautiful oak double doors were horribly warped and buckling at their hinges. The booming sound came again, and they buckled further. Someone—or something—was pounding on the doors.

His heart beating quickly, Stanley stepped back from the railing and looked at Uncle Jack. The old man met his gaze and pursed his lips. Stanley cast a final glance at the doors, then went over to where Alabaster and Nell were standing.

"*What's going on?*" he whispered, as yet another *boom* shook the house.

"*Dunno,*" Alabaster whispered back, "*but I don't think it's the paper boy!*" He seemed excited rather than frightened, unlike Nell, whose eyes were wide and haunted.

"*I think we're under attack,*" she whispered, just before another window broke somewhere below.

Stanley paused for a moment to let the implications of Nell's words sink in. Just then, a final *boom* rang out, followed by a loud, tearing *crack* of breaking wood. He peered down into the entrance hall just in time to see the front doors burst free from their hinges, and fall crashing to the floor. Moonlight poured in through the ruined doorway, revealing several dark shapes as they came bounding into the entrance hall. It was impossible to discern any of their features, but they looked like people. Who could they be? Robbers and thieves, perhaps? Somehow, a gang of brutal ruffians seemed out of place in the sleepy seaside town of West-port. Perhaps they were from somewhere else ... perhaps they were ... pirates?

Stanley's speculation was cut short as another dark figure stepped through the doorway. This one was quite unlike the others. For one thing, it was monstrously tall and massive, and had to stoop to come in through the door. Stanley couldn't guess for sure how tall this strange figure was, but had he taken a moment to compare it with its comrades, he would have surmised that its height had to have exceeded nine feet. The giant was clad in a dark robe that billowed about it in the night air, and he seemed to be wearing some sort of spiked helmet on his head.

The tall one stepped over the wrecked doors, and, two strides later, was standing in the centre of the hall, beneath the great chandelier. Stanley tried to get a better look at him, but the gloom was too deep, even with moonlight pouring in through the doorway. He felt someone tap his shoulder, and turned to see Uncle Jack looking at him.

"*Over here, laddie,*" the old man whispered, "*get 'round the corner an' hide in the shadows.*"

Stanley obeyed. He withdrew from the banister and hunkered down beside Alabaster and Nell, but soon after, got up on his knees so he could see down into the entrance hall. The tall one was still standing there. He suddenly raised a hand and made a slashing gesture which his men seemed to understand. They all sprang into action and disappeared into rooms and down hallways, their footsteps echoing eerily off the marble floors. The tall one stood alone for a moment in the middle of the hall, then, with a quick movement of his behelmetted head, glanced up to where Stanley and the others were hiding. Stanley ducked down a split second after, and breathed a sigh of relief when no sound of huge booted feet came from the nearby stairs. He raised himself back up off the floor, and had to clap a hand over his mouth to keep himself from screaming. The tall one was at the top of the third floor landing. He had ascended the steps without making a sound. He seemed to be trying to decide what to do next, when a sharp, piercing whistle rang through the hall. One of his men had appeared on the second floor landing, and was motioning for him to follow. The giant descended the stairs silently, pausing to examine the fish head mounted on the wall, and followed the smaller fellow down the east wing hallway.

"*Now's our chance,*" whispered Uncle Jack. "*Follow me!*"

He crept out onto the landing and made his way to the top of the stairs. Not a sound came from below, and he signaled that it was safe for the others to follow. Stanley fell in line behind Benjamin, and soon they were all at the bottom of the staircase. Uncle Jack waved them into the corner to the left of the stairs, where the shadows were deepest. Stanley sat down beside Nell, and was thinking about what a miracle it was that they hadn't been seen, when two dark shapes went running by. They went into the dining room, and as soon as they were gone, Uncle Jack stood up and went over to a telephone sitting on a nearby end table. Stanley thought he was calling the police, but instead, the old man entered five numbers on the old-fashioned rotary dial, and dropped the receiver back onto its holder. There came a brief, and mercifully quiet rumbling from under the floor, and suddenly a whole section of the staircase lifted up. Uncle Jack went around to the front of the stairs, motioning for everyone to follow. The stairway had lifted up to reveal a second stairway beneath it, this one leading down. It was, in fact, the fifteenth secret passage in Uncle Jack's mansion, and the only one that Stanley and Alabaster hadn't been able to find—and with good reason, for this one was the most secret, most important one of all.

"Follow me," said Uncle Jack, as he led the way down the secret stairway.

They started down the stone steps, and the secret door closed behind them. The stairway wound down, down, down, far past the mansion's basement. Lanterns placed at regular intervals provided light for the otherwise dark descent. The walls, ceiling, and steps were made of rough-hewn stone; this was no natural tunnel, and Stanley marvelled at the time and effort it must have taken to build this secret stairway. He tried counting the steps, but lost count somewhere after a hundred and fifty.

They descended in silence, the only sound coming from their footfalls, which echoed loudly in the small tunnel. Stanley became aware that Nell, who was behind him, was breathing rather heavily. A moment later, her footsteps stopped, and Stanley looked back to see what was the matter. Nell was standing still, eyes closed tightly, her suitcase held at her side.

"Nell," said Stanley, "are you okay?"

"I don't like closed-in spaces like this," she said through gritted teeth. "I'm claustrophobic."

"Oh," said Stanley.

"You may as well keep going, Stanley, because I can't go any further."

"What? Yeah, right—we can't just leave you here." He tried to think of something encouraging to say. "Um, look, just don't think about it. We must be almost at the bottom, anyway." Nell didn't answer.

"We've already come this far," said Stanley. "Might as well see it through." He held out his hand, and after a moment, Nell grabbed it tightly in her own, which was unpleasantly clammy.

"There, you don't even have to open your eyes," said Stanley, starting down the steps once more.

Minutes later they reached the last step, went through a doorway, and into an enormous cavern. Pericles fluttered over and landed on Stanley's shoulder.

"Well, what took you two so long?" asked the parrot.

"Uh, just helping Nell with … her suitcase," said Stanley. Nell quickly let go of his hand, which was starting to throb (it still hadn't had a chance to heal, and as such, was still bandaged). Nell noticed him wincing, and said and embarrassed *sorry*.

Alabaster's voice suddenly echoed through the cavern. "Stanley, Nell, look!"

Stanley turned his attention away from his hand, to take in his first look at his surroundings.

The cavern was vast, about a hundred yards from end to end. It was lit by several large lanterns which hung down from the ceiling far above, and bathed in their glow was an old sailing ship. It was a small vessel, perhaps sixty feet long, and quite sleek-looking. The bow jutted forward elegantly, like the head of some proud beast, poised and waiting patiently for its chance to burst forth from the cave and slice its way across the open sea. A single mast rose from the middle of the deck, and what looked like a tiny house was located towards the rear. The ship bobbed serenely in the water of a subterranean lake. The cavern floor jutted out into the water, forming a natural dock, to which the ship was moored.

The towering Benjamin Stone walked by, carrying a huge wooden crate. He nodded to Stanley and Nell, and made his way towards the ship.

"Well? Let's go!" said Pericles impatiently. Stanley and Nell followed Benjamin up the ship's gangplank, where they were met by a very excited Alabaster.

"Isn't this great? It's a real ship, and it's got a sail, and a wheel, and an anchor, and Uncle Jack says it's really fast! It's not as big as I expected, but a big one wouldn't fit into this cave, would it? It's probably better that it's small, anyway— we'd need a big crew for a big ol' warship! I kind of hoped there'd be a big one down here, but this one was, instead, but that's okay, I think it's awesome! I mean, I haven't had much of a chance to look around, 'cause I just got here a few minutes before you did, but it looks like a great ship to me!"

"Easy there," said Pericles, when Alabaster finally paused to draw breath. Benjamin took the opportunity to take his box down a staircase near the bow.

Nell said, "Alabaster, you *do* realise that we only just barely escaped from those burglars upstairs, don't you?"

"Pff!" said Alabaster. "We don't have to worry about *those* goons! We're safe in this secret cave, and we're on Uncle Jack's ship! His *ship*, Nell!"

Uncle Jack suddenly emerged from the small hut behind them. He looked tired, but not nearly as worried as he had back upstairs. "Everyone here?" he asked as he closed the door behind him. "Good. You okay, Stanley? Nell? Alabaster?"

Stanley and Nell nodded silently.

"We're great, Uncle Jack!" Alabaster said with unearthly enthusiasm.

"Alright," said Uncle Jack. "Well, let me welcome ya aboard. A pirate's gotta have a ship, an' this one's mine—the *Ogopogo*. Ya won't find a sturdier vessel on this, or any other ocean." He stood there for a time, as if putting his thoughts in order, before continuing. "As you three know, I'm leavin' tomorrow—er, today—on an important journey. I told ya that I wasn't gonna be able to bring ya along, but, well, things've changed a bit since then."

"Who are they, Uncle Jack?" said Stanley, anxious to get right to the point. "Who attacked your house?"

There was a pause, and then Uncle Jack shrugged. "I've been tryin' to figure that out since Pericles woke me. I've no idea who they are or what they want, but I *do* know that I ain't leavin' you three here if there's a crew like *that* in the area."

Stanley took a moment to consider Uncle Jack's words. "So ... are we coming with you?" He asked.

"Aye," said Uncle Jack.

"Yay!" said Alabaster.

"Now don't go thinkin' that this is some pleasure cruise," said Uncle Jack, raising an index finger. "I wasn't kiddin' when I said it'd be dangerous. Things bein' as they are, though, I figure ye'll be better off with me, Benjamin, an' Pericles close by."

"Are we leaving right now?" asked Nell.

"Aye, that we are," said Uncle Jack. "The sooner the better."

"But what if that ... *giant* is still there when we get back?" said Stanley.

"Then we'll deal with 'im when the time comes. Right now, we got a big adventure ahead of us, so let's get ready to make sail! Benjamin! Pericles! What say you?"

Pericles fluttered over to Uncle Jack and landed on his shoulder. "We're good to go, captain. We await only your command."

Benjamin, who had just finished pulling up the gangplank, saluted and stood at attention.

"Right then!" said Uncle Jack, "I'll man the helm. Pericles, to the crow's nest with ya! Benjamin, weigh anchor! You three," he said, turning to the children, "enjoy the ride!"

Pericles fluttered up to the top of the mast while Uncle Jack limped over to the wheel. Stanley watched as Benjamin turned a large winch fixed to the starboard side of the ship. The anchor cable slowly wound round and round until at last, the heavy anchor was out of the water. Benjamin flipped a switch, locking the winch in place, then went over to stand beside Uncle Jack.

"Anchor's aweigh!" shrieked Pericles, and Stanley felt the ship lurch forward.

"Nothin' to worry about," called Uncle Jack as he operated the wheel. "The current's just got us now—it'll take us right out o' the cave."

The subterranean lake was actually a river, and the Ogopogo was now riding its current towards an opening in the cavern wall. This opening led to a tunnel, which apparently led all the way out to sea.

They entered the tunnel, leaving behind the glow of the cavern's lights. Benjamin disappeared down the staircase, and returned with a large lantern, which he lit, and placed at the Ogopogo's bow.

"Thank you kindly, Benjamin," said Uncle Jack.

The lantern illuminated the dark tunnel, casting more than enough light for Uncle Jack to steer by. The tunnel seemed to be a natural one, probably carved out by this very river over millions of years.

While Nell inspected the anchor cable winch, Stanley stood at the bow with Alabaster, leaning on the bulwark and watching the walls of the tunnel go past. He was feeling a bit apprehensive now that the reality of the journey was starting to sink in. He nudged Alabaster, and said, in an undertone,

"Hey, Alabaster, are you ... worried about this?"

"About what?" said Alabaster.

"About, you know, what we're going to do. About this adventure."

"Worried? Hmm. Nope, can't say that I am. I'm more hyperactively excited about it than anything else! Why, are *you* worried?"

"Well, yeah, a little ..."

"Because it'll be dangerous?"

"There's that, yes ..."

"Because we're journeying into the unknown?"

"Ummm, sort of ..."

"Because of the mystery and spontaneity?"

"That too, but ..."

"Because there's a fantastic adventure ahead of us and it doesn't quite seem real?"

"I guess those are all part of it, but, it's just that I'm, um ... sort of going to miss my Mom and Dad. A lot."

"Ohhhh," said Alabaster.

"I mean, we could be gone for a long time. Doesn't that bother you?"

"Not really," said Alabaster, "but my Mom and Dad go away a lot—I'm used to not having them around. Besides," he said, clapping Stanley on the shoulder, "I've got my best buddy right here! How could I be lonely?"

Stanley laughed. "Yeah, that's right! No reason for two best friends to be lonely!"

"What are you two discussing so seriously?" said Nell, joining them at the bow.

"Oh, uh, nothing," said Stanley, "just ... guy stuff."

"Oh, really?" said Nell, sounding vaguely amused. She left it at that, though, much to Stanley's relief. For some reason, he didn't really want Nell to know that he missed his Mom and Dad.

After several minutes, it occurred to him that Uncle Jack's house was not this far from the sea. No one was saying anything, though, and he decided not to mention it just then. Instead, he listened to the sound of the water as it flowed swiftly through the tunnel. It was a peaceful, pleasant sound, and it echoed soothingly off the smooth stone walls.

Several more minutes passed, and Stanley was wondering how long this tunnel could possibly be, when he saw it: a tiny point of light far ahead. The light got closer and closer, and larger and larger, until it started to reflect on the damp rock of the tunnel, and on the surface of the water. Stanley heard Uncle Jack say,

"Benjamin, would ya mind putting out the lantern?"

Moments later, Benjamin took the lantern and blew it out, plunging the tunnel into a rapidly fading semi-darkness. The mouth of the tunnel was now clearly visible, getting closer and closer until ...

CHAPTER EIGHT:
THE HIGH SEAS

The Ogopogo cleared the tunnel mouth and cut swiftly through a small wave, carried still by the current of the subterranean river.

Stanley closed his eyes against the glare; the sunlight was blinding after the darkness and gloom of the tunnel. Had he been less caught up in the moment, he may have wondered how it could possibly be morning already.

"WHEEE-HAAAAA!" cried Uncle Jack as the ship sliced through another wave. Stanley opened his eyes and squinted, trying to get used to the light. Before he could see, though, he could feel the wind blowing against him, and smell the salt air as the ocean sprayed up around him.

Finally able to open his eyes completely, Stanley gave a "Whoa!" of amazement as he took in his surroundings. The Ogopogo was now in the middle of a chain of tiny islands. Many of these islands were only big enough to accommodate a few small shrubs, but some had thickets and groves of trees on them, with enough room for a good-sized house. The sea itself was the picture of oceanic beauty, as blue as the cloudless sky above it, with a hint of turquoise. The whole scene looked like something out of a postcard from some tropical paradise. Stanley marvelled at the palm trees covering some of the islands.

Alabaster, of course, was beside himself with excitement. "WOO-HOO!" he cried, jumping up onto the railing and spreading his arms like a bird, "I'M THE KING O' THE WORRRRLD!"

Nell grabbed him by the shirt tail as he swayed forward dangerously, and pulled him back down to the safety of the deck. "Alabaster, be careful!" she scolded.

Stanley, however, was feeling just as excited as Alabaster, and proceeded to jump up on the railing himself, letting fly a "WOO-HOOO!" of his own. He hopped back down just as Nell cried, "*Stanley!*", and grinned hugely. "You should try it!" he said.

Nell just sighed and shook her head, muttering something that sounded like '*boys*'.

Stanley turned to look at Uncle Jack, who was laughing merrily.

"Ahh, it's good to be back on the high seas again!" the old man called loudly. "The sun, the wind, the spray, an' crystal ocean as far as the eye can see!"

Stanley, still grinning, looked past Uncle Jack, towards the tunnel from which they had just come. His grin faded immediately, and he raced astern to get a better look.

"Stanley, where are you going?" said Alabaster, running after him.

Stanley didn't answer. He was staring incredulously at the tunnel, which, he assumed, would have Uncle Jack's Mansion and the town of Westport somewhere above it. Instead of a cliff, however, the tunnel opened out of a large, rocky island. The mainland was nowhere to be seen.

"Uncle Jack!" cried Stanley, racing back to where his uncle stood operating the wheel, "Where are we? Where's Westport? Where's your house?"

"We're a long way from Westport, m'lad," said Uncle Jack cryptically.

"But we only just went through that tunnel! We should have come out below the cliffs, and we're not sailing very fast, so we should be able to—"

"Easy now, Stanley," said Uncle Jack, taking a hand off the wheel and putting it on Stanley's shoulder. "Listen to me when I say, we're nowhere near Westport, or East Stodgerton, or Costa Rica, or anywhere you've ever been." Stanley stared at him, eyes wide.

"You mean …?"

"Aye, lad. I believe the expression is, *we're not in Kansas anymore.*"

Stanley put a hand on his forehead. He could scarcely believe it—he was in another world. He was in a world that was far from his own, where pirates still sailed the seas, and kings and queens ruled as in the days of old. And somewhere in this world, this world which was so close, and yet so far from his own, a vast treasure waited to be discovered.

"It might take a while to sink in," said Uncle Jack, not sure how the children were taking this. "I would've told ya before now, but, well, I thought you three would figure it out. Yer a clever bunch, that's for sure."

Nell was nodding slowly. "I guess I suspected," she said. "After you told us about your life and everything, but … I just couldn't believe there was a whole other world out there …"

Uncle Jack nodded his understanding. "It'd be tough for anyone to believe, I think. Ya probably thought all that stuff happened on some obscure corner o' the globe. You okay, Stanley?"

Stanley tore his eyes away from the mainland that wasn't there and said, "Yeah. Yeah, I'm fine." And the odd thing was, he *was* fine. Now that the initial shock had worn off, he expected to feel worried or scared, but he didn't. "I feel great! This is just … amazing!"

He gazed ahead, past the bow. They were clearing the island chain, and between them and the horizon, there was nothing but ocean.

"So, are we on another planet?" said Alabaster excitedly. "Did we go through some kind of portal, and travel half way across the galaxy to an alien world?"

"Well now, Alabaster," said Uncle Jack, "I don't think it's quite a question of travelling to another planet. Did you ever read *The Chronicles of Narnia*? C.S. Lewis?"

"I did," said Stanley, "My Mom read them to me when I was little."

"Well," said Uncle Jack, "I think that's the sort of *travelling between worlds* that we're dealing with here. 'Course, to answer yer question, Alabaster, I haven't the faintest idea how it works, so for all we know, we *could* be halfway across the galaxy. I'd say it's best not to think about it too hard," he said with a chuckle.

Stanley wasn't interested in how they had come to be here; he wanted to see everything there was to see, starting with every corner of Uncle Jack's ship.

"So then," said Uncle Jack, as if reading his mind, "how would you three like the grand tour?"

"Yeah!" said Stanley and Alabaster in unison. Nell smiled, but said nothing.

"Alrighty then, follow me! Benjamin, mind the helm for a bit, will ya?" And with that, Uncle Jack limped off towards the small hut at the rear of the ship. Stopping in front of the door, he turned and said, "This here's the main crew quarters, where you three'll be stayin'. Go on in an' have a look around."

He opened the door and the children went in. The interior of the cabin wasn't exactly spacious, but it was very cosy. There were six bunks set into the walls on the left and right, three on top, three on the bottom. Each bunk had a small round porthole beside it, which let in a modest amount of light. Uncle Jack explained that screens could be pulled out to hide each bunk.

"Just in case ya want a little privacy," he said, mostly to Nell.

Stanley looked around the room one more time. It really seemed larger inside than it did from the outside. There were shelves, a chest of drawers, and cabinets for each bunk. For a moment, he wished that he was back home in East Stodgerton with his parents close by. But then Uncle Jack was ushering him outside towards the stairway at the bow.

"Incidentally," said Uncle Jack, when Alabaster asked where the stairway went, "The front of a ship is called the bow. The rear is the stern, the left side is port, and the right side is starboard. Easy, eh? An' these stairs, Alabaster, lead to the Orlop deck, an' the hold.

Additional crew cabins, including Uncle Jack' s and Benjamin's, were located on the Orlop deck. Below it, the hold held the Ogopogo's cargo. As Uncle Jack explained, pointing out piles of boxes and barrels, most of it was food.

"Non-perishables, of course," he said, checking the labels on the boxes. "Oatmeal, lots o' that—plenty o' nuts an' dried fruit; dried peas—for pea soup, popular naval dish; some meat, beef jerky, mostly."

Stanley hadn't thought about food until now, and, listening to Uncle Jack, his hopes of high-sees gastronomic delights became smaller and smaller. Salty beef was, after all, a poor substitute for fresh lobster.

"And," said Uncle Jack, opening a nearby locker, "all the fish you can eat!" He produced three fishing poles from the locker and held them out to the children, smiling widely.

"Cool!" said Alabaster, grabbing one of the poles. Stanley and Nell were a bit more hesitant.

Stanley was thinking back to his first—and only—fishing experience. His family had been up at the cottage a few summers back, and Mr. Brambles had taught him how to fish. Stanley had rather enjoyed it, until his father reeled in a decent-sized rainbow trout. At that point, Stanley had realised that the hook actually punctured the fish's mouth. That hadn't been so bad, but to his horror, the hook had tragically gone right through the hapless ichthyoid's left eye.

"Er, well, that happens from time to time," Mr. Brambles had said apologetically, as he extracted the hook with less than surgical precision. "But, er, they don't feel a thing!" He had then proceeded to behead, gut, scale, and fry the fish for dinner. Tasty though the fish had been, Stanley hadn't touched a fishing pole since.

"What's the matter, Stanley?" said Uncle Jack, after he had been silent for a time. "Don't ya like fishin'?"

Stanley hesitated for a moment, and then, not wanting to hurt Uncle Jack's feelings, said, "Oh, sure I like it—I just haven't done it for a while."

"Ah, no worries," said Uncle Jack happily.

"I've never fished before, at all," said Nell, looking much more interested than Stanley.

"Well you'll soon learn, both o' yeh! You can help me teach 'em, Alabaster, what'ya say?"

"Sure!" said Alabaster, beaming.

"Alright," said Uncle Jack, taking back the fishing poles and replacing them in the locker, "That's about it for the tour. Let's head back up to the main deck." With that, he limped up the steps, followed by the three children.

A strong wind had kicked up while they were below decks, and it was slowly pushing the Ogopogo back towards the islands.

"Blast," said Uncle Jack as he took over for Benjamin at the helm and squinted into the wind. "This won't do at all. The wind is comin' right out o' the north-east."

"Is that bad?" asked Stanley.

"It's bad for *us*. Ethelia is about thirty-five degrees north-east o' here, an' this wind is gonna slow our trip down, that's for sure."

"What are we going to do?" said Nell. "You can't sail into the wind, can you?"

"There *is* a way to use the wind that's blowin' right at you," said Uncle Jack, "It's called *tacking against the wind*. You turn the ship from side to side, which lets you sorta catch the edge o' the wind, if you see what I mean. But," he said raising an index finger, "I prefer a quicker, less complicated method. Benjamin, would ya mind fetching the wind crystal?"

Benjamin saluted and disappeared down into the hold. He returned minutes later with a small wooden chest in his hands.

"Thank you," said Uncle Jack, taking the chest from Benjamin. "Now then," he said, producing an old-looking key from his coat pocket, "I'll wager you three have never seen anything like *this* before." He unlocked the chest, opened it, and drew forth an odd-looking jewel. It was colourless, and looked like two crystal pyramids attached at their bases. It was large enough that Uncle Jack couldn't close his hand around it.

"Neat," said Alabaster.

"Ooh, how pretty," said Nell. "Look, you can see clouds inside it."

Taking a closer look, Stanley saw that she was right. Moving around very quickly inside the crystal were what looked like tiny clouds. They were moving so fast, though, that they looked more like steam.

"That," said Uncle Jack, "is wind. Only time yeh'll ever see wind is when it's inside a wind crystal."

"That's incredibly amazing!" said Alabaster. "How did you get the wind *in* there?"

"Oh, ya don't put wind in a wind crystal," said Uncle Jack with a small chuckle, "It *makes* wind!" He gripped the crystal with two hands, and twisted in opposite directions. There was a tinkling click as the two halves rotated, and the three children were nearly blown off their feet by a powerful gust of wind.

"Whoa!" said Stanley and Alabaster in unison.

"Wow!" said Nell.

"Not bad, eh?" said Uncle Jack, turning the two halves of the crystal back to their original positions. "This little wonder'll give us all the wind we're gonna need. Pericles," he called, "will ya do the honours?"

The parrot fluttered down and grasped the crystal in his talons, carrying it to a small metal shelf half way up the mast. The crystal hovered above the shelf, held there by some invisible force. Meanwhile, Benjamin had opened a long, thin trapdoor in the deck no wider than one of the deck planks, and was hauling on a rope attached to the mast.

The thin compartment held the ship's large, square sail, and its yard (the horizontal pole to which the sail was attached). As Benjamin pulled on the rope, the yard rose higher and higher until the sail was fully unfurled. Then, Uncle Jack flipped a switch on the mast, the wind crystal turned itself, and WHOOOSH! the sail was filled with wind. The Ogopogo lurched ahead, and Stanley nearly lost his balance.

"YEE-HAAAA!" shouted Uncle Jack as the ship ploughed through wave after wave, "Now *this* is what sailin' is all about! Slicin' through the waves at top speed, the wind an' spray in yer face! YEE-HAAA!" he cried for the second time, as he grasped the wheel and turned the ship thirty-five degrees north-east.

The ship was indeed going very fast. Within less than a minute, the small island chain behind them was out of sight. Stanley leaned over the railing and watched the waves go by. Alabaster and Nell were standing at the bow, talking, and he was about to go over and join them when Pericles fluttered down and landed on the railing beside him.

"Impressive, isn't it?" said the parrot.

"I'll say," said Stanley. "This is all so … incredible! I don't even know what to say."

"Yes, I know how you feel. It's an amazing world, to be sure." Pericles gazed out at the endless, glittering ocean. Stanley did the same, then looked back at Uncle Jack, who was gripping the wheel and looking towards the horizon with a smile on his face.

"He misses it, doesn't he?" said Stanley, turning back to Pericles. "This world, I mean."

"Yes," said Pericles, "he misses it terribly. It's his home—mine, too, and Benjamin's. We miss it, too, of course, but not nearly as much as Jack does."

They were silent for a moment, then Stanley said, "What do you call this world? I mean, we call Earth *Earth*, but what do you call *this* one?"

"We sometimes call it Earth, as well, or simply The World … but the proper name is *Terra*."

"Terra?"

"Yes. I understand the proper name for *your* Earth is *Gaia*?"

"Oh, uh, I don't really know."

Pericles nodded. "I'm quite sure it is."

"Pericles," said Stanley, after another moment of silence.

"Hmm?"

"Why can you talk? Do all the parrots in this world talk? For *real*?"

"Oh, yes," said Pericles proudly, "We parrots are among the most intelligent birds in the world. Why do you ask? Surely the parrots in your world talk? I've seen them on television …"

"Oh, no," said Stanley, "They aren't actually talking. I mean, they're saying things, but they're only repeating what people teach them to say. They can't, you know, make conversation, like you."

"What? *Repeating what people teach them*? How preposterous! Next time I'm in Westport, I'll make inquiries at the nearest pet shop."

"You've never gone looking for other parrots?"

"Well, yes, but I've been unable to find any. I usually prefer the company of people, anyway. Parrots tend to be rather haughty and overbearing at times."

"Surely not," said Stanley, trying to keep a straight face.

"Oh yes," said Pericles, waving a wing idly. "Why, Jack's sister—your grandmother—had a scarlet macaw who was so uppity, that—"

"*My grandmother?*" interrupted Stanley. "That's right, she's Uncle Jack's sister! She's from this world, too!"

"Oh, well, yes, I thought that went without saying," said Pericles.

"She never mentioned it, though," said Stanley. "In fact, I don't think she ever even talked about Uncle Jack."

"No, I don't suppose she would have. They had a bad falling-out after their father died. I think she partially blamed him for Steven's death. Preposterous, of course. And then, when she found out that Jack had taken up a life of piracy, she grew even more angry with him. When Tyrone the Tyrant began hunting down pirates, your grandmother was harassed for being the sister of the most wanted pirate in history. Finally, Chamberlain declared her a traitor and locked her up. It was all a ploy, of course, a plot to catch Jack when he came to rescue her, and rescue her he did, right from the dungeons of the King's palace." Pericles chuckled. "They thought they had him, but he was just a bit too quick, a bit too smart." He sighed. "Of course, after that escapade, Jack decided that his homeland was no longer safe, for him, for his men, or for the last surviving member of his family, his sister, Emma.

"None of his crew wanted to leave, though, except for Benjamin and I, so he took this very ship, and set sail for a place where Chamberlain's men could never find him."

"Our world," said Stanley. "*Gaia.*"

"Correct," said Pericles. "On that last voyage, five souls were aboard: your uncle, Matilda (his wife-to-be), your grandmother, Benjamin, and myself. Jack bought the mansion and decided to settle down with Matilda. Benjamin lived with them for a while, then got his job down at the docks. I stayed with your uncle and aunt most of the time … and your grandmother moved away, got a job as a teacher, just like she'd had back in Rhedland. She met your grandfather—a teacher, as well—and they got married and had your mother."

"Wow," said Stanley, "I never knew my grandma was … well, from another world! It sounds so incredible."

"Oh yes," said Pericles, looking at him intently. "The blood of Terra flows in your veins. I'd say there are precious few people who can claim a Terran and Gaian ancestry."

Stanley was at a loss for words. "I … I … my … wha … I never could have imagined!"

"No, I suspect not. And you know what I think? I think that explains why you were so eager to come on this voyage. Your Terran blood wanted to come home. Subconsciously, you wanted to return to the world of your ancestors. You didn't feel scared or sad when we sailed out of the tunnel, did you?"

"No, not after the, you know, the surprise wore off. I felt great, I still do."

"There you go! Your Terran side, as it were, is so glad to be home, you have no time to be apprehensive! Ahh, genetics is truly an amazing thing. Well, if you'll excuse me, Stanley, I really should get back to my lookout duties."

He flapped into the air and fluttered back up to the crow's nest. Stanley watched him go, then looked out at the sea, then down at his bandaged hand. He gingerly removed the bandage and stared at the wound in his palm, which had scabbed over nicely. As he regarded the dark red gash, Pericles' voice echoed through his thoughts:

The blood of Terra flows in your veins.

CHAPTER NINE:
ARMOURED AND
DANGEROUS

"Lunch time!" called Uncle Jack. Stanley, who had been daydreaming for some time, started in surprise and turned to see Uncle Jack standing in the middle of the deck, holding four fishing poles. He went over to where his uncle was already handing poles to Alabaster and Nell.

"We'll drop anchor here," Uncle Jack called to Benjamin, who turned off the wind crystal and unlocked the winch holding the anchor cable. As the anchor fell into the water with a splash, the big man joined the rest of the crew, a fishing pole of his own in his hand.

"Right then," said Uncle Jack, "In the spirit of high-seas adventure, I thought we'd catch our lunch today. These here are prime fishin' waters, so we shouldn't have any trouble! Now then, ya bait yer hook like this." He proceeded to put a fat, yellowish worm on his hook. The worm wiggled, not looking at all pleased with its situation. Uncle Jack handed out similar worms to the rest of the crew, who then baited their own hooks.

Stanley watched Nell, who was apparently not fazed in the least by the act of impaling an invertebrate on a sharp piece of metal. Alabaster was having a bit more trouble, and ended up reducing his worm to a squishy, unidentifiable ruin. As Alabaster sheepishly asked a laughing Uncle Jack for another worm, Stanley wrestled his own onto his hook. The worm sat there, seemingly resigning itself to its fate. Satisfied, Stanley looked up at Uncle Jack.

"Right!" said the old man. "Now, the cast. It's all in the wrist, watch me." He drew back his pole, then flicked it sharply forward. The hook, worm and all, went sailing gracefully over the ship's railing, landing *plunk!* in the water about ten feet off the port bow. "There, nothin' to it!" said Uncle Jack, beaming.

The children imitated the action, and soon four red-and-white bobbers were bobbing merrily in the water.

"Now," said Uncle Jack, "we wait."

And wait they did. A good half hour went by, before Uncle Jack said,

"Harr, confusticate these fish! What could they be doin' down there? They should be goin' for those glow-worms like there's no tomorrow!"

Stanley, who had been hoping not to catch anything, looked down into the water. On the starboard side, the shadow cast by the ship reduced the sun's glare, allowing him to see several feet below the surface. Suddenly, a great mass of fish went zipping by, right under the boat.

"Here's some fish," he called, but the others had already begun reeling in their catches.

"Well done, well done!" said Uncle Jack as he, Alabaster, Nell and Benjamin dropped four gasping, flopping, silvery fish on the deck. The fish were a foot long each, at least, and if you looked at them a certain way, colours reflected off them in the sunlight.

"Prism fish," explained Uncle Jack. "Very plentiful in this region, a real delicacy, they are! I wonder why they took so long to bite?"

"Look," said Nell, "they didn't even try to eat the worms; they haven't been touched."

"Guess we baited the hooks pretty well," said Uncle Jack with a chuckle. "Now, these fish are pretty hearty, so I think one apiece will be more than enough ... Stanley, m'lad, haven't ya caught one yet?"

"Oh, no, not yet. But a whole school of them just went by, I'll wait for another one."

Uncle Jack frowned at this. "A whole school, ya say? You saw them?"

"Yeah," said Stanley, "they were going really fast, too, it's a wonder you guys caught any at all."

"Going really fast," muttered Uncle Jack. "Hmph, that certainly is uncharacteristic o' this type o' fish. They usually swim about pretty slow, lookin' for little shrimp to eat."

While Uncle Jack was speaking, another large school of prism fish swam by at top speed, travelling in the same direction as the first. Stanley was mentally willing the fish not to grab onto his hook, when he heard Alabaster exclaim,

"Whoa, look at the size of *that* sucker!"

Seconds after Alabaster had spoken, a monstrously large shape passed under the ship. Stanley saw it, and began to get nervous.

"What? Where?" said Uncle Jack uneasily. "How big was it, Alabaster?"

"Uh, gee, I don't really know."

But Stanley could make a pretty good guess. The shape had to have been at least thirty feet long.

"Maybe the prism fish were fleeing from the big one," Alabaster said brightly. Uncle Jack was looking worried.

"Er, Stanley, lad, maybe it'd be a good idea to take yer line outta the water."

No sooner had Uncle Jack finished speaking, when something tugged at Stanley's line. Or, more accurately, hauled on it like a freight train. The spool made a loud buzzing sound as it spun round and round, releasing foot after foot of fishing line. Stanley was so mesmerised by this that he forgot he was still holding his fishing pole very tightly, with both hands.

"*Stanley, let go!*" cried Uncle Jack.

But it was too late. The line ran out, the pole went taut, and Stanley was yanked off his feet, over the railing, and into the deep, dark ocean. SPLASH.

"STANLEY!" cried Alabaster.

"OH NO!" shrieked Nell.

"GREAT FLIPPIN' FLOUNDERS!" shouted Uncle Jack.

Stanley, of course, heard none of this. He hit the water hard, and was aware of a cacophonous bubbling sound in his ears as he was dragged down. He regained enough sense to let go of the fishing pole, whose handle scraped painfully over his injured hand on its way down into the briny deep. He had become slightly disoriented, and for one panicked moment, forgot which way was up. As the bubbles caused by his splash dissipated, he looked down past his feet to see nothing but deep, dark blue. Coming towards him out of that deep, dark blue was an even darker shape. It was very large, and, deciding that he didn't want to find out what it was, Stanley kicked madly towards the bright surface.

Suddenly, something fell into the water right beside him, and he exhaled in surprise, letting in a mouthful of salty sea water. He felt a large, thick arm lock itself around his waist, and the next thing he knew, he was out of the water, being carried up a rope ladder by Benjamin Stone.

Stanley coughed and spluttered, trying to speak, but was interrupted as the water just beneath him erupted and thrust towards him a monstrous, nightmarish face. Razor-sharp jaws, large enough to bite a car in two, snapped shut like a steel trap only inches from his face. With a snarl of rage, the face disappeared into the foaming water.

Stanley had only seen the face for an instant, but an instant was all it took for him to fully appreciate the horror of a live Dinichthys. It was just like the head mounted on the wall at the top of the stairs in Uncle Jack's mansion: undeniably fish-like, a rounded head covered with smooth armour plates, a vast, gaping maw, toothless, but equipped with jagged blades of razor-sharp shearing bone, and on either side of the head, glaring orange bowling-ball sized eyes.

Gaining the top of the rope ladder, a dripping Benjamin vaulted lightly over the railing and set a soggy Stanley down on the deck. Benjamin pulled up the ladder as Stanley was instantly set upon by Alabaster, Nell, and Uncle Jack.

"Stanley, are you alright?" said Nell breathlessly. There were tears in her eyes and she sniffed them back as she knelt beside him. Alabaster knelt as well, looking very pale, even more so than usual.

"That thing almost had you," he said shakily. He had a haunted look on his face, and Stanley briefly mused that it was strange seeing him without a smile.

"Stanley, laddie!" said Uncle Jack, swooping down and putting his hands on Stanley's shoulders, "Are yeh alright? Mercy, it's a good thing Benjamin's quick on the uptake! My stars, if somethin' happened to ya, I ... Are yeh alright, lad? Say somethin'!"

The enormity of the situation was just beginning to hit Stanley, and he jumped up, shouting, "ARMOUR FISH!" His legs were shaky and his head was swimming, but he managed to keep his feet.

"Aye, an armour fish it is," said Uncle Jack grimly, as he got to his feet. "An' yer bleedin', Stanley." Stanley looked down at his injured hand, which had reopened and was indeed bleeding, if less profusely than before.

"Blood in the water," said Uncle Jack. "That'll attract every carnivorous fish within sixty miles. Look lively, mates! We're not out o' this yet! Benjamin, weigh anchor an' ready the main gun! Pericles, start the wind crystal an' stay on the lookout for more armour fish! We're gettin' outta here!"

Orders were obeyed, and soon the Ogopogo was moving again. Benjamin was still hauling up the anchor when there came a sharp tug on the cable. To everyone's horror, the bow of the ship was then pulled down towards the water, the stern consequently rising up into the air at a surprising angle.

Stanley, who had grabbed hold of the port railing, caught Nell by the hand as she slid towards the tip of the bow, which was slowly submerging. Alabaster had been less fortunate, and tumbled down the stairs to the hold with a series of thumps that might have been comical, had the situation been less dire.

The bow dipped even lower into the water, and the hull groaned under the strain. His right hand howling with pain as Nell clung to it, Stanley looked back to where Benjamin was trying frantically to cut the anchor cable with a long, wide-bladed knife. Uncle Jack was nowhere to be seen.

Nell suddenly screamed. Whipping his head round to see what had caused her outburst, Stanley was horrified to see the now familiar shape of an armour fish's head emerging from the water.

"AARRRGH!" he cried, "THERE'S MORE THAN ONE!"

The fish opened its mouth and roared loudly; it was a sound like nothing Stanley had ever heard, a sort of shrieking howl that made his eyes water. The fish lunged towards Nell, who was dangling well out of reach. Still, the seven-foot-wide jaws bit savagely into the deck, splintering the boards and leaving a gaping hole in the bow. Water immediately rushed into the breach, and Stanley heard Alabaster cry out from down in the hold.

With another rage-filled roar, the fish reared up out of the water, aiming another ferocious bite at Nell's dangling legs. Suddenly, a thunderous blast rang out from somewhere behind them. A blazing fireball shot past Stanley's head and disappeared into the fish's mouth, where it exploded, sending the armour fish flying backwards into the water with a tremendous splash. Glancing behind him, Stanley was not surprised to see Uncle Jack standing behind a big black cannon, whose barrel was smoking incriminatingly.

"HAH! That'll show these overgrown piranhas!" he shouted. "You alright there, Stanley? Nell?"

"Been better!" said Stanley truthfully. Nell clenched her teeth and said nothing.

There was a loud snap, and to everyone's surprise and relief, the Ogopogo's bow bobbed out of the churning water, returning the ship to its ideal sailing position; Benjamin had finally cut the anchor cable.

"Well done, Benjamin!" said Uncle Jack. Stanley, who was just getting back on his feet, was thrown off balance as something ran into the port side of the ship with a loud *thud*. Moments later, a similar *thud* was heard from the starboard side.

"They're rammin' us!" spluttered Uncle Jack, "The ruddy blighters are rammin' us! It's always the same ol' thing, I tell ya!" and with that, he fired another cannon blast into the water. The ship shook from the blows, and Uncle Jack fired repeatedly off the port side, but the water was churning and foaming so much that he probably didn't hit anything.

Alabaster came clambering up from the hold, shouting, "They're breaking through! Water's starting to come in through the cracks!" The Ogopogo was jolted sharply as another armour fish rammed the hull, and Alabaster fell back down the stairs.

"Blast it!" snarled Uncle Jack, firing another shot into the churning foam, "Benjamin, would yeh please see to the damage in the hold?"

"I can help him," said Nell stepping forward, her face flushed.

"A'right, good fer you, lassie," said Uncle Jack. "Keep me informed, you two—an' make sure Alabaster's okay, would ya?"

Benjamin saluted and was down the stairs in an instant, followed closely by Nell. The savage pounding, however, had stopped.

"*Whew*, you scared them off!" said Stanley to Uncle Jack. Uncle Jack, though, did not look the slightest bit relieved.

"Scared 'em off? No such luck," he said, panting with fatigue. "They're still here, four or five of 'em, I think. I can see 'em circlin' the ship."

Stanley, who was feeling less and less confident that they would get out of this alive, followed Uncle Jack's gaze. Sure enough, at least five armour fish could be seen circling the Ogopogo, just beneath the surface of the water.

"What are they doing?" he said. "What are they waiting for?"

Stanley's question was answered almost immediately. With a surge of foam and a roar of fury, the head of yet another armour fish broke the surface. This one was even larger than the others, and looked much older. Its armoured head was pitted and dented, with many cracks marring the once smooth surface. The razor-bladed jaws were more jagged, looking as if parts of them had broken off over the years. The fish's right eye glared fiercely, but all that remained of the left one, was a gaping, ruined socket, blackened around the edges.

Stanley expected Uncle Jack to blast the fish in its good eye, removing it efficiently from the picture, but was surprised to see the old man take his hands off the cannon and stand up straight, staring in disbelief at the disfigured fish.

"*One-Eye*," he muttered darkly.

The fish, who seemed to have heard this, opened its mouth wider than ever and made a disturbing sound. It was a hideous, rasping hiss, but there was no mistaking it; it sounded exactly like

"*LEEEEEEEEEEE …*"

"Recognise me, do ya?" said Uncle Jack loudly. "I must say, One-Eye, I didn't expect to see *you* again."

"*SSSSURPRISE*," hissed One-Eye.

"Aye, quite the surprise, indeed," said Uncle Jack. "An' seein' *yer* ugly mug reminds me why I *hate* surprises."

"Er, maybe you shouldn't be insulting it," Stanley whispered nervously.

Uncle Jack waved the suggestion aside. "Quiet, lad; I know what I'm doin'. So, One-Eye," he shouted at the fish, "Whatcha been up to these past forty years?"

One-Eye made a gurgling, growling sound, then hissed,

"*HHHUNTING.*"

"Hunting, eh? I never woulda guessed. And, pray tell, *what* have ya been huntin'?"

"*YOU.*"

Stanley's mouth had gone dry, and it felt as if a block of ice had dropped into his stomach. This fish obviously meant to devour them all, and Uncle Jack was making it angry.

"*Me?*" said Uncle Jack, "My my, how very flattering. Have ya had any luck?"

One-Eye growled menacingly. "*TODAY.*"

"Aye, o' course, o' course," said Uncle Jack casually. "And, ah, why, exactly, have ya come to get me today?"

"*REVENGE.*"

"Ha ha!" laughed Uncle Jack, "Well, it's good to know ya haven't been wastin' yer time!"

One-Eye had just started to growl again, when an exuberant young armour fish leaped high out of the water, jaws wide, and flew straight at Uncle Jack, obviously meaning to bite him in two, if not three. Stanley cried out and cowered down behind the bulwark. Uncle Jack, however, stood stock still, glaring defiantly up at the razor-sharp jaws sailing towards him.

Quick as a flash, One-Eye leaped after the younger fish and clamped his jaws down on its tail, dragging it out of the air. The surprised fish shrieked loudly before it and One-Eye disappeared below the waves. The water churned for a few moments, then turned red. One-Eye surfaced again. The other fish did not.

"Tisk tisk, One-Eye," said Uncle Jack, as the fish's large red eye fixed on him, "I'd've thought yeh'd be able to exert a bit more control over yer school, get a bit more respect!"

At this, One-Eye roared loudly and thrashed his head wildly from side to side. The other armour fish were now floating a ways off, their smooth, shiny heads bobbing in the waves.

"This is the way to deal with armour fish," Uncle Jack said quietly, glancing sideways at Stanley. "Make 'em angry, an' they start actin' stupid, makin' mistakes. The blood in the water is helpin'—the smell makes 'em crazy, so they'll be havin' a hard time keepin' their heads clear, even ol' One-Eye."

One-Eye, who was still thrashing about madly, let out another loud roar as the other armour fish looked on. Stanley could have sworn they looked afraid.

"He's got the bloodlust, he has," said Uncle Jack with grim satisfaction. "He's been tryin' to hide it since I started tauntin' 'im, but I knew he wouldn't be able to hold it in for long. That other fish's attack was what did it—no one gets to eat me but One-Eye, an' he's at the point where he'll kill anyone who disobeys 'im."

"He … he killed his own … fish," Stanley said with horror and revulsion.

"Aye," said Uncle Jack, "that one lost control of its anger—lost its common sense. It probably didn't even know what it was doin'. Okay, laddie, quiet now, he's calmin' down."

One-Eye had stopped thrashing, and his good eye was glaring, if possible, more fiercely than ever.

"Temper temper, old boy," called Uncle Jack. One-Eye growled, but said nothing. Uncle Jack continued his taunt.

"Look at you! Yer a wreck! Ya been searchin' the seas for the past forty years, lookin' for me! It's a waste o' life, is what it is! Revenge, ya call it? Ha! How 'bout *pathetic, sad obsession*? Does the name *Ahab* ring a bell?"

"*AHAB?*" roared One-Eye; this was clearly the last straw. The other armour fish roared as well, then sped towards the Ogopogo at top speed. Upon seeing this, though, One-Eye thrashed harder than ever, turned, and lunged at the others. Soon, the enraged armour fish were all tearing at one another in a savage frenzy, while the sea boiled and churned around them.

"Now's our chance!" said Uncle Jack, "Pericles, the wind crystal! Get us movin'!"

Pericles obeyed instantly, flicking the switch and filling the sail with wind. Uncle Jack dove for the wheel, and turned the ship away from the battling armour fish.

"It won't be long before they realise we've left," said Pericles, as he fluttered back up to the crow's nest.

"Let's just hope I made 'em angry enough to buy us some time," said Uncle Jack.

No sooner had he spoken, when a thunderous roar rang out behind them. Moments later, Pericles shrieked,

"THREE ARMOUR FISH, CLOSING FAST!"

"Not angry enough, I guess," said Uncle Jack.

Stanley leaned over the port railing and gazed astern. Travelling in the Ogopogo's wake were three smaller wakes, and they were overtaking the speedy little ship with disheartening ease.

"Uncle Jack, we've got to go faster!" said Stanley.

"Can't do it, lad," Uncle Jack answered. "We've taken on too much water—the hold's flooded! We're carryin' too much weight … we're gonna have to fight!"

Stanley took a deep breath and let it out slowly. Their situation was a dismal one; the ship was slowly sinking, making it impossible to outrun the pursuing armour fish. The fish, themselves were big and strong enough to eventually batter the ship to pieces, and devour each member of her crew in a single bite.

Uncle Jack interrupted his thoughts. "Stanley," he began gravely, "I need ya to man the ship's cannon."

Stanley gawked at him. "Me? But I can't …"

"Benjamin's down in the hold, tryin' to keep us afloat, lad. I need to be steerin' the ship. All ya gotta do is aim, an' pull that lever on the side o' the gun. Ya don't have to hit anything, just scare 'em a bit, keep 'em on edge. You can do it, lad."

Stanley was about to protest further, when the battered head of One-Eye broke the surface twenty feet off the port beam, roaring with fury.

"No time to sit an' chat about it," said Uncle Jack.

Stanley looked at him, then at One-Eye's monstrous visage, then at the ship's gun. How hard could it be? Making up his mind, he strode purposefully up to the cannon and positioned himself behind it.

"Don't forget to put the lever back into place after ya fire," Uncle Jack cautioned. Stanley nodded slightly, more to himself than to anyone else. Gripping the cannon's lever, he aimed the gun in One-Eye's general direction.

Suddenly, one of the smaller armour fish surfaced right beside the ship. Surprised by the roaring beast, Stanley unintentionally pulled the lever. With a loud booming noise, a jet of fire exploded from the cannon's mouth, washing over the astonished armour fish. The creature shrieked more with surprise than pain, and dove beneath the waves. Stanley was just as surprised as the fish, and lost control of the cannon, which proceeded to swing wildly left to right, up and down, spewing a constant stream of searing, red-gold flame. Above the roar of the flames, Stanley heard Uncle Jack shouting,

"THE LEVER! PUSH IT BACK!"

Stanley leapt on the wild gun and pushed the lever back, shutting off the stream of fire. Mortified, he looked back at Uncle Jack, who waved and said,

"No worries, no harm done—just remember for next time! There's a fire crystal in that gun, lad! Gotta go for short, controlled bursts to get the strong fireballs!"

So that's it, thought Stanley, *a fire crystal!*

There was no time to be amazed, though, for the next instant, One-Eye came streaking towards the ship at an acute angle, dealing a glancing blow to the hull with his armoured head. Stanley grabbed the lever again, this time concentrating fully on aiming. The cannon had a crosshair above its barrel, and this Stanley focused directly on One-Eye's good eye, which was now glaring balefully at Uncle Jack.

His face set, Stanley prepared to pull the lever, but then something happened. The ghastly red eye fixed on *him*. Stanley gazed into the eye, and for an instant, saw the rage and anger drain out of it. He saw fear in that eye, and resignation. One-Eye had made a costly mistake, and was now about to pay for it.

Very well, the eye seemed to say to Stanley. *Finish me off, then.*

Stanley held his aim for a full ten seconds, the fish staring straight up into the crosshair. He tried to pull the lever, but his mind had filled with images of a small fish, a rainbow trout, gasping in the early evening air, a hook protruding from its left eye. Stanley closed his eyes and took his hand off the lever.

Suddenly the ship lurched sharply to the left, then to the right. Stanley lost his balance and clung to the railing for support. He glanced back at the water, and was not surprised to see it devoid of any trace of One-Eye. The ship continued to lurch three or four more times, and then there was a loud, groaning crack from the stern. Stanley looked over at Uncle Jack, who was spinning the ship's wheel; it appeared to be malfunctioning.

"Useless!" said the old man angrily, sending the wheel into another wild spin. "Those blasted fish broke the rudder!" He clasped his hands behind him and paced back and forth briefly, then stopped and looked up at Stanley. "It's not lookin' good," he said bluntly. "We can't make top speed, an' we can't take evasive action. If we keep goin' like this, it's a cinch they'll bash us to pieces." He sighed heavily, then limped over to the mast and turned off the wind crystal. The ship slowly reduced its speed, until it was drifting quite calmly.

Stanley had never felt so ashamed in his life. He had had the chance to end this battle, but hadn't taken it. Uncle Jack had been relying on him to protect the ship, and he hadn't even had the nerve to fire on a huge, murderous fish, who obviously wouldn't have thought twice about devouring him. Staring at his shoes, he said,

"I'm sorry, Uncle Jack."

The old man looked at him intently. "Sorry, lad? Sorry for what?"

Stanley was so frustrated by his own incompetence, that he was on the verge of tears. He fought them back and said, "I had the chance to … to *get* One-Eye, but I … I couldn't do it. The way he looked at me, I just couldn't bring myself to …"

Uncle Jack stared at him, mouth slightly open with surprise, then shook his head as if to clear it. "Why Stanley, as I live an' breathe!" He limped over and put a hand on Stanley's shoulder. Taking off his hat, he said, "Laddie, I don't know what to say!" Stanley sniffed and fought to keep a neutral face. "Ya shouldn't be sorry, m'lad. *I'm* the one who should be apologisin' to *you*! Imagine, me expectin' you to be able to handle a cannon, right off the bat! I'm sorry, Stanley, I was thinkin' back to me glory days. I should never have put so much pressure on ya!"

"No, it's not that," said Stanley, wiping his nose with his hand, "I *could* handle it. I had One-Eye right in my sights, I could have gotten him easily. But I just …" He paused, staring down at his shoes again. "I felt sorry for him," he mumbled.

Uncle Jack was silent for a moment. When Stanley looked up at him, he had a thoughtful look on his face. Finally, he said, quietly, "Ya had 'im in yer sights, ya say?"

"Yeah," said Stanley miserably. "He just stared right back at me. I could have hit him five times, but instead I … chickened out."

"Sounds to me like yeh can handle a gun better than I could've expected," said Uncle Jack.

"Huh? But I—"

"If ya had 'im in yer sights, if yer sure ya coulda had 'im … then ya probably coulda!"

"You don't understand," said Stanley, "I let him go!"

"Aye, an' I'm proud of ya for it."

Stanley stared. He had expected Uncle Jack to be furious with im, but instead, he was saying that he was proud!

"But I don't—"

"Stanley, lad, over the years, I've fired that cannon so many times I've lost count. An' just now, ya got me thinkin', ya did. Whether ya meant to or not, ya showed concern for One-Eye back there. Ya held yer fire when ya knew right well that ya coulda finished 'im off. Ya say ya felt sorry for 'im, an' ya may call it chickenin' out, but d'ya know what *I* call it?"

Stanley shook his head.

"I call it *compassion*. Here's a beat-up ol' fish, missin' an eye, face all banged up, a right mess. He's out for blood, true, but you're thinkin', maybe it's not just the fish's fault; he's obviously had a rough life, an' is that any reason to hurt someone, just 'cause he's angry at the world? ... and other things ..."

Uncle Jack had a distant look in his eyes. "Ya got me thinkin', lad. Ya got me thinkin' that maybe if I hadn't fired that gun so much ... maybe I'd've made a few less enemies."

"*You* shot out his left eye, Uncle Jack?" said Stanley quietly.

"Aye. Er, that is, *yes*, I did. That's why he's out to get me. One-Eye was the first sea-monster, the first foe I ever fought, way back when I was just an ensign, before I'd ever even dreamed of becomin' a pirate. There he was, probably the biggest armour fish that ever lived, circlin' the ship with some of his mates. They hadn't attacked us yet, but as soon as that red-eyed head broke the surface, I, bein' the hard-headed fellah that I was, hopped behind an un-manned cannon (inappropriate conduct fer an officer, if ya want to know) an' dealt 'im one, right in the eye. I'd heard enough about armour fish, ya see—how they're merciless, wicked things that can smash a ship to pieces, an' would kill ya as soon as look at ya.

"Anyway, it did the trick ... for awhile, anyway. I got a medal for bravery, an' became a hero, at least to the crew of a wee cargo freighter. Started callin' me *Blackout Jack*, for a while, they did—cause I'd *blacked out* one o' the big fish's eyes, I guess—'till they just shortened it to *Black Jack Lee*.

"But I'll tell ya, a little glory sure wasn't worth the price. One-Eye wasn't dead, an' he came back to haunt me many times during me years on the high seas. I lost some good men to 'im. He was just the first of a whole line of enemies, but in many ways, he was the worst." He sighed.

"An' now, for the first time in I dunno how any years, I feel guilty about it. Makin' him my enemy, I mean. I'm thinkin' that maybe if I'd taken a leaf outta *your* book, Stanley, we wouldn't be in this mess we're in." He sighed again and leaned against the bulwark. "I'm not gonna let 'em take this ship, though," he said gruffly. "They say old hatreds never die, but these armour fish will, mark my words. We'll get outta this, lad, never fear."

"What if you apologised?" said Stanley.

"Eh? Apologise?" said Uncle Jack. "To a fish?"

Stanley shrugged. "My Dad always says that an apology is the best kind of band-aid."

Uncle Jack looked uncomfortable. "But Stanley, lad, there's no reasonin' with armour fish, they're bloodthirsty maniacs, every last one of 'em, an' what's more, only a few of 'em are bright enough to *really* understand when yer talkin' to 'em!"

"Like One-Eye?"

"Aye, like—right." He gave a little smile, then turned and gazed out over the ocean. "AHOY, ONE-EYE!" he called loudly. Stanley followed his gaze, and moments later, the familiar mangled face broke the surface. One-Eye opened his mouth and hissed menacingly, but did not attack.

"You really think this'll work?" Uncle Jack asked Stanley.

"Couldn't hurt," said Stanley with a shrug.

Uncle Jack nodded and took a deep breath. "One-Eye, old boy, I've been talkin' to me nephew here, an' he's got me thinkin'." He paused, waiting for some kind of reaction. One-Eye, however, just continued to stare.

"Ahem," coughed Uncle Jack. "After all these years, I think it's only right to tell ya …" he glanced briefly at Stanley, who nodded encouragingly. "That I'm sorry. I'm sorry for hurting ya. I was young an' foolish back then, an' I acted thoughtlessly, and, er, uh, well … I'm just sorry for everything I put ya through." Uncle Jack gripped the railing tightly with both hands, holding his breath. Stanley heard footsteps behind him, and turned to see Alabaster, Nell, and Benjamin coming up from the hold. He put a finger to his lips, signalling that they should be quiet.

Meanwhile, One-Eye and Uncle Jack were staring at eachother, two old enemies, met for what would likely be the last time, finally able to resolve their old hatreds.

Suddenly an odd gurgling hiss emanated from One-Eye's throat. It sounded as if he was repeatedly breathing outwards in short, quick bursts. The sound grew louder, and Stanley's heart sank when he realised that One-Eye was laughing. He took a pained look at Uncle Jack, who was still staring stone-faced at the fish.

One-Eye's laughter escalated into roaring, bubbling guffaws (if it's possible for a fish to guffaw), and was joined by two other armour fish, who were trying half-successfully to imitate the noise.

"THINK THAT'S FUNNY, DO YA?" shouted Uncle Jack, grabbing the cannon and aiming at the laughing One-Eye. He was about to pull the lever, but then he cast a glance at Stanley. Stanley looked back at him. He felt so bad for Uncle Jack, that he was about to say, *go ahead, finish him off*. Instead, though, he held his tongue and watched the anger drain from his uncle's face. The old man took his hand off the lever and sighed deeply. He paused for a moment, then said, "Fine, One-Eye, have it your way. But this years-long feud between us is over. I'll not fight yeh any more, so be on yer way, an' I'll do the same."

One-Eye, who had stopped laughing, was clearly not ready to let things end this way. He snarled and sped towards the Ogopogo. As he reached the side of the ship, the massive fish leaped up out of the water and let out a ferocious roar. Almost as if by reflex, Uncle Jack levelled the cannon and fired. One-Eye took the blast full in the face, and was blown backwards into the water with a great splash. He surfaced a moment later, floating on his side. He didn't move again. The other armour fish shrieked loudly and disappeared below the waves. Uncle Jack grimly regarded One-Eye's lifeless body.

"I shoulda known," he said quietly. "A band-aid doesn't help a wound that's been left open so long." With that, he limped past Stanley and made his way down the stairs to the Orlop deck. Alabaster joined Stanley by the cannon.

"That was scary," said Alabaster. "You okay, Stanley?"

"Yeah, I'm fine."

"What about Uncle Jack?"

Stanley didn't answer. He leaned on the railing and stared down at One-Eye, floating there in the water.

"He did what he had to do," said Pericles, alighting on Stanley's shoulder. "Those fish would have killed us."

"Yeah," said Stanley. "I know."

CHAPTER TEN:
MINOR REPAIRS

For the next few hours, the Ogopogo drifted aimlessly. With no anchor and no way to steer, the ship was at the mercy of the wind and waves, both of which seemed indifferent to the vessel's plight. Uncle Jack barricaded himself in his cabin for the better part of the afternoon, even refusing food when Benjamin served them all a late lunch, so Pericles took command as acting captain.

"Might as well take down the sail, Benjamin," he said, after ordering Alabaster and Nell to man the ship's pump, in hopes of ejecting the three feet of sea water which now filled the hold. "No sense in getting blown right back to where we started." The wind was indeed still blowing out of the north-east, and with no rudder, they were better off staying put, rather than barrelling off in a random direction.

"Is there anything I can do?" asked Stanley.

"No, you can relax," said Pericles, as he perched on the motionless steering wheel. "The pump isn't particularly complex, and Benjamin doesn't need any help with the sail. I think we all deserve a rest after today's insanity."

Stanley found himself agreeing. "Should I go talk to Uncle Jack?"

"No, I think he should be left alone for now," said Pericles. "Facing one of your worst enemies isn't easy, even for Jack, and he hasn't done it for a long time. He usually just needs to recover for a spell after a battle. Give him some time."

Just then there came a very high-pitched shriek from below decks.

"EEEEYAAAA! WHAT ARE YOU DOING, YOU ... YOU ... YOU *TWIT!*"

Moments later, Nell came storming up from the hold, looking more than a little harassed. She was soaking wet, as was Alabaster, who was close behind her.

"What happened?" asked Stanley, trying not to smirk.

Nell cocked her thumb back at Alabaster. "*This* idiot put the pump on reverse, and it sucked in about three more feet of seawater before I could shut it off! Anything that was still dry down there is now soaking wet! It's a complete disaster!"

"Yeah!" said Alabaster. "I mean, just when you think nothing else can possibly go wrong, something like *this* happens!"

"*It was your fault!*" Nell snarled.

"I know, that's what makes it so *frustrating!*" said Alabaster, clenching his fists.

Nell, who was so vexed that she was temporarily unable to speak, bared her teeth at Alabaster and made a noise of profound disgust and annoyance, before stalking furiously off to the cabin.

"Wow!" said Stanley, "Is she ever mad!"

"Yeah!" said Alabaster, "That was amazing!"

"Amazing?" echoed Stanley, "More like terrifying! I thought she was going to bite your face off or something!"

"Yeah!" said Alabaster, not sounding particularly terrified, "I've never seen anything like it! I mean, girls at school usually just ignore me or roll their eyes at me. They never almost kill me!"

"Uh, yeah," said Stanley.

"I guess the lesson here would be to tread softly around Nell when she's doing something important," said Alabaster thoughtfully.

Stanley folded his arms and regarded his friend sceptically. Alabaster seldom learned his lesson on the first try.

"Well," said Alabaster after a moment or two, "how 'bout a game?" And he strode off confidently towards the cabin to get his Monopoly board.

While they were setting up the game, Pericles fluttered down to the deck with a fat sunfish clasped in his beak. He landed by the Monopoly board, flipped the fish into the air, and swallowed it in one gulp. Stanley briefly considered the fact that he had never heard of a parrot eating a fish.

"Scrumptious!" said Pericles, making a sound that was the equivalent of smacking one's lips, only with a beak. "I say," he said, looking at the game board, "may I play, too?"

*   *   *   *

Pericles proceeded to thoroughly trounce the boys at Monopoly. "My, my," he said as Stanley handed him two five hundred dollar bills and the deeds to every property he owned, "This game seems rather advanced for youngsters. Real estate trading, taxes, deeds, mortgaging … it really requires a quick mathematical mind, not to mention some real business savvy."

"It's a *game*," Stanley said testily, "It's supposed to be *fun*."

"Ah, yes of course," said Pericles. "Well, ah, that's enough for me—I'll leave you two to it."

"I hope he realizes I need that Monopoly money back," said Alabaster, as Pericles fluttered away with a stack of colourful bills grasped in his talons.

Deciding that they had had enough Monopoly for one day, the boys began packing up the board. There came a sound of movement from the stairway, and Uncle Jack's behatted, white-haired head came into view.

"Ahh," he breathed as he made his way up the stairs and onto the deck, "I never get tired o' lookin' out at the open sea." He leaned against the port bow railing and stared out over the water.

"How are you, Uncle Jack?" asked Stanley after several minutes had gone by. Uncle Jack turned towards him and said,

"Fine, Stanley, an' thanks for askin'." He sighed and turned his gaze back to the horizon. "I just needed a bit o' time to meself, ya see. But," he said, turning around once more, "now that I've had it, and am feelin' right as rain again, we can get back down to business." He let go of the bulwark and walked, quite easily, over to where Stanley and Alabaster were sitting.

Stanley noticed with some surprise that Uncle Jack had swapped his artificial metal leg for a battered old wooden one. Noting Stanley's surprise, Uncle Jack grinned and said,

"I always liked this old wooden one better. That metal contraption they gave me never fit right!"

They all laughed at this, although Stanley found himself wondering exactly how Uncle Jack attached and detached his artificial legs.

"You've probably been wonderin' how we're gonna get outta this mess we're in," said Uncle Jack. To be perfectly honest, the thought hadn't crossed their minds until now, but they nodded anyway.

"Well, so have I," continued Uncle Jack, "but I think I've got a plan. First—"

Just then the cabin door burst open, and Nell came striding out onto the deck, a small stack of papers in her hand. She brushed by Stanley and Alabaster, and made a beeline for Uncle Jack.

"Mr. Lee," she said, "if you don't mind, I'd like to talk to you about repairs."

Uncle Jack stared for a moment. "Repairs?"

"To the Ogopogo," said Nell.

"Oh, er, right, o' course," said Uncle Jack. "Well, ah, what about the repairs?"

"Well," said Nell, "the leaks have been stopped, but the hull has been severely weakened at certain key points." She held up a diagram of the Ogopogo, which she had presumably drawn herself. Indicating certain areas marked in red, she continued,

"The damage in these areas is so bad that they can't be patched up permanently. These sections of the hull are going to have to be replaced."

"Oh," said Uncle Jack, staring at the diagram. He passed it to Benjamin, who glanced at it briefly, then nodded.

"Also," said Nell, flipping through her sheets of paper, "I've been thinking about the destroyed rudder. Now, I think I can temporarily solve that problem, too—long enough to get us where we need to go for repairs—but I'll need a bit of help." She held up another sheet of paper. "I've drawn up some rough blueprints, and made a list of some of the tools and parts I'll need."

Uncle Jack examined the list and the blueprint with wide eyes. "Er, well," he said, after a moment or two, "these plans're very, uh, *thorough*, that's true enough, but, ah, well …"

"What's the matter?" said Nell.

Uncle Jack took a deep breath. "I think buildin' an engine from scratch might be a wee bit drastic, given our current situation, lass."

"Oh," said Nell, looking a bit put out.

"What!" cried Alabaster, "You know how to build engines, Nell? That's awesome! *You're* awesome!"

"Well, I could do it if I had the right parts and stuff," said Nell, going a bit red in the face, "And it wouldn't really be from scratch; I'd just work around the principle of the boiler, and borrow a few parts from the stove. Like I said, it would only be temporary, and not very powerful, but I designed it so that we could steer it, and … and … uh, I guess it *is* a bit complex …"

"Well, for our purposes, anyhow," said Uncle Jack, looking again at the blueprints. "I gotta say, though, I'm flat out impressed with these plans o' yers—the parts I can understand, anyways! Ya got a real knack for machinery there, lassie!"

"Where did you learn so much about engines, Nell?" asked Stanley, as Nell took her blueprints back from Uncle Jack.

"From my Dad, mostly," said Nell. "He's a mechanic—he can fix anything."

"That's all very well and good," said Alabaster, "but I think I should point out that these so-called '*blueprints*' of yours are actually *white*."

Nell stared at him.

"I just wanted to clear that up," said Alabaster. "Just to save you from embarrassing yourself later on." He tapped the side of his nose obnoxiously.

Before Nell could injure Alabaster, Uncle Jack piped up,

"Listen up, mates! As I was sayin' before, I think I have a plan to get us outta this fix we're in. Now, currently, we're unable to steer the Ogopogo, but I think if we can rig up some kinda—er, Nell, didja have a question?"

Nell had raised her hand and was waiting patiently for a chance to speak. "Sorry to interrupt," she said, "but I also had an idea for, um, building a new rudder."

"Really?" said Uncle Jack.

Nell held up another sheet of paper. "Yeah, just in case the engine didn't work. The design is pretty simple, and it won't work quite like the old one ..."

"Ah, I see where yer goin' with this," said Uncle Jack, examining the diagrams. "Yer plan is to keep the rudder at the stern ..."

"Yeah," said Nell. "If we can drill a hole in the deck about, oh, eight centimeters in diameter, we could insert a wooden peg, which would allow us to turn the new rudder left and right. Um, the only thing is, the rudder blade is going to have to be pretty long; it has to reach down below the water level."

"Aye, that's true enough," said Uncle Jack. He scratched his chin in thought for a moment or two. "But I don't see why we can't make it work! Nell, Benjamin, you two come with me—let's see how much extra wood we can scrounge up."

*   *   *   *

Nell, Uncle Jack and Benjamin spent the rest of the afternoon working on the new rudder. Stanley and Alabaster spent the time watching and feeling useless. The boys had tried to help at first, but Stanley just couldn't seem to hammer the nails in straight, and Alabaster dropped *his* hammer on Nell's foot. Fortunately, Nell had been wearing shoes at the time, but she still suggested that things might go a bit more smoothly if the boys would leave the work to the people who 'knew what they were doing'.

Stanley yielded to Nell's logic, but Alabaster insisted on hovering close by, watching with wide eyes as Nell nailed planks together with professional ease.

At length, Nell put down her hammer and wiped her forehead with her arm. "Whew!" she said, standing up and stretching, "It's finally done!"

"Not bad, not bad," said Alabaster. "So what's next?"

"Well, now we just have to get the thing into position," said Nell, clearly pleased with her work. "And you can help with *that*, if you want."

"Sweet!" said Alabaster.

They all helped to lift the new rudder and heave it into position. It was a rather ungainly piece of wood, and moving it wasn't easy, nor was standing it on its end at the stern without dropping it overboard. Stanley was glad for the chance to help, even though Benjamin Stone was doing most of the work. They had to balance the rudder on its end and lower it down into the water. The section at the top had been built to overlap the deck—this was the control point for the rudder, since it couldn't be attached to the ship's wheel. After a few tense moments, there came a satisfying *thunk* as the rudder's pivot peg dropped into the hole that Benjamin had drilled.

"Well done, mates," said Uncle Jack, clapping his hands, "well done indeed. An' well done on designin' an' buildin' the new rudder, Nell—ye'll be an engineer someday, I'll warrant!"

Nell went bright red at this. "Oh, well," she said, shuffling her feet, "I'm just glad I could help."

"Right!" said Uncle Jack, turning back to the rest of the crew, "Look lively, mates—we've gotta make up for lost time! Let's get back in gear! Pericles, to the crow's nest with ya! Benjamin, yer on rudder duty! Stanley, Alabaster, this deck could use a good ol' fashioned swabbin'. Would ye mind? There's mops down in the hold. Nell, ya worked hard today—ye can take a break if ye'd like."

"No, that's okay," said Nell, "I'll help Stanley and Alabaster."

✳   ✳   ✳   ✳

Stanley, Alabaster and Nell spent about half an hour swabbing the deck, while the Ogopogo sped eastward across the sea. The sun was starting to sink low behind them; evening was approaching.

"Uh, by the way," said Nell, looking up from her swabbing, "Alabaster, I'm sorry for, um, getting mad at you earlier and calling you a … twit and an idiot."

"Oh, that's okay," Alabaster said cheerfully as he scrubbed some grime out of the port scupper, "I know you didn't really mean it—you were just mad, that's all. It's *Stanley* you should be apologizing to—you really scared him!"

"What!" said Stanley, almost dropping his mop. Nell looked at him, a surprised smile on her face.

"Really?" she said, going slightly pink, "Did I scare you, Stanley?"

"No!" Stanley almost yelled.

"But Stanley," said Alabaster, looking confused, "when Nell yelled at me, didn't you say it was terrifying?"

"Well, yeah, I did, but I didn't mean—I mean, it wasn't really ... uh ..." Stanley looked helplessly from Alabaster to Nell, who was looking somewhat amused.

"I'm sorry I scared you," said Nell, patting Stanley playfully on the head.

"S'okay," Stanley said uncomfortably, "I mean, you didn't!"

Nell laughed. "I know, I know, I'm just teasing."

"Hey, I just thought of something," said Alabaster. "Maybe Stanley was just *joking* when he said you terrified him, Nell!"

"I'm sure that's what it was, Alabaster," said Nell, winking at Stanley.

Stanley sighed and went back to his mopping. He paused for a moment and gazed out over the ocean. The sun, sinking low in the west, had stained the water a vibrant red. Pericles alighted on the railing beside him.

"Good weather tomorrow," commented the parrot.

"Yeah? How do you know?" said Stanley.

"*Red sky tonight, sailor's delight,*" recited Pericles. "A red sunset like this always means fine weather the next day."

"What if you get a red morning?" asked Stanley.

"Then you'd better take warning!" said Pericles, laughing shrilly.

Stanley gave a small laugh, and looked down at the water rushing by the Ogopogo as the ship sliced its way through the waves.

"If you're almost through with the swabbing," said Pericles, "dinner is just about ready. Nothing too fancy tonight—Benjamin is too busy steering the ship, and the stove is probably out, anyway. Come down to the galley when you're ready.

✳   ✳   ✳   ✳

Stanley opened his eyes, only to find himself underwater. Panicking, he swam about wildly, looking for the surface, but all was dark and gloomy, and the bubbles he made went off in a hundred different directions.

I'm going to drown, he thought fearfully.

"No, you're not," said a voice. "You're safe."

Looking around, Stanley saw a beautiful mermaid swimming towards him. "Help!" he said, "I can't find the surface! I'm going to drown!"

The mermaid smiled and said, "Don't worry, you can't drown." She pointed at Stanley's feet. Looking down, Stanley was surprised to see a shimmering fish's tail where his legs used to be.

"See?" said the mermaid with a smile.

Stanley gasped, and breathed in a lungful of sea water, but to his surprise, it was just like breathing air. "I can breathe!" he said with elated relief.

The mermaid laughed. "I know! You've always been able to, you just didn't realize it."

Stanley suddenly noticed that the mermaid looked like Nell, only a few years older. "Nell?" he said incredulously, "You're a mermaid?"

The mermaid looked confused for a moment, then her expression turned to one of fear. Without another word, she turned and swam off into the watery gloom.

"Hey, wait!" cried Stanley, "What's the matter?"

As soon as he had spoken, though, an icy shaft of fear lanced through his stomach. His heart began to race, his breath coming in quick gasps. Something else was down here, something monstrous and terrible, and Stanley was alone with it, all alone in the deep, dark ocean.

Looking down past his tail, he could see something huge and dark coming towards him; a shapeless mass of darkness, blacker than the darkest night. He tried to flee, but the thing was instantly upon him. It reached out with great constricting strands of itself, and wrapped him tightly in darkness. A harsh, cold voice rasped in his ear.

"*MINE.*"

"NOOOOO!"

Stanley opened his eyes to the sleepy, comfortable darkness of the Ogopogo's crew cabin. Not sure where he was, he looked around the room, breathing loudly, a cold sweat bathing his face. Finally remembering that he was safely aboard the

Ogopogo, he sighed with relief. He tried to move, but his blankets were wrapped tightly around his body like a mummy's bandages. He fought his way free, then threw his blankets on the floor and lay back, gasping.

"Just a dream," he muttered. He could hear Alabaster breathing peacefully in the bunk above him, and Nell's quiet breath from across the cabin was barely audible over the soothing sound of the waves outside.

Peaceful and comforting though the scene was, Stanley was now wide awake. He got out of bed, grabbed his housecoat, and quietly made his way out the cabin door and onto the main deck.

The night air felt heavenly as he shuffled over towards the port beam. A loud snort issued from the crow's nest, and he looked up to see Pericles perched on the edge, his head tucked under a wing. Grinning at the comic image, Stanley leaned on the railing and gazed out over the dark water.

Looking up at the sky, he was amazed by what he saw. The stars shone brilliantly, and there were thousands upon thousands of them, far more than he had ever seen in the skies over East Stodgerton. The stars, however, weren't the most amazing things in the sky; that title belonged to the moons—there were three of them. One looked very small, and was a bright royal-blue. The second was larger, and emerald green in colour. The third was very large, and coloured a light reddish-brown. It looked very close. Stanley stared at the moons. "I really am in another world," he whispered.

Something far off on the ocean, near the horizon, caught his eye. It was a cool, blue light, and as he stared at it, it seemed to grow brighter. A second blue light appeared, a bit closer to the ship, and from what he could see, it seemed to be a flame. A third flame sprang up much closer, perhaps three miles away; it looked as if it was burning right on the surface of the ocean. Stanley was transfixed by the blue fire's eerie glow, unable or unwilling to look away.

He snapped out of his trance, though, and gave a *whoof!* of surprise when somebody tapped him on the shoulder.

"Oops, sorry, Stanley," said Uncle Jack. "Ya weren't sleepwalkin', were ya? I hear yer not supposed to wake up someone who—"

Stanley shook his head. "Oh, no, I was just looking at the stars and stuff."

"Can't sleep, huh?"

"Well, I had a ... bad dream," Stanley said, slightly embarrassed.

"Ah well, nothin' like night air to clear the head," said Uncle Jack, taking a place at the railing beside Stanley. "Especially night air on the high seas!"

"There's three moons," said Stanley, looking up at the sky, "and the sky is so clear! The stars are amazing!"

"Aye," said Uncle Jack, gazing up as well. "Sailors have a very special relationship with the stars. We use 'em to navigate, for one thing."

"Really? How?"

"Well, if ya know the positions of the stars, yeh can figure out yer own position without too much trouble. Yeh can use a sextant, o' course, an' there's loads of charts an' books filled with star maps an' such—they tell ya where above the world a star is at any given time, an' if ya know where a star is, ya know where *you* are, in relation to that star."

"That's amazing," said Stanley.

"An' what's more," continued Uncle Jack, "once yeh've spent a lifetime navigatin' by the stars, yeh can do it without even consultin' a chart! Look there." He pointed to a very bright star, high above the horizon. "That there's the north star, *Norvus*. It's always over the north pole, so no matter where y'are in the world, if yer lookin' at Norvus, yer lookin' north."

"Do all the stars have names?" asked Stanley.

"Oh, I think so," said Uncle Jack, "Astronomers've spent centuries namin' 'em. Let's see, the easy ones are Norvus, Caleas, Brantes, Marifus, Torathal, Dentrius, Estalia, Vannar, Ecceltria, Westron, Borial, Quinta, Robinus, Oracus, Sentius, Garlus, Bellus, Damicus, Kiren, Poreal, and Sudovus."

"Those are the *easy* ones?"

"Oh, aye, a piece o' cake compared to the rest."

"And you know them all?"

"Yep, sure do. An' judgin' by the angle of Norvus, Westron and Caleas, we're still on an easterly course."

"Shouldn't we be going north-east?" asked Stanley.

"Ideally we would be," said Uncle Jack, "but we need repairs as soon as we can get 'em, an' Ethelia's a bit far."

"Where are we going now?"

"We're headed for Port Silverburg. It's a good-sized port city; it's a good deal closer than Ethelia. We should be there by tomorrow evenin', assumin' we get an early start tomorrow. Plus, one o' me old lieutenants owns an inn there, I'm told, so accommodation won't be a problem while the Ogopogo's gettin' fixed."

"How long will the repairs take?"

"Depends on who we got workin' on 'em, but I'd say at least three or four days. I hate to waste so much time, but there ain't much we can do about it. We took some heavy damage from those blasted armour fish, an' Nell knew what she was talkin' about when she said the repairs she and Benjamin made were only temporary."

Stanley looked down at the waves as they lapped against the ship. The ocean looked dark and secretive compared to the shining splendour of the starry sky. "Do you think there are any more armour fish down there?" he asked.

"Oh, I think we'll be pretty safe from armour fish," said Uncle Jack. "They usually sleep at night, an' Benjamin an' I're keepin' an eye out for anything *fishy* ... get it?"

"I get it," said Stanley, forcing himself to chuckle at Uncle Jack's monumentally weak joke. He glanced up at the old man, and was surprised to see that his hair, which had been snowy white, was now shot through here and there with streaks of grey and black. The difference was plain, even by the faint light of the moons. "Uncle Jack, your hair!" Stanley exclaimed.

"You noticed, eh?" said Uncle Jack.

"Yeah," said Stanley, "it's not all white anymore. What happened?"

Uncle Jack shrugged. "This sea air must be doin' me some good!" he said cryptically.

"How old are you, Uncle Jack?"

"Why Stanley!" said Uncle Jack, pretending to be affronted, "Ye should never ask a gentleman his age! Heh heh, just kiddin'. I'll be 109 in October, me lad! An' I hope to see the lofty heights o' 150 'fore I sleep in the cold earth!"

"Wow!" said Stanley, "You sure don't look like you're 109!"

"No, I s'pose not," said Uncle Jack with a grin.

"But *how?*" cried Stanley, "How can you possibly be that old? And you're going to live to be 150? I don't understand!"

Uncle Jack shrugged. "As far back as I can remember, the average life expectancy 'round these parts has been a hundred an' thirty, an' there're plenty o' wrinkled old coots who live long after that. There's alotta differences between this world an' the one you live in. Folks from Terra just live longer than those from Gaia."

"But why?" said Stanley. "How?"

"Dunno, haven't the foggiest. I mean, I'm sure Gaia's pollution is partly to blame, but there must be somethin' else, somethin' Gaia doesn't have, that keeps the Terran people alive longer. So I still got some time, an' plenty to do, 'fore I head for Davie Jones's Locker—which, as I already told ya, shouldn't be for some time yet." He took a deep breath, and let it out contentedly. "I still ain't quite spent enough time lookin' at the sky, fer one thing."

"I'm not sure *anyone* could ever do that," said Stanley, following his gaze. As he looked up at the moons, though, something else caught his attention: the strange, blue fire he had seen earlier. Once again, Stanley found the fire strangely mesmerizing.

"Uncle Jack?"

"Hmm?"

"What's that light there? See it? It looks like blue fire, or something."

"Saint Elmo's Fire," answered Uncle Jack. "Best not to pay too much attention to it."

"What is it, though?" asked Stanley.

"Well," said Uncle Jack, still looking up at the moons, "some folks say it's gasses in the air, ignitin' spontaneously. Others think it's torches carried by mer-people. 'Course, any sailor worth his salt knows it's not either o' those."

"What is it *really*?"

"Spirits."

Stanley's eyes widened, and he studied Uncle Jack's face, looking for a smile, a wink, anything to suggest that he was joking. There was nothing.

"Spirits?" Stanley echoed. "Like *ghosts*?"

Uncle Jack nodded. "The fire marks their territory—an' warns others to stay away. Those are probably restless spirits of men who sailed these waters long, long ago."

"Why are they still here, on Earth?" asked Stanley, nervous and curious at the same time.

"Who knows?" said Uncle Jack, "Maybe they were cursed in life, maybe they still have unfinished business, maybe they have some penance to pay. Maybe there's somethin' keepin' 'em here; there may be somethin' deep beneath the sea that they're bound to—a ship, a treasure, I dunno, spirits are a mysterious lot."

"Are they dangerous?" asked Stanley.

"Most of 'em are harmless enough," answered Uncle Jack. "Some of 'em are very unpleasant, though, which is why it's a good idea to stay away from 'em. If you stare at the fire for too long, they might decide to come after ya."

A funny feeling shot through Stanley's stomach, and he quickly looked away from the spirit fires.

"Now don't worry," said Uncle Jack, noting Stanley's nervous expression, "we're plenty far enough away; they probably don't even know we're here—we'd have to be right up beside 'em for them to notice us, an' even then, they'd probably let us be."

"Have you ever seen them?" Stanley asked solemnly. "The spirits, I mean?"

Uncle Jack pursed his lips. "Aye, I've seen 'em. Once, long ago."

Stanley thought his uncle would say more, but when he didn't, he said, "What happened?"

"Er … I'd prefer not to talk about it right now," Uncle Jack said uncomfortably. "Some things shouldn't be spoken of at this time o' night."

They stood silently for several minutes, and then Uncle Jack said,

"Well, I think I'm ready fer bed again. See ya tomorrow, Stanley lad." He turned and made his way towards the bow, but before descending the staircase, he looked back and said, "Don't you be worryin' about spirits an' armour fish now, Stanley. It's too nice a night to spend thinkin' on such things."

Stanley watched him disappear below decks, and listened as his cabin door opened and shut. Looking back at the eerily-glowing Saint Elmo's Fire, Stanley felt inclined to be afraid. But then he looked up at the breathtaking expanse of the sky, and found himself agreeing with Uncle Jack; it *was* too nice a night to waste on fears and worries. He made his way back to the cabin and lay down in the comfort and security of his bunk. He fell asleep with the sound of the waves in his ears, and did not have any more nightmares.

CHAPTER ELEVEN: PORT SILVERBURG

Much to everyone's relief, the next day was completely monster-free. Stanley and Nell were a bit worried about a second armour fish attack, while Alabaster, who was never fazed for long by any amount of danger, kept going on about how cool the armour fish were. Uncle Jack assured them that no armour fish would dare come near the Ogopogo, especially after One-Eye's dramatic demise.

As Pericles had predicted, the weather was fine, indeed, and there was not a cloud in the sky from dawn until dusk.

There really wasn't a lot to do on board a small ship like the Ogopogo, but Stanley found he never tired of standing at the bow, watching the white-capped waves roll and flow around him. This is how he spent the greater part of the day, looking out over the crystal sea, the wind blowing in his hair, feeling the ship bobbing up and down beneath him. How fine it was to be out on the open sea, with nothing but sky and ocean in every direction. How wonderfully alive the ocean seemed, compared to the stubborn solidity of dry land. As the waves rolled and the wind blew, Stanley felt himself falling in love with the sea; here was a vast and open expanse, where every moment was an adventure, a realm of endless possibility, with the constant promise of wonders just over the horizon. It was a realm of danger and beauty, a place where nothing was certain, but despite all the dangers, all the uncertainty, Stanley felt right at home.

*　　*　　*　　*

The Ogopogo sped eastward all that day. While Stanley and Alabaster busied themselves swabbing the deck or playing Monopoly, Nell spent much of the time bustling back and forth from the hold to the stern, checking and re-checking the repairs, and making sure the new rudder was holding together. At about six o'clock that evening, Port Silverburg appeared on the horizon. Stanley was in the bathroom (a small hut at the Ogopogo's stern with a bench with a hole in it, which led to the ocean below), and had just sat down to do his business, when Pericles shrieked,

"LAND HO! LAAAAAND HO!"

Ignoring any further call of nature, Stanley made himself decent, threw open the door, and dashed to the bow, where Alabaster, Nell, Benjamin, and Uncle Jack were standing. Far ahead, a great slab of land had appeared, and was coming closer and closer to the tiny ship. A rocky coast ran to the north and south, and further inland, great forests could be seen. Directly ahead of the advancing Ogopogo was a large town. It looked like a larger version of Westport, with a few differences. For one thing, the impressive harbor was filled with sailing ships, all of which were made of wood, and none of which had ever seen an engine. The town proper was built into a gradually sloping, rocky cliff, which was topped by forestland. Most of the buildings were white and old-fashioned-looking, and the whole scene was like a picture from a post card.

"Ahh, Port Silverburg," said Uncle Jack happily. "An' in record time, too!"

Within the space of about twenty minutes, the Ogopogo was brought to rest in the harbour beside a sturdy wooden pier. Uncle Jack and Benjamin lowered the gangplank, and the crew prepared to disembark.

"AHOY THERE!" came a loud voice from over the starboard side. Everyone looked down onto the pier to see a short, thin man with greying hair, glasses, and a faded shirt and trousers. His round head had a shapeless black hat perched haphazardly upon it, and in his left hand he clutched a thick folder which was packed with papers.

"Ahoy!" Uncle Jack called back as he made his way down the gangplank. Stanley and the others followed.

Stopping in front of the bespectacled man, Uncle Jack held out his right hand in a friendly fashion and said, "Hello, my good man, how are ya this fine evenin'?"

The man regarded Uncle Jack coolly, and did not shake his hand. Instead, he opened his bulging folder, took a pen from its perch behind his ear, licked the tip obnoxiously, and began to scribble on a sheet of paper.

"Name, please," said the man, without looking up.

"Name?" said Uncle Jack, clearly taken aback by the other man's poor manners. "Name, right, er, *John Silver*, esquire, at yer service, I'm sure."

Scribble, scribble, scribble.

"And is this, er, *ship* yours?" said the man, glancing disdainfully at the battered form of the Ogopogo.

"Aye, that she is," said Uncle Jack, folding his arms across his chest. "Ya got a problem with that?"

The man ignored the question, as well as Uncle Jack's tone of voice.

"And the name of the, er, *ship* is …?"

"The Ogopogo, an' she's the sturdiest vessel to ever sail the—"

"Just the name will do," interrupted the man. "How do you spell it?"

"O-G-O-P-O-G-O," said Uncle Jack through clenched teeth.

Scribble, scribble, scribble.

"What is the purpose of your visit to Port Silverburg?" said the man, still refusing to make eye contact with Uncle Jack

"Well, repairs, for one thing," said Uncle Jack. "We also plan to visit an old friend o' mine—Bartholomew Crane."

The other man stopped writing, and looked up for the first time. "You're a friend of Mr. Crane's?" he said skeptically.

"Aye, that I am," said Uncle Jack, "Now, are we just about through with this little interrogation?"

The man regarded him briefly with one eyebrow raised and a doubtful look on his face, then closed his folder, put his pen back behind his ear, and thrust his hand towards Uncle Jack, palm up.

"It's ten shillings to moor your ship. Repairs are extra."

"*Ten shillings!*" echoed Uncle Jack, "Since when do ya charge ten shillings? Last time I was here it was *three!*"

The other man rolled his eyes, as if he had heard this same speech many times before. "Ten shillings," he repeated, still holding out his open palm.

Uncle Jack muttered something about thievery, then produced a small canvas bag from a pocket inside his coat, from which he drew three coins; these he placed in the man's palm.

"There, two crowns fer the dockin' fee, an' a shillin' fer yer trouble."

The man looked down at the coins in his hand with something like contempt.

"Yer lucky I'm feelin' generous today," said Uncle Jack.

And with that, he pushed by the bespectacled man and made his way up from the dock towards town, followed by his crew. As they reached the short stone stairway leading up to the street, Stanley glanced back at the short, thin man. He was watching them go, arms akimbo and a frown on his face.

What a jerk, he thought as he followed Nell up the steps.

*   *   *   *

The members of the Ogopogo's crew made their way up the sloping main street of Port Silverburg. Like Westport, the town had a distinctly old-fashioned look and feel; the similarity ended there, however. This was no retirement community. Port Silverburg was a town in its prime, and obviously a place of some importance. The buildings, almost all of which were made of gleaming white brick and topped with black roofs, stood proud and tall, their corners keen, their walls smooth. The town had a sharp, alert feel to it; there was none of the comfortable sleepiness of Westport.

It was indeed a good-sized town, and very clean and cheerful, with trees and patches of greenery here and there, to offset the monotonous white of the houses and shops. Most of the buildings on either side of the cobbled street were two stories high, with shops and restaurants on the ground floor, and apartments above. The company passed by a handsome-looking pub, through whose windows could be seen a crowd of people enjoying their evening meal. Loud singing, accompanied by a guitar and fiddle issued from the pub's open windows, filling the early evening with music. On the sidewalk, a young man was lighting street lamps with what looked like a very long match. As the sun set, the street began to get busy. Groups of people were scuttling about, setting up market stalls, and putting up decorations. It looked like there was to be some kind of festival that night.

"Uncle Jack," said Stanley, tugging on the old man's sleeve, "what's happening? Is there a party going on?"

"Got me, Stanley," said Uncle Jack with a shrug, "I was just wonderin' that meself." Then, glancing to his left, he stopped suddenly and said, "Ah, here we are!"

"Where's here?" asked Alabaster.

They were standing outside a building very much like any other along the street. The sign above the door proclaimed, *The Silverburg Inn*, and judging by the sounds of music and loud voices emanating from within, it was a popular establishment.

"Follow me," said Uncle Jack, opening the door and leading the way in.

Stanley stepped over the threshold, and peered around at the dimly-lit interior. The room was long and rectangular, with a bar running three quarters of the way along the left wall. Behind the bar, a large bald man with a face like a bulldog's was polishing pint glasses, pausing now and then to fill one for one of his many customers. In addition to those hunkered at the bar, throngs of patrons were crowded around small, round tables which were so close together that no one could get past without a good deal of squeezing. In the back corner, a small band was playing a merry tune that Stanley didn't recognize, but that everyone in the pub was singing along to.

We've sailed the broad ocean
For many a year,
We ain't got no worries,
We ain't got no fears,
All we need is a star
And some rum in the jar
And the greatest of pirates we'll be
Oh, the greatest of pirates we'll be!

Stanley was not surprised to see Uncle Jack singing along, his face drawn up in a huge smile as he swayed from side to side in time with the music. He was interrupted by a loud voice.

"*Oy! You there!*"The voice belonged to the massive bartender, who was now scowling in Uncle Jack's direction.

"Eh?" answered Uncle Jack, "Who, me?"

"Yeah, you!" said the bartender, "You can't bring young 'uns in 'ere! This's no place for the likes o' them!"

"Now just a moment, matey," said Uncle Jack, approaching the counter, "We're not here to drink."

"Well in that case," said the barman, leaning forward menacingly, "*you* can get out, too."

"Ya don't understand," said Uncle Jack, also leaning forward, despite the fact that the barman could easily have picked him up and flung him out the door, "I'm lookin' fer someone—an old friend o' mine."

"Good luck with that," said the barman sarcastically, as he turned away and resumed wiping his glasses.

"His name's Bartholomew Crane," said Uncle Jack loudly, "an' unless things have changed fer the worse 'round here, he runs this very inn!"

The barman paused in his wiping, then turned back around to face Uncle Jack. "You're a friend of Mr. Crane's?" he asked in the same skeptical tone that the man at the pier had used.

"Aye, he's a good friend o' mine," said Uncle Jack, "what's so ruddy hard to believe about that?" He folded his arms and waited for an answer. "Well? Is 'e here, or not?"

"No, he ain't here," growled the barman, "so I suggest you an' yer posse here hit the road, 'fore I—"

"*Andrew!*" A voice from behind caused Uncle Jack, Stanley and the others to turn around in surprise. Standing in the doorway was a portly man with short, brown hair and a neatly-trimmed mustache. He was dressed in an impeccable grey suit, which looked very old fashioned to Stanley. A maroon waistcoat barely contained the man's belly, and his pants looked as if they might rip the moment he sat down. His round, pudgy face was drawn in a disapproving frown, but it was clearly a face which was more accustomed to smiling and laughing.

"Well, what do you have to say for yourself, Andrew?" said the portly man as he marched towards the now sheepish-looking bartender. "Imagine, acting in such a fashion, especially towards strangers!"

"Beggin' yer pardon, Mr. Crane, sir, but I just thought as you wouldn't want to be disturbed, sir."

"Disturbed?" repeated Mr. Crane, "I think *I'm* a better judge of whether or not I want to be disturbed!" He turned to Uncle Jack and smiled imploringly. "I must apologize for Andrew's poor manners. Port Silverburg really is a friendly place, as I'm sure you'll agree, if you give it half a chance. Tourism really is very important to us, and we're usually very glad to—"

"We're not tourists," said Uncle Jack, interrupting him.

"Oh," said Mr. Crane, "Well, still, we appreciate and welcome any visitors to our town. Er, why did you want to see me, if I might be so bold?"

Uncle Jack, who until now had been grinning with barely-controlled mirth, began to laugh out loud. Mr. Crane looked very confused.

"Bart! Barty Crane!" laughed Uncle Jack, "Look at ya! All dressed up—it's just too much!" He reached out for Mr. Crane, grabbed him by the collar, and dragged him into a joyful embrace. Mr. Crane's eyes were wide as saucers, his arms held tight against his sides.

"Er," he said, as Uncle Jack pulled back, "do we know each other?"

"*Know eachother!*" cried Uncle Jack, "Blisterin' barnacles, Bart, I never thought I'd live to have yeh ask me *that!*"

Mr. Crane continued to stare wide-eyed at Uncle Jack, but soon a look of dawning comprehension crossed his face. "Is it … is it really you?"

"Of course it's me! An' if yeh were still part o' me crew, I might have somethin' to say about it!"

"*Captain Jack!*" cried Bartholomew Crane, as a huge smile lit up his features, "Jackson Lee, you scalawag!" he said, now taking his turn to hug Uncle Jack. "It's been ages! Bless you! Bless you, Captain!" He released Uncle Jack and turned to Andrew, the bartender, who was staring, open-mouthed.

"Andrew, you daft ape! Do you know who this man is?"

"C-c-cap'n Jack!" Andrew stammered, "My apologies, cap'n Jack, sir, I didn't recognize ya!" He saluted, a look of absolute mortification on his face. "Andrew Scrubb, beggin' yer pardon, sir!"

"Andrew Scrubb!" said Uncle Jack, "As I live an' breathe! Ye were part o' the best gun crew under my command!"

"Yes sir, thank you sir," said Andrew, still saluting.

"Ye were just a wee lad back then, Andrew! How yeh've grown! At ease, at ease, lad."

Andrew exhaled heavily.

"Well now," said Uncle Jack, "Andrew, ya must surely remember *this* man?" He waved Benjamin over, who stepped forward, smiling brightly at Andrew.

"Why, that's Benjamin Stone!" cried Andrew, "Benjamin Stone, th' best gun captain t'ever light a fuse!" He hopped over the counter and grabbed Benjamin's hand, shaking it vigorously.

"Benjamin, m'boy!" said Mr. Crane, looking up at the towering man before him, "you're looking well, and that's an understatement!" Benjamin beamed, and shook hands with Mr. Crane.

"And look!" said Mr. Crane, noticing Pericles, who was perched on Stanley's shoulder, "It's Pericles!"

"I thought you'd never notice," said Pericles, fluttering over to land on Uncle Jack's shoulder, "A pleasure to see you again, Bartholomew, and you, Andrew."

"Likewise, Mr. Pericles," said Andrew, addressing the parrot as if he were a superior officer.

"Well, I must say," said Mr. Crane, "this is a most unexpected and wonderful surprise! We've got so much to catch up on! Please, let's get out of this drafty doorway and find a more comfortable place to sit and talk. This way, this way!"

He motioned for the rest of the group to follow, then made his way past the crowded tables to a door beside the bar. Uncle Jack, Benjamin, and Pericles followed, while Andrew went back to his bartending duties. Stanley, Alabaster, and Nell hesitated for a moment.

"Well!" sniffed Nell, "They certainly didn't pay any attention to *us*!"

"Do you think we're supposed to go with them?" said Alabaster.

"I think so," said Stanley, "After all, Uncle Jack brought us in here with him."

"C'mon, you three!" Uncle Jack had come back and was motioning for the children to follow him. "Let's go, I wanna introduce ya to Bart! Don't worry, he's a fine fellow!"

"Guess that settles that," said Stanley, as he, Alabaster, and Nell followed Uncle Jack out of the room.

*   *   *   *

Moments later, they were all seated at a round table in a small, private parlour, removed from the noise and bustle of the main room. A lantern hung down from the ceiling, casting its comfortable glow about the small room, which had grown dark with the setting of the sun.

"Well now!" said Mr. Crane, once they had all settled down, "Just look at these lovely children!"

Stanley, Alabaster, and Nell glanced awkwardly at one another.

"Jackson, are they yours?"

"Oh, no, they ain't mine," said Uncle Jack, "Stanley, here is me great nephew, an' these are his friends, Alabaster and Nell."

"Well it's a pleasure to meet you all," said Mr. Crane, shaking each of their hands in turn. He then turned back to Uncle Jack and sighed happily. "Jackson, I can't tell you how good it is to see you again! My, how you've changed!"

Uncle Jack laughed. "Yeah, forty years'll do that to ya! An' speakin' o' changes, look at *you*! Yeh've, er, filled out a bit since I saw ya last."

"Ah yes," said Mr. Crane with a chuckle, "Well, I don't get as much exercise as I used to."

"An' yeh've become quite the snappy dresser, too! Look at yeh, decked out in the latest finery, you are!"

"Ah, well, I'm not exactly strapped for cash these days, now am I?" He and Uncle Jack both laughed at this.

"So what've ya been doin' with yerself?" asked Uncle Jack, "Had alotta free time on yer hands?"

"Actually, no," said Mr. Crane, "The demands of my office keep me quite busy."

"*Office?*" said Uncle Jack with a grin, "Since when do *you* have an office?"

"Since I became Lord Mayor!" said Mr. Crane, with a little smile.

Uncle Jack's mouth fell open. "Yer the Lord Mayor of Port Silverburg?" he asked with astonishment.

"That I am!" said Mr. Crane proudly. "I've been running the show these fourteen years, been re-elected twice. It's a busy job, but I think I'm cut out for it."

Uncle Jack was shaking his head in wonder. "Barty Crane, a Lord Mayor! Heh, I was hopin' to find ya well, but not *this* well! Yer a wonder, Bart, as I've said many times before!"

Mr. Crane beamed. "You're too kind, my friend! But please, what brings you to Port Silverburg? Surely you're not here just to visit *me?*"

"Aye, yer right about that," said Uncle Jack in a much more serious tone, "though I wish that was the only reason for us showin' up. We're on an important mission …"

Mr. Crane brought a hand to his chin and inhaled sharply. "You don't mean …"

Uncle Jack nodded. "The treasure's in danger, Bart, an' we have to find it before our friend, Chamberlain does."

"Chamberlain!" growled Mr. Crane, as he bopped the table with his fist, "He's always up to something, that man. But Jack, how did you get word of this?"

"Diego sent me a letter," said Uncle Jack.

"Diego, of course!" said Mr. Crane, "He's been spying on Chamberlain for years. I've not seen him for some time now."

"That's 'cause he's in prison," said Uncle Jack gravely.

"Say it isn't so!"

"It's so, alright," said Uncle Jack, "He found out that Chamberlain is real interested in the treasure. He's probably out there lookin' for it as we speak."

"Ever since he was appointed Regent, Chamberlain's been taking less and less interest in the affairs of the Empire," said Mr. Crane. "Things have been pretty good of late, especially compared to the way things were under Tyrone. In fact, Chamberlain is very popular with the people—those people who don't know him personally, of course."

"Yer sayin' people *like* 'im?" said Uncle Jack.

"Oh yes," said Mr. Crane, "he's very charming, apparently—in public, at least. But like I said, he's not paid a visit to any cities or towns for quite some time."

"Probably too occupied with treasure huntin'," said Uncle Jack.

"That would certainly make sense, given the news you've just brought me," said Mr. Crane. There was a brief pause, and then he said, "So, what's the plan?"

"The plan," said Uncle Jack, "is to get to the treasure before Chamberlain does. First, though, we spring Diego from prison in Ethelia."

"Ethelia!" exclaimed Mr. Crane, "You're going to rescue Diego right from under Chamberlain's nose?"

"That's the plan," said Uncle Jack.

"But, but Ethelia is the most fortified, well-guarded city in the Empire! You'll have to go through a dozen security checkpoints before you even get near the palace!"

"I expect so," said Uncle Jack.

"Jackson, please," said Mr. Crane imploringly, "it's too dangerous. Diego wouldn't want you to risk your neck for such a foolish mission."

"Foolish, is it?"

"You know what I mean, Jack. Chamberlain has a personal vendetta with you, and we both know what would happen if he found you walking the streets of his city. He leaves me alone, but he won't forgive you."

"I don't want 'im to forgive me," said Uncle Jack, "an' you shouldn't, either."

Mr. Crane sighed. "Trust me, Jackson, in my situation, it's better to be on good terms with the lord of the Empire. My pirating days are behind me, and now I just want to live my life as Lord Mayor of Port Silverburg, and run this town with honesty and decency. I'm sorry if I've brought dishonour on myself for saying so."

Uncle Jack closed his eyes. "Bart, don't speak of such things. Yer not dishonoured. You stay on good terms with Chamberlain, if that's what it takes to keep this town in the fine state it's in. As long as ya keep yer honesty an' yer decency, yeh'll keep yer honour, as Lord Mayor, and as a former member of me crew."

A tear rolled down Mr. Crane's cheek, and he sniffed loudly. "Thank you, captain," he said as he fumbled for a pocket handkerchief, "and bless you. You're a good man, and I'm proud to be your friend. I hope Diego appreciates the lengths to which you're going to save him."

"I'm sure 'e will," said Uncle Jack with a grin, "after 'e tells me off fer riskin' me neck in such a *foolish* fashion!"

Mr. Crane blew his nose loudly, then folded the handkerchief and put it back in his pocket. "Right then," he said, wiping his eyes with the back of his hand, "now that I know your mission, I want to help you in any way I can. Please, anything you need, tell me, and I'll see what I can do."

"Well, for starters, the Ogopogo is in need of some serious repairs," said Uncle Jack.

"Ahh, the Ogopogo," said Mr. Crane nostalgically, "So you brought her back, eh? She's a fine ship. I'll get the best crew in town to work on her. Anything else?"

"No, I think that's it, and thank ya kindly, too. Oh, wait, we'll be needin' a place to stay, perhaps ya could rent us a couple rooms here at the inn?"

Mr. Crane held up a restraining hand. "Tut tut, my friend, I won't hear of it! You and your crew will stay at my house 'till the repairs are complete."

"Yer house?" said Uncle Jack, "Well, we wouldn't wanna impose ..."

"Not at all!" said Mr. Crane, getting up from the table, "Nothing would make me happier, and besides, Jenny will be overjoyed to see you!"

"Jenny?" echoed Uncle Jack, "Bart, do you mean—?"

"This way, please," interrupted Mr. Crane, with a wry smile. "I'll summon a carriage to take us to my home, and I'll have your things brought up from the ship."

"Well!" said Uncle Jack, also getting up from the table, "I didn't expect such a royal treatment, I'll tell ya that!"

Mr. Crane beamed, and ushered them out of the room.

✳   ✳   ✳   ✳

The horse-drawn carriage swayed rhythmically as it made its way up the cobbled street, which had become very crowded. People were milling about, talking loudly, or singing along with musicians, who had appeared on just about every street corner. Colourful streamers were suspended between the buildings, forming a kind of rainbow roof over the street below.

Stanley watched the people singing and dancing to the music, and couldn't help but wonder what in the world was going on. He thought about asking Mr. Crane, but, being a bit shy around strangers, decided against it.

"Mr. Crane," said Alabaster, who was never shy around anyone, "what's going on? Is this some kind of party?"

"That it is, lad!" said Mr. Crane, "It's a grand celebration! It's the fifteenth anniversary of the fall of the Old Empire, and the death of Tyrone the Tyrant, not to mention the downfall of his entire family line!"

"You're celebrating a man's *death*?" said Nell, a tad reproachfully, "Isn't that a bit morbid?"

"Not at all!" said Mr. Crane, "The death of Tyrone the Tyrant was the beginning of a new era of peace and prosperity! The people of Rhedland no longer live in fear and poverty. You might say it's kind of a golden age. We were all afraid of what Chamberlain would do as Regent, but things have really never been better. Despite our past enmity with him, he really is a man of the people. I don't think Tyrone would have made Chamberlain Regent, had he known his plans for the future. So you see, we're not just celebrating the death of the old king; we're celebrating freedom, peace, a new life! And I think that's something worth celebrating."

"Well said, old chap!" said Pericles.

"Aye, well said, indeed!" said Uncle Jack, "I'll tell ya, though, I didn't expect the situation to have improved so much. From the way Diego described it in 'is letter, yeh'd think Chamberlain was just the next Tyrone."

"Well, if Chamberlain captured the poor fellow, it's not surprising that he'd describe him in a less than favourable light," said Pericles.

"Quite right," said Mr. Crane, "I've no love for Chamberlain, myself, but he's done enough for the people of Rhedland that I can honestly call him a good and just ruler ... for now."

"Well I, fer one, ain't convinced," growled Uncle Jack. "It ain't easy to believe that a man who was Tyrone the Tyrant's lap dog, could turn around an' become a champion o' the people. The things Chamberlain did, the misery him an' his ilk brought to Rhedland, an' the rest o' the world ... I don't care how 'good' an' 'just' a ruler he seems to be—I'll bet ya my share o' the treasure he's got somethin' up 'is sleeve."

"Well, whatever his motives," said Mr. Crane, "he's made Rhedland a better place to live these past fifteen years. But please, enough about all that! The Freedom Festival is on all month long, and I won't have this joyous occasion dampened by grim talk of times past!" The carriage lurched to a halt, and he flung open the door, smiling warmly. "You are all my guests, and while you are here, I must insist that you enjoy yourselves!"

They all exited the carriage, and found themselves standing in front of a massive three-story house of noteable magnificence. It was chiefly white, with bright blue borders around its numerous windows. The front yard was well tended, with flower beds all along the front of the house, and a closely-cropped, vibrantly green lawn. A tall hedge ran all the way around the property, with a wide gap opening onto a stone pathway, which led up to a large semi-circular porch supported by stout white pillars. As they made their way up the path, Stanley marveled at a large shrub which had been trimmed to look like a sailing ship.

"Wow, Mr. Crane!" said Alabaster, "Your house is almost as nice as Uncle Jack's!"

"Nicer, I think!" said Uncle Jack, "The Lord Mayors sure do know how to live in style, don't they?"

"Well, perhaps it is a tad extravagant," said Mr. Crane, "but it's home. Besides, we're always entertaining guests, so the extra room helps. But please, do come in!"

As he was waving them towards the porch, the front door opened.

"Bartholomew, you're back early." A lean, fair-haired woman was standing in the doorway. She was more handsome than pretty, and was dressed in a sensible blouse and skirt. She smiled as she came down the steps, and kissed Mr. Crane on the cheek. "Darling," she cooed, "what brings you back so early?"

"Why, I couldn't bear to be away from you, my dear!" said Mr. Crane, while Alabaster turned to Stanley and pretended to throw up. "Oh, and I've brought some very special guests!"

"Oh, how wonderful!" she said.

"Uncle Jack stepped forward and took off his hat. "Jenny? Jenny Goldsmith?"

"Yes, that's me, only it's Jenny *Crane* now. Do I know you, sir?"

Uncle Jack laughed out loud. "Jenny Crane! Whallopin' Walruses! So you two finally got hitched, did ya?"

"Er," said Mrs. Crane.

"My dear!" said Mr. Crane, "Don't you recognize our old captain?"

Mrs. Crane stared at Uncle Jack for a moment, then gasped, covering her mouth with her hands. "Jack?" she whispered from behind her hands, "Jackson Lee?"

Uncle Jack nodded.

"Captain Jack!" Mrs. Crane shrieked, before leaping at Uncle Jack and embracing him. "What are you doing here? What have you been doing? What a wonderful surprise! Oh, captain Jack!" she said again, before burying her face in his shoulder.

"Whoa now!" said Uncle Jack, easing her back. "Let me get a good look at ya!" He held Mrs. Crane by the shoulders and looked into her eyes. "My word!" he said, "It's really you, Jenny! Look at ya! Yer a noblewoman! Me two top lieutenants, married! It's almost too much, it is!"

Mrs. Crane blushed and put an arm around Mr. Crane. "A lot has happened since you went away," she said.

"Don't I know it!" said Uncle Jack.

"Well, won't you all come inside?" said Mrs. Crane, "You're just in time for supper, if you'd like to join us."

"Sounds great," said Uncle Jack, and they all followed Mr. and Mrs. Crane inside.

Stanley was the last one up the steps, and as he reached the front doorway, he suddenly felt an odd prickling sensation between his shoulder blades. It felt as if someone was watching him. He glanced over his shoulder, but no one was in the yard, or on the street beyond the hedge.

"You okay, Stanley lad?" said Uncle Jack, who was waiting just inside the doorway.

"Yeah, fine," said Stanley, as he followed the old man inside.

Neither of them saw the figure across the street, hidden in the bushes. The figure was dressed in a long cloak, the colour of damp ashes, and in the growing darkness, it was all but invisible. The cloaked one watched as the small group across the street disappeared into the Lord Mayor's house.

"So you've arrived at last," the cloaked one whispered from under its hood, "so you've arrived at last …"

CHAPTER TWELVE:
THE HOSPITALITY OF THE
CRANES

Soon they were all seated at the Cranes' dining room table, getting ready to tuck into the most outlandish meal Stanley had seen yet. There were several different kinds of fish (Stanley recognized the prism fish), as well as an assortment of odd vegetables. One serving dish was heaped with what looked like a cross between broccoli and asparagus, while another was covered with purple carrots. There were lobsters on the table, as well, although they were bright blue, instead of red. There were also several different kinds of shellfish, but nothing on the table was as novel as the centre piece, a spiny shelled creature as big as a thanksgiving turkey, with a long, curving tail.

"That's a sea scorpion," said Mr. Crane, in answer to Alabaster's frantic questions and gesturing. "You can have the tail, if you'd like."

Alabaster's expression was that of one who had just won the lottery, as Mr. Crane broke off the tail and placed it on his plate. Nell looked on with what could only be mild revulsion.

Mrs. Crane was overjoyed to see Pericles and Benjamin, and was delighted to meet Stanley, Alabaster, and Nell.

"Nell," she said, when Nell introduced herself, "what a lovely name. Is it short for Prunella?"

"Yes," said Nell, "although, to be honest, I don't like it very much. I think Jenny is a much prettier name."

"Oh, but your name has so much history behind it, dear!" said Mrs. Crane, "Did you know that the second queen of Rhedland was named Prunella?"

"Oh. Well, no, I didn't," said Nell.

"They called her the warrior-princess," said Mrs. Crane. "She led the Rheddish army against the Saurian hordes in the battle of the Blue Coast. Her father, the king, and her older brother, the prince, both fell in that battle, and it seemed like all was lost, but then Prunella took up her father's sword, and her brother's shield, rallied the troops, and slew the Saurian warlord with a single stroke!" She paused for effect, making sure the children were captivated. They were. "So, the battle was won, and Prunella was crowned queen of Rhedland. You should be proud of your name, Nell." She smiled and pulled off one of the sea scorpion's claws, before going back to her dinner.

Nell looked completely blown away. "I will, from now on," she said.

"Mrs. Crane?" said Stanley, "Does my name have any history behind it?"

"Sure it does!" said Alabaster, "The Stanley Cup!"

They stayed at the table long after the meal was over and the butler, Charles, had cleared away all the dishes. After the Cranes had finished bombarding the children with questions, the conversation turned to fond memories of days gone by, as is often the case when friends get together after not having seen eachother for a long time.

By the time ten o'clock rolled around, Stanley was finding it very difficult to stay awake; the past couple of days had been very busy, to say the least, and it suddenly felt as if all the tiredness he had avoided since early yesterday morning, had finally caught up with him. Indeed, the only thing keeping him from falling asleep was the loud laughter of the adults, as they reminisced about their apparently hilarious adventures.

Stanley didn't mind sitting quietly and listening, though; after all, he had wanted to hear some ripping pirate stories from Uncle Jack, and now they were flowing forth like water from a broken tap. He listened as Uncle Jack wrapped up another one:

"… So there was Wilkins, carryin' a barrel full o' rotten apples, completely oblivious to the fact that there's a two hundred-foot-long sea-serpent starin' at 'im, makin' ready to devour us all! An' everyone's shoutin' at 'im to get outta the way, but Wilkins, 'e thinks they're tellin' 'im to get rid o' the apples! So what does 'e do? He dumps the whole stinkin' mess overboard, right into the serpent's mouth! I swear, ya never saw a sicker-lookin' sea-serpent than that one, poor fellow!"

The adults roared with laughter at this, and it wasn't until Alabaster nodded off and let his head flop down on the table, that anyone took any notice of the three obviously exhausted children.

"Good heavens!" exclaimed Mr. Crane, "The poor lad's out like a light!"

"Oh dear, look at the time!" said Mrs. Crane.

"Sorry 'bout that, mates," said Uncle Jack, consulting his watch, "Look at us, talkin' away while you three sit there, dozing off!"

"We must apologize!" said Pericles with indignation.

"Indeed!" said Mr. Crane, "Please, my good children, forgive our rudeness. Would you like to be shown to your rooms?"

Stanley and Nell nodded in unison. Alabaster snorted loudly and muttered something about not wanting to go to school.

"Well then," said Mrs. Crane, "I suggest we retire to the lounge, and let these tired children get to bed! Mrs. Pennyfeather, would you mind showing these three to their rooms?"

"Not at all," said Mrs. Pennyfeather, the Cranes' housekeeper, who had just appeared in the dining room doorway. "This way," she said, and left the room.

Stanley elbowed Alabaster in the ribs to wake him up, then dragged himself away from his chair to follow Nell out into the main hall and up the grand staircase.

"Here we are," said Mrs. Pennyfeather, stopping at the end of a long, cozily-lit hallway. "Your rooms are here, here, and here," she said, indicating three doors, side by side, "and the bathroom is across the hall. If you need anything, my room is at the top of the stairs, alright? Feel free to knock."

"Thank you very much," said Nell.

"Yeah, thanks," said Stanley and Alabaster.

"Oh, it's no trouble," said Mrs. Pennyfeather, "you just have a good night, now." She turned and disappeared down the hallway.

"Well, g'night, guys," said Alabaster sleepily.

"Goodnight, Alabaster," said Nell.

"Night, Alabaster," said Stanley, as Alabaster's door closed. "G'night, Nell," he said, as he opened his own door and started to go inside.

"Wait, Stanley," said Nell.

Stanley paused, turning to look at her. "Hm?"

"Uh," said Nell, as if she wasn't quite sure what she was trying to say. She stayed silent for a few seconds, then said, "Uh, have a good sleep."

"Oh," said Stanley, "thanks, you too. 'Night."

"Night," said Nell, as she went into her room.

What was that all about? Thought Stanley as he closed his door behind him; tired as his was, though, he didn't give it much thought. Instead, he retrieved his pyjamas from his suitcase, which had been brought up to his room, and got ready for bed. He could hear the sound of lively music and singing coming from outside; the Rhedland Freedom Festival was in full swing. Looking out the window, he could see the rest of the town sloping away towards the harbour. Colourful lanterns hung from the buildings, and the street lamps blazed brightly, illuminating the throngs of people crowding the streets. Some were talking, some were singing, some were dancing, all were happy, as far as Stanley could see. There must have been a great many musicians playing, for the night was filled with merry music. It drifted up through the night and through the window, and brought a smile to Stanley's face. He wondered just how many people were dancing and singing right now, glad to be alive, and to be free. He also wondered why they'd never had a similar festival back in East Stodgerton. After all, they'd never had a tyrant king lording over them there; they had *always* been free. The people of Rhedland knew how lucky they were, but did the people back home know?

"I wonder," Stanley said to himself.

Soon he was sleeping peacefully, warm and comfortable in the massive, king-sized bed, oblivious to the sounds of joyful celebration in the street outside.

*   *   *   *

Stanley awoke the next morning at 10:30, feeling very well-rested, indeed. He got dressed and made his way downstairs, where he found Uncle Jack, Pericles, and the Cranes enjoying a hearty breakfast in the dining room.

"Mornin', Stanley," said Uncle Jack, as Stanley entered the room.

"Morning, Uncle Jack," said Stanley.

"Please, have a seat, and some breakfast," said Mr. Crane.

"Did you sleep well?" asked Mrs. Crane.

"Yes, very well, thanks," said Stanley, as he sat down and helped himself to some eggs and sausages.

"Alabaster an' Nell not up yet?" said Uncle Jack.

"No, I guess not," said Stanley, looking around. "That's the first time I've ever been up before Alabaster. Is Benjamin not up either?"

Benjamin Stone was indeed not present at the table.

"Actually," said Mr. Crane, "Benjamin is down at the docks right now, help-ing to repair the Ogopogo. I went down there earlier this morning, to get a crew working on her, and, well, he insisted on coming along. They'll be at it now, but the repairs will take the better part of three days—she needs a complete overhaul, for one thing, and the damage was extensive. But, my *point* is that we'll have to find some way to keep the rest of you people entertained! Is there anything you'd like to do while you're here, Stanley?"

Stanley swallowed a mouthful of food and thought for a moment. "Er, could we look around town? Maybe go down to the docks and see the ships?"

"A capital idea!" declared Mr. Crane. "I'll take you all on a tour of Port Silver-burg, harbour and all. Sound good?"

"Sounds great," said Stanley. He was anxious to see some of those massive sail-ing ships up close.

Alabaster and Nell finally decided to get up, and after breakfast, they piled into the carriage with Stanley, Uncle Jack, and Mr. Crane. It was a wonderful day for a tour of the city; the sun shone brightly down on the white buildings, and a cool breeze was blowing gently in from the ocean.

Mr. Crane showed them all around town, from the gates to the docks. They spent a great deal of time looking at the ships in the harbour; there were many different kinds, from sleek, speedy clippers to fat, sluggish merchant ships, all of them crawling with sailors working hard to prepare for their next sea voyage.

"Port Silverburg is an important centre for trade and commerce," explained Mr. Crane. "There are always plenty of merchant ships moored here. We get a lot of goods from further inland, too—grain, timber, flax, textiles, and such—which get picked up here, and taken all over the Empire."

Stanley nodded as Mr. Crane spoke, but he was really only interested in look-ing at the ships. Some of them were massive, and many he recognized from books.

They even got to watch the Ogopogo being repaired. The workers had hauled the ship right out of the water and placed it on a wooden frame to make their work easier. Benjamin Stone was there, hammering fresh, new planks into place, and making it look like the easiest thing in the world.

"Don't you worry now," said Mr. Crane, "these boys are the best shipwrights around, and I'll say the same of Benjamin Stone! You'll have the old girl back as good as new, and better!"

"I'm not worried!" said Stanley.

"I know," said Mr. Crane, "I was talking to your Uncle!"

They all laughed, and then Mr. Crane said, "Well, on with the tour!"

As they started to head back towards Main Street, Nell cleared her throat and said,

"Er, Mr. Lee? Mr. Crane?"

"Something wrong, Miss Hawthorne?" said Mr. Crane.

"Oh, no, nothing's wrong, I just … I was just wondering if … would you mind if I stayed here and maybe helped with the repairs?"

"Oh," said Mr. Crane, a bit taken aback. "Well, I … hmmm, what do you think, Jackson?"

Uncle Jack scratched his chin. "I think Nell here is just as capable a carpenter as any o' those lads workin' away aboard me ship—maybe even more so! Nell, I'd be honoured if ye'd help with the repairs to the Ogopogo. Why don'cha go team up with Benjamin over there?"

"S-sure!" said Nell, her face bright red. She jogged over to where Benjamin Stone was working. The big man beamed down at her, and handed her a hammer.

"Keep an eye on 'er, Ben," called Uncle Jack, "An' Nell—you keep an eye on Benjamin, will ya?"

Nell and Benjamin both waved, then went back to work.

"Alright then," said Mr. Crane, "shall we go?"

It took them the rest of the day to see the sights of Port Silverburg; they went to the art gallery (which Stanley found a bit boring), and then to the park for a picnic lunch. After lunch, they went to the Port Silverburg Little Theatre, where they watched *The Misadventures of Sir Bumbleroll,* a hilarious play about a scatterbrained knight. Then, it was off to the Port Silverburg museum of antiquities, which Stanley enjoyed very much; a new museum was a real treat, especially after having been to the East Stodgerton Museum of Natural History a hundred times.

After the museum it was getting close to dinner time, so they returned to the docks to pick up Nell and Benjamin, and took the coach back to the Cranes' house. Nell couldn't stop talking about the work she and Benjamin had been doing, and Stanley found himself wishing that he could have helped with the repairs, too.

*   *   *   *

They spent the next day at a beach just outside of town; it was a popular place for tourists and holidayers. After hours of swimming and sunbathing, they returned to the Cranes' house for supper. They were all having a splendid visit, but Uncle Jack was getting noticeably restless. Stanley was a bit surprised to find that he was getting restless, too.

*   *   *   *

"Today's our last day in Port Silverburg," said Uncle Jack at breakfast the next day.

"Is the Ogopogo all fixed?" said Stanley.

"The repairs will be done by late afternoon," said Mr. Crane, "but please, wait 'till tomorrow. You don't want to set out with evening coming on, do you?"

"Well, we don't want to wear out our welcome," said Uncle Jack.

"Not at all!" said Mr. Crane, "please, I insist!"

"Well, alright then," said Uncle Jack, "I've never been one to refuse a friend's hospitality." He looked out the window. It was a grey, gloomy morning—a good morning for staying indoors and curling up with a good book. "Looks like we've got some rain on the way."

And rain it did. Soon after breakfast was over, a loud thunderclap announced the coming of the storm. The rain came down in buckets, pelting the streets of Port Silverburg with drops the size of almonds

"This sure puts a damper on things," said Alabaster to Stanley, who was sitting at a window sill, chin cupped in his hands.

"Kinda," said Stanley absently, "but I also sort of like to just sit and watch the rain. It's neat."

Alabaster glanced out the window at the cloud-covered sky and the soaking streets. "Well," he said with a shrug, "Nell and I are starting up a game of Monopoly with Mr. and Mrs. Crane, if you want to join us."

"Nah, that's okay," said Stanley, "you guys go ahead."

"Okay," said Alabaster, heading for the lounge. "See you later."

Alone with his thoughts once more, Stanley went back to his rain watching.

*   *   *   *

The rain continued all that day and into the evening with the relentless intensity that only a summer storm can muster. Just as dinner was being laid out on the table, there came a loud knock at the front door. Charles, the butler strode into the dining room shortly after answering the door, followed by a bedraggled-looking man with greying hair and glasses which were all fogged up and speckled with water droplets. It was, in fact, the same man who had questioned Uncle Jack the day they'd arrived.

"Winston!" said Mr. Crane, as he stood up from the table, "What brings you here, especially on so ghastly a night as this?" He turned to his guests at the table and said, "This is Winston MacNeil, the harbour-master."

"Aye, we've met," said Uncle Jack coolly.

"Frightfully sorry about that, Mr. Lee, sir," said Winston, "if I'd've known it was *you* docking in our harbour, well, I ..."

"No worries," said Uncle Jack, "water under the bridge, an' all that."

"Thank you, Mr. Lee," said Winston, looking relieved.

"Please, Winston, tell me what's brought you here," said Mr. Crane.

"Yessir, of course, sir," said Winston, turning to face Mr. Crane. "Well, ah, to put it plainly, sir, ah, the, ah, the Regent's ship just docked at pier one!"

"The Regent?" said Mr. Crane, "You mean *Chamberlain*?"

"The very same."

"*Chamberlain*?" said Uncle Jack, getting up from the table, "What the devil's *he* doin' here?"

"I haven't the foggiest," said Mr. Crane, "he hasn't been here since last year, and he always sends a telegram to notify us that he's coming. Winston, did *you* know about this?"

"No sir, Mr. Crane, I most certainly did not."

"Jackson," said Mr. Crane, his face very white, "I think you and your crew had best make yourselves scarce—it will be very bad if Chamberlain finds you here."

"Right," said Uncle Jack, "we gotta leave, *now*. Benjamin an' I'll go upstairs an' grab the luggage. Pericles, you an' the young 'uns head out the back door, an' we'll meet yeh there in a minute."

"Use the servant's stairway in the back," said Mr. Crane to Uncle Jack, "It's much more discreet, and it will take you right down to the back door."

"Makin' fer a clean getaway," said Uncle Jack. He reached out and grabbed Mr. Crane's hand, clasping it in his own. "Bart, I'm sorry we gotta part ways again, but, well, thanks fer everythin'. I'll see ya again before this is all over, I hope."

"My house is always open to you, Captain," said Mr. Crane, saluting with his free hand.

"G'bye, Jenny," said Uncle Jack, turning to Mrs. Crane.

"Goodbye, Captain Jack," said Mrs. Crane, throwing her arms around him. "Be careful, and good luck."

There was a loud knock at the front door. They all went silent for an instant, and then Mrs. Crane said,

"*Go! Now!*" and they all sprang into action.

"*Kitchen!*" hissed Uncle Jack to Pericles and the children, before bounding up the stairs with Benjamin close behind. Mrs. Crane herded the children into the kitchen and closed the door behind them.

"Let's go," said Pericles, who was perched on Stanley's shoulder, "out the back door."

Stanley was about to turn the doorknob, when Nell grabbed him by the arm.

"*Wait!*" she hissed, and pointed at the curtained backdoor window. A moment later, a flash of lightning illuminated the darkness outside, revealing the silhouette of a person standing just outside the door. The children froze in their tracks.

"*There's someone out there,*" whispered Stanley.

"Who could it be?" said Alabaster quietly, "Do you think it's one of Chamberlain's goons?"

"*It's a trap,*" whispered Nell, "*they've probably got the place surrounded.*"

"I must warn Jack," said Pericles. He took off from Stanley's shoulder and disappeared up the servant's stairway.

"Now what?" said Alabaster.

"I'm going to see what's going on out in the main room," said Stanley, creeping towards the kitchen door.

"*Stanley, wait!*" Nell whispered loudly.

Stanley put a finger to his lips, signaling for silence. Nell closed her mouth, but her eyes begged him to get away from the door. Heart racing, Stanley grasped the handle and pulled. *Please don't squeak*, he silently implored. The door opened noiselessly, just a crack, but enough to see through. He needn't have bothered with his stealth; Mr. Crane still hadn't opened the front door.

As the loud knocking resounded once more through the house, Mr. Crane took a deep breath, grabbed the handle, and flung the door wide. The sound of falling rain came rushing in, and there was a dramatic flash of lighting and roll of thunder, as three figures stepped into the room.

Once of them could only be Chamberlain himself, dressed in a fine blue naval uniform with gold buttons and epaulettes. His chest was adorned with medals, and his posture was perfect. His chin, covered in a day's growth of stubble, was thrust out proudly over his collar, which was so high that it touched his jawbone. The Regent's face was a permanent mask of disapproval, his lips pursed tight and his jaw set. His right eye was covered with a black eye patch, but the left one, a cold ice-blue, gazed appraisingly around the room. He looked like a man of late-middle-age, his face lined from years of frowning, and his short, neatly-trimmed hair gone completely grey.

Stanley's first view of Ezekiel Chamberlain did not disappoint; he had the look of a villain down pat, and was an impressive man to behold, to say nothing of his two escorts.

The Regent's escorts (or, perhaps, bodyguards) were both at least seven feet tall, and much more massive even than the towering Benjamin Stone. They were clad from head to toe in identical suits of shining armour, and their faces could not be seen, so well did their helmets conceal their features. In fact, the concealment seemed almost too good. It was almost as if there was nothing inside the helmets at all, nothing but blackness. For a time, all Stanley could do was stare. He had never seen such a huge person, let alone two at the same time. There was something else, though, something strange and haunting, even disturbing about these two giant soldiers. Maybe it was their size, maybe it was their invisible faces, maybe it was the way they stood there, as still and as silent as statues, not even so much as twitching a finger of their huge, armoured hands. Whatever it was, it sent a chill up and down Stanley's spine.

As imposing as the scene was, Stanley had to stifle a snicker as one of the huge soldiers folded up an umbrella which he had been holding over Chamberlain's head. Stanley lost all will to laugh as he caught sight of the soldier's sword, which couldn't have been less than five feet long. Chamberlain's eye came to rest on Mr. Crane.

"Well, Crane," he said in an accusing tone, "it certainly took you long enough to answer the door. It's almost as if you didn't want to let me in. Do you usually leave guests on the doorstep until they get thoroughly soaked, before admitting them?"

Chamberlain was obviously not thoroughly soaked, was, in fact, fairly dry, but Stanley was quite sure Mr. Crane knew better than to point that out.

"Certainly not, Lord Chamberlain," said Mr. Crane with a bow, "It's just that you caught us a little off guard with your sudden arrival."

Chamberlain cocked his head to one side. "Does my spontaneity displease you, Crane?"

"Not at all, not at all!" said Mr. Crane, getting a bit red in the face, "It is always a pleasure to have your lordship as my guest. Please, to what do we owe this unexpected treat?"

Chamberlain *Hmphed*. "You may dispense with the pleasantries, Crane, I find them rather tiresome."

Stanley remembered Darth Vader saying something similar in *Return of the Jedi*.

"Yes, of course," said Mr. Crane uncomfortably. "Er, how about something to drink for you and your men?"

"Coffee," said Chamberlain.

Mrs. Crane took the coffee pot from the dining room table and filled a mug for the Regent.

"Er, you've met my wife, Jennifer," said Mr. Crane as Mrs. Crane handed the mug to Chamberlain.

"*Of course I have*," snapped Chamberlain, before taking a sip.

"And what would *you* fellows like?" said Mr. Crane to the two soldiers, who had not moved an inch since their arrival. The soldiers did not respond, or give any indication that they had heard what Mr. Crane had said.

"Nothing for them," said Chamberlain, taking another sip of coffee. "They're on duty."

"Ah, yes, of course," said Mr. Crane.

There was a very awkward silence as Chamberlain finished his coffee. Mr. Crane shuffled his feet nervously as the Regent paused to stare at him fixedly between sips.

"Er, what brings you to Port Silverburg, your Regency?" said Mr. Crane, in an attempt to dispel the awkwardness.

"It certainly wasn't your wife's coffee," said Chamberlain, setting the empty mug down on a nearby lampstand.

"I'm terribly sorry you didn't like it," Mrs. Crane growled sarcastically. Chamberlain took no notice; instead, he strode over to the dining room table, tracking mud all over the carpet as he went.

"Entertaining some guests, Crane?" he said over his shoulder.

"Er, no," said Mr. Crane. Chamberlain turned to face him.

"Awfully large meal for *two*, don't you think?" He indicated the eight place settings at the table.

"Er, ah …" said Mr. Crane, now very red in the face.

"We thought you might like to join us for dinner," said Mrs. Crane coolly.

"Is that right?" said Chamberlain, looking squarely at her with is good eye. "So you decided to set six extra places at your table, did you?"

Mr. Crane was looking absolutely terrified, but Mrs. Crane simply folded her arms and said,

"We had no idea you'd only bring two of your men along. We thought we'd have a full table when you arrived."

"And how did you know I was arriving, at all?" said Chamberlain, advancing on Mrs. Crane with his hands clasped behind his back.

"Er, I can field that one, m'lord," said Winston, who had been cowering in the lounge.

"*You?*" Chamberlain rounded on Winston and glared balefully at him. "What the devil are *you* doing here, *harbour-master?*" he spat out the words *harbour* and *master* like sour milk.

"Begging your pardon, m'lord, but I thought they'd want to know of your arrival, s-so as to make ready to entertain you properly."

"Is *that* what you thought," sneered Chamberlain. "Well, you're a regular *saint*, aren't you, harbour-master? What a relief it is to know that the Cranes are ready to entertain me properly! What a shame it would have been, if I had arrived without their knowledge! What a predicament, what a scandal! Ahh, but there's no reason to think about that, is there? After all, there's a feast on the table, coffee in the pot, and three slack-jawed bumpkins in the front hall to welcome me! What more could I ask for?" He glared from Mr. Crane, to Mrs. Crane, to Winston, then sighed heavily. "Very well," he said, running a hand through his hair, "I suppose I'll have to accept the fact that you are hospitable to the point of absurdity. I can only trust that your reputation as an honest and honourable man, is not unfounded, *Mayor* Crane, and that you would not keep anything hidden from me."

Mr. Crane cleared his throat and adjusted his tie, but said nothing.

"Very well then," said Chamberlain, once it became clear that there was nothing else forthcoming, "I'll be on my way. I've other business in town this evening." He made for the door, and just as he was about to turn the handle, he paused and looked over his shoulder. "Oh, that's right," he said, pretending to suddenly remember something, "there was one more thing I meant to ask you about."

"Y-y-yes?" stammered Mr. Crane.

Chamberlain put his back to the door. "As I made my way along the docks," he began conversationally, "I noticed an interesting little ship moored at pier twenty-one. Do you know the vessel of which I speak, *harbour-master?*"

"Who, me?" said Winston, pointing at himself.

"*No, I meant the* other *harbour-master standing behind you! Of course, you! Do you know the vessel?*"

Winston's eyes were wide as he stammered out, "Y-y-yessir, I-I-I know it!"

Chamberlain smiled unpleasantly. "And, perchance, would you happen to know who that ship belongs to?"

Winston glanced briefly at Mr. Crane.

"I AM SPEAKING TO *YOU*, HARBOUR-MASTER," roared Chamberlain, "NOT THE LORD MAYOR, *YOU!*"

"Y-yessir, of course, sir! Er, the ship is … that is, sir, the ship you're, ah, referring to, is … j-just a fishing ship, sir! Many fishermen around here have them!"

"Is that so?" said Chamberlain interestedly, "So it's a commonly-seen type of ship, then, is it? A popular design?"

Winston nodded.

Chamberlain scratched his chin. "Well, harbour-master, I find that fact very interesting, very interesting, indeed. You see, I've been a navy man all my life, and I've sailed in and out of every port in the Empire countless times, and only *once* have I ever seen a ship like the one at pier twenty-one. It was a unique design, actually—a custom-built vessel … and do you know who that ship belonged to, harbour-master?"

Winston shook his head slowly.

"It belonged to the most wanted man in the history of the Empire," said Chamberlain, "the traitor-pirate, *Black Jack Lee*!" He glared at Mr. Crane. "Now, either that ship down at pier twenty-one is a damn clever replica, or it is the *exact same ship* that escaped my clutches forty years ago. So I ask you, *Mayor* Crane, *why* would Jack Lee's ship be moored in *your* harbour?"

Mr. Crane had finally composed himself, and, his face set, he answered, "I can see where you're going with this, Lord Chamberlain, and I can assure you that even if Jack Lee *were* in town, he wouldn't be daft enough to come to the house of the Lord Mayor!"

Chamberlain scowled darkly, then snapped his fingers. "Search the house, men!" he called to his soldiers, who sprang immediately into action. "We'll see just how daft Jack Lee really is."

Chamberlain and his men searched high and low, basement to attic, but found no trace of Uncle Jack, or his crew.

"Now do you believe me?" said Mr. Crane, as Chamberlain stomped angrily down the stairs and into the entrance hall. As one of his soldiers opened the front door, Chamberlain stuck his index finger in Mr. Crane's face, and said,

"Maybe Lee was here, and maybe he wasn't, but know this: if I find out that he *was*—and I will find out, either way—your life, Crane, will be forfeit. I've forgiven you your past transgressions, but I'll not suffer your treachery again. I *will* be back, Crane, and you won't see me coming."

Thunder crashed again, making Chamberlain's words all the more menacing. "Come," he called to his soldiers, "to the harbour. We'll find the owner of that ship yet."

And then they were gone. Mr. Crane watched them go from the front window. As they made their way down the front walk, a third soldier appeared from around back and joined the other two, and they all disappeared down the dark street.

"Whew!" breathed Mr. Crane, "I thought we were done for! You were wonderful, my dear!"

"But where could Jack and the others be?" said Mrs. Crane.

They searched the house themselves, calling for Uncle Jack, but the old man and his crew were nowhere to be found. The only clue they discovered was an open window at the end of the third floor hallway. Chamberlain had apparently thought nothing of this, but Mr. Crane stuck his head out the window and smiled.

"Good old Jack," he said as he pulled his head back in and closed the window. "He sure knows how to make an exit."

"That he does," said Mrs. Crane, "That he does."

Perhaps you're wondering exactly how Uncle Jack, Stanley, and the others got away without Chamberlain noticing, and at what point they made their escape. As you can probably guess, Stanley wasn't eavesdropping for long; just as Chamberlain asked for coffee, Uncle Jack appeared at the bottom of the servant's stairway and signaled for Stanley, Alabaster, and Nell to follow him. They made their way up to the third floor, went to the end of the hallway, out the window, down the latticework, through the hedge, and down main street towards the harbour. Benjamin Stone amazed them all by carrying the children's suitcases the entire way, and soon they found themselves at pier twenty-one, gazing up at the glistening form of the Ogopogo.

"Well, it appears as though the repairs are done," observed Pericles.

"Aye," said Uncle Jack, "Bart's men do good work, that's fer sure, not to mention all the help Nell an' Benjamin gave 'em. Good work, by the way, you two." He glanced briefly over his shoulder at the rain-soaked streets of Port Silverburg, then turned back to face the Ogopogo. "Well, step lively, mates," he said, heading for the gang plank, "We need to get outta here, pronto."

By the time Chamberlain and his men arrived at pier twenty-one, the Ogop-ogo and her crew were long gone. Chamberlain's cursing could be heard for miles.

CHAPTER THIRTEEN: KRAKEN WISE

Stanley stepped out of the cabin and into the bright morning sunshine. He rubbed the sleep from his eyes, then joined Alabaster, who was fishing off the port beam.

"Morning, Stanley," said Alabaster as he reeled in his line. "Nell's down in the galley ... the stove's busted, or something, and she's helping Benjamin fix it. Pretty nice weather, eh?"

"Yeah," said Stanley, looking up at the cloudless sky and feeling the warm sun on his face. The storm had blown itself out during the night, and now there was nothing to suggest that it had ever happened. Stanley leaned on the railing and gazed out at the surrounding area. The Ogopogo was currently anchored in a small, quiet cove surrounded by dense woodland. "Where are we?" he asked to no one in particular.

"We're in Woodman's Cove," said Pericles, who came fluttering down from the crow's nest to land on the railing between Stanley and Alabaster, "about eight hours north of Port Silverburg."

"Eight hours!" Stanley said with surprise, "How'd we get so far?"

"Jack was up most of the night, guiding the ship through the storm," answered Pericles. "He finally sailed in here at around four-thirty this morning, after I insisted that he get some sleep."

"Is he still in bed?" asked Stanley.

"Yes, and we'll let him sleep as long as he wants. He's done more than his share in getting us away from Chamberlain."

Chamberlain. Stanley wondered if he had gotten anything out of the Cranes, and if he had noticed that the Ogopogo was gone. He wondered if Chamberlain had left Port Silverburg right after they had, and even now was closing in on Woodman's Cove. He looked nervously astern, at the entrance to the cove, half expecting a huge man o' war to come sailing in, guns blazing, with Chamberlain at the helm.

"I doubt that Chamberlain would have left Port Silverburg before the storm ended," said Pericles, noting Stanley's nervous look. "Even if he did, his chances of finding us are slim." The parrot cleared his throat. "Er, even so, I think we'll get under way right after breakfast."

Soon after breakfast, the Ogopogo was sailing north along the coast, with Benjamin Stone at the helm. Stanley, Alabaster, and Nell had just started a game of Monopoly, when Pericles swooped down and landed in their midst.

"Well," he said, "I'm relieved to report that there are no other ships around, as far as my eyes can see."

"How far *can* your eyes see?" asked Alabaster.

"*Very* far," said Pericles smugly.

"How long will it be 'till we get to where we're going?" asked Nell, as she landed her tiny metal dog on *Oriental Avenue*.

"The journey to Ethelia will take about four days," said Pericles, "It would take less time if we had a full crew, but we'll have to drop anchor at night if we want to get any sleep."

Stanley didn't much like the sound of this. Four days, with stops at night, seemed like plenty of time for Chamberlain to catch up with them.

"I wouldn't worry," said Pericles, when Stanley voiced his concern, "we won't be dropping anchor out on the broad ocean—there are hundreds of coves and bays up and down the Rheddish coast, most of which are far too small to admit a massive vessel like the *Maelstrom*."

"Is that Chamberlain's ship?" asked Stanley.

Pericles nodded. "The waters along the coast are very shallow—much too shallow for a ship of that size. It's the biggest vessel to ever serve in the Imperial Navy. Chamberlain would be mad to follow us this close to the shore."

"He's sure mad at Uncle Jack," said Alabaster.

"Mad as in *crazy*," said Nell.

"Well, crazy or not," said Stanley, "I'd say he's a huge jerk."

"You have no idea," said Pericles.

*   *   *   *

Soon after eleven o'clock, Uncle Jack emerged from below decks and bid them all a very cheerful good morning. "How's everythin' goin', Benjamin? Pericles?"

Benjamin gave the thumbs up.

"Everything is ship-shape, captain," said Pericles.

"An' how 'bout you three?" said Uncle Jack, turning to the children, "Ya doin' alright?"

"Ship-shape!" said Alabaster, saluting ridiculously.

"Yes, Mr. Lee," said Nell politely.

Stanley wanted to respond positively, but he found that he was not feeling ship-shape at all. An odd feeling had come over him after breakfast, and it wasn't a result of Benjamin's cooking; it was a kind of nervous apprehension, very vague, but very real.

Uncle Jack's tone became more concerned. "Somethin' wrong, Stanley? Ya look a bit peaky."

"I ... I dunno," said Stanley, "I just have a funny feeling."

"Like you're gonna barf?" said Alabaster, trying to be helpful.

"No no, I'm not sick, it's more like ... oh, I don't know, it's probably nothing."

"If you're worried about Chamberlain," said Pericles, "I'll remind you that the Maelstrom would bottom out if it tried to—"

"No, it's not Chamberlain," interrupted Stanley, waving the parrot's words aside. "It's nothing, really." He was lying, of course, and the expression on Nell's face suggested that she knew.

"Well, if yer sure yer okay, then," said Uncle Jack, not sounding very convinced. When Stanley said nothing more, he ordered Pericles back on lookout, and took Benjamin's place at the helm. The children went back to their Monopoly game.

"Okay, my turn," said Stanley, rolling the dice. "Eight! One, two, three, four, five, six, seven, eight," he counted, as he jumped his favourite playing piece, the car, around the board. "Woo! Kentucky Avenue!" he exclaimed, landing on the so-named space, "I'm buying it!"

He looked up at Alabaster, who always made a fuss if anyone bought the red properties (which were his favourite), and was surprised to see him staring back intently.

"Alabaster, what's the matter?" said Stanley.

Alabaster pursed his lips, then said, "Um, what was that funny feeling you had just now?"

"I told you, it was nothing," said Stanley, slightly annoyed that Alabaster wouldn't let the subject drop.

"Come on, just tell me," said Alabaster.

Stanley was about to tell him to lay off, but stopped. It was unusual for Alabaster to be acting so seriously, and if Alabaster wasn't joking or smiling about something, it *had* to be serious.

"Okay," said Stanley. After all, if you couldn't confide in your best friend, who *could* you confide in? "It's sort of like …" he searched for the right analogy. "Like, you know when you're watching a scary movie, and you know something bad is about to happen? It's like that. Why? Why are you so interested in a weird feeling I had?"

"Cause I have it, too."

An audible silence fell over the Monopoly board.

"What do you mean?" said Stanley.

"What I just said," said Alabaster, sounding a bit fearful, "I have the same weird feeling, like something bad is going to happen."

They both looked at Nell, who had gone rather pale.

"I have it, too," she whispered. "A feeling of apprehension."

"Okay, wait a minute," said Stanley, closing his eyes and shaking his head, "you mean to tell me we're all feeling the same thing, for some reason? You guys both said you were fine, just a few minutes ago."

"I lied," said Nell.

"Er, me too," said Alabaster sheepishly, "I thought it was nothing, but then *you* said you had a funny feeling …" He trailed off, a worried look on his face.

There are few things that would cause Stanley to feel afraid in broad daylight, and a worried look on Alabaster Lancaster's face is one of them.

"Maybe we share some kind of telepathic link," said Alabaster, looking slightly less worried at the prospect of something so cool.

"Let's be rational here," said Nell, a tad harshly, "Nothing like this has ever happened before, right?" Stanley and Alabaster both nodded. Nell spread her hands in a 'there you go' gesture. "So there's got to be a reason for it."

"But it's the middle of the afternoon," said Stanley, "It's sunny, it's warm, and we have friends close by. What could possibly make us feel scared?"

The more they talked about it, the worse the feeling became, until Stanley found his voice quavering when he tried to speak.

"Okay, look," he said, "this isn't helping, and to be honest, it's making me a bit freaked out, so let's just—"

He was interrupted by a loud shout from Uncle Jack.

"*Pericles*," called the old man, "what'ya make o' *that?*"

Turning around, Stanley gazed past Uncle Jack, and past the bow. Not far ahead, a thick fog had sprung up over the surface of the water.

"Fog bank, captain," said Pericles, "Just appeared from beyond that peninsula, there."

The fog did indeed seem to be billowing out from behind the peninsula in question.

"It's that fog," said Alabaster shakily, "that's what's causing it."

"But it's just fog," said Nell, "condensation in the air. How could *that* make us feel like … like …"

"Like there's something *in* the fog?" said Alabaster.

"Oh, stop it," said Nell, "You're scaring me."

"No I'm not," said Alabaster, "*it's* scaring you."

"Guys, quit it!" said Stanley. This conversation was not helping matters. "Look, let's ask Uncle Jack. He's probably seen this sort of thing before."

This was deemed an acceptable course of action, so they joined Uncle Jack by the wheel, and waited patiently while he finished a hushed conversation with Pericles, who was perched on his shoulder.

"All I know is, it came out of nowhere, and it's giving me a bad feeling," muttered the parrot.

"Aye, me too," said Uncle Jack, "a very bad feelin' indeed."

Stanley cleared his throat, causing Uncle Jack and Pericles to jump in surprise.

"Whoa!" said Uncle Jack, "I didn't see yeh standin' there, mates!" He was trying to sound cheerful, but Stanley could hear the uneasiness in his voice. "What's on yer minds?"

Stanley glanced sideways at the not-so-distant fog. "Er, Uncle Jack, we have a bad feeling about that fog, too."

Uncle Jack stopped trying to seem cheerful. "You too, eh? The three of yeh?"

The children nodded, and Alabaster stepped forward.

"Don't go into the fog, okay, Uncle Jack? I think we should stay away from it."

"Yeah … yeah, I think yer right," said Uncle Jack, turning the wheel and steering the ship away from shore, so that it was now sailing parallel to the mysterious fog. "We'll just give 'er a wide berth as we go by," he said conversationally, "stay well out of 'er way."

The Ogopogo sailed in a very wide arc around the peninsula, which was now invisible, thanks to the thick fog. As they went past, though, the fog began to billow towards them alarmingly, as if a strong wind were propelling it away from shore.

"Don't get *closer* to it!" suggested Pericles.

"I'm not," said Uncle Jack, "*It's* getting' closer to *us*."

The word '*us*' died in Uncle Jack's throat, as the fog enveloped the Ogopogo. In the space of a heartbeat, the beautiful afternoon sunshine was replaced by a cold, damp twilight, with nothing but grey in every direction. The sun, the shoreline, the horizon, everything further than a few metres from the Ogopogo had been swallowed and blotted out by the thick mist.

Pericles wisely turned off the wind crystal, and the ship came to a drifting stop. An oppressive silence had descended on the scene, and the crew hardly dared to breathe, lest they disturb it.

"Well, that was certainly unexpected," said Pericles.

"It was that," muttered Uncle Jack.

Stanley was more than a little unnerved at this point. The strange fog seemed to have removed them from the rest of the world. There was no movement of air or water, and Uncle Jack's voice sounded muffled and distant, though he was standing only a few feet away. As the others stood listening to the eerie silence, Stanley walked over to the starboard railing, his footsteps clunking mournfully as he went. He peered down at the water, which, minutes ago had been rolling and alive, but was now as calm as a stagnant pond. Without the clear blue sky to reflect upon it, the water had taken on a dark green hue, but as Stanley gazed down at it, it seemed to go black. At first, he assumed that the water's appearance was due to the fog's interference, but the more he looked at it, the more it seemed to be completely, utterly black.

"It's like an oil slick," he muttered, but it was not like an oil slick. The water seemed to radiate blackness, and Stanley's heart began to beat very fast. He was about to call to Uncle Jack, when Alabaster piped up,

"Pee-yoo! What stinks?"

Nell wrinkled her nose. "Yuck, it smells like bleach!"

Stanley took a big whiff, and coughed. It smelled like the laundry room in his basement, only a hundred times worse. "I think there's some kind of chemical in the water," he said, hoping against hope that that was what it was. "There might have been a spill, or a leak from a town around here? It's made the water all black." The bleach smell grew stronger, and something told him that this was no chemical spill.

"This ain't no chemical spill," said Uncle Jack. "That's ammonia yer smellin'. It's a kraken."

Pericles made a funny noise, like a squeaky shriek. "It … it *can't* be!"

"A kraken?" said Alabaster, "A crack in *what*?"

"A *kraken*," said Uncle Jack, "kay, arr, ay, kay, ee, enn. A sea monster with many arms, like a giant squid."

Stanley froze. He had read all about giant squids, seen drawings, diagrams, and the model in the East Stodgerton Museum of Natural History. It had scared him when he was little, and for a long time he wouldn't go past it without closing his eyes. Once he had turned ten, though, he'd decided that enough was enough, and confronted the model squid. It wasn't as scary as it had been when he was five, but it was still a fearsome sight. The model was life-size—about forty feet long—but Stanley had read in a book, that giant squids could grow to be eighty feet long, maybe more. He remembered the ten grasping arms, two of which were longer than the others, and used to capture prey. He remembered the fierce, parrot-like beak hidden among the tentacles, and the huge, staring eyes, bigger even than those of an armour fish. For all its hideousness, though, the giant squid wasn't supposed to be ferocious or aggressive, but then, Stanley wondered how anyone could know that, since no one has ever seen one alive.

"I didn't know giant squids stank so much," said Alabaster to no one in particular.

"That they do," said Uncle Jack, releasing the ship's wheel and going around behind the cabin. They heard him rummaging around back there until he returned, pushing before him the cannon which he had used against the armour fish.

"A squid's body is coated with ammonia," said Uncle Jack, as he set up the gun, "That's why it stinks. It must be very close."

"But giant squids never come to the surface," said Stanley, "They live deep in the ocean."

"That's the giant squids *you* know," said Uncle Jack, "A *kraken* is another matter, entirely. They'll come near the surface, lookin' fer sharks, or whales, even armour fish. An' if a kraken spots a ship, it'll go for it, sure as anythin'. A nasty lot, they are."

"But what is a kraken doing *here*?" said Pericles indignantly. "They live in the southern ocean, and they never come near the coast!"

"There's somethin' wrong with it, I think," said Uncle Jack, as he leveled the cannon and prepared to fire at anything that wiggled. "It's blackened the water with its ink, so it's upset, an' its smell is off, so it might be sick."

"And the fog?" said Pericles, a touch of hysteria in his voice, "I've never heard of a kraken making *fog!*"

"Nor I," said Uncle Jack, "but I got a feelin' that the two are connected. I'm willin' to bet that this ain't no ordinary kraken."

The situation was sounding worse and worse to Stanley. Not only were they close to a dangerous animal, they were close to a dangerous animal that was upset, sick, and could control fog. He took a fearful look overboard, and was more than a little surprised to see something looking back at him.

It was a huge, horrible, bloodshot yellow eye, which had to have been at least two feet across. Stanley made a frightened gagging noise and fell backwards onto the deck with a 'thud'.

"Stanley!" said Nell, as she and Alabaster rushed to his side, "What's the matter?"

Stanley pointed wildly over the railing and stammered, "Eye! B-B-BIG!"

Uncle Jack wheeled the cannon over to the starboard side, locked the wheels in place, and prepared to fire. "You three may want to get inside," he said without looking at them, "this could get ugly."

The children were about to act on Uncle Jack's advice, when something long and snakelike rose dripping out of the water. This was no snake, though; it was a tentacle, one of the two longer arms of a giant squid. The tentacle was jet black, just like the water from whence it rose. The suction cups lining the tentacle's underside were almost invisible, and at its tip, where one would usually find a flat, oval surface used for grabbing fish, a huge eye had opened and was staring down at Uncle Jack.

"That ain't right," said the old man, sounding awed and disgusted at the same time. "There's somethin' seriously wrong with this overgrown dish o' calamari."

The tentacle-eye stared a few seconds longer, and just as everyone was thinking that their fears may have been misplaced, a second tentacle shot out of the water quick as a flash, wrapped itself around the mast, and began to pull. The Ogopogo rocked alarmingly on its starboard side, nearly sending everyone sprawling onto the deck.

It was fortunate that they had stopped off in Port Silverburg; Mr. Crane's repair team had replaced the Ogopogo's mast with a new one, one with a great steel pole at its core. This steel pole was the only thing preventing the mast from snapping in two as the kraken held it in its impossibly strong grip.

Uncle Jack steadied the cannon and fastened it to the railing with a rope, before firing a flaming blast at the tentacle-eye. The thing dodged the fireball with incredible agility, and watched it disappear into the fog. Before Uncle Jack could fire again, another tentacle shot out of the water and knocked him aside. Seconds later, six more of the beastly things surfaced and began flailing about in a very unsettling manner.

Stanley rushed to help Uncle Jack, who had rolled down the now sloping deck and bumped into the bulwark. "Are you okay?" he gasped, as he helped the old man to his feet.

"Aye, thanks to you, laddie—LOOK OUT!" He grabbed Stanley and dove aside, just as the tentacle crashed into the place where they had been standing.

Stanley and Uncle Jack both stared open-mouthed as the tentacle pulled back. Its tip had opened like a flower, revealing an impressive set of jaws, lined with equally impressive teeth.

"*What the devil* is *this thing*?" yelled Uncle Jack, as he and Stanley dove aside again, narrowly avoiding the wickedly gnashing teeth.

Stanley looked wildly around him. The horrible tentacles were everywhere, twisting and flailing in the air, wriggling across the deck, latching onto the ship. A few of them had actually wrapped themselves around the hull, and judging by the groaning noises coming from the ship, they were squeezing. Fortunately, back in Port Silverburg, Mr. Crane's men had installed a steel support frame on the inside of the hull—a good thing, since without it, the Ogopogo would have been reduced to splinters.

"*Crush my ship, will ya*?" cried Uncle Jack, as he drew a short cutlass from inside his coat, and leapt upon the nearest tentacle.

Stanley saw that Alabaster and Nell had found a pair of oars, and were waving them threateningly at another one of the foul appendages.

"*Back, back*!" shouted Alabaster as the thing twisted about, trying to find an opening. It suddenly thrust itself at Nell, jaws snapping, but she swiftly brought up her oar and knocked it away with a loud, wet '*whack*'. A dribble of thick, black fluid proclaimed that she had wounded it. The tentacle hissed angrily and curled itself up, protecting itself from further attack.

The Ogopogo's hull groaned again under the strain of the kraken's crushing grip. Stanley saw that Uncle Jack was skillfully hacking at one of the tentacles which had encircled the hull. The thing shuddered and twitched as the wound grew deeper, but it refused to release its grip.

Stanley raced around the deck, looking for a weapon of his own, when all of a sudden he felt something wet and squishy latch onto his leg. With a sharp yank, the horrible thing pulled him off his feet, and wrapped itself around his entire body. He cried out in horror as he was lifted into the air, where he found himself staring into the vicious jaws of the tentacle. Just as the slavering monstrosity was about to attack, though, it gave a funny lurch and fell, '*thplatt*' onto the deck, taking Stanley down with it. The foul thing's grip had mysteriously relaxed, and he was able to fight his way free of the slimy black coils. He clambered to his feet, wondering what had happened. His answer stood before him: Benjamin Stone. He was holding a hefty-looking axe, whose blade was dark and dripping with kraken ichor. He had arrived just in time, and severed the tentacle with one clean chop.

"Thanks, Benjamin," Stanley said lamely, as he tried to catch his breath. Benjamin nodded once, then went to work on the tentacle wrapped around the mast. Two mighty hacks later, he was rewarded with a drenching spray of black ichor, and another severed, lifeless tentacle.

Stanley couldn't believe how strong Benjamin was, but his attention was suddenly monopolized by a great disturbance in the ocean just off the starboard bow. The black water had begun to bubble and boil, and the smell of befouled bleach grew even stronger. A great, dark mass began to rise slowly from the churning, blackened sea; the kraken, itself had come to join the battle, and it was nothing like the model in the museum back home.

It had a long, sleek, ridged shell which radiated the same darkness as the water. In fact, the creature's entire body seemed to be darkening the fog; it was as if the kraken were a light bulb, except that instead of shining with light, it shone with darkness, and that is what made it truly horrible.

The monster's body was more octopus-like than squid-like; squat and lumpy, instead of long and thin. It had a pair of eyes in its 'head', in addition to those found at the end of its two longer arms. These glared about fiercely, leaving no room for doubt that behind them lurked a terrible intelligence. The creature's mouth, which was clearly not a beak, opened wide and let out a thunderous roar. The mouth was little more than a gaping, round hole lined with rows and rows of sharp, needle-like teeth.

It was almost too much to bear, and Stanley began to feel as if he might faint. A dizzy feeling came over him, and everything seemed to slow down. Cowering beside Alabaster in front of the cabin door, he watched as the kraken's tentacles twisted and flailed about in ridiculous slow-motion. He watched as Nell spent what felt like half an hour savagely jabbing her oar into one of the bloodshot tentacle-eyes, before she dropped her weapon and put her hands over her ears. He saw the beast itself, thrashing and bellowing in the black water as the air around it became hideously dark and shadowy. The dizziness grew worse, and Stanley crouched down, head lowered and eyes closed.

Don't pass out, he told himself, *stay awake—you can't pass out now.*

A loud explosion caused him to open his eyes, just in time to see a fireball crash into the kraken's shell. The monster shrieked with fury, and unwrapped its arms from the Ogopogo's hull. Stanley stood up, the dizzy feeling vanishing as he watched Uncle Jack aim the cannon at the kraken's horrendous mouth.

Uncle Jack, the only person on board who had kept his head when the kraken had surfaced, had leapt behind the cannon while everyone else was stunned by the creature's unnatural roar, and fired off a shot.

The kraken's shell was stronger than steel, and the fireball hadn't so much as dented it, but the shock value of the attack had surprised the beast long enough to make it release the ship. Now, though, realizing that it hadn't been injured by the blast, the kraken hissed with fury and raised its tentacles threateningly, obviously intent on counterattacking.

Uncle Jack, though, stayed as cool and level-headed as ever. "I wouldn't try anythin' if I were you," he called from behind the cannon.

The kraken's eyes narrowed, and it gave a long, low hiss, dripping with malice, but it did not attack. Instead, it stared hatefully at the old man, as if it were trying to figure him out.

In all its long existence, it had never faced such a foe. How did the prey command such bright, cruel flame? It had seen flames before, but never one that burned so brightly, and certainly not one that could be thrown about in such a fashion. What would happen if it were touched by the flame? The flame had touched its shell, but nothing could harm the shell. If the flame were to touch the flesh ... but that was a risk that had to be taken. The prey had harmed it, cut off two of its precious limbs. No. It would not retreat, it would not allow the prey to escape unpunished. If it was quick enough, it could kill them all before the fire-thrower could react. Then, it would drag them to its lair, and feast.

The kraken, however, had underestimated Uncle Jack's prowess with a cannon. While the monster was thinking its horrible thoughts, the old man discreetly unhitched the gun from the starboard railing, and released the wheel locks, just in case he had to make a quick move.

And a quick move he made. The kraken suddenly thrust its tentacles at Stanley, Alabaster, and Nell with unearthly speed, and that would have been the end of them, if not for Uncle Jack. Instead of watching the creature's tentacles, he had been watching its *eyes*, and the second before it attacked, he had seen those eyes look away and focus on the children. The instant he saw the eyes move, he shoved off from the bulwark and rode the cannon sideways across the deck, firing as he went. The monster had been so intent on catching the children, so sure of it victory, that it hadn't noticed Uncle Jack, hadn't seen the fireballs flying towards it, until it was too late.

Two of the fireballs exploded harmlessly on the kraken's shell, and a few others didn't hit at all. But one of them flew right into the monster's tooth-filled cavern of a mouth. A gargled shriek was cut short as the fireball exploded, sending a hideous spray of kraken-ichor into the stratosphere. The Ogopogo's deck was instantly drenched by the wave of foul, black fluid, but the crew members were too shocked to be disgusted as they watched the kraken's ruined form slump lifelessly into the black water.

Just as all seemed quiet, one of the beast's tentacles rose nightmarishly out of the water. It quivered for a moment, then the jaws at its tip opened wide. An odd gurgling sound came forth, and the thing coughed, sending something small and black flying out like an arrow shot from a bow. The projectile flew right into Stanley's left shoulder, and knocked him backwards onto the deck, while the tentacle went limp and dropped into the water with a splash.

Nell screamed as Stanley fell, and rushed to his side, followed closely by Alabaster.

"Stanley! Stanley!" cried Alabaster, "Speak to me!" He grabbed Stanley by the front of his shirt and shook him with both hands.

"Ow!" said Stanley, "Stop, Alabaster, that hurts!"

"Are you okay?" said Nell, her voice full of concern.

"Uh, I think so." He turned his head so that he could see his shoulder. Sticking up out of a hole in his sleeve was something long, sharp, and black. He suddenly felt sick.

"'Scuse me, you too," said Uncle Jack as he and Benjamin crowded in. "Sufferin' sea horses, Stanley! Are ya all right? Can ya sit up?"

"I think so." With an effort, and a lot of groaning, Stanley managed to sit up and prop himself against the cabin wall. He was starting to feel lightheaded again, and his shoulder, which sent bolts of pain up and down his arm every time he breathed in, was starting to tingle unpleasantly. Grimacing, he looked down at the black kraken spike. It looked like a big needle, and was about a half inch in diameter. The visible part was six inches long, but there was no telling how much more of its length was buried in Stanley's shoulder. It hadn't gone through to the other side, and he supposed that was a good sign.

"Does it hurt?" asked Alabaster, his curiosity getting the better of him.

"*Well of course it hurts!*" snapped Nell, before Stanley could respond, "*He has a big spike stuck in his shoulder!*"

"Take it easy there, Nell," said Uncle Jack gently, "no sense in gettin' all worked up over this. How ya doin', Stanley?"

Stanley tried to smile bravely. "Not bad," he managed, through gritted teeth.

"Now, y'know, laddie," said Uncle Jack, leaning forward, "that thing's gonna have to come out."

Stanley nodded, his face set; this was obviously going to hurt, a lot. He had been stung by bees before, and gotten his share of splinters, but this ...

"Look!" said Uncle Jack suddenly, "The fog is clearin' up!"

Stanley forgot about his shoulder for a moment, and followed Uncle Jack's gaze skyward. Sure enough, the thick, impenetrable fog was dissipating. Beams of sunlight stabbed down through rents in the fading mist, and patches of blue sky began to appear.

Stanley was so busy staring up at the returning sunlight, that he didn't notice as Uncle Jack reached forward, grabbed the kraken spike, and yanked. He yelped loudly as searing pain exploded in his shoulder, and was very surprised to see the offending projectile clasped in Uncle Jack's hand.

"Way to go, Uncle Jack!" said Alabaster, as the old man tossed the seven-inch kraken spike away.

"Whoa!" said Stanley, surprised at how quickly it had all happened, "Thanks, Uncle Jack."

Uncle Jack smiled. "Don't mention it, lad. Now, let's see about gettin' ya patched up."

Minutes later, Stanley's shoulder was bandaged up nicely, and was already feeling better.

"Here, lad, take one o' these." Uncle Jack produced a pill bottle from the first aid kit, and shook a small, green capsule into his hand.

"What is it?" asked Stanley, taking the pill and the cup of water which Benjamin had fetched for him.

"An anti-venom," said Uncle Jack, as Stanley swallowed the pill. "Extra strength, available without a prescription, an' all that."

"Anti-venom?" said Nell, "Was that thing poisonous?

"Not sure," said Uncle Jack, "I've never seen a kraken shoot barbs at people." He noticed the worried look on Stanley's face, and said, "Not to worry, lad. If that spike had any poison in it, that wee pill will get rid of it, ye can be sure o' that."

"How are you feeling, Stanley?" said Alabaster.

"Tired," said Stanley. He was feeling more and more lightheaded, and all he wanted to do now was sleep. He was feeling cold, too, despite the fact that the warm sun was fighting its way though the clearing fog. It felt as if ice water was flowing through his veins, and he hoped the anti-venom pill really was extra strength.

It wasn't long before the fog vanished completely. The day was once again bright and clear, the sky cloudless and full of sunshine. A pleasant breeze was blowing from the southeast, and the sea had resumed its usual movement and rolling. It was good to see everything returned to normal, but something very interesting began to happen. As the warm afternoon sun shone down on the Ogopogo, the disgusting kraken ichor, which had covered the deck, began to evaporate. Even more surprising was what happened to the two severed tentacles which were lying by the mast. With an unsavoury sizzling sound, they dissolved and evaporated as well, and it wasn't long before all traces of the kraken were gone, leaving the Ogopogo's deck completely spotless.

"By all the currents o' the sea, that has to have been the most unusual monster I've ever had the misfortune of meetin'," exclaimed Uncle Jack, as he watched the last of the black goo disappear from his coat, leaving the material like new.

"It totally disappeared," said Alabaster, closely examining the deck boards.

"So the fog and the kraken *were* connected," mused Nell, "Sunlight is harmful to it, so it created the fog to keep itself out of the sun."

"A kraken creatin' fog?" said Uncle Jack, "It just doesn't add up."

"What do you mean?" said Nell.

"I mean that this was no kraken. I've seen krakens before, an' lemme tell ya, they were nothin' like this beastie."

"But you knew what it was, before we even saw it," said Nell, "You knew the smell."

"Aye, that's true. Lemme rephrase it: That thing was not a kraken *anymore*. Maybe a long time ago it *was* a kraken, but somewhere along the line, somethin' happened to it, to make it … like *that*."

"There has never been a black kraken," put in Pericles, "and there has never been a kraken with an anatomy like that of the one we just saw, and a kraken has never been able to control the weather. Jack's right—this thing was more than just a kraken, and if you ask me, we're all extremely lucky to be alive."

There was a brief silence before Uncle Jack said, "Alright, Pericles, that's enough. We're safe now, an' that's what counts."

The parrot '*hmphed*', but did not argue.

"It's time we got back under way," Uncle Jack continued, "we've a long way to go yet, an' sittin' here chattin' won't get us any closer to Ethelia. All hands, make sail! Stanley, how're ya doin' over there?"

But Stanley didn't answer.

"I don't think he's doing well at all, Mr. Lee," said Nell, who was kneeling beside him, "He's unconscious."

Abyss

Stanley found himself underwater, once again. "I'm dreaming." He said it aloud, and watched as bubbles came out of his mouth and floated away like balloons on a summer breeze. He was deep under water, and it was very dark, but there were beams of light coming from every direction, as if he was surrounded by flood-lights.

Suddenly, he became aware of movement in the water. He felt a presence somewhere nearby, and his blood turned to ice. He didn't know what the thing was, but he did know he didn't want to be anywhere near it. He swam off in the direction of one of the lights, but stopped suddenly. The light he had been swim-ming towards had gone out. Somehow, Stanley knew that those lights were not supposed to go out. He looked around him and was horrified to see another light go out, and then another, and another, and another after that. He swam franti-cally towards yet another light, only to see it go out, too, along with several oth-ers. For what seemed like hours, he swam about, trying to reach the lights, only to have them go out just as he came close. Finally, the last light was extinguished, and he was left in total darkness.

"NO!" he yelled, and then began to cry with anger and frustration. It was all so unfair. He hadn't been able to save any of the lights, not even one.

"*Not even one,*" came a cruel, hissing voice from somewhere off in the dark-ness.

Stanley sniffed back the last of his tears. "Who are you?" he called. His voice was shaky and weak.

"*Who are you?*" replied the same cruel, hissing voice. It sounded like an echo, but was clearly not.

"What are you?" Stanley insisted, "What do you want?"

"*What are you?*" the voice repeated, "*What do you want?*"

"Why are you repeating everything I say?"

"*Why are you repeating everything I say?*"

"Leave me alone!"

"*Alone.*"

Stanley could feel the presence getting closer. It was coming for him.

"Get away from me!"

"*Alone.*"

He kicked frantically, trying to swim away, but it was useless; the thing was right behind him. Suddenly, he felt something drop into his pocket. It felt like a large marble. He drew the object forth, and was amazed by what he saw. In his hand, he held a small sphere of brilliant white light. It looked like a star, and felt pleasantly warm in his hand. He felt his fear melt away, and turned around. Floating not far away was a shapeless black mass. Stanley held up the sphere of light, and the dark mass shrank away from it.

"You don't like this, do you?" said Stanley.

"*You don't like this, do you?*" hissed the mass.

"Go away."

"*Away.*"

But the dark mass did not go away. It began to get bigger and bigger. It didn't come any closer, but soon it had formed itself into a great, hollow sphere, with Stanley at the centre. The dark mass would not come within a certain distance of the light cast by the small white globe. Stanley was relieved by this, but wondered how he was going to get away.

Suddenly, the sphere of light grew larger. It grew and grew, and then its white light turned gold, and Stanley saw that it was now filled with blue, and he realized that he was no longer looking at the sphere of light …

CHAPTER FOURTEEN:
THE MASKED MAN

... He was looking at the porthole beside his bunk in the Ogopogo's cabin. The blue he had seen in his dream was the clear blue sky, and the golden light was that of the sun. He blinked several times, wondering at what point he had opened his eyes, then looked at his watch. 6:08.

Have I been asleep since yesterday afternoon? He wondered. He remembered the fog, and the kraken attack, and ... his shoulder. The kraken had shot some weird spike into his left shoulder. He looked down at the shoulder in question, and saw that the bandage was still in place. There was a dark, brownish stain in the middle of the white dressing, and he touched it gingerly. Surprisingly, the wound didn't hurt anymore. Curious, Stanley peeled back the bandage, and was astounded by what he saw: nothing. There was no red, scabby hole in his shoulder, nor was there anything to suggest that there ever had been. Only the blood-stained bandage betrayed the fact that there had been a wound beneath it.

Stanley pulled the bandage back completely, and poked himself in the shoulder. Nothing. No pain, no stiffness, not so much as a tingle. As if that wasn't enough, his surprise redoubled when he took a look at the palm of his right hand. There had been a deep, angry gash across that palm since the day he'd met Nell, and he kept finding ways to irritate and reopen it so that it just would not heal. He'd been worried that it might be getting infected, but now it was gone. Gone without a trace, no scar, no mark, just a fully-functional, slightly dirty palm. *"How is this possible?,"* he asked himself.

Now that he was fully awake, Stanley decided to get up and ask his friends for some answers. How could he possibly have been asleep long enough for his wounds to heal so completely?

Judging by the deep, peaceful breathing coming from elsewhere in the cabin, Alabaster and Nell were still fast asleep. Stanley was feeling much too impatient to wait for them to get up, so he got out of bed, drew back Alabaster's bunk screen, and poked him repeatedly in the forehead.

"Nurrf," Alabaster murmured in his sleep. Refusing to awaken, he rolled over against the wall and snorted loudly.

"Come on, wake up," said Stanley, grabbing hold of Alabaster's pyjama shirt and shaking him.

"I don't *wanna* go to school today, Mom, can't I sleep in?"

"Alabaster!" Stanley said loudly.

Alabaster rolled over and opened his eyes. "Oh, morning, Stanley." He rolled back over, then sat bolt upright an instant later. "Stanley!" he exclaimed, "You're awake! Boy, what a relief! You just sort of conked out there, and we couldn't wake you up! We thought you might've been poisoned, but you were still breathing, so we knew you weren't dead! But still, we sure were worried, and Nell and I took turns sitting by your bed, and I tried to wake you up a couple times, but you just kept on sleeping, so I gave up after a while, and Nell said that if I didn't stop bothering you, she'd throw me overboard! Anyway, it sure is good that you're finally awake. I wonder why you slept so long?"

"You guys sat beside me?" said Stanley, deeply touched.

"Yep," said Alabaster, "we wanted to keep an eye on you."

"Well, uh … thanks," Stanley said lamely, "that was really nice of you guys."

"No problem," said Alabaster, "So, how does it feel to sleep for three days?"

"*Three days!*" said Stanley, "I've been sleeping for three days?"

"Yeah, amazing, isn't it?"

Just then, Nell drew back her bunk screen. "Stanley!" she said happily, "You're awake! I thought I heard your voice. How are you?"

"Fine," said Stanley, "I'm better than fine—look, my shoulder's all healed up, and so's my hand." He rolled up his sleeve to display his wound-free shoulder.

Nell stared, mouth open. "But that's amazing!" she exclaimed, as she hopped out of bed, "That should have taken weeks to heal, months, even!" She poked Stanley's shoulder rather roughly. "There's not even a mark!"

"Same thing with my hand," said Stanley, displaying his right palm, "Remember when I cut *this*?"

"Oh yeah, right," said Nell, turning a bit pink, "But ... but *that* cut is completely healed, too!"

"Awesome!" said Alabaster, "You're like Wolverine, Stanley!"

"Nice!" said Stanley, "I'll have to start calling everyone *bub* from now on."

"Ugh, please don't," said Nell, "It was probably just that pill your uncle gave you, Stanley. Who knows what kind of medicine they have here?"

"... Yeah, you're probably right," said Stanley, looking again at his right palm.

"Let's go find Uncle Jack," said Alabaster, "He'll be glad to see that you're okay."

*   *   *   *

Uncle Jack was indeed very glad to see Stanley up and about.

"Stanley! Am I ever glad to see ya up an' about! Ya gave us all quite a scare, that's fer sure. How's the shoulder?"

Stanley rolled up his sleeve. "It's fine!"

"Holy halibuts!" said Uncle Jack, "Yer all healed up! That's incredible, I've never seen anythin' like it!"

"So you don't know how it happened?" asked Stanley, "It wasn't the anti-venom pill?"

"Narr, a wee pill like that doesn't speed the healin' process—it just neutralizes an' eliminates poisons in the blood stream. I dunno how ... what could've caused ... seems impossible ... yer a marvel, Stanley, m'lad!"

"See?" said Alabaster, giving Nell a small nudge, "It *wasn't* the pill. Stanley's Wolverine!"

"What's a wolverine got to do with this?" Uncle Jack asked curiously.

While Alabaster explained who Wolverine was, Stanley and Nell headed down to the galley to see what was for breakfast. Benjamin was standing at the tiny stove, with Pericles on his shoulder.

"Ah, good morning, Nell, and a *very special* good morning to you, Stanley!" said the parrot, as they entered the room. Benjamin beamed and waved at them.

"Most intriguing," said Pericles, when Stanley showed him his mended wounds.

"What's for breakfast?" asked Nell, trying to change the subject.

"Ah, Benjamin is frying up some moonfish he caught yesterday. Quite delicious, if I may say so."

"Hey, we must be pretty close to Ethelia by now," said Stanley.

"That we are," said Pericles, "We've been making excellent time these past few days. I believe we'll arrive soon after lunchtime, if we weigh anchor right after breakfast.

*　　　*　　　*　　　*

Breakfast was indeed delicious, and it wasn't long before the Ogopogo was once again sailing north, on the final leg of its journey to the city of Ethelia. Shortly after eleven o'clock, they came upon a long line of buoys, spaced about fifty yards apart. The line of buoys extended from the shoreline to somewhere beyond the visible horizon.

"Those buoys mark the territory of the Imperial Capital," explained Uncle Jack, "They go for miles an' miles, formin' a big semi-circle around the city. We've a little less than an hour to go now, mates."

Just as Uncle Jack finished speaking, a shadow flitted across the Ogopogo's deck.

"What was that?" said Stanley.

"What was what?" said Alabaster, who hadn't seen it.

"Must have been a bird," said Nell.

"Prob'ly an albatross," said Uncle Jack, "They're good luck, y'know."

The shadow passed over them again.

"Bit big for an albatross," commented Pericles.

Stanley squinted up into the bright morning sky. Sure enough, something with wings was circling the Ogopogo, and it was definitely too big to be an albatross.

"I see it, I see it!" cried Alabaster, pointing skyward excitedly. "That's no bird—it's a *person!*"

"A person?" said Uncle Jack, "Mercy, me eyes ain't as good as they used to be! Ya sure it's a person, Alabaster?"

"Pretty sure."

"A person? With wings?" said Pericles, "The very idea!"

"But it's true!" said Alabaster, "I can see his feet. Come on, Pericles, you can see a long ways, look for yourself!"

"Oh, very well, I'll take a good look, but pluck me bald and call me a turkey if that oversized gull catches me staring at him!"

"Pericles ain't very friendly with other birds," explained Uncle Jack.

"Especially not sea birds," said Pericles, "Rude and uncouth, the lot of them. Oh, I say, how odd!"

"What?" said Uncle Jack, "What's odd?"

"It *is* a person. And he does indeed appear to have a pair of wings!"

"See? I told you," said Alabaster.

"Must be a hang-glider," said Stanley.

But it wasn't. The figure circled closer and closer, lower and lower, until it landed swiftly and smoothly in a crouching position on the Ogopogo's deck. The figure remained crouching for a moment, then stood up, flexing a pair of huge, black, bat-like wings. The wings suddenly stiffened, and began folding themselves up like pieces of paper. In a matter of seconds, they were gone. Without wings, the figure did indeed look like a person, although its features were concealed by a long, dark cloak the colour of damp ashes, and a blank, white mask with two eye holes and several vertical slits for a mouth.

They all stared at the mysterious masked figure, and the mysterious masked figure stared right back.

"If this is another monster attack," muttered Pericles, "I think I may moult."

"Take it easy, Pericles," said Uncle Jack quietly, "let's find out what this fellah's about 'fore we start gettin' jittery." He cleared his throat. "*Ahoy there!*" he called, taking a few steps towards the mysterious figure, "Welcome aboard the Ogopogo. I'm the captain. Er, who might you be?"

No answer. The figure simply stood there and stared. Uncle Jack tried again.

"So, what brings ya out here on this fine day?"

Still no answer. Uncle Jack shuffled his feet uncomfortably.

"Er, mighty impressive wingspan ya got there."

"You are travelers from afar," came a hoarse, rasping voice from behind the mask. The words seemed to carry a low rumble as they were spoken.

"Ahh, aye, that's true enough," said Uncle Jack, relieved to have gotten a reaction. "We sailed outta Port Silverburg a few days ago."

"You came from afar," repeated the masked man, "You hail from the land where one moon rises."

There was a brief pause as Uncle Jack glanced back at his crew. Stanley heard Nell whisper,

"*One moon*? Does he mean *our* world?"

"An' what d'you know about a land where one moon rises?" inquired Uncle Jack.

"I know what was foretold," rasped the masked man.

"Uh-huh. An' *what*, exactly, was foretold?"

"That is not for you to know."

"Oh really? Well, I'm sorry to disappoint ya, mate, but ya got the wrong ship. Like I told ya, we just came outta Port Silverburg ..."

"You came from far beyond Port Silverburg, old man. I saw you arrive, with my own eyes."

"Assumin' ya did," said Uncle Jack, folding his arms, "what is it ya want with an old sailor like me?"

"Nothing," croaked the masked man, "My business is with the boy of the two bloods." He shoved Uncle Jack out of the way, and made a beeline for Stanley. Benjamin Stone stepped in to block his path, but was tossed aside as if he had been made of straw. Alabaster rushed forward.

"Hey, knock it off!"

Before he could say anything else, the masked man picked him up with one hand and tossed him neatly beside Benjamin.

"*Hey!*" shouted Stanley, suddenly furious, "*No one throws my friends around!*"

"Stanley, no!" cried Nell, as she jumped forward and pulled him out of the masked man's reach. She was flung aside for her trouble, and landed in a heap on top of Alabaster.

"AVAST, YA SCURVY SCOUNDREL!" Uncle Jack bellowed, as he charged forward, cutlass drawn.

The masked man raised a gloved hand, and a translucent wall of darkness rose up, cutting him and Stanley off from the rest of the group. Uncle Jack crashed into the wall and started pounding on it as if it were made of solid rock.

"Harr!" he shouted, "Get this wall o' yours outta here, an' face me like a man!"

The masked man took no notice, but turned to Stanley and took a menacing step forward.

"What devilry is this?" squawked Pericles, who was trying unsuccessfully to fly over the strange wall.

Stanley backed away until *bump*, he hit the cabin wall. He thought briefly of ducking inside, but decided against it. Two steps later, the masked man stood before him, staring down from behind that blank, featureless mask.

"All this has been foretold," came the rasping, rumbling voice. "Your protectors have failed you, and now you are mine."

"They're not my protectors!" Stanley shot back, "They're my friends, and you didn't have to go throwing them around like that! Just tell me what you want from me, and get out of here!"

The masked man let out a short, oddly shrill bark of laughter, then reached into his robes and drew forth a long, curving black sword. Stanley gasped and shrank back, trying to melt into the cabin wall.

"*Stanley!*" screamed Nell, rushing forward and squashing her nose against the wall of darkness.

"*Look out, Stanley!*" shouted Alabaster, as if Stanley hadn't noticed the sword raised above him.

The masked man's shadow seemed to grow longer, spreading across the deck like spilled ink, until it touched Stanley's shoes. This appeared to have trapped his feet, for he could no longer move them. All poor Stanley could do was watch as the masked man turned the sword blade-down, the tip pointing rock steady at his chest.

"It is over before it has even begun," the masked man said hissingly, as he raised the sword and made ready to strike. Stanley closed his eyes and hoped against hope that being impaled on a sword didn't hurt as much as he thought it did.

He waited. And waited. The seconds ticked by. What was the masked man waiting for? Was he still holding the sword, waiting till he saw the whites of Stanley's eyes?

An entire minute passed, and then the tension became too much to bear. Stanley risked a peek, opening one eye ever so slightly. Then, he opened both of them, a confused look on his face. The masked man had lowered his sword, and was staring blankly at him. What could it mean? He then sheathed the sword completely, and knelt in front of Stanley, so that their faces were level. Stanley stared at the mask's eye holes. He couldn't see the eyes, themselves, but he knew they were there, gazing searchingly into his own. The masked man suddenly stood up.

"Interesting," he rumbled, "Very surprising. This eventuality was *not* foretold." He turned away from Stanley and unfolded his massive wings. "You may live for now, boy," he called over his shoulder, "but only because you intrigue me." He leapt, cat-like, onto the starboard railing and crouched there, wings spread wide.

"Wait!" said Stanley, trying unsuccessfully to follow, "Who are you? Why did you want to kill me?"

The masked man ignored the questions. "Farewell, Stanley," the voice rasped, "until next we meet." Then he dove off the railing, flapped his wings, and soared off on a warm air current, disappearing into a bank of cloud. Stanley watched him go, his mind spinning with questions. The wall of darkness dissolved moments later, and he found himself surrounded by Alabaster, Nell, and the others.

"Who *was* that guy?" said Alabaster, excitement and horror mixing in his voice.

"*How the heck should I know?*" Stanley shouted, quite a bit more harshly than he had intended. "Sorry," he said, seeing Alabaster's slightly hurt expression, "I didn't mean to yell. It's just a bit upsetting, almost getting killed by a psycho with wings and a mask."

"Whoever he is," Pericles piped up, "he is a very powerful sorcerer. I can't imagine why a sorcerer would seek to destroy *you*, of all people, Stanley."

"Yeah!" said Stanley, "I never did anything to him! I don't even *know* him! Hey, you don't think he's working for Chamberlain, do you? He said he saw us in Port Silverburg, maybe he's a spy."

"And he went after *you* as a way of taking a shot at Uncle Jack," said Alabaster sleuthily. Uncle Jack was shaking his head.

"Narr, that fellah wasn't workin' fer Chamberlain. In all the time I've known the man, he's never employed sorcerers—not even decent ones. Besides, if our flyin' friend *had* been workin' for Chamberlain, he'd've been holdin' that sword over *me*, not Stanley."

"What bothers *me*," said Nell, "is that he knew who Stanley was, or, at least, he knew who to go after. What did he mean about all this being *foretold*? How could he possibly know that Stanley would be here, today?"

"Sorcerers and magicians are a mysterious lot," said Pericles, unintentionally stating the obvious, "Divination is a rather common (if unreliable) skill of those who practice the magical arts."

"That's foretelling the future," Nell whispered to Alabaster, noting his blank look.

"Oh, right," said Alabaster, "but what could anyone foretell, that could make them want to hurt Stanley? He's a nice guy."

"An' yer a good friend, Alabaster, lad," said Uncle Jack, "but that doesn't mean everyone's gonna like ya."

"That maniac was probably wrong, anyway," said Pericles scoffingly, "Everyone knows that divination is not a precise form of magic. After all, he didn't follow through with his little 'mission', now did he? He said himself that something hadn't been foretold. He obviously made a mistake."

"But he knew my name," said Stanley, wishing he could agree with Pericles, "And he called me *the boy of the two bloods*."

Pericles sniffed dismissively. "He heard your name when Miss Hawthorne called to you." Nell turned slightly red at this.

"As for *two bloods*," Pericles went on, "why, that could mean just about any-thing; a child born of a duke and a peasant woman—the mixing of 'noble' and 'common' blood, as it were. Or it could mean a boy who has undergone a blood transfusion, perhaps. In fact, you could apply *two bloods* to every single person in the wide world, if you consider the fact that a child is made up of genes from both father and mother …"

"Wow, Pericles, are you ever smart!" said Alabaster.

"Oh, not really," said Pericles, the words oozing with false modesty, "I am merely an assiduous student of reason."

"*And* of babblin' till yer blue in the face," Uncle Jack muttered audibly.

"I merely thought we should examine every possibility, and not lose our heads," said Pericles snippily.

"Well, I guess we can't blame ya for that," said Uncle Jack, "Yer probably right, anyway, Pericles, it's soundin' more an' more like Mr. Spooky back there messed up, in a big way." He turned to Stanley. "What'ya think, lad? Feel any better 'bout this business?"

"Yeah," said Stanley truthfully. It had been a harrowing experience, but he seemed to be getting used to these, and already the whole thing seemed rather distant. He had been in grave danger, but here he was, alive and well, surrounded by friends, with the sun shining brightly, and the sea rolling beneath him. It was a good day to be alive. "I feel much better."

CHAPTER FIFTEEN: ETHELIA, CAPITAL OF THE EMPIRE

"Y'know, lad," said Uncle Jack, "I've been in plenty o' scrapes meself." He tapped the deck with his wooden leg. "An' as ye can see, I didn't always get away unscathed!"

Uncle Jack had been trying to put Stanley's mind at ease for the past forty minutes. Stanley's mind was *already* at ease, but he appreciated the gesture, and was glad for the opportunity to hear some tales of danger and adventure.

"The open sea ain't the safest place," the old man was saying, "but ya gotta remember that danger is a part of everyday life, 'specially for a man o' the sea."

Stanley was thinking about how life back home in East Stodgerton could hardly be called 'dangerous', when Pericles squawked,

"LAAAAAND-HO!"

"What'ya mean, *land-ho*, ya daffy bird?" Uncle Jack called, "We're barely fifty yards from the coast!"

"I *mean* we've arrived!" said Pericles.

The Ogopogo rounded a tall, white cliff, and there, sprawled magnificently on the shore of a great, wide bay, was Ethelia. It was absolutely massive. The harbour was a least ten times the size of Port Silverburg's. Hundreds of ships, big and small, were moored at scores of massive stone piers, while hundreds more sailed around the bay, coming and going on business of their own. Beyond the crowded harbour was the city proper, where cobbled streets could be seen meandering off among an uncountable collection of sandy-coloured buildings with terra cotta roofs. To the left and right of the harbour were the mouths of two rivers, beyond which the land rose up to form the cyclopean cliffs at the mouth of the bay; a watchtower stood atop each.

Even more buildings could be seen hugging the far banks of both rivers, some of them built right into the cliffs. The city continued far into the distance, its limits invisible from this vantage point.

"Ethelia," said Uncle Jack reverently, as the children gawked at the sweeping urban panorama. "Biggest city in the Empire. Half a million people livin' here—course, that was forty years ago, there's probably more now."

"Look at the castle!" said Alabaster excitedly.

Rising out of the distance, towering high above even the tallest buildings in the city, was a colossal white castle, its spires shining in the early afternoon sun, its pennants caught in the warm summer breeze.

Stanley loved castles. He read about them often, and enjoyed looking at the pictures and diagrams, imagining what it must have been like to live in one.

"Someday I'm going to visit every castle in the world," Stanley had told his mother the first time she had shown him the photographs she and his father had taken of some of the world's most famous castles. And now, here he was, staring at the real thing—not some mouldering, decrepit ruin, but a flawless, shining fortress in its prime.

"It's like something out of a fairy tale," Nell marveled.

"That's the imperial palace, mates," said Uncle Jack, "the centre of the Empire, folks call it. In there yeh'll find all the administrative offices, the house of Parliament, the Senate, the Bank o' Rhedland's head office, and, o' course, the seat of the King …"

"Or in this case, the Regent," said Pericles, alighting on Uncle Jack's shoulder.

"It's huge!" exclaimed Alabaster, "I've never seen such a big building!"

"Biggest building in the Empire, maybe even the world," said Uncle Jack, "Ya think it's big now, wait'll ya get right up close to it. Ya can't really tell from here, but the castle's way on the other side o' the city, built right on the tip o' the Rheddish Delta."

"The reason Ethelia is so important," said Pericles, "is its location. It sits right at the mouth of the Rheddish River, the biggest, most efficient trade route in the Empire, which flows 3,972 miles from its source in the southeast, to empty into the ocean. Anything going up the river has to go through Ethelia, as does anything that's going overseas. It's a fascinating city. People from all over the place coming and going …"

"Aye, it's a pity we can't stay for a bit," said Uncle Jack, "but we're here on business."

Stanley knew what he meant. "Your friend, Diego, right?"

"Aye. I wanna be half way 'cross the ocean 'fore they realize he's gone."

By now, they had sailed much closer to the harbour, close enough to see the citizens of Ethelia milling about. Aboard the many ships moored in the harbour, sailors could be seen loading and unloading cargo, working on repairs, and clambering about the rigging like monkeys. Pericles turned down the wind crystal, so that the Ogopogo's speed became much more city-friendly; a wise move, since the bay was absolutely teeming with ships. Tiny sailboats, big enough for only a few people, went zipping about, dodging recklessly between huge, lumbering warships.

As they approached the harbour, a ship like a large tug boat came chugging towards the Ogopogo. It was the first boat they had seen with an actual engine; puffs of white smoke were billowing out of a stout smokestack, which stuck up out of the vessel's cabin. As the tug drew up alongside the Ogopogo, a man in a dark blue uniform appeared on deck, and began to wave a pair of flags. Uncle Jack seemed to know what this meant, and waved back before turning off the wind crystal and ordering Benjamin to drop anchor. The tug stopped, too, and the man in the blue uniform stepped up onto his boat's port railing and hopped easily over the space between the two vessels.

"Welcome to Ethelia," said the man, shaking hands with Uncle Jack. His tone was friendly enough, but Stanley thought it seemed a bit forced.

"Thank you kindly," said Uncle Jack, "What can I do for ya?"

The man produced a clipboard and pen. "This is a security checkpoint, sir. I've just got to ask you a few questions before you dock."

Uncle Jack looked a bit confused, but answered a series of questions, just like he had back in Port Silverburg. "Er, forgive me for askin', lad," said Uncle Jack delicately, as the man packed up his clipboard, "but aren't ye a marine?"

The man sighed and nodded reluctantly. "Aye, Imperial Naval Guard, Lieutenant, Second Class."

"Well what's a Lieutenant, Second Class doin' on harbour security detail? Er, no offense, but isn't this sorta work beneath someone like yerself?"

"Yes, it is," the marine said irritably, "I take it you haven't been to Ethelia in a while?"

"No, I haven't," said Uncle Jack.

"Well, the reason we've been reduced to glorified customs agents, is the induction of the Knights of the Silver Sword.

Uncle Jack stared blankly.

"Big huge guys?" offered the marine, "All dressed up in these massive suits of armour? Never show their faces?"

"Oh yeah!" piped up Alabaster, "We had a run-in with *them* back in Port Silverb—*oof!*"

Stanley and Nell had both elbowed him in the stomach. The marine laughed and shook his head.

"Yeah, right. If you'd had a 'run-in' with the Knights of the Silver Sword, I don't think you'd be standing here today."

"We saw 'em, though, that's fer sure," said Uncle Jack, shooting a look at Alabaster, "Marchin' around the streets o' Port Silverburg like they owned the place." He neglected to mention that they had barely escaped the knights' clutches.

"That's them, alright," said the marine, "About a year ago, Chamberlain disbanded the Imperial Naval Guard, and brought in the Knights of the Silver Sword as his elite military unit. I don't know where he gets these guys, but every time I turn around, there seems to be more of them, and thanks to *them*, I'm stuck here chatting with tourists all day. Er, no offense, sir."

"None taken," said Uncle Jack. "But this is a right *scandal*, it is! The Imperial Naval Guard has history, tradition! It goes back hundreds o' years!"

"Were you in the marines, sir?"

"Nah, but I was in the navy, an' I knew many good marines, meself. I'd wager you lot're none too happy 'bout things these days."

"Definitely not. Er, well, I'd like to stay and continue this discussion, sir, but I really do have to get back to work. I am on 'duty' after all. You can dock at pier three-forty-one."

"Thank ye kindly, lad," said Uncle Jack, taking a docking permit slip from the marine, who then saluted and leapt back aboard his tug. "Nice fellah," he commented as he turned on the wind crystal. Benjamin pulled up the anchor, and minutes later, they had all disembarked at pier three-forty-one.

"Need any work done on your ship, sir?" said a young man wearing blue overalls and a filthy shirt.

"Check 'er for cracks an' leaks, if ya wouldn't mind," Uncle Jack told the harbour worker, putting a few coins in his hand.

"Yessir, thank you, sir."

"Right then," said Uncle Jack, as they made their way up from the harbour, "as you three already know, I've got some very serious business to take care of here in Ethelia. *But*," he said, before Alabaster could blurt out the exact nature of that business, "I won't be about it 'till much later tonight, so we might as well enjoy the rest o' the day."

"Yeah!" said the children in unison.

They spent the afternoon wandering around the city, poking about in all kinds of shops, exploring the vast market area, and taking an informative city tour in a horse-drawn carriage. Every so often, Stanley saw marines in their blue uniforms walking by. They all looked very disgruntled, and he felt sorry for them.

Uncle Jack treated them all to dinner that evening at a very fancy restaurant. They had to trek back to the Ogopogo and change into some nice clothes, because you weren't allowed in the restaurant wearing shorts and a T-shirt. Dinner was a fabulous production, and there was plenty to talk about, but no one spoke much while they ate. Stanley wasn't very hungry, and sat poking distractedly at his shrimp spaghetti. He was more than a bit worried about Uncle Jack, and the plot to break Diego out of prison, and what part he would have to play.

"Right," said Uncle Jack, once they had all finished eating, and were waiting for the bill, "after we're done here, we're all gonna head back to the Ogopogo. A bit later on, Benjamin an' I'll be off to do you-know-what. I'll be needin' you three to stay put, an' be ready to leave. Pericles'll stay with ya, an' he can show ya how to get the Ogopogo ready to sail. We might be needin' to leave in a hurry."

They left the restaurant and made their way down the street in silence. Stanley was pondering exactly how Uncle Jack would pull off the prison break, when he saw a lady drop something on the ground as she walked past. Breaking off from the group, he went to pick it up. It was a gold bracelet, whose clasp had come undone. He caught up with the lady and tapped her on the arm, saying,

"You dropped this, ma'am."

The lady looked at Stanley, then at the bracelet, and said, "Oh, thank you so much, young man!" She leaned down and kissed him on the cheek. "I don't know what I'd have done if I'd lost this!"

Stanley waited till the lady walked away, before wiping his cheek in disgust. Feeling rather pleased with himself all the same, he looked around for Uncle Jack and the others. They were nowhere to be seen. He was suddenly alone, and he had no idea where he was.

Stanley felt panic trying to rise up inside him, but was relieved to see a wisp of wild, white, grey-streaked hair not far down the street. He caught up with the hair's owner and tugged on his sleeve, saying,

"Aren't we going to the harbour, Uncle Jack?"

But it wasn't Uncle Jack. It was a surly-faced old man with a crooked nose and pointed chin. His face looked like it had been punched one too many times.

"Ere, what's this, then?" growled the man, "Tryin' t' pick me pockets, are yeh, yeh grubby wee urchin? Begone with yeh, lest my cane find yer backside!"

Stanley was so surprised and embarrassed that he muttered a barely audible 'sorry' and ran off down the street.

"Harr, yeh better run!" the man called after him, "Yeh can't pull anythin' off on ol' Pete, an' sure!"

Stanley raced around the crowded street, looking for any sign of Uncle Jack and the others, but to no avail. *Okay,* he said to himself after a minute or two, *don't panic. Uncle Jack can't be far off, and he's probably looking for you right now ... and if he's not, he* will *be when he gets back to the harbour.*

"The harbour!" he cried aloud, earning him funny looks from passers by. All he had to do was get to the harbour; then he could find the Ogopogo at pier three-forty-one and wait for his friends there. The only problem was, he didn't know in which direction the harbour lay. From where he was standing, he couldn't see the ocean, or even the palace. Plucking up his courage, he stepped out into the street and stopped a young couple, who looked friendly enough.

"Er, excuse me, but can you tell me how to get to the harbour from here?"

Neither the man, nor the woman answered. Instead, they were staring wide-eyed at something behind Stanley, something that was apparently very tall. Stanley turned around slowly and let out a surprised gasp. A Knight of the Silver Sword was standing there, its polished armour glinting in the cool light of the rising moons. It stared straight down at him, unmoving, unflinching, and for all outward appearances, unbreathing. Stanley gawked at the faceless knight, not noticing that the young couple had begun to slowly back away. Unconsciously, he imitated the action, but just as he had taken his first step backward, a huge armoured hand reached out and grabbed him by the shoulder.

"*You're coming with me,*" came a deep, rumbling voice from the depths of the knight's helmet.

Terrified, Stanley struggled mightily, and broke free of the knight's grip, tearing his good shirt in the process. Not wasting a second, he bolted, running as fast as he could down the street, dodging crowds of bewildered onlookers, and hearing the knight's armour clanking from somewhere behind him.

Hoping that the knight's heavy armour would prevent it from attaining any kind of pursuit velocity, Stanley raced around a corner and ran blindly into the middle of an intersection, where he was almost run over by a passing carriage.

"Watch where you're goin, boy!" shouted the driver, shaking a fist.

Breathing heavily, Stanley cast around for any sign of the knight. There was none, and his heart leapt as he gazed down the street. There in the distance, rising high above the city, silhouetted menacingly against the large, red moon, was the Imperial Palace. His heart leapt again, as he turned around and saw the lights of the harbour not far off; now it was just a matter of getting to the Ogopogo and waiting for Uncle Jack.

But then his heart sank. Three knights of the Silver Sword had just appeared a ways down the street, between him and the harbour. His heart sank again, as they began to march towards him. Looking down the streets to his right and left, Stanley was dismayed to see several more knights coming towards him. The crowds of people gave them a wide berth, allowing them to march freely and swiftly; indeed, they seemed to be closing with unearthly speed. Stanley ran off again, forced to flee in the opposite direction of the harbour. Deciding that heading towards the palace was a bad idea, he tore off down a narrow side street, hoping to take a roundabout route that would lead back to the harbour, while at the same time throwing the knights off his trail.

After about a quarter of an hour, breathing heavily and clutching at a stitch in his side, Stanley peered cautiously around a corner, and saw the harbour, closer now than ever. Unfortunately, a pair of knights had also just rounded a corner a few streets over, and were heading his way. Stanley crept carefully backwards, and ducked into a wide, dark alleyway between two warehouses. Still breathing heavily, he waited for the two knights to pass by, and was just about to go make sure all was clear, when he heard a noise behind him. He turned around, and felt a block of ice drop into his stomach. Two more knights were stepping out of the shadows, into a splash of moonlight shining down from the small, blue moon. Had they been there all along, waiting for him?

He tried to make a fresh break for it, but reconsidered as the first pair of knights stepped silently into the alley, blocking out the light of the street lamps. Stanley looked about wildly for an escape route, but there was none. Exhausted and frustrated, he glared up at the advancing knights.

"*What do you want?*" he yelled angrily.

But the knights did not answer. Instead, they stopped moving and raised their heads slightly, so that they seemed to be looking at the back of the alley. Stanley turned around and saw that the knights behind him were acting strangely; they seemed to be struggling, and were holding their arms close at their sides. As he looked closer, Stanley saw that the knights were being wrapped up in what looked like long, black lengths of rope. He marveled at this strange development, then jumped with surprise as the two massive knights were yanked off their feet and into a dark corner of the alley. There was a loud, metallic *crunch*, like the sound of a pop can being crushed, and then the two knights came flying out of the shadows and into the moonlight, horribly mangled.

Stanley cried out upon seeing the knights, who looked as though they'd been through a trash compactor. He peered fearfully into the dark corner, then down at the lifeless knights. There was something *else* in this alley, something that could easily crush a seven-foot-tall armoured knight. Stanley could feel it lurking in the shadows, but it wasn't just in the corner—it was all around him.

The knights behind him had drawn their massive broadswords, and were looking around with what could only be apprehension. With an unearthly *whooshing* sound, something long and black rose up out of the shadows at the end of the alley, and shot straight at one of the knights. The thing narrowly missed Stanley, who toppled over to one side and collapsed against the brick wall. Several more of the strange black rope-things shot out of the darkness, from different directions, and wrapped themselves around the knight's armoured torso. The hapless knight didn't even have time to swing his sword, before his armour collapsed under the thing's grip, his head flopping forward, his arms and legs dangling grotesquely, like those of some giant rag-doll. The dark thing lifted the knight into the air and threw him to the ground with an earth-shaking smash.

Horror-stricken, Stanley stumbled over the remains and out into the street. The last knight tried to flee as well, but as he left the alley, hot on Stanley's heels, something like a huge, clawed hand reached out of the darkness and dragged him back again. A terrible crunch told Stanley that the knight had met a fate similar to that of his comrades.

Stanley reeled drunkenly across the street. He was feeling very dizzy. The world was spinning, the street was rolling like waves on the ocean. He could still feel the thing close by. The stars above were spinning, too, leaving trails of light behind them. His vision blurred more and more until he had to close his eyes, then the dizziness became even worse, and he vomited, before falling to the pavement, unconscious. He did not dream.

CHAPTER SIXTEEN: PRISON BREAK

"Is he alive?"

"Yeah, he's breathing, and he's got a pulse."

"But why won't he wake up?"

"He's awfully pale."

Voices penetrated the darkness. They sounded distant and muffled, as though coming from very far off.

"I wonder what happened to him. There are no signs of injury."

"Looks like he was ill. Maybe that's all, just a flu."

"But he's so cold."

"Lord deliver me, look at this!"

"What? ... oh ... my ..."

"They ... they've been ..."

"What could have done this?"

"Oh man, oh man, oh man ..."

"Keep it together, boys. We've all seen stuff like this before."

"Not like *this*, we haven't! Look at them!"

"Whatever it was that got 'em, it must be about as big as a house. We'll find it."

"Are you kidding? You think we can handle something that can take out four knights?"

"Uh-oh. Speak of the devil. What are *these* guys doing here?"

"*We are taking over this crime scene.*"

"Begging your pardon, sir knight, but we were here first."

"*Irrelevant. This action directly concerns the Knights of the Silver Sword. It is our duty, and ours alone, to investigate the situation.*"

"Hey, what are you doing with him? We need to ask him some questions, he might know something."

"*This boy is* already *wanted for questioning. We have orders from the Regent, himself. We will inform you if there is anything we feel you need to know.*"

Shouts of outrage and indignation faded into silence. All was darkness for a long time, until …

✳   ✳   ✳   ✳

… A faint light … the sound of dripping water …

Stanley opened his eyes. He was in a strange, dark room with no windows, lying on a rough wooden cot. A lantern hanging from the ceiling fought valiantly to illuminate the room, casting its dim, flickering light on stone walls, which were slick with condensation, and covered here and there with patches of scruffy-looking moss. The air was stale, and had a damp, musty smell. Stanley sat up and dangled his legs off the edge of the cot, listening to the sound of water dripping annoyingly from somewhere not far off. He jumped suddenly, as something darted out from under the bed: a big, wicked-looking rat, which turned and regarded him insolently, before scurrying through a slot at the bottom of the room's only door. The door was made of some kind of metal, and looked very solid.

"Where am I?" Stanley wondered aloud.

"You're in a prison cell," said a voice.

Stanley looked up in surprise; he hadn't considered that there might be someone in here with him. "Who's there?" he asked a tad nervously.

"That would be me," answered the voice. It was a dark voice, low and harsh, and hoarse, as if its owner hadn't spoken in a long time. Stanley peered across the room, looking for the speaker. At first, he couldn't see anyone, but then he caught sight of a pair of yellow eyes glinting in the shadows of the room's darkest corner. Perhaps it was a trick of the light, but the shadows in that corner seemed suddenly to recede, revealing the unmistakable shape of someone huddled there. The someone sat there, staring impassively at Stanley.

"Er," said Stanley uncomfortably, "this is a prison?"

"That's what I said."

"Are … are we still in Ethelia?"

"Yes."

"… Do you know why I'm here?"

"No. You must have broken the law."

"What? No!" said Stanley, slightly shocked at the idea, "I didn't break any law!"

The someone in the corner shrugged. "Don't bother trying to convince *me*."

"But they can't put kids in jail!"

"You'd be surprised what *they* can do."

Stanley sat there for a moment, staring at a puddle on the floor. He was in jail. Someone had found him and taken him to this dark, dank cell … but why? What had he done? He looked up again to see the yellow eyes still watching him. "Who are you, anyway?"

A pause. "They call me *Grey*."

"Grey? Like the colour?"

"Something like that."

"Is that your actual name?"

"It's what they call me."

"But is it your *name*?"

Grey didn't answer.

"Uh," said Stanley, after the silence had become uncomfortable, "So, are you a criminal?"

"I'm in prison, aren't I?" said Grey, not quite answering the question.

"How long have you been here?"

"A very long time."

"What did you do?"

"What?"

"Uh, what did you do to get thrown in jail?"

Grey suddenly stood up and stalked towards Stanley. He knelt down, grabbed him by the shirt, and pulled him forward, so that their faces were inches apart. "You ask too many questions," he hissed.

"S-sorry," said Stanley, more than a little alarmed. Grey shoved Stanley back and stood up, folding his arms and glaring at the cell door.

Seeing Grey clearly for the first time, Stanley couldn't help but stare. Grey was very tall, almost as tall as Benjamin Stone. He was dressed in a tattered, mouldy shirt and trousers, which looked about a hundred years old. His body had a lean and muscular look to it, but was covered from head to foot in bandages that may once have been white. He looked like a mummy, and the only parts of his face not covered in bandages were his eyes. These were devoid of pupil or iris, and seemed to glow with their own yellow light.

Stanley noticed that Grey's face seemed rather flat; there was no lump in the middle of it to betray the presence of a nose, and it was more than possible that there were no ears sticking out of the sides of his head. Had Grey's nose and ears been cut off sometime in the past, as part of some unspeakable act of torture?

"What are *you* looking at?" Grey said, noticing Stanley staring up at him.

"Nothing," Stanley said quickly.

"You're wondering what's under these bandages, aren't you?"

"Um …"

"You want a peek at the freak, is that it?"

"What? N-no, of course not! … Er, I *was* wondering about the bandages, though."

"It's none of your business."

"No, I guess it isn't," Stanley said unhappily, as he stared down at the floor. He noticed the puddle again, and it made him think of the open sea, which, in turn, made him think of Uncle Jack, Alabaster, Nell, Benjamin, and Pericles. He wondered if he would ever see them again. Then he thought of his Mom and Dad back in East Stodgerton, and wondered if he would ever see *them* again. Was he doomed to spend the rest of his days in this damp, mouldy old prison, with a jerk named Grey for a cellmate? He suddenly felt very lonely, lonelier than he had ever felt in his life. A huge sob had been fighting its way up from his stomach, and it suddenly burst forth in a flood of tears and heartache. He put his hands over his face and wept loudly, while Grey watched with a mildly surprised look in his yellow eyes.

"Hmph," said Grey after a couple minutes, "What, did I hurt your feelings?"

Stanley sniffed loudly. "No," he said sulkily.

"Then what's the matter?" said Grey.

Stanley sniffed again, then said, "I miss my Mom and Dad, okay? I'm never going to see them again, now, and they'll never know what happened to me." He tried to say more, but a fresh bout of sobbing negated his ability to speak. It was horribly embarrassing to be crying in front of Grey, and he tried mightily to stop. He finally got himself under control, and looked up, expecting to see Grey laughing at him. To his surprise, though, Grey was keeping very quiet, looking at him in an odd way.

"It's been a long time since I've seen anyone cry," he said softly.

"Yeah, I bet you *never* cry," said Stanley. "You never get lonely, or miss your Mom, or *anything*, right?"

"I don't remember my mother," said Grey.

They stared at eachother for a time, then Grey reached up and started to unwrap the bandages from his face. When he was done, Stanley could only stare. Grey's face was completely devoid of scars or deformities, but it was a face unlike anything he had ever seen. Grey's skin was black—not the natural deep brown of human skin—*really* black, like a shadow in a forest at midnight. His hairless head, though shaped like a human's, bore no trace of a nose, ears, or even a mouth.

"What are you?" said Stanley, in an awed voice.

"I am what I am," Grey answered cryptically. "Nothing more, nothing less."

Stanley looked down at Grey's hands, and noticed for the first time that the fingers were not wrapped in bandages. They were long, black, and claw-like, their tips pointed and hooked.

"Are you … human?" Stanley asked timidly.

"Our appearance isn't what makes us human," Grey said, as if he had recited it many times before.

"No, I know, I just … I didn't mean …" Feeling that it was very important not to offend Grey, Stanley wisely decided not to put his foot any further into his mouth. "Um, so why do you wear the bandages?" he asked, trying to ask the most harmless question possible.

"The guards think they make me easier to see."

"Really? Do they work?"

"No."

Stanley gave a small laugh at this, but stopped abruptly. Grey's impassive stare was rather unnerving. He coughed uncomfortably, and said, "Er, I'm Stanley, by the way." He tentatively offered his hand for Grey to shake, but Grey made no move to accept the friendly gesture. Stanley pulled his hand back after a moment, half expecting Grey to bite it off. He stared back down at the floor, cupping his chin in his hands, and let out a heavy sigh. He was starting to wish he had never decided to come along on this adventure. He wondered where Uncle Jack and the others were, and if they were even looking for him. For all he knew, they could be half way across the ocean by now. When he looked up again, he saw that Grey was still silently staring at him.

"What?" said Stanley, "Why are you staring at me?"

"I can see you more clearly than I see other people."

Stanley's expression was quizzical. "What do you mean?"

"I mean, I see you more clearly than I see other people."

"Yeah, but what does *that* mean? Do people look blurry to you? Do you need glasses?"

"I don't know."

Just then, there came the sound of footsteps from the hall outside. Suddenly relieved to hear signs of other human life, Stanley jumped up and pounded on the door.

"*Hey!*" he shouted, as he hit the door with the palm of his hand, "*Hello out there! Hey!*"

The footsteps stopped outside the cell, and a small slot window near the top of the door slid open. A pair of eyes peered through into the cell.

"What's all this noise, then?" said a man's voice, "Keep it down in there."

"Wait!" said Stanley, as the slot began to close.

"Hold on," said a second voice from the other side of the door, "that sounds like a kid."

A second pair of eyes appeared at the slot, and widened when they caught sight of Stanley. "Hey, I know you," said the second voice, "You came into the harbour yesterday, around noon, in that little ship, with your Grandpa, or something. Sylvester, right?"

"Stanley," said Stanley, relief flooding though him. "You must be that marine who talked to my uncle."

"That's right. Er, what are you doing down here in the dungeons?"

"I don't know!" said Stanley, "I just woke up in here, I don't know how I got here." He thought back to the events leading up to his incarceration. "I got lost after leaving this fancy restaurant … *The Golden Goblet*, I think it was called. Then, I got chased by a whole bunch of Knights of the Silver Sword."

"And they captured you? Brought you here?"

"No! They were … they were …" The strange occurrence in the dark alley came flooding back to him. "They were … killed by some kind of … monster! There's a monster loose in the city! You've got to do something!"

"A monster?" the first voice said skeptically, "You're telling us that there's a *monster* running around the city?"

"Yes! It killed four knights before they knew what was happening!"

"And yet, somehow, you escaped? Why didn't the 'monster' get you, too?"

"I just … got away quickly, I guess," Stanley said, but he knew it wasn't true. The thing in the alley had taken out two of the knights in the space of a few seconds; it was definitely fast enough to catch a small boy who happened to be standing still at the time. Why had the creature not gone after him?

"It was probably too busy with the knights to care about a kid," the second marine said.

"What?" said the first marine incredulously, "Rick, you don't actually *believe* this clap-trap?"

"I overheard Commander Wardman talking about finding four knights in an alley off Harbour Street. He said they'd been crushed and mangled ..."

"What? I never heard about that!"

"They're supposed to be keeping it quiet," said Rick. "Chamberlain is in a state about it, and the knights are none too pleased that the marines tried to get involved."

"But seriously," said the first marine, "anything that can kill a Knight of the Silver Sword, let alone four of them, must be, I dunno, the most dangerous thing in the world! Chamberlain would want it dealt with, not covered up." He looked at Stanley. "What did this *monster* of yours look like, anyway?"

"Uh, well," said Stanley, trying to think, "I didn't really get a good look at it ..."

"You must have had *some* impression of its size? Shape?"

"Er, uh, it had long, thin arms, with claws."

"That's it? Well that certainly narrows it down, thank you."

Stanley was starting to develop a real dislike for the first marine. Why wouldn't he believe his story? "You'd believe me, if you'd been there," he said.

"Yeah, I'm sure."

"Take it easy, Bill," said Rick, "Look, it seems to me that Stanley, here, was just in the wrong place at the wrong time." He looked at Stanley. "I don't know why those knights were after you in the first place, but I'm going to talk to Chamberlain about it, and see if I can get you out."

Stanley's heart leapt. "Really? You can get me out of here?"

"I can give it a shot, but don't get your hopes up too high—Chamberlain's word is final, after all."

Stanley couldn't believe his luck. Minutes ago, he'd been feeling sorry for himself, ready to accept a life behind bars, and now he was close to being free again.

"Uh, hold on a second, Rick," said Bill.

"What?" said Rick, "You don't want to talk to Chamberlain? Come on, you can't put a kid in a dungeon! They probably want him for questioning, there's just been a mistake."

"I don't know about that," said Bill, now sounding worried, "Do you know which cell this is?"

"Yes, it's nine-twenty ... *three* ..." Rick's voice trailed off unpleasantly.

"Nine-twenty-three," echoed Bill. "That's Grey's cell."

"Why on *earth* would they put a kid in with Grey?" said Rick, sounding both worried and disgusted.

"Why would they put *anyone* in with Grey?" said Bill.

Rick's eyes appeared at the window again, and widened to the size of saucers when he saw Grey standing behind Stanley like a dark, bandaged statue. "Okay, Stanley," he said stiffly, "I'm letting you out." There was a loud *clink-a-link-a-link* as Rick fumbled with his key ring.

"Wait!" said Bill, "Maybe we should leave them both in there."

"What?" said Rick, "Are you nuts? You're saying we should leave the kid in there with *him?*"

"All I'm saying," Bill began carefully, "is that this is a maximum security cell, and no one gets put in there without good reason."

"Yeah, but ... wait a second, you don't think—"

"It *might* be possible ... that a monster ... could disguise itself as a kid."

"*What?*" said Stanley, outraged by the very idea, "No! I'm not a monster! I'm a kid, *really!* My name is Stanley Brambles, and I live at number twenty-five, Bubbletree Lane, in East Stodgerton! Find my Uncle Jack, he'll tell you that I'm a regular kid!"

There was a pause, then Rick said, "Come on, Bill, I met this kid, *and* his uncle yesterday. They're good people."

"This boy is no monster." It was Grey who had spoken, and Rick and Bill stared in surprise.

"Wh-wh-what?" said Rick.

"This boy is no monster," Grey repeated.

"Sh-shut up!" said Bill, his voice rising to a girlish pitch, "Why should we believe anything *you* say?"

Grey's yellow eyes glared fiercely out of his black face, but his tone remained even. "You don't have to believe me, but consider this: a dungeon is no place for a child. He should be outside in the sun, learning about the world, not locked up in a dank cell."

Stanley slightly resented Grey's use of the word *child,* but he was really too surprised to care. Grey had just said something rather profound, and had, seemingly, shown concern for him. Stanley turned round and gazed up into Grey's fierce eyes, but they were devoid of warmth or compassion. Had he really meant what he'd just said? Regardless, the words seemed to have their desired effect.

With a sharp *click*, the heavy metal door swung slowly open. Rick craned his neck around the door, a pistol in his hand and a fearful look on his face.

"Right. Stanley, come on out. Grey, if you try anything, I'll be forced to shoot you." Grey didn't answer, but he appeared to have accepted Rick's terms. Stanley allowed Rick to lead him out into the hall, but glanced back briefly at Grey. What was going to happen to him?

"What did Grey get put in jail for?" Stanley asked as Rick started to close the cell door.

"Got me," said Rick, "He's been in here as long as anyone can remember. Everyone on prison duty knows he's dangerous, though. He can—" He trailed off and cocked his head to one side, listening. An ominous clanking sound could be heard from somewhere not far off, and it was growing steadily louder. Stanley had a pretty good idea of what could be making the sound, and his suspicions were confirmed, when a Knight of the Silver Sword rounded a corner halfway down the hall, and stopped, as if trying to make sense of what he was seeing.

"Uh-oh," Rick muttered. It was looking as if Stanley wasn't going to escape, after all. He tried to think of a way out of this situation, but his mind had gone blank. He looked despairingly up at Bill, who now had a very strange look on his face. His eyes were wide, and his round, slightly pudgy face was bathed in sweat. He suddenly started to stammer,

"B-b-ba-m-ma-muh-j-j-juh-juh-ja-ja-ja-jail-JAIL BREAK!"

At Bill's loud cry, the knight sprang into action and stalked clankingly towards them.

"Bill!" shouted Rick, "What are you *doing?*"

"Sorry, Rick," said Bill breathlessly, "but I can't let you do this. I won't go to jail just because you have a hunch about this kid." Stanley noticed that Bill had drawn his own pistol, and was pointing it at Rick.

"No one's going to jail," said Rick, raising his hands in a gesture of peace, "C'mon, Bill, put the gun down."

"N-no!" said Bill, now grasping his weapon with both hands, "Look, Rick, I won't turn you in, if you'll just cooperate with me—I'll tell Chamberlain that this wasn't your fault. I'll tell him the kid tricked you, and got hold of the keys. I'll tell him ... I'll tell him—" Bill's ranting was suddenly interrupted, as something bounded out of the prison cell and knocked him viciously into the stone wall of the corridor. A shot rang out as Bill accidentally pulled the trigger, and the bullet whizzed by Rick's head, bouncing harmlessly off the wall.

It had been Grey, of course, who had sent Bill flying, and who was now dragging the struggling marine to his feet. "Fool!" he growled, his face inches from

Bill's. Bill's face wore an expression of sheer terror, as Grey grabbed him by the throat and lifted him off the ground.

"Fool," Grey repeated, as Bill choked and struggled.

"Put him down, Grey," said Rick, his pistol pointed at Grey's head. This did not have the desired effect, however, as Grey somehow closed the distance between himself and Rick, and knocked the gun out of his hand, all in the space of a heartbeat.

Stanley was at a complete loss. He stared around him at Rick, who had backed away against the cell door, at the knight, who had stopped beside Rick, and was apparently content to watch the scene play out, at Grey, whose glaring yellow eyes showed fury in his otherwise blank face, and at Bill, who was grasping at Grey's arm, and whose struggles were growing more and more feeble. Stanley knew that something had to be done. Deep down, he didn't think Grey was a killer, (he would later wonder why on earth he'd been so certain of this), but he might *become* one, if someone didn't step in.

"*Grey!*" he shouted, and it sounded loud and strange in the dungeon corridor, "*No!*"

For a moment, it seemed as if Grey was ignoring him, but then he turned his midnight-black head, and stared at Stanley with those burning yellow eyes.

"Don't do it," said Stanley. It was barely a whisper, but it seemed Grey had heard. He gave Stanley a very strange look—was it sadness? Pain? Or just reluctant obedience?—and released Bill, who slid down the wall and lay gasping and coughing in a heap on the floor. There was a long silence, broken only by Bill's choking coughs, and then the knight, who was apparently tired of being an audience member, drew his massive broadsword and stepped forward, pointing the blade at Grey.

Grey's eyes narrowed, and, where none had been visible until now, a mouth opened up, as if it had been there all along. It was a vicious mouth, filled with sharp teeth and a long, serpentine tongue. Grey snarled ferociously and leapt upon the knight. There was a spectacular row, but it was soon brought to an end, as several more knights came marching down the corridor. Grey jumped off his foe and backed away from the approaching knights. He glared defiantly at them, and then, to Stanley's surprise, appeared to sink right into the stone wall and disappear. The shadows in the area seemed to flicker for a moment, and then, nothing. Grey had gone.

"He's disappeared!" spluttered Bill, who was struggling to get up, "Now we'll *never* find him! I thought he couldn't do that when he was wearing those bandages!"

Stanley stared at the spot where Grey had been. How had he just disappeared like that? It didn't really matter; he was gone now, probably on his way outside, on his way to freedom and whatever was waiting for him beyond these slick, damp walls. Stanley hoped that Grey would be careful outside, and not give anyone a reason to imprison him again. He was happy for the strange fellow, but also somewhat disappointed that Grey hadn't taken him along.

His thoughts were interrupted, as a heavy, armoured hand fell on his shoulder, and grasped tightly.

"You're coming with us," said the knight's deep, menacing voice.

Stanley had no choice but to obey.

CHAPTER SEVENTEEN:
THE NEW KING

The knights propelled Stanley through the dark dungeons of the Imperial Palace, swords drawn and ready, as if they were escorting the most dangerous criminal in the land. As they passed cells on either side of the corridor, prisoners inside would come to the doors (barred doors, unlike the door of cell nine-twenty-three) to see what was going on. Many of them called out to the knights, saying things that are far too rude to repeat here. More than once, Stanley saw filthy, greasy faces leering at him from between the bars of certain cells. At one point, someone reached out through the bars and tried to grab his shirt, but the knight walking directly behind him caught hold of the prisoner's arm and wrenched it sideways. The man screamed as a loud *crack* proclaimed that his arm had been broken. Stanley quickened his pace and pulled his arms tightly to his sides. He needn't have bothered; the rest of the prisoners kept their hands and arms safely in their cells.

*　　　*　　　*　　　*

After what seemed an age to Stanley, he and the squad of knights reached a staircase, which wound up out of the dungeons. These they climbed, up and up, higher and higher, until it felt to Stanley that his legs would surely fall off if he went on much longer. Finally, when he was starting to feel as if he couldn't go another step, he saw the knight in front of him stop before a large wooden door. The knight opened the door, and beckoned for Stanley to follow, which he did, due mostly to the broadsword pointed at his back. Beyond the door was a long hallway, with many more doors along its length, all large and wooden, all identical, right down to the last metal stud.

This new hallway couldn't possibly be part of the dungeons; the floors were shiny, probably made of marble, and the smooth, gleaming walls were decorated with beautiful tapestries and paintings. The air seemed wonderfully fresh and fragrant after the damp mustiness of the dungeons. Stanley looked about for an avenue of escape, but there was none. Even if he *did* make a successful break for it, he had no idea where he would go, and he assumed that the knights knew the palace a good deal better than he did.

His assumption was confirmed, as the knight ahead of him stopped at one of the many doors, pulled it open, and led the way through. Where were they taking him? Why were they leading him out of the dungeons? Could they be setting him free? *No*, Stanley thought, *that would be a little too much to hope for*. More likely they were taking him to his place of execution. He shuddered briefly at the idea, but temporarily forgot his anxiety, as he looked up at his surroundings.

The hall through which he was now being led was so breathtakingly beautiful, that he stopped walking for a moment to take it all in. Uncle Jack's entire house could have fit into this place, which made even that mansion's grand entrance hall look like the inside of a cardboard box. The walls and floors were made of a shiny blue-white stone, which looked like marble. Huge pillars rose up in long lines on either side of an elegant red carpet which ran the length of the hall, and was about as wide as a football field. Wedge-shaped windows in the vaulted ceiling, high above, let in generous amounts of sunlight, which shone down on scores of pearl-white statues standing at the foot of each pillar. Balconies could be seen, high up on either side of the hall, leading to and from the palace's upper floors. Stanley would have loved to stay here for a bit and explore every inch of this magnificent hall, but the knight behind him tapped him on the shoulder, and shoved him rather roughly to get him moving again. He trotted quickly forward to catch up with the knight ahead of him, who was leading the way towards a pair of monstrous double doors.

Stepping through the doors, Stanley found himself in a circular room which, while considerably smaller than the hall he had just passed through, was still vast in its own right. The room's walls and floor were made of the same blue-white stone as the great hall, and the same wedge-shaped windows were built into the domed ceiling, which also had a large, round window right at its apex. Tall windows were placed between the pillars, which were spaced at wide intervals around the room. The red carpet from the great hall continued into this room, where it ran up a short flight of wide steps, to a raised platform in the centre, upon which stood a magnificent golden throne.

Someone was seated on the throne.

It wasn't Chamberlain.

Sitting there in a very relaxed, almost lazy fashion, was a person wearing a hooded cloak the colour of damp ashes. The person's face was concealed behind a blank, white mask with two eye holes and vertical slits for a mouth. Stanley was shunted forward by one of the knights, stopping at the foot of the steps, where he stared up at the throne in shock.

"Well, well, well," said the masked man in his low, rumbling voice, "we meet again." He shifted in his seat, sitting up straight and placing the tips of his gloved fingers together. He seemed to be in much better spirits today; indeed, when he spoke, his words carried a hint of suppressed glee. Stanley closed his eyes and shook his head, as if this were all just an illusion.

"Hm hm hm," chuckled the masked man, "Surprised to see me, are you?"

"Er, well, yes?" said Stanley, not knowing what else to say.

"Yes, of course you are," said the masked man, regarding Stanley over the tips of his fingers. He seemed to be enjoying this. "You were expecting someone *else* to be seated on the throne? Chamberlain, perhaps?"

Stanley nodded silently. Yes, this was certainly the last person he would have expected to meet in the throne room of the Imperial Palace.

The masked man laughed shrilly; it sounded very strange, especially compared to his low, rumbling speaking voice. "Yes, of course you did," he said with obvious amusement. "Everyone does." The masked man sighed contentedly and eased himself back into the throne's soft, red padding. He glanced over at the closest knight. "Leave us," he commanded, and the words carried a distinct rumble, as from distant thunder.

The knights obeyed immediately, turning around and marching out of the throne room, closing the doors behind them.

"Well," said the masked man, once the doors had boomed shut, "well well well well well."

Stanley wanted to say *well what?* but kept his mouth shut. He stared up into that blank, white mask, into those dark eye holes. Questions were spinning through his head, but he wondered how prudent it would be to start demanding answers from a powerful and dangerous sorcerer.

"Do you know why you are here?" the masked man inquired, clutching the throne's arm rests.

"No," said Stanley.

"You have absolutely no idea?"

"Uh, you're not going to kill me, are you?"

"HA!" laughed the masked man, making Stanley jump with surprise, "Kill you? Oh, I don't think so."

"You didn't seem to think it was funny yesterday," said Stanley, before he could stop himself. The masked man went quiet, putting the tips of his fingers together again.

"No, indeed," he said, all traces of amusement gone from his voice. "If everything had proceeded as I had foreseen, you would now be dead. The fact that you still live, has thrown my plans into disarray, if you must know. This unforeseen outcome—your continued survival—has given rise to a host of other unforeseen outcomes. You are an enigma, Stanley, and if I am to understand any of this, I must first understand *you*."

None of this made any sense to Stanley, who couldn't see how he could possibly be part of *anyone's* 'plans'. "So ... that's why Chamberlain told the knights to put me in jail?"

"*I* told the knights to put you in jail. Chamberlain hasn't been here for well over a week. He should be back soon, though." As if it had all been planned in advance, the throne room doors burst open, and in marched Ezekiel Chamberlain, flanked by a pair of Knights of the Silver Sword.

"Ahh, speak of the devil," rumbled the masked man, as the doors closed again.

To Stanley's surprise, Chamberlain, who had seemed proud and powerful back in Port Silverburg, marched to the foot of the stairs without even looking at him, and knelt down, head bowed.

"My lord," he said gruffly.

"Rise," the masked man rumbled. Chamberlain obeyed, standing up quickly.

"Did you succeed in your errand?" asked the masked man.

"It was a false alarm, my lord," said Chamberlain briskly. "There is no plot to overthrow the Empire."

The masked man leaned forward, and Stanley could tell he was staring very hard at Chamberlain. "But that is not why you went to Port Silverburg, is it, Ezekiel?"

"My lord?" Chamberlain's expression was one of polite confusion, but Stanley could see sweat on his face.

"You didn't go to Port Silverburg to uncover a plot. You went there to capture the notorious pirate, Black Jack Lee." The masked man's voice had grown soft and dangerous. Chamberlain tugged at his collar.

"My lord, I didn't—"

"DO NOT LIE TO ME!" roared the masked man, his shouted words carrying a distinct roll of thunder as he leaped up from the throne, pointing at Chamberlain, who shrank back involuntarily. Suddenly, just as it had done yesterday aboard the Ogopogo, the masked man's shadow seemed to grow longer, and began to creep down the steps and across the floor towards Chamberlain. The shadow reached the Regent's boots, then started to ooze up his legs. Stanley stared in wonderment as Chamberlain's uniform went dark. The shadow stopped just beneath his stubbly chin, and he made a gagging noise, as if he were choking.

"You know I hate being lied to," said the masked man, slowly descending the steps, as Chamberlain choked and struggled, and Stanley looked on in horror. "I can almost always tell, you know. And *this* time, I'm absolutely sure. Do you know how I know, Ezekiel?"

Chamberlain, who was in no position to answer, choked louder, and tried to shake his head.

"You received a telegram," said the masked man, "telling you that Black Jack Lee had arrived in Port Silverburg."

Chamberlain's eyes widened.

"I sent the telegram myself," rumbled the masked man. He turned, made his way back up the steps, seated himself once more on the throne, and snapped his fingers. His shadow retreated immediately, and Chamberlain fell to the floor, gasping and coughing horribly.

"Y-*you*? But why?" Chamberlain said, once he had regained his ability to speak.

"I have my reasons," said the masked man, waving a gloved hand impatiently. "It was a test, for one."

"A *test*?" said Chamberlain, still coughing every few seconds.

"Yes, a test," said the masked man. "A test of your ability to follow orders. A test which, I am less than pleased to say, you failed miserably."

By now, Chamberlain had regained his feet, and was standing at attention, arms held close at his sides. He was trying to put on a proud and dignified air, but his face was reddening furiously.

"If you will recall, Ezekiel," the masked man went on, "I gave you a direct order to cease your inane quest for vengeance. You were to leave your old foes well enough alone, and strive for the higher goal. Do you not remember agreeing to those terms?"

Chamberlain did not answer at first; he was staring down at the floor, his lips pursed, his hands clenched and shaking at his sides.

"I'm sorry, I didn't hear you," said the masked man, leaning forward and raising a gloved hand to his head, as if cupping his ear in an effort to improve hearing.

"I remember, my lord," said Chamberlain, barely moving his lips.

"Of course you remember," said the masked man, "which means, you consciously and intentionally disobeyed me. So I ask myself, why, Ezekiel, *why?*"

Chamberlain cleared his throat and took a deep breath. He cleared his throat again as the masked man stared down at him, gloved hands cupping his chin, like a child listening to a grandparent's stories.

"I thought," began Chamberlain, "that if I could just bring Lee in, under my own strength, that your lordship might—"

"Liar," rumbled the masked man, before Chamberlain could finish his explanation. Once again his shadow lengthened, darting down the steps this time, creeping swiftly up towards Chamberlain's throat.

"M-my lord, please!" cried the Regent, before gagging as the shadow worked its cruel choking magic.

"We both know that you did not have my best interests at heart, when you set out to find Lee," said the masked man, standing up and waving a finger at Chamberlain, as if he were scolding a child. "You thought you would sweep down upon Port Silverburg, apprehend Lee with your bare hands, and put an end to this tiresome vendetta that you've been keeping alive these forty years."

Chamberlain choked and struggled.

"And you would tell me that you did it for *my* benefit, perhaps even going so far as to say that Lee posed a threat to me?" The masked man laughed mirthlessly. "We both know that the only thing on your mind, was the expression Lee would have on his face, as you plunged your sword into his heart." He chuckled again, then turned away. As he did so, his shadow released the Regent once more, and zipped back up the stairs. The masked man waited for Chamberlain to stop coughing, then turned back around to face him. "I need not describe what would have happened to you, had you succeeded in killing Lee," he said in a soft and very dangerous tone. "I will leave that to your imagination, just in case you ever feel compelled to embark on another lovely little 'crusade'."

Chamberlain gulped audibly.

"You're a slow learner, Ezekiel," the masked man sighed, flopping back onto the throne. "But I'm not worried. I'm sure you'll learn your place, eventually ... either that or I'll end up obliterating you. Frankly, I'm interested to see which happens first."

Chamberlain grimaced. "If that is *all*, my lord—" he said curtly.

"It is *not* all," said the masked man, leaning forward. "I have things to tell you."

"Indeed?" said Chamberlain, "I am pleased that your lordship has finally chosen to confide in me."

"Believe me," said the masked man, "I've been putting it off for as long as possible." He put his fingers together and stared down at Chamberlain. "As I told you when we first met, I have plans, Ezekiel, *big* plans." Chamberlain remained silent, his hands clasped regally behind his back. "And I hope," continued the masked man, "that I can count on you to help me carry out those plans."

Chamberlain's chest swelled. "My lord, I swear to you that I will never again allow my personal feelings to interfere with your orders. You have my full support."

"Good," said the masked man, not sounding entirely convinced, but satisfied for the moment. "Headstrong though you may be, your work in the political sector has been good. You have done an admirable job of representing me in parliament. Now, though, I must ... *you* must undertake an important mission." There was an overly dramatic pause, and then the masked man said, "I seek the *Black Jack Bonanza*."

Chamberlain and Stanley gasped in unison. The Black Jack Bonanza! The masked man was talking about Uncle Jack's treasure!

"Oh yes," said the masked man, a hint of amusement in his voice, "I know all about that fabled hoard. I also know that *you* have been seeking it for a long, long time." Chamberlain looked stunned. "You've been keeping it a secret, I know. You never thought to tell *me* about it though, did you?"

"Er, well, no, my lord, I ... didn't think you would be concerned with it. After all, I ceased my search when you came to power, and, well, if you didn't want me to search for Lee, I thought you *surely* wouldn't want me to search for Lee's gold."

There was a long silence as the masked man regarded Chamberlain over the tips of his gloved fingers, and Stanley expected that horrid shadow to come creeping down the steps once more. This, however, did not happen. Instead, the masked man sat up straight and said, in a reasonable tone,

"Yes, I understand. With the wealth of Rhedland at my fingertips, why would I be wasting time on a treasure hunt. You," he said, indicating Chamberlain, "seek it for the purpose of vengeance, and personal financial gain."

Chamberlain cleared his throat nervously.

"Whereas *I* have, shall we say, more *high-minded* reasons for seeking it. Oh yes," he said, noting Chamberlain's raised eyebrow, "like you, I have been seeking that treasure hoard for many years, but as you can see, I've had no more success than you."

This sounded like good news to Stanley; it seemed as though the masked man was the likeliest candidate to find the treasure, and if *he* couldn't find it, it must have been well-hidden, indeed.

"I've spent a great deal of time scouring the world for the Black Jack Bonanza," said the masked man, "and I have nothing to show for it, but ten dead pirates and a theory."

"A theory, my lord?" said Chamberlain, barely containing the eagerness in his voice.

"Yes, a theory," the masked man said grimly. "I have deduced that ancient and powerful magic protects the treasure, magic which renders it impossible to find ... *unless the seeker knows where it is.*"

"I didn't know such magic existed," said Chamberlain.

"*Of course you didn't,*" snapped the masked man. "But now you do, and, unless you are more thick-skulled than I think you are, you will even now be piecing together the next logical inference."

Chamberlain frowned darkly. "Lee," he breathed. "Lee knows where the treasure is buried. None of his old cronies know, but *he* does, he *must!*" He flushed furiously. "If you had allowed me to hunt him down with the full strength of the Imperial Navy, we would be sitting upon the treasure at this very moment!"

"If I had allowed you to hunt him down with the full strength of the Imperial Navy," said the masked man, "you would have killed him, and we would *never* find the treasure."

"I will find him!" spluttered Chamberlain, "I will find him, and I will bring him to you, unharmed, and he will lead us to the treasure!"

"Tut tut, Ezekiel," the masked man said patronizingly, "No need to get worked up. I've taken matters into my own hands, and ensured that Jack Lee will come to *us*. By the way, have you met his nephew, Stanley?"

Stanley jumped at the sound of his name. Chamberlain looked sharply at him, apparently seeing him for the first time.

"Wh, *what?*" said the Regent, blinking several times with his good eye.

"This is Jack Lee's nephew," said the masked man. "Or, *great*-nephew, I suppose, isn't that right, Stanley?"

Stanley looked up at the masked man, then at Chamberlain's disbelieving face. Thinking quickly, he answered, "No, I'm not his great-nephew, I don't even know who you're talking about. My great-uncle is John Silver, and he—"

"Stanley, please," said the masked man, in a good-humoured tone which carried no hint of good humour, "You mustn't lie. Lying is wrong. You must always tell the truth." He stared piercingly down at Stanley, who had to look away from those dark, blank eye holes. "I'll ask you again, Stanley … you are Black Jack Lee's great nephew, are you not?"

Stanley stared at the red carpet for a moment, remembering what had happened when Chamberlain had lied to the masked man. Finally deciding that it would be prudent to tell the truth, he nodded, and muttered, "Yeah."

Chamberlain made a triumphant noise and stalked forward, kneeling in front of Stanley as if to get a better look at him. "So!" he hissed breathlessly, staring intently at him with his ice-blue eye, "So!"

Stanley grimaced. Chamberlain had looked villainous enough at a distance, but up close, he truly looked like an evil maniac.

"Out for a little holiday, eh?" Chamberlain said mockingly. "Your jolly old uncle thought he'd bring you on a lovely sailing trip? Thought he'd stop off in Port Silverburg to visit his old friend, Bartholomew Crane?" Stanley tried to back away, but Chamberlain grabbed his arm and pulled him forward. "*I* was in Port Silverburg, too, you know," he said in a soft, menacing whisper. Stanley could see flecks of spit flying out of the Regent's mouth whenever he pronounced his *s*'s and *t*'s. "Your uncle didn't want to see me, though," said Chamberlain. "Thought he'd make me look the fool once again, for old time's sake, did he? Slipped right out of my grasp, right from between my fingers. Thought he was pretty clever, hmm? Proud of his daring escape?"

"No!" said Stanley suddenly, wrenching free of Chamberlain's grip. "He didn't think he was being clever at all!" He was shouting now, angry that Chamberlain would say such things about Uncle Jack, that Uncle Jack would want to make him look like a fool, that he would consider his escape from Port Silverburg a clever bit of sport.

"He ran because he knew you wanted to kill him!" Stanley yelled, pointing accusingly at Chamberlain. "He knew you were still obsessed with hunting him down for no good reason!"

Chamberlain's face was a mask of fury, as he stood up and took a threatening step towards Stanley. "Shut your mouth, boy," he snarled, but as he raised a hand to hit Stanley, he suddenly jerked backwards and was flung across the room, where he landed in a heap in front of the doors. He lay there for a time, more than a bit dazed.

Stanley gazed from Chamberlain to the masked man, who was dusting off his hands in a satisfied way. The masked man had descended the steps while Chamberlain was raging at Stanley, and had personally tossed the unsuspecting Regent with incredible ease.

"I must insist that you refrain from harming the boy," rumbled the masked man, as the two knights helped Chamberlain to his feet. "He is our special guest."

"Guest?" Stanley echoed, "But you had me put in jail! Er," he said, his indignation fading as the masked man stared blankly at him.

"If you're worried about damaging the hostage," Chamberlain said contemptuously, making his way back towards the masked man, "I can assure you that Lee will be *more* willing to cooperate if he thinks—"

"Hostage? Oh, please!" scoffed the masked man, waving Chamberlain's words aside, "Do you really think I am *that* small-minded, Ezekiel?" Chamberlain looked affronted, clearly having thought that he'd finally grasped his master's plan. "I do apologize, Stanley," said the masked man, "but your stay in the dungeon is a precautionary measure. It's nothing personal, I assure you." He turned away from Stanley, clearly not expecting his consent.

"But my lord, don't you see?" said Chamberlain imploringly, "This boy is an ideal hostage! When Lee learns that we have him, he'll come to rescue him! He'll walk right into our hands! Besides, what possible use could you have for the boy, if not—"

"I will remind you not to question me, Ezekiel," said the masked man, "And that I am in control of the situation."

Chamberlain muttered something under his breath.

"What was that?" the masked man asked sharply. Chamberlain paused for a second or two, then said,

"I only wish that your lordship would ... confide in me more often."

"Keep you in the loop, so to speak?" offered the masked man. "Ezekiel, I've told you before, that to speak too freely of one's plans, is to invite disaster. Revealing my plans to anyone, even someone as *loyal* as you (he put an absurd emphasis on the word *loyal*) could result in their irreparable damage." Chamberlain did not appear satisfied with this explanation. "Oh, very well," sighed the masked man, "If you're going to sulk about it, I'll let you in on this juicy tidbit: I did not summon you to Port Silverburg solely to test you. I did it to fulfill a prophecy, one that has awaited fulfillment for a long, long time." He cleared his throat loudly, and paused for effect. "I refuse to relate to you the entire prophecy, but the part which concerns *you*, is thus: *The one I seek would evade the clutches of my disobedient servant.*

Chamberlain's expression was expectant. "*And?*"

"And," said the masked man, "that is all I'm going to tell you."

Stanley's mind raced. What did it all mean? He had certainly evaded Chamberlain's clutches (with Uncle Jack's help), and from what he'd been hearing, Chamberlain certainly seemed to be a disobedient servant, but really, this 'prophecy' didn't sound too difficult to fulfill. He looked up and saw the masked man watching him.

"You are skeptical," the masked man rumbled softly.

"Er," said Stanley.

"Most people are, especially when a prophecy concerns them personally." The masked man's voice had taken on a thoughtful, musing tone. "Yes, indeed. We like to think that we are the supreme masters of our destinies; that is why many find the power of prophecy so difficult to accept." He began to pace back and forth, his hands clasped behind his back, while Chamberlain rolled his eyes impatiently. "The future lies before us, but time hides it from our view. Oh, to be able to gaze ahead, and see all the days of our lives laid out before us, to look forward and face the future with surety and courage, instead of fear and doubt ... but alas, even those gifted with prophetic powers can see but minute glimpses of the yet-to-come ... visions and riddles, which must be pieced together." He stopped pacing and looked at Stanley. "But each of those pieces is a priceless treasure to the astute seer."

"What do you see?" Stanley was slightly surprised to hear himself asking the urgent question. "Er," he said, averting his gaze from the dark chasms of the mask's eye holes, "I mean, what do you see about *me?*"

The masked man laughed darkly. "I've seen great discouragement ... but also new hope."

Frustrated by the cryptic response, Stanley pressed further. "But what's *my* future? What is it that happens, that involves *me?*"

"I don't know."

"What? But you said—"

"I said that prophecies are never clear ... but they are never wrong."

"So how can you not know what *my* prophecy is?"

The masked man folded his arms and stared at the floor, as if uncertain of what to say next. "Because," he rasped quietly, "I can no longer see your future."

Stanley gaped, not entirely sure what these words meant.

"My lord!" said Chamberlain, "You should not be revealing such things to the boy!"

"But you could see my future yesterday," said Stanley, trying to keep the masked man's attention.

"Yes," said the masked man, "But you will recall that I let you live."

"So you really *did* plan to kill me, right up until the last minute! Something happened that you hadn't foreseen, you said it yourself!"

"Indeed," said the masked man, "You—"

KA-BOOM!

An explosion suddenly rang out through the throne room, and the great wooden doors were blown off their hinges, flattening the two knights who had been standing before them. The masked man, who had obviously been on the verge of revealing something crucial, stopped in mid-sentence and wheeled around to face the smoking wreckage of the throne room doorway. Chamberlain, who had been standing closer to the doors, was picking himself up after having been knocked off his feet by the blast.

"*WHAT IN THE BLOODY BLUE BLAZES?*" he roared as he stood up, drawing forth a sword and pistol.

Stanley's interest in the masked man's explanation evaporated, as he watched three figures clamber into the room.

"Great scott, Benjamin!" said a familiar voice, "How much powder didja use? What're ya tryin' to do, bring the whole place down on top of us?"

Stanley's heart leapt higher than it had ever leapt before. Emerging from the smoke were Uncle Jack, Benjamin Stone, and a disheveled-looking man, whom Stanley had never seen before.

"Mercy!" exclaimed Uncle Jack, surveying the damage and coughing loudly, "Me ears're still ringin' (cough cough) an' I can hardly see a blessed thing!"

Stanley wanted to cheer. He wanted to run, jump, do a backflip, punch Chamberlain, sing a song. Uncle Jack hadn't left him behind. No one had forgotten him, left him to live out the rest of his life in a dungeon, written him off as an unfortunate loss. Uncle Jack had noticed that Stanley was missing, and had blasted his way into the throne room of the Imperial Palace to find him.

"Uncle Jack!" Stanley cried, waving his arms and jumping up and down. Uncle Jack looked over, and his wrinkled old face lit up with a joyful grin.

"Stanley, lad!" he yelled, spreading his arms wide. Stanley ran towards his uncle, but a big black boot got in his way, and he was forced to stop. The boot belonged to Chamberlain, who pointed his pistol at Stanley and snarled,

"Stay where you are, boy!"

Stanley backed up a few steps, and watched as Chamberlain turned to face Uncle Jack, whose happy grin had been replaced by a look of depthless fury. Chamberlain smirked and pointed his pistol at Uncle Jack.

"Well, well," he said silkily, "we meet again. It's been a long time, Jackson."

"Not long enough," Uncle Jack replied, his fists clenched at his sides. Chamberlain's smirk grew more pronounced.

"Jackson, please," he said, "Must our first conversation in forty years be filled with angry words?"

"Must you put on yer same old big-shot act, playin' all cool an' suave when I know damn well that yer boilin' inside over the way I 'ruined yer life'?"

Chamberlain's smirk vanished, replaced by an ugly grimace. "You know me so well, Jackson, even after all these years."

"Not like I could forget," said Uncle Jack bitterly, "Any more than you could."

Chamberlain scowled. "No, you're quite right about that."

"Well then stop actin' like we're old chums, *Ezekiel*, 'cause it's bloody annoyin'!"

"Yes, you're right, Jack," said Chamberlain savagely, as he cocked his pistol's hammer, "No more games. Goodbye."

A shot rang out.

A spark flashed from the pistol's barrel.

The gun kicked back.

The shot's echo rebounded off the marble walls.

Stanley was aware of a loud, constant, high-pitched sound coming from somewhere close by. Slowly, the realization hit him: the noise was coming from his own mouth. He was screaming, he was screaming *NOOOOO!* at the top of his voice. He felt anger, rage like he had never felt before. It was everywhere, in his blood, in his mind, in the air around him, and he knew why. Chamberlain had fired his gun, fired it at Uncle Jack. He had killed Uncle Jack, Stanley's great uncle, a good man who did not deserve to die like this.

Stanley couldn't see, couldn't hear, couldn't even think; all that mattered now was that he hurt Chamberlain, hurt him as badly as possible, punch him, kick him, beat him, tear him to pieces. Stanley could see Chamberlain. He was standing there with his back to him, the smoking gun in his hand. Stanley rushed towards the Regent. He stretched out his arms, his hands and fingers ready to attack.

But they weren't his hands.

Instead of fingers, he had long, black claws, sleek and sharp. The hands to which the claws belonged were large and brutish, with huge knuckles and smooth, black skin. Stanley stopped and stared at the claws with shock and wonder. *These aren't my hands*, he thought, and then a great (and somehow familiar) dizziness seized him. He stumbled and landed on his knees, instinctively holding out his arms to keep from smashing his face on the floor. He blinked dazedly and tried to bring his hands into focus. The dizzy feeling subsided, and he found himself staring at two perfectly normal twelve-year-old human hands. His hands. Stanley blinked several more times, then held a hand up to his face. He stared at it, as if daring it to turn back into a claw. It didn't. Shaking his head, he looked up at Chamberlain, who was still facing the other way. Had he not even heard Stanley charging at him, screaming like a wild man?

What was Chamberlain staring at, anyway? Then Stanley remembered. Chamberlain had shot Uncle Jack. Anger began to boil again behind Stanley's eyes, but it fizzled out abruptly as he saw what had grabbed Chamberlain's attention so completely. Uncle Jack was still alive. Stanley could barely see him, but there he was, standing on the other side of an almost opaque wall of darkness which had sprung up between him and Chamberlain, at the exact moment the pistol had been fired. There, on the floor, at the foot of the wall of darkness, was a shiny lump of metal: the bullet which had flown from Chamberlain's gun, intending to bury itself in Uncle Jack's heart.

Stanley knew at once what had happened. He turned around and saw the masked man standing there serenely, his left arm held out in front of him. The hooded head turned slightly, and the mask stared blankly at him for a moment, before turning towards Chamberlain, who was firing off more shots at the mysterious wall.

"That will do, Ezekiel," said the masked man sternly, and his shadow shot across the floor towards the Regent. This time, instead of creeping up to Chamberlain's throat to strangle him, the shadow actually rose up from the floor like something emerging from a pool of tar. The shadow seemed to turn 3-D, and took on the shape of a large hammer, which swung heavily at Chamberlain, knocking him sideways across the floor. The Regent landed hard on the polished marble, where he lay, unconscious but still breathing.

The wall of darkness vanished, and Uncle Jack, who had been straining to see through it, stumbled forward, staring incredulously from the prone form of Chamberlain, to Stanley, to the masked man.

"*You!*" he said, pointing at the masked man.

"Me," the masked man agreed.

"What the devil're *you* doin' here, ya great loony?" growled Uncle Jack, "What're ya doin' with *him?*" he indicated Chamberlain.

"I'm exercising my authority," said the masked man matter-of-factly.

"Authority?" Uncle Jack echoed, "An' what *authority* would that be?"

"Why, my authority as ruler of the Rheddish Empire," said the masked man.

Uncle Jack looked as though he thought this was a grand joke. "Ahh, o' course, I see now," he said, "So all this talk of Chamberlain, here bein' the Regent Lord o' the Empire is codswallop, then, is it? An' I s'pose *you* must be some long-lost relative o' the Royal Family, eh? Tyrone the Fifteenth's cousin's half-brother's nephew, p'raps?"

"The Royal Family? PAH!" spat the masked man. "Thieves and usurpers, all. No, my claim to the throne goes back long before the Tyrones ever arrived in Rhedland."

Uncle Jack did not look convinced. "But Chamberlain—"

"Is not fit to run an ice cream parlour, much less an empire," stormed the masked man, looking disdainfully at the unconscious Regent. "*His Lordship* is little more than an errand boy, I'm sorry to tell you, and a poor one at that, although I'll admit he has his uses ..." The masked man trailed off as Chamberlain stirred and opened his eye.

"What ... happened?" the Regent murmured blearily.

"In case you haven't noticed," said the masked man, ignoring Chamberlain and addressing Uncle Jack, "his Regency desires nothing more than your destruction."

"I've realized that, thanks," said Uncle Jack sourly.

"Of course," said the masked man, "and that is why he is such a nuisance. You see, I need you, Jackson Lee, I need you to help me ... and you can't help me if you're dead, now can you?"

"Oh, ya think I'll be helpin' ya, do ya, Mr. Mask?" Uncle Jack took off his hat and pressed it against his chest in a ludicrously exaggerated gesture of respect. "An' what can this humble ol' sailor do to help ye, oh great ruler of the Rheddish Empire?"

Stanley was inclined to laugh at this, but the masked man was not.

"I need you to tell me the location of the Black Jack Bonanza," he said in the slow and deliberate fashion of someone who is trying valiantly to keep his anger in check. Uncle Jack, himself, no longer seemed to see the humour in all of this.

"An' what," said Uncle Jack, his expression darkening as he placed his hat back on his head, "d'*you* know about the Black Jack Bonanza?"

"Everything," said the masked man maliciously, "Everything, that is, except *where ... it ... is.*"

Uncle Jack was shaking his head, his expression one of puzzlement and disbelief. "Who *are* yeh? *What* are yeh? Yeh show up outta the blue, land on me ship, frighten me nephew ... an' the next day, I run int'ya in the throne room o' the

Imperial Palace, of all places, where ya have the gall to tell me that yer after me treasure! An' apparently, yer the new king! Now tell me, *who are yeh?*"

"In time, *all* will know my name," rumbled the masked man, as he slowly ascended the steps to the throne, "but until I choose to reveal it, I will remain anonymous."

"Oh yeah?" said Uncle Jack as the masked man sat down, "Well, Mr. Anonymous, I can tell ya that I won't breathe a word to ya 'bout me treasure, so ya might as well forget about makin' a name for yerself as the man who brought home the fabled Black Jack Bonanza."

At this, the masked man laughed shrilly. "You think I seek the treasure for fame and glory, Lee? You think I seek riches? Wealth?" He sighed pityingly, and said, "You people are all so predictable. You see nothing but the blatantly obvious. The scope of your minds is so … limited. You, Chamberlain … *everyone*, you never look beyond what's right in front of you, never bother to hazard a glance at what's further down the road … and *that*," he said with a sinister chuckle, "Will make my task all the simpler."

"Think that way, if it'll make ya happy," said Uncle Jack, "But we're leavin'. C'mon, Stanley."

Stanley glanced quickly up at the masked man, who was making no move to stop him, and then hurried over to where Uncle Jack, Benjamin, and the disheveled man were standing. They all backed away from the throne, and were just about through the shattered doorway, when there came an ominous clanking sound from the hall outside.

Seconds later, no less than fifty Knights of the Silver Sword came marching into the throne room, swords drawn.

"Aw heck," muttered Uncle Jack as the knights formed a tight circle around the four of them. Stanley cast around at the wall of armour and swords, and all the relief and happiness he'd experienced on seeing Uncle Jack suddenly vanished, leaving an empty, despairing feeling in the pit of his stomach.

"I neglected to mention," said the masked man, getting up from the throne, "that I will not be letting you go. I thought you might have assumed that, but, well, there it is. Take them away," he said to the closest knight, and the circle closed in.

CHAPTER EIGHTEEN:
THE LURKER

It was a grim procession that made its way down the winding staircase, to the deepest, darkest, dankest dungeons of the Imperial Palace, some minutes later. Stanley kept his gaze on the slimy floor, wondering what was going to happen now. They had been so close, so close to escaping from this horrible place, and now ...

Now it looked as if this fantastic adventure was really going to end in a foul, mouldy old prison cell.

Stanley glanced sideways at Uncle Jack, wondering if the old man was entertaining similar thoughts. To his surprise, the look on his great-uncle's face was not one of sadness or defeat, but of sharp alertness. His eyes were darting this way and that, and his jaw was set. Something was going on here, but what? Stanley peered all around, and then the realization hit him: they were being led through the dungeons by two Knights of the Silver Sword. Two knights? Only two knights? There had been fifty of them flanking the prisoners as they were escorted out of the throne room, and now there was one at the front of the group, one at the back. The others must have peeled off along the way. At first, Stanley was inclined to feel hopeful and optimistic at this unforeseen twist of fate, but then he reminded himself that two knights were probably more than a match for a boy and three men, and besides, even if they did escape the knights, where would they go?

Stanley was still thinking gloomy thoughts, when it happened. The small procession was passing by an innocent-looking alcove in the damp stone wall, when something leapt out of it, and collided with the rear knight. The knight, caught completely off guard, toppled sideways and smashed into the wall, leaving an impressive display of cracks in the rough-hewn stone. The knight slumped to the floor and did not move again. Stanley stared from the prostrate knight, to the knight's attacker, who, after making sure the knight was down for good, stood up and bounded forward, leaping right over Stanley as he and the others ducked, and landed on top of the lead knight, knocking him to the floor. A brief scuffle ensued, finishing with a sickening cracking sound, and an abrupt end to the knight's struggles. The attacker rose from the knight's still form, and turned to glare at the prisoners with fierce, yellow eyes. It was Grey.

"Grey!" Stanley cried.

"Stanley," said Grey flatly, giving an almost imperceptible nod.

Uncle Jack, who had been regarding Grey apprehensively, gaped at Stanley. "Stanley lad, you ... you *know* this fellah?"

"Er, well, sort of," said Stanley, forcefully reminding himself that he didn't exactly *know* Grey. "We were, uh, in a cell together, and—"

"You were in a cell with Grey?" said the scruffy man, looking either deeply impressed or deeply skeptical.

"Uh, for a bit," said Stanley, glancing over at Grey, who stared back unhelpfully.

"Is he friend or foe, Stanley lad?" Uncle Jack asked hurriedly.

"F-friend," Stanley answered, not exactly sure what he was basing his answer upon.

"Good enough for me," said Uncle Jack, moving forward. "We're gettin' outta here," he said to Grey, as he retrieved his pistol from the lead knight's tool bag. "Yeh helped us with those knights, so feel free to tag along 'till we're outta here." He turned to the others and said, "Right, lads, let's move out! Dame fortune has smiled on us, so I say we get while the gettin's good!" And with that, he jogged down the dark corridor, his wooden leg not slowing him down in the slightest.

Benjamin and the scruffy man quickly followed after Uncle Jack, but Grey didn't move until Stanley passed by him. Stanley raced along the corridor, doing his best to keep up with the others. Grey, who was obviously not giving his all, stayed beside him.

Moments later, they reached the end of the hall, stopping in front of a metal door with a sign on it, which read,

-UTILITY ROOM-
DANGER:
AUTHORIZED
PERSONNEL ONLY

Beyond the door could be heard the sound of running machinery.

"This is it," said Uncle Jack, slightly winded after running the length of the corridor. "I'll have this door open in a jiff." He reached into an inner pocket of his coat and produced two long, thin bits of metal. They looked like paper clips that had been straightened. He stuck the wires into the keyhole and began to move them about ever so slightly. Stanley and the others looked on for a moment or two, and then Grey stepped forward and tapped Uncle Jack on the shoulder.

"Not now," said Uncle Jack distractedly, as he tried to concentrate on picking the lock.

"Step aside," said Grey curtly.

"Eh?" said Uncle Jack, looking up from his work.

"Step aside," Grey repeated.

Uncle Jack shot a questioning glance at Stanley, who shrugged uncomfortably. What was Grey planning to do?

"Well, alright, matey," said Uncle Jack coolly, as he moved out of the way, "If ya think ya can get this door open any faster 'n I can, be my gues—"

CLANG!

As soon as Uncle Jack was out of the way, Grey turned a shoulder to the door and kicked with incredible speed and power. The lock broke instantly as the door buckled inwards, then Grey reached out and pulled it open, as if it had been unlocked the entire time. He stood expectantly by the doorway, looking like some kind of nightmarish porter, waiting for Uncle Jack to lead the way through. Uncle Jack stared wide-eyed at the massive dent in the three-inch-thick door.

"Er … ah … well done," he said to Grey as he passed through the doorway.

The others followed, Stanley and Grey bringing up the rear. The utility room was long, low, dimly-lit, and slightly wider than the hall outside. Set into alcoves at intervals of about twelve feet were all kinds of machines, all of which were emitting loud, annoying mechanical noises. The *chug-chug-chug* and the *clank-clank-clank* mingled with the *rum-rum-rum* and the *fss-fss-fss* to form an awful din that made Stanley long for the relative peace and quiet of the dungeon corridors. He clapped his hands over his ears and glanced sideways at Grey, who didn't seem to care a whit about the noise.

At the back of the utility room there was another, smaller alcove with nothing in it except for a large manhole. The small group squeezed into the alcove and stared down at the round metal cover. Stanley looked from Grey, to the scruffy man, to Benjamin, to Uncle Jack, who was the only one who seemed to know what he was doing.

"Right," Uncle Jack shouted over the roar of the machinery, "This is it—our way out! Let's get this manhole open!"

Stanley looked down at the cover. It looked heavy, and there was no handle. How were they supposed to get it open? His unasked question was answered, as Benjamin Stone unhooked a stout-looking length of metal from his belt: a crowbar. Benjamin jammed the crowbar into a small opening between the manhole cover and the stone floor, and tried mightily to lever the heavy piece of metal out of the hole. Muscles bulging and teeth gritted against the strain, Benjamin managed to lift the cover a few inches, but then, dishearteningly, the crowbar broke with a metallic snap.

But the manhole cover did not fall back into place, for Grey had swooped in at some point, and eased his fingers under the lid. With a mighty heave, Grey flipped the manhole cover open. They all stared wonderingly at him for a moment, then Uncle Jack said,

"Okay, let's go," and pointed at the metal ladder which led down into the darkness of the manhole, from which a supremely vile smell was issuing, accompanied by the sound of swiftly-flowing water. Benjamin went first, then the scruffy man, then Uncle Jack, Stanley, and finally Grey, who pulled the manhole cover back into place.

Reaching the bottom of the ladder, Stanley slipped on the wet, slimy ground, and was mercifully caught by Uncle Jack.

"Steady, lad," said the old man as he helped Stanley regain his feet, "Ya don't want to be slippin' too far down here." A slimy *thud* indicated that Grey had chosen to drop down from above, rather than climb safely down the ladder.

Stanley peered around him. They were somewhere very dark, cold, damp, and stinky. The sound of rushing water was very close now, probably only a few feet away, and Stanley stayed stock still for fear of falling blindly into an underground river.

"Benjamin," came Uncle Jack's voice, echoing strangely off the unseen walls, "a light, if ye would." There was a sharp *click click click*, and Benjamin Stone appeared from out of the darkness, bathed in the flickering light of a torch. The torch, though rather feeble, was bright enough to reveal their new surroundings. They were in a wide, tubular tunnel with smooth, slick walls. Beneath their feet was a stone (or perhaps concrete) walkway which ran, it could be assumed, the entire length of the tunnel. The sound of flowing water came from what seemed to be a great river, flowing down the middle of the tunnel, its water dark and foul. Stanley was very glad that he'd fought the urge to move; a half-step to his left would have landed him in the nasty river of sludge.

"This is the Ethelia Sewer System," said Uncle Jack, as he lit another torch for himself. "These tunnels run under the entire city, an' eventually empty into a water treatment plant down by the harbour. That's where we wanna be. Now, it's a long walk, an' there're ... er ... *things* livin' down here, so I want us to stick close together, an' don't wander off, no matter what y'hear or see, a'right?"

Stanley nodded silently, as did Benjamin and the scruffy man. Grey made no indication that he'd heard what Uncle Jack had said.

"Right," said Uncle Jack, "Let's move."

They went in single file along the narrow, slippery walkway, the only light coming from their torches. Uncle Jack had offered a third torch to Grey, who was bringing up the rear, but Grey merely shook his head in response. It was a long, dark journey through those sewers, and a damp one, and a smelly one. Stanley had thought the dungeons were bad, but right now, they seemed like the Ritz compared to this place. He had been hoping that after a while, his sense of smell would become numb to the horrendous odor, but, even after an hour of walking, the smell still made him feel like throwing up.

But the smell was not the only thing bothering him. The journey was made all the more unpleasant by Uncle Jack's warning that there were *things* living in the sewers. Stanley had become a bundle of nerves, and jumped at the slightest drip of water. When he asked Uncle Jack what sort of things were down here, the old man just shook his head, as if to say, *you don't want to know.*

The tunnel went on an on, never veering from its course. This was probably a good thing, Stanley decided, as it reduced their chances of getting lost. He had the distinct feeling that it would be exceedingly easy for one to lose his way down in this dark, stinking underworld.

They periodically passed by openings in the wall, most of them much smaller than the tunnel they were in. These side-tunnels connected to other parts of the city, but Stanley noted, with no small amount of curiosity, that some of them had caved in. At one point, they were passing by an innocent-looking side-tunnel, when the scruffy man, who was walking in front of Stanley, suddenly stopped. He was peering into the tunnel, holding his torch before him for improved lighting. Stanley peeped around the corner to see what the man was looking at, and when he saw what it was, he gasped. Less than ten feet into the small side-tunnel sat a huge, wooden treasure chest, its lid wide open, the gold and jewels inside spilling out onto the damp stone floor.

Stanley couldn't believe it. All that treasure, just lying there, waiting for someone to claim it ... waiting for *him* to claim it! Yes, why not? It seemed such a waste to just leave the gold and jewels. Why leave a heap of treasure in a place like this? The scruffy man was having similar thoughts, it seemed, for he exchanged a glance with Stanley and proceeded slowly down the side-tunnel with a greedy look on his face. Not wanting the man to have the treasure all to himself, Stanley followed. They were mere paces away from the treasure, when a pair of hands reached out from behind and grabbed them by the shoulders.

"We were told not to wander off," said Grey, pulling Stanley and the scruffy man backwards, out of the side-tunnel.

"Yes, but—" said the scruffy man, struggling to free himself from Grey's grip.

"The treasure!" said Stanley, struggling as well, "We're just gonna get the treasure, we're not wandering off!"

"What treasure?" Grey asked tersely.

"*That* treasure!" said Stanley, pointing ten feet into the side-tunnel.

But it was gone. The tunnel was empty.

"There's nothing there," said Grey, his voice impassive.

"But it was right there!" spluttered the scruffy man, "We both saw it!"

"Yeah!" said Stanley, "It's there! It's just a little further along ..." He strained to see deeper into the tunnel, but it was obviously devoid of any scrap of treasure. He blinked a few times, then shook his head as if to clear it. It was true, there was no treasure down that side-tunnel. But how could he have imagined it?

"We should keep moving," said Grey.

*   *   *   *

They walked and walked for another full hour, and still the tunnel's end was nowhere in sight. Stanley's shoes were covered in slime, and the foul air was giving him a headache. They passed many more side-tunnels, but Stanley didn't see any more treasure. More than once, though, he thought he saw movement in the tunnels, as if there were creatures lurking there, just out of sight. He knew that there were indeed creatures down here in the sewers, because he could see their eyes shining out from side-tunnels across the water. Sometimes more than ten pairs of yellow, red, or green eyes could be seen gleaming at him from the darkness. The things, whatever they were, didn't seem to be dangerous, or, perhaps they were merely content to watch the procession go by like some kind of odd little parade.

Stanley's least-favourite part of the sewer walk happened shortly into the third hour of the journey. The group had stopped to rest at a huge intersection of tunnels, and Stanley had just sat down reluctantly on the slimy floor, when he heard it:

Someone was calling his name.

Stanley ... Stanley ...

Stanley jumped immediately to his feet, not sure if he was hearing correctly. He cocked his head to one side, trying to discern where the voice had come from.

Stanley ... Stanley ...

He heard it again, a voice calling his name.

Stanley ... come help me ... Stanley ...

It was a girl's voice, which Stanley found very strange, because the only girl he knew around here was Nell, and she was back at the harbour, waiting on board the Ogopogo with Alabaster and Pericles ... or was she?

Stanley, please help me ... I'm lost ...

A horrible thought began to grow in Stanley's mind. What if Nell and Alabaster had decided to come looking for him? Uncle Jack had said that the sewers led to a water treatment plant down by the harbour. What if Nell and Alabaster had found their way into the sewers through the treatment plant? What if they'd been wandering down here for hours, hopelessly lost, hurt, maybe unable to move?

Stanley ... please help me ... please ...

It had to be Nell. Did it sound like her voice? *Of course* it was her voice, no other girl around here knew him. What did Nell's voice sound like, anyway? Like *this*, of course. Almost without thinking, Stanley headed back up the tunnel, back the way they had come.

Help me, Stanley ... please ...

"I'm coming," Stanley muttered to himself. He passed by a few side-tunnels, pausing at each one to listen for the voice. Finally, stopping beside a rather large one, he leaned against the tunnel mouth, listening hard.

Stanley, help me ...

It was definitely coming from down here.

"Yecch!" Stanley jumped away from the wall in disgust. He had been leaning against a patch of greenish slime, which had soaked the side of his shirt, and smelled like burning rubber. He wiped the slimy mess off as best he could, and saw that the entire tunnel mouth was covered in the stuff.

Stanley, help me ...

Taking a deep breath and squaring his shoulders, Stanley set off down the side tunnel. He noted that the green slime was all over the tunnel's interior, as well. In some places it was very thick, and bulging, as if there were something underneath it. In other places, the slime seemed stringy, and hung down from the tunnel roof like stalactites.

Stanley, help me …

He had reached another side-tunnel, this one leading away to his left. The voice was coming from this smaller tunnel, Stanley was sure of it. Approaching the mouth of the new side-tunnel, he discovered that it was completely closed off by a covering of slime.

Stanley … Stanley, help me … please …

The voice was coming from right behind the wall of slime. How was he supposed to get through it? "Uh, hello?" he said tentatively, his voice echoing strangely. "Is that you, Nell?"

Stanley, said the girl's voice, *come closer …*

The wall of slime parted with a horrible wet tearing sound, seeming to open inwards, like the double doors of a cathedral.

Stanley … please … come in …

"Is that you, Nell?" said Stanley, starting to feel a bit uneasy.

Help me, Stanley … come in … help me …

The extremely bizarre and unsettling nature of this situation was finally starting to dawn on Stanley, who found it necessary to blink several times and shake his head to clear it. He felt as if he were just waking up from a long nap. This whole thing suddenly made very little sense. Nell was claustrophobic. Why would she be in the sewers, hiding behind a door made of slime, in a slime-filled tunnel? How could she be calling out to him without anyone else hearing? Anyone else … why had he gone off by himself without telling Uncle Jack? Why did he suddenly have a horrible feeling in the pit of his stomach?

Stanley … please come in … I need you to come in … now … please, Stanley …

Now that he thought about it, the voice really didn't sound all that much like Nell's; in fact, it didn't sound like a voice at all. It sounded like a deep, gurgling hiss, and it wasn't speaking any language that Stanley recognized. He backed away from the slime door, and as he did, saw movement just beyond it. Something was getting up, and it was big. There came a skittering sound, as if many clawed legs were scrabbling to lift a heavy body … that sharp, gurgling hiss again …

And the thing emerged from its lair. Stanley didn't pause to look at it, choosing to run for it before the creature could get any closer. As might be expected, he slipped on the slimy floor and tumbled headlong into a large, squishy lump, which, he realized with a pang of real horror, was an egg the size of a basketball. He scrambled to his feet as quickly as the slimy floor would allow, and felt something sharp rake across his back. A frustrated hiss indicated that the thing had not intended him to survive. Slipping, sliding and stumbling, Stanley ran for the tunnel mouth, all the while expecting to feel the thing's claws ripping into him again. He was close, so very close, and then, horribly, tragically, nightmarishly, he slipped again, and fell face-first onto the stinking, slime-covered floor.

But something was happening. Golden light flared before him. Figures were standing at the tunnel mouth. A voice rang out, clear and strong:

"STANLEY, LAD, GET DOWN!"

Not even considering the needlessness of this advice, Stanley flattened himself as much as he could. The skittering was right behind him, the terrible, gurgling hiss almost in his ear. A foot, a human foot, took a step forward and was right beside his face. Not knowing why, he turned around, and looked up at the dark shape bearing down on him.

BANG!

An explosion. A gunshot.

A flash of light. An inhuman scream.

The gun's muzzle-flash lit the slime-ridden tunnel for a fraction of a second, but it was enough time for Stanley to see the face of his attacker.

It was a ghastly face, a face from a deep, dark, unspeakable nightmare, a face that should not have existed, a face that was insectoid, yet also reptilian, but, most horrible of all, vaguely humanoid. Pale, slimy skin stretched over a strange, alien skull ... a mouth which opened sideways, like an insect's mandibles, but which contained rows of sharp, ghoulish teeth ... slits for a nose ... and two huge, round, bulging black eyes, eyes filled with hunger and madness.

Stanley screamed and closed his eyes, but the image of the face was burned into his retinas. It seemed worse with his eyes shut, but he kept them that way just the same.

There came another hideous, gargled scream—a scream of pain and fury—and then a heavy, squelching *thud*, as the thing collapsed. Stanley lay there for a moment, breathing heavily and gaping at the shapeless lump before him. He felt very tired, but also relieved.

He let out a surprised squawk, as hands gripped his shoulders and dragged him out of the slime tunnel, to the safety of the stone walkway. He lay down on the cold stone floor, panting and staring up at the faces which swam before him, willing them to come into focus. A hand pushed against this shoulder, helping him into a sitting position, where he found himself looking into Uncle Jack's anxious face.

"Stanley lad, speak to me! Are ye all right?"

"Yeah," said Stanley bravely, "I'm okay."

"Are ya hurt?"

"Yeah, I think so … my back …"

Someone prodded him in the back, between his shoulders.

"There's no wound," said Grey's voice.

"Well good," said Uncle Jack. "Stanley, lad, what the devil d'you mean by wanderin' off on yer own? Yer just lucky we had Grey along, he's the one who found ya."

Stanley looked around at Grey, who stared back impassively.

"S-sorry!" said Stanley, now feeling like the world's biggest idiot. "I don't know why … I thought I heard someone calling my name … and … then I realized it couldn't be her …" He looked up at Uncle Jack, tears welling up in his eyes. "I'm sorry!" he bawled into Uncle Jack's shoulder, getting slime all over the old man's coat. "I don't know why I was so stupid! I sh-shouldn't h-have gone off on m-my own!"

"There there," said Uncle Jack, a bit taken aback by Stanley's outburst, "Yer okay now, that's what counts." He patted Stanley gingerly on the head.

"What *was* that thing?" said the scruffy man, sounding horrified.

"A lurker," said Grey.

"How d'you know *that?*" inquired the scruffy man. "Have you seen one before?"

"No," said Grey.

"Then how do you know it's called a lurker?"

"It lurks," Grey said simply.

"Well y'know what *I* think it is?" said Uncle Jack, standing up and helping Stanley to his feet.

"What?" said the scruffy man.

"A siren," said Uncle Jack.

"A siren?" repeated the scruffy man, "Oh, come on, Jack."

"I'm serious," said Uncle Jack. "A creature, a monster that lures people to their doom with its sweet voice. From what Stanley's said, I think this beastie fits the bill." He turned to Stanley and said, "T'wasn't yer fault, lad. If that thing was anythin' like in the old stories, I'd say *no one* could've resisted its call."

They were silent for a moment, then the scruffy man said, "Well, *whatever* it was, it went down after one gunshot. Excellent aim as always, Jack."

Grey shook his head, but said nothing.

"Okay," said Uncle Jack, "I don't know 'bout you lads, but I'm really itchin' to get outta this place. Stanley, you okay to go?"

Stanley nodded. "Yeah, let's go."

"A'right, then let's move, double time!" said Uncle Jack, "An' if ya hear a sweet voice callin' for ya, me lads ... bloody well ignore it!"

CHAPTER NINETEEN:
BACK ON TRACK

"Is it just me, or is it getting brighter?" The scruffy man lowered his torch and peered ahead into the darkness of the tunnel. Stanley looked, too, and was sure he could see, far in the distance, a minuscule speck of light.

"Not long now," said Uncle Jack, cheerful for the first time since they'd entered the sewers. They had now been walking for almost four full hours, and Stanley, though tired, cold, and covered in siren slime, felt re-energized as the point of light drew closer and closer.

It wasn't long before the small group was standing at the mouth of the main tunnel, which was blocked off by thick, vertical metal bars, between which flowed the nasty-smelling river which carried the refuse of the entire city. Beyond the tunnel mouth was the interior of a colossal building filled with enormous cylindrical water tanks, connected to one another by a network of pipes. The biggest tank lay just beyond the tunnel mouth, and the foul sewer water was pouring directly into it, where it frothed and steamed unpleasantly.

"That'll be the treatment plant," said Uncle Jack in a satisfied tone, peering in at the water tanks with an almost nostalgic look on his face. "C'mon, let's get outta these sewers."

Grey suddenly stepped forward and gripped two of the bars, straining with all his might in an effort to bend them, but even his unnatural strength proved insufficient to move them even a fraction of an inch.

"Don't waste yer time," said Uncle Jack, "Those bars'll be made of adamant—no one could hope to bend 'em. This way." He pointed to a metal ladder which ran up the wall to their right, and disappeared into a vertical tunnel just big enough for a person to fit through. Uncle Jack led the way up the ladder, which ran upwards for a good fifty feet, before stopping beneath another manhole. They all stopped briefly, waiting for him to open the metal cover. There came a series of grating metallic squeaks, then a sharp click, and light flooded down from above. Stanley followed the scruffy man up the ladder and through the manhole.

"Up we go, laddie," said Uncle Jack, hoisting Stanley out. "Merciful mantas, Stanley, yer a sight!"

Stanley did indeed seem to have come off the worse from their sojourn in the sewers; a more filthy, bedraggled sight you've never seen. He was covered from head to foot in all manner of filth and slime, his clothes torn, frayed and soiled beyond any stretch of the imagination, his shoes little more than slimy, muddy lumps, his hair looking like a clump of matted seaweed. Filthy though he was, Stanley found that he didn't really care, and the smell, which wafted off him like some ethereal being ready to take on solid form, didn't bother him that much. He was glad to be out of the sewers, out of the dungeons, out of the castle, and on his way out of the city, with Uncle Jack and the rest of his friends still intact.

Stanley peered about at his new surroundings, squinting in the light which, after so long in the sewers, was blindingly bright. Little by little, though, his vision adjusted, and he saw that they were now standing in what seemed to be a small office, or perhaps a control room for the water treatment plant. Beneath three windows which looked down upon the interior of the plant was a long control panel covered with buttons, levers, gauges, dials, and blinking lights. Stanley found it interesting that, though Rhedland (what he'd seen of it) had a distinctly old-fashioned look and feel to it, the technology of the time was advanced enough to allow for the creation of high tech control panels and noisy machines in the dungeons of castles.

The control room was on the same level as the city proper. Through another set of windows across from the control panel, Stanley could see the streets and buildings meandering off towards the horizon, and, in the distance, towering above everything else, the Imperial Palace. The sun was shining outside, and he wondered what time it was. He looked at his watch which, although plastered with slime, was still ticking resolutely. Its smeared face read 11:17.

A door to the left of the control panel led to the interior of the treatment plant, but Uncle Jack crossed the room and opened a second door, which opened onto the street outside. The fresh, brisk breeze blowing in off the ocean felt like the breath of life to Stanley. He had almost forgotten what wind felt like, and after four hours of breathing stagnant, fetid sewer air, he vowed never to go underground again, if he could help it.

He gazed down Harbour Street, then at the innumerable stone piers to which a multitude of ships were moored. The great bay was alive with activity, just as it had been yesterday, when they'd first arrived. Scores upon scores of ships were bouncing and bobbing on the white-capped waves, as the tiny steam tugs went zipping about, performing their security duties. Seeing the tugs flying the Rheddish flag made Stanley think of Rick, the marine who had welcomed them to Ethelia, and who had also almost helped him escape from the dungeons of the palace. He hoped that Rick hadn't gotten into trouble over that whole fiasco.

"Hop to it, mates," said Uncle Jack, almost skipping with glee; the fresh sea air had clearly affected him in a positive fashion, as well. The small group made its way down along the harbour, past hundreds of ships, weaving in and out of rows of freight boxes, crates, loading devices, and sailors. Finally, they saw it, barely twenty yards away: the Ogopogo, bobbing serenely in the water, moored at pier three-forty-one.

Unfortunately, it was being guarded. Stanley's heart sank. Two marines in dark blue uniforms were standing at attention in front of the Ogopogo's gangplank.

"*Proteus's pimply patoot!*" growled Uncle Jack, "We've come all this way, an' they've got a coupl'a flunkies guardin' me ship!"

"I'll take care of them," Grey said grimly.

"Wait!" said Stanley, reaching out a restraining hand which, to be perfectly honest, could not have restrained Grey any more than it could have jumped off Stanley's arm and done a dance on its fingers. All the same, Grey stopped, glared down at Stanley's hand, then at Stanley, who said,

"What … what are you gonna do? *Kill* them?"

"If necessary," said Grey, sounding unconcerned at the prospect.

"What? No!" said Stanley vehemently. "No! You can't just go around killing people!"

Grey glared fiercely. "Why not?"

"*Why not?*" said Stanley, aghast, "Because it's *wrong!* It's bad! Murderers are bad people!"

"Maybe I'm a bad person," said Grey.

"I don't think you *are,*" said Stanley, staring defiantly up into those ferocious yellow eyes. "You helped us. You could have left us down there in the dungeons, but you stayed, and helped us get out. I don't think you're a bad person. You didn't kill those two knights, *did you?*"

"How would you know?"

"I dunno—I could just tell they weren't dead."

There was a brief pause, then Grey said, "No, I didn't kill them, but only because they're extremely difficult to kill." He added this last bit almost like an afterthought. Stanley gave him a small smile, but Grey turned away. "The knights are undeserving of mercy."

He said nothing more, which seemed to indicate that the discussion was over. At any rate, he made no move to harm the marines guarding the ship, but took a few steps away from the group, looking morose, as usual. Uncle Jack stepped towards Stanley and whispered,

"I'm proud of ya, laddie." The he backed up a bit, and said, gruffly, "Well, Stanley, lad, have ya got a plan?"

"I don't think we *need* a plan," said Stanley, looking back at the two marines. There was something familiar about them. As Stanley began to walk purposefully towards the marines, one of them grinned brightly and waved, saying,

"*Hey, Stanley!*"

It was Rick, and standing to his right was a gloomy-looking Bill.

"What are you doing here?" asked Stanley as Uncle Jack and the others came closer as well.

"Waiting for you guys," said Rick cheerfully. His smile faded, though, as he caught sight of Grey. "Oh," he said nervously, "Grey's with you then, is he?"

"Yeah," said Stanley, "D'you have to arrest him or something?"

"Well, no," said Rick, still eyeing Grey apprehensively, "but, well, we really don't *have* to anything."

"What d'you mean?" said Stanley.

"We got sacked," said Rick shortly. "Chamberlain found out that I let you out of your cell, and he sent me and Bill packing."

"I just wanna say I'm sorry," Bill blurted out, an anguished look on his round face. "I got scared, and panicked—I didn't know what to do! I'm really sorry for—for—"

"That's okay," said Stanley, whose opinion of Bill had not improved until now. "But if you two got sacked, why are you guarding the ship?"

"We're not technically supposed to be guarding it," sad Rick impishly, "What with being disgraced former members of the Imperial Marine Corps ..."

"But when we found out that your boat was being guarded," Bill said quickly, "we decided to step in and help you guys."

"So we marched up to the guys on guard duty—Belanger and Montgommery, a real pair of gutless rat-finks—and told them we had orders to take over. So here we are, waiting to see you off!"

"And hoping to high heaven that Belanger and Montgommery don't find out we've been sacked," added Bill.

Uncle Jack stepped forward and seized both Rick and Bill by the shoulders. "Bless you lads, both o' ya," he said, pulling them into a fatherly hug, "Yer a proud testament to the ancient naval tradition. Always do what you know to be right—"

"Especially when a great ghoul like Chamberlain would have you do otherwise," said Rick, freeing himself from Uncle Jack's emotional outpouring. "Besides, I wanted to see the great Black Jack Lee one last time."

Uncle Jack looked surprised and impressed. "So ya knew it was me? How long've ya known?"

"Oh, about three seconds," said Rick, "I wasn't sure 'till just now." He grinned roguishly.

Uncle Jack laughed. "Blisterin' barnacles, I sure walked into that one! Fooled by a coupl'a young 'uns, I never thought I'd see the day. Heh, seems to me you two woulda made good pirates!"

Rick and Bill beamed.

"What'll you do now?" Stanley asked.

"We're leaving town," said Rick. "We booked passage to Port Silverburg."

"My family lives there," put it Bill.

"And then I'll head inland to Darenville," said Rick, "I've got an, er, engagement there that I have to keep."

"Well, tell 'er Black Jack Lee sends his blessing," said Uncle Jack with a wink.

"That I will!" said Rick, saluting.

"Well," said Uncle Jack, as Stanley started to ask what they were talking about, "I guess it's high time we set sail. You two," he said to Rick and Bill, "thanks for yer help, from the bottom o' me heart."

"It was an honour assisting you, sir!" said Rick and Bill in unison, saluting again, and then turning to march briskly away.

"Right then, mates," said Uncle Jack, once the marines had marched out of sight, "let's get this ol' girl ready to sail!"

Benjamin Stone and the scruffy man obeyed instantly, rushing up the gangplank and setting to work immediately. Stanley hung back and looked up at Uncle Jack, who turned and walked over to where Grey was standing.

"Up the gangplank with ya, laddie," said Uncle Jack over his shoulder. Stanley pretended to obey, but stopped at the foot of the plank, listening stealthily.

"Well Grey, here we are," said Uncle Jack. Stanley turned around and saw Grey incline his head ever so slightly.

"Ya got any plans?" asked Uncle Jack.

"Plans?" Grey echoed emotionlessly.

"Aye, plans," said Uncle Jack. "D'you know what yer gonna do now, where yer gonna go? Yer a free man now, after all."

Grey seemed to consider this for a moment. "I have nowhere to go," he said in that same emotionless tone, "There is nothing for me to do."

"Nothin'?" said Uncle Jack.

"Nothing," said Grey.

"No family?"

"No."

"No home to go back to?"

"No."

"Yer just gonna stand there for the rest o' yer life, then?"

Stanley cringed. What was Uncle Jack trying to do, make Grey angry? He looked at Grey's face. If Grey was indeed getting angry, he was doing a good job of concealing it. Of course, Stanley mused, it was probably difficult for Grey to make himself look angrier than he already did.

"Grey," said Uncle Jack, "I'm gonna tell it to ya straight. Yeh helped me nephew an' the rest of us outta some tight spots back there, an' I want ya to know that I appreciate it."

Grey scowled.

"I don't know what yer motivation was," continued Uncle Jack, "an' I don't know what yeh did to get yerself locked up in the first place, but I *do* know that ye could do great things with those skills o' yers. I also know that, if yeh were willin', yeh'd be a big help to us on board the Ogopogo, an' I've got plenty o' room for new crew members."

"Are you asking me to join your crew?" Grey asked disinterestedly.

"Nope," answered Uncle Jack, "I'm just sayin' that if ya got nothin' better to do, an' ya feel inclined to help out on an important mission, an' yer ready to work for yer keep, then heck, I'd be glad to sign yeh up. But I'm not gonna ask ya to do anythin'—I'm gonna leave the choice entirely up to you, matey ... but choose quick, 'cause we gotta leave, pronto."

Grey continued to scowl, but said nothing.

"Right lads!" called Uncle Jack, turning away from Grey and heading for the gangplank, "No more dilly-dallyin'! We don't know how long it'll be 'fore our friends back at the Palace realize we're missin', so let's move! Stanley! What'ya think yer doin'? Up the gangplank with ya! Where's Pericles?"

Benjamin walked by and pointed at the crow's nest, from which could be heard the unmistakable sound of a parrot snoring.

"Asleep at a time like this!" said Uncle Jack, shaking his head. "*Ahoy, Pericles!*" he bellowed. There was a surprised squawk from the crow's nest, and Pericles dove down and swooped onto Uncle Jack's shoulder.

"All clear, captain," said the parrot, saluting briskly.

"All clear for nap time, is it?" said Uncle Jack.

Pericles cleared his throat embarrassedly, then his beady eyes widened. "My goodness!" He exclaimed, "Miss Hawthorne and Mr. Lancaster are still hiding in the hold! I told them not to come out 'till I said so!"

"Ya daffy bird!" said Uncle Jack, "How long've they been down there?"

"What time is it?"

"Almost eleven-thirty!"

"My word! I sent them below decks at six this morning!"

"Well then go get 'em, ya sleepy overgrown squab!"

"Right away, captain!" said Pericles, and he took off for the Ogopogo's hold.

"Unbelievable!" said Uncle Jack in exasperation, "Some lookout! Falls asleep when he's supposed to be keepin' an eye out! Anyone could've come aboard!"

Stanley fought to keep a straight face. Pericles was, after all, a parrot. He turned around at the sound of his name.

"Stanley!"

A huge grin lit his face. Emerging from the hold were Alabaster and Nell. They looked tired, but very glad to see him.

"Alright, Stanley!" yelled Alabaster, running towards him, his right hand raised for a high five. As he got closer, though, a look of surprise replaced his ecstatic grin. "Whoa!" he said, coming to a complete stop.

"What happened to *you?*" said Nell, stopping beside Alabaster. Their gazes ran from Stanley's slime-caked shoes to his filthy, matted hair.

"Uh, bit of trouble in the sewers," said Stanley awkwardly, reminded once again that he was filthy beyond description. Nell looked vaguely repulsed, but Alabaster's face lit up.

"Awesome!" he exclaimed. "You went through the sewers? Wow! Boy, do you ever stink! C'mon, Stanley, what was it like?"

"Story time *after* we're on the high seas," said Uncle Jack, hauling up the gangplank. "Besides, right now I wanna introduce ya." He turned and called, "Ey, Diego, c'mere!"

The scruffy man came over and said, "What's up, Jack?"

"I'd like ya to finally meet the youngest members o' the crew," said Uncle Jack beaming. "This here is Nell, Alabaster, an' ye've already met me great nephew, Stanley. Mates," he said, clapping the man on the shoulder, "this here is Diego Montigo, me best friend in the whole world!"

A light went on in Stanley's head. Of course! They had come to Ethelia for the sole purpose of rescuing Uncle Jack's long time friend, Diego Montigo, the man who had written the mysterious letter. And here he was, looking somewhat the worse for his months in prison, but smiling happily nonetheless.

"You wrote that letter!" Alabaster blurted out excitedly, pointing at Diego.

"Oh, you read it?" said Diego, looking interested, "I'd have thought your uncle might have hidden it somewhere."

"He's not actually my uncle," said Alabaster, bouncing up and down on the balls of his feet, "I'm his *honourary* nephew!"

"An' I *did* hide yer letter," said Uncle Jack, "but these three're far too clever for me! They found the secret room where I stashed it, an', well, here they are!"

Diego shook Stanley's hand, then Alabaster's. "And you're Nell?" he said shaking Nell's hand. "That's a lovely name."

Nell said nothing, but blushed furiously for some reason. Just then, Pericles appeared from nowhere and alighted on Uncle Jack's shoulder.

"Everything's ship-shape, captain," squawked the parrot. "We're good to go. Diego," he said, turning towards Diego and bowing humourously, "It is a great pleasure to see you again."

"And you, Pericles," said Diego, returning the bow.

"Right!" said Uncle Jack, "Hoist the mainsail! Weigh anchor! Make sail!"

Diego rushed off to hoist up the sail, while Benjamin Stone hauled up the anchor. The Ogopogo gave a lurch backwards. Uncle Jack himself was at the wheel, guiding the ship along the pier.

Stanley suddenly remembered something. Rushing to the bow, he looked at the spot where the Ogopogo had been moored, and saw Grey standing there, watching the ship pull out of the harbour. Stanley felt a great swell of disappointment. He had genuinely thought that Grey might accept Uncle Jack's offer and join the crew. But then again, Stanley really didn't *know* Grey. It wasn't like they were friends or anything. He looked back at Uncle Jack, who met his eye and shrugged; he had clearly guessed what Stanley was thinking. Returning his gaze to the harbour, Stanley was not surprised to see that Grey had gone.

"Oh well," he muttered to himself.

"Whoa! Look at *that* guy!" Alabaster exclaimed.

"What's he doing?" said Nell.

Stanley joined the two of them at the starboard beam. "What's going on?" he asked.

But before they could answer, he saw what they were looking at: someone was running swiftly along the pier, catching up with the departing Ogopogo.

It was Grey.

"*Grey!*" Stanley shouted.

Grey looked up briefly, then seemed to speed up, bowing his head in concentration.

"He doesn't look grey to me," commented Alabaster.

"Do you know him, Stanley?" Nell inquired.

"Yeah, sort of," said Stanley distractedly as Grey sped closer and closer.

The Ogopogo cleared pier three-fort-one completely, but Grey was still a good thirty yards away.

"He's not gonna make it!" said Stanley desperately. "Uncle Jack, stop the ship!"

"Eh? Stop the ship, Stanley? What's up?"

Stanley didn't answer. Instead, he watched as Grey raced to the end of the pier, and, without hesitating for even a fraction of a second, took a flying leap off the edge. Stanley, Alabaster, and Nell gasped in unison as Grey cleared the twenty-foot gap between the pier and the Ogopogo, to land roughly on the forecastle deck. Nell and Alabaster stepped back cautiously as Grey stood up and flexed his limbs.

"Grey!" said Stanley happily, rushing forward with the intention of hugging him. At the last moment, though, he reflected that Grey was probably not the type to accept hugs, and so stopped short and beamed up at him.

"Stanley," said Grey flatly, as if unaware that he had just made a spectacular entrance.

Stanley heard Uncle Jack order Diego to take the wheel, followed by the uneven *clunk* of the old man's wooden leg as he came over to join them.

"Welcome aboard," said Uncle Jack to Grey, holding out his right hand. Grey glared down at the outstretched appendage, and after a moment's pause, reached out and shook hands with Uncle Jack.

"Right," said Uncle Jack briskly, "Now, am I correct in assumin' that ya wish to join me crew?" Grey glared at Uncle Jack for another moment's pause, then inclined his head ever so slightly. "Great!" said Uncle Jack. "Yeh'll be workin' to earn yer keep, o' course. Ever sailed before?"

Grey shook his head.

"No problem," said Uncle Jack cheerfully. "We'll show ya the ropes, so to speak. Welcome aboard, crewman Grey." He stood up straight and saluted. Grey stood there and stared. "Ya salute and say *yes sir* when the captain addresses ya formally," said Uncle Jack, gazing steadily up at Grey. Grey scowled more darkly than before, but then, instead of seizing Uncle Jack and heaving him overboard, straightened his posture and placed his right hand against his temple.

"Yes sir," he said in a surprisingly respectful tone. Stanley's mouth dropped open. Alabaster and Nell looked on uncertainly.

"At ease," said Uncle Jack, smiling. "We're just a small crew with a small ship, so we're pretty relaxed 'round here, ain't we, mates?" He looked hopefully at the children.

"Huh? Oh, oh yeah, nothing to it," Stanley said helpfully, elbowing Alabaster in the ribs.

"Yeah!" said Alabaster brightly, "Uncle Jack's the best captain ever!" His smile faltered slightly, as Grey graced him with a ferocious scowl. Nell remained silent, eyeing Grey apprehensively.

"A'right, crewman Grey," said Uncle Jack, looking at Grey appraisingly, "I think the first order o' business is to get ya some decent clothes. Benjamin! C'mere, will ya?" Benjamin appeared from behind the main cabin and came over to where Uncle Jack was standing. "Benjamin," said Uncle Jack, "would ya mind if our new friend Grey, here, borrowed some o' yer spare clothes? I wouldn't ask, but, well, yer the only fellah 'round here who looks about his size."

Benjamin glanced at Grey, then gave a good-natured nod and headed for the stairs. Grey followed wordlessly.

"Right," said Uncle Jack, turning now to Stanley, "Laddie, I'm afraid I've had to make a very important decision, an' ya may not like it." Stanley felt his insides squirm uncomfortably. "As captain o' this ship," Uncle Jack continued, "I always have to keep the best interests o' me crew in mind. That's why I'm afraid I'm gonna have to—"

He paused, and Stanley leaned forward unintentionally.

"Insist that ya take a bath!" Uncle Jack finished, with a short chuckle.

"A … bath?" said Stanley.

"'Fraid so, lad," said Uncle Jack, "Ya stink to high heaven! I can't, in good conscience, subject me crew to such an offensive odour!"

*   *   *   *

Stanley had never thought that a bath could feel so good. A large, round wooden basin had been filled with warm water and placed behind the cabin, with some bed sheets hung around it for privacy. He sat in the basin and scrubbed and scrubbed until at last, he felt reasonably clean. The water had turned a nauseating green from the siren slime, and he was glad to see that the beastly stuff washed off with soap and water.

Nell had retrieved some fresh clothes for him, and as he toweled himself dry, he looked down at the filthy, slime-soaked shirt and pants he'd been wearing in the sewers.

"Won't be wearing these again," he muttered, but then something caught his eye. The back of his shirt (which had once been one of his best) had a large horizontal rip in it from where the siren had attacked him. Unsettlingly, a dark, brownish stain ran several inches down the back of the shirt, as if it had been soaked with blood. Almost reflexively, Stanley reached back and ran his fingers over the area between his shoulders. He distinctly remembered searing pain in exactly that area, the siren having taken a swipe at him with a clawed limb.

But Grey had said that there was no wound, and it seemed he'd been right; there wasn't so much as a scratch on Stanley's back, as far as he could tell.

Where, then, had the blood stain on his shirt come from? The only possible explanation he could think of, was that the blood had come from the siren, and splattered on him when Uncle Jack shot it. Stanley shuddered at the violent image, then tossed the shirt aside and started to put on his clean clothes. Just as he was pulling up his jeans, though, he remembered something Alabaster had said the day before:

You're like Wolverine, Stanley!

Could it be true? *Had* the siren injured him, sliced a deep cut across his back? Had the cut bled profusely for a few seconds, then miraculously healed itself? Could it be that he, Stanley Brambles, possessed superhuman healing powers?

Don't be ridiculous, said a reproving voice in his head. *You know perfectly well that the siren didn't cut you. You imagined the pain, and ripped your shirt when you fell.*

That had to be it, Stanley thought resolutely, buckling his belt and picking up his filthy shirt and pants, *No one has that kind of ability*, especially *not me*.

*   *   *   *

The Ogopogo sped swiftly away from Ethelia, and before long, all traces of the mainland had disappeared over the eastern horizon. It was now half past twelve, and the crew members were seated on the warm, sunny deck, enjoying a lunch of grilled prism fish.

"Diego, take it easy, mate!" said Uncle Jack heartily as Diego consumed the last of his second fish and started on a third, "Yer gonna make yerself sick!"

"I can't help it, amigo!" said Diego thickly through a mouthful of fish. "It's amazing what three months of prison rations'll do to a man's appetite!" Diego already looked much healthier than he had back at the Imperial Palace, mainly because he'd had a bath and a change of clothes, as well as a shave and haircut. His dark hair, which had been greasy and stringy, was now clean, trimmed, and tied back in a short ponytail. His face, which had been grimy and covered with a scraggly growth of beard, was now clean and smooth, and sported a neat, pointed goatee. He really was a handsome fellow, his features chiseled but friendly, his face that of a man who loved to laugh.

"I like him," Alabaster whispered to Stanley. "He's cool, like a rock star, or something." Stanley agreed. Diego *was* cool.

"What d'*you* think, Nell?" he whispered to Nell, who was staring very intently at Diego.

"Huh? What?" she said, starting slightly and looking around as if she'd been dreaming.

"*What do you think of Diego?*" Stanley repeated.

"Oh?" she said, going a bit pink, "Why do you ask?"

"Uh, just wondering," said Stanley, slightly confused.

"Oh. Well, he's alright," said Nell, and then she became very interested in her meal, which she hadn't touched yet.

"Mr. Diego?" said Alabaster, in the tone of someone addressing a famous actor, "how old are you?"

"Mr. Lancaster!" squawked Pericles, "It is impolite to ask a gentleman his age!" But Uncle Jack and Diego were laughing.

"Yeh can always count on Alabaster to get right to the point," said Uncle Jack, clapping Diego on the shoulder.

"Well that's a quality I can admire," said Diego, grinning and raising his water glass. "I'm one hundred and five years old."

"But you look so young!" Nell blurted out, and then clamped her hands over her mouth, blushing a deep scarlet.

"Gracias," said Diego, ignoring Nell's obvious mortification, "You're too kind, Nell."

Stanley stared at Diego. The man didn't look a day over thirty.

"Mr. Diego," said Alabaster, "do you use *Just For Gents*, the hair colouring system designed specifically for a man?"

"Alabaster, *shut up!*" said Stanley.

"*What?*" said Alabaster, "Nine out of ten barbers can't tell the difference!"

Diego smiled. "No, Alabaster, this is my natural hair colour. The reason I look like this, is … well, something happened to me while I was in prison …"

"Diego," said Pericles, "you don't have to—"

"It's alright," said Diego, "I don't even remember it, really … I was taken to a strange room filled with all sorts of odd equipment … and the next thing I knew, I was back in my cell, and I looked like I was fifty again."

"You don't *look* fifty," said Alabaster.

"Don't forget, folks 'round here don't age the way they do where you come from," said Uncle Jack, addressing the three children. "'Round here, fifty, isn't even middle age. It sure was a surprise to see me old friend lookin' like *this* when I busted open his cell!"

"I was surprised by you, too, amigo," said Diego. "You look a little rough for a hundred and ten."

"A hundred an' *eight*," Uncle Jack corrected. "I may look like a coot, but I'm as spry as ever, right mates?"

"Yeah!" said Stanley and Alabaster in unison.

As Diego, Uncle Jack, and Pericles went on chatting, Stanley looked over at Grey, who was sitting cross-legged in front of his untouched plate, looking morose.

"Aren't you hungry, Grey?" Stanley asked tentatively.

"No," said Grey, staring fiercely at nothing in particular.

"Oh, well Benjamin could probably just save it for—"

"Tell him not to bother," Grey interrupted, standing up suddenly, and without another word, he left the group and disappeared down the stairs to the hold.

"What was that all about?" Nell asked Stanley.

"Got me," said Stanley, shrugging.

"Really!" said Pericles indignantly, "How very rude. Imagine, leaving the table halfway through a meal, without a single word of apology!"

"We're not exactly at a table, Pericles," Diego said fairly.

"Oh, you know what I mean!" spluttered the parrot. "There are certain rules of etiquette that should not be ignored under any circumstances! Why—"

As Pericles continued to rant, Stanley, Nell, and Alabaster put their heads together.

"Why'd he leave, Stanley?" asked Alabaster.

"I dunno, there was no reason—"

"He seemed angry about something," said Nell.

"He always seems angry about something," said Stanley. "Anyway, I only just met him, and he's not really the talkative type, so … oh, who knows, maybe fish offend him."

The meal ended, and once again the Ogopogo was zipping west across the open sea. "Now we've got a decent-sized crew," said Uncle Jack, as Benjamin stepped up for a turn at the wheel. "We'll be able to rotate helm shifts so's we don't hafta stop at night—we can keep sailin' 'round the clock."

This sounded good to Stanley. At some point, Chamberlain and the masked man were bound to find out that he, Uncle Jack, Benjamin, and Diego were not locked up in a cell, and that the Ogopogo was no longer moored at pier three-forty-one. Having someone at the helm day and night would cut their travel time in half, and give them a decent head start for when Chamberlain finally decided to come after them. He felt his stomach drop, though, as he remembered that the masked man could fly.

Oh well, he thought to himself, *they'll have to find us before they can catch us, and it's not like they know where we're going.* Deciding that worrying was pointless right now, he pushed the thoughts out of his mind and joined Alabaster and Nell for a game of Monopoly.

*   *   *   *

On his way to bed that night, Stanley was surprised and pleased to see Uncle Jack showing Grey how to steer the ship. Grey was either not listening to a word Uncle Jack was saying, or else he understood so completely that he didn't even have to nod his head.

"Just hold this course," said Uncle Jack, indicating the ship's compass, "an' call me if there's any trouble."

Wordlessly, Grey took the wheel, and Uncle Jack, apparently satisfied, headed off to his cabin for the night. There came the sound of a door opening and closing, and Diego appeared from around behind the cabin; he'd been in the bathroom doing his evening business.

"Hola, Stanley," he said cheerfully, when he noticed Stanley standing by the cabin door.

"Hi," said Stanley as Diego passed by.

"Oh, that's right, I was meaning to have a word with you," said Diego, snapping his fingers and turning back around.

"Oh," said Stanley, slightly surprised, "Er, what about?"

"Step over here," said Diego, leading the way along the side of the cabin and stopping to lean against the ship's railing. Lowering his voice, he said, "So you were in a prison cell with Grey?"

"Er, yeah," said Stanley, lowering his voice as well. "For a little bit, but then I got out."

Diego *hmmed*. "And did you speak with him?"

"Only a little," said Stanley, trying to remember what Grey had said to him. "Nothing too interesting."

"Did he tell you anything about himself?"

"No, not really. Just his name, pretty much. Er, do you know anything about him? Did you hear anything when you were in prison?"

"Rumours," said Diego, looking up at the moons. "The guards talked about a dangerous prisoner in a maximum security cell, and, of course, all the other inmates—the guys who'd been in there a long time—all had their own stories."

"Stories?"

"Yeah, about what he supposedly did to get locked up in a maximum security cell."

"What did they say?" asked Stanley, his curiosity getting the better of him. Diego looked at him for a moment, then looked out to sea.

"I'd rather not repeat any of it. It was probably all lies, anyway, just a bunch of idiots trying to get attention."

"I got the feeling he really didn't belong there," said Stanley. "Like me. Like he just got put in there for no good reason."

"What makes you think that?"

"I—er—I dunno—just the way he talks and acts and stuff. It's hard to describe." He glanced over at Diego. "Do *you* think he's dangerous?"

Diego sighed. "I dunno, amigo. He hasn't lain a finger on you or any of us, and it's not like he didn't have the chance to do us all in. He could've finished us off in the sewers and got out of there scott free."

"But he helped us," said Stanley, smiling to himself. "He saved us from those knights, and kept us away from whatever that weird treasure was, and helped me when I—"

"Got attacked by the lurker. Or siren, or whatever it was. He led us right to you, found you in seconds."

Stanley nodded. How could Grey be a dangerous criminal? Criminals and murderers didn't show concern for people they hardly knew. And now, here he was on the Ogopogo, working as a member of the crew.

"And," said Diego, "your uncle seems to trust him, and Jack Lee is an excellent judge of character."

"Do *you* trust him?" asked Stanley. "Do *you* trust Grey?"

Diego was silent for a moment. "Honestly, Stanley, I don't. Not completely, anyway. Unlike your uncle, I have trouble giving people the benefit of the doubt. My trust in a person starts at the bottom—it needs time to build itself up. And," he said, turning now to look at Stanley, "I don't know if I should bring this up, but … there are certain similarities between him and someone else we know."

Stanley thought about that one for a moment. Grey was unlike *anyone* he knew. He was dark and mysterious, maybe not even human, and he was secretive and shadowy, and …

Shadowy. An image flashed through Stanley's mind, an image of a robe the colour of damp ashes, and a blank, white mask … an image of a shadow creeping across the floor as if it were liquid, creeping up the body of a man in a naval uniform, creeping up to strangle him …

"The masked man," Stanley breathed.

Diego nodded grimly. "I've heard stories about *him*, too, seen firsthand what he's capable of."

"Me, too," said Stanley nervously, scanning the night sky for any trace of a dark, winged shape. "Pericles said he's probably a powerful sorcerer."

"Pericles is probably right," said Diego. "A *dark* sorcerer. The guys unlucky enough to have had a personal 'meeting' with him, called him the shadow man. He can manipulate darkness, make shadows do his bidding, even in broad daylight."

Stanley shuddered. "Yeah, I've seen some of the things he can do. Did *you* meet him before?"

"Yes," said Diego heavily, "a few times."

A thought crossed Stanley's mind. "Was he the one who made you … younger?"

Diego shook his head. "I'd rather not talk about it."

Stanley nodded understandingly; any experience Diego had had involving the masked man must have been horrible. "Is it ... is it true?" he asked. "Is *he* really the new king? Has he really taken over the Empire?"

"Looks that way," sighed Diego. "Otherwise, he wouldn't be treating Chamberlain like a rag doll. Believe me, no one messes with Chamberlain, unless they're *in charge*."

"But ... so, does this mean that Grey is a sorcerer, too?" said Stanley. "I mean, I don't know if he can do all the things the masked man can, but if he *can*, what does it mean?"

"I honestly don't know," said Diego. "They might have nothing to do with each other, but if they *do* ..." He glanced meaningfully at Stanley, then smiled and shook his head. "Look, don't base your opinion on what I've told you. I mean, Grey has already proven that he's able and willing to look out for us—for *you*, Stanley. It's like you two have some kind of connection or something ... But listen, a lifetime as a pirate has taught me that you can't judge someone by what others say; you have to figure people out for yourself. And all I'm saying is that I wouldn't want Grey as my enemy."

He sighed, took a last look at the moons, then said, "Well, I dunno 'bout you, but I'm in need of some serious sleep. Buenos noches, Stanley."

Stanley watched him cross the deck and descend the steps to the hold without looking at or speaking to Grey. Sighing, Stanley looked over at Grey, who was still at the helm. He'd barely moved since he'd first taken the wheel, and had given no indication that he'd seen Diego pass by. Could Grey really be a dark sorcerer? Was he evil and malevolent like the masked man? Somehow, Stanley didn't think so. He found it hard to imagine Grey hurting people just because he could, or because he enjoyed it. No, Grey didn't seem the type, and Stanley couldn't shake the feeling—the feeling he'd had since he'd first met Grey—that behind the fierce, menacing exterior was something more, not something evil or sadistic, but something good and decent.

He shook his head. He had very little to back all this up with, having known Grey for only a day or so, and, he realized, he was very, very tired. It had been, after all, a harrowing day. With one last glance at Grey, Stanley opened the cabin door and went in.

The Ogopogo sailed on all through the night, with Grey at the helm.

CHAPTER TWENTY:
THE MEMORY MIRROR

Stanley awoke very early the next morning. It was just before five o'clock, and the first rays of the rising sun were reflecting off the ocean, and shining obnoxiously through the porthole beside his bunk, right into his face. Opening his eyes blearily, he noted that he had forgotten to close the curtains last night. "Uurrg," he groaned, forcing his eyes closed and rolling over.

But the damage had been done. The more Stanley tried to go back to sleep, the more awake he became, until finally, he sat up in his bunk and reluctantly prepared to face the coming day. He hopped out of bed and dressed quietly, taking care not to disturb Alabaster and Nell, who were still sleeping peacefully. He pulled on a sweatshirt to guard against the early morning chill, and stepped out onto the Ogopogo's deck.

The morning was brisk and breezy, and Stanley shivered as he closed the cabin's door behind him. The three moons were still dimly visible high above, as they fought a losing battle for control of the sky against the steadily rising sun. Golden rays of light shot across the water, shimmering and dancing on the surface, making Stanley squint against the glare.

It was very peaceful here on deck, in the quiet of the morning, with no company save for the blowing wind and the rolling waves, and the soft creaking of the ship. And, of course, Grey, who was still at the wheel.

"Grey!" said Stanley, heading over to the helm.

"Stanley," said Grey, refusing to surprise Stanley with a hello or a good morning.

"Have you been up all night steering the ship?" Stanley asked.

"Yes."

"Aren't you tired?"

"No."

"But you haven't slept since yesterday morning!"

"That's right."

"You *do* sleep, though, right?"

"Sometimes. If there's nothing else to do."

"But you don't *have* to?"

"No."

"So you stay up all day, all night, twenty-four hours a day?"

"Yes."

"Do you ever get lonely?"

"What?"

"Do you ever get lonely? Like, in the middle of the night, when everyone else is asleep and you're all by yourself?"

There was a long pause, which Stanley found a bit uncomfortable. Finally, Grey spoke again, but instead of answering Stanley's question, he said,

"Why are you up so early?"

It wasn't a harsh or accusatory question, as might be expected from him; it was just a question.

"Oh, er," said Stanley, slightly taken aback. He was, after all, used to asking questions and having Grey reply brusquely, not the other way around. "I just … woke up and couldn't get back to sleep."

"Mmm," said Grey.

"The sun was shining right in my face," Stanley continued, trying to keep the conversation going. The attempt seemed to have succeeded, for Grey turned his head slightly and looked askance at him.

"The sun bothers you, too?"

"Well, yeah, when I'm trying to sleep, and it's shining right in my face." Stanley looked up at Grey, who was once again staring forward. "It doesn't bother me once I'm up, though. Does it bother *you?*"

A pause. "Yes," said Grey.

"You're not supposed to look right at it, you know," said Stanley, not meaning to sound smart-alecky.

Grey shot him a ferocious scowl. "I know," he growled.

"Right," said Stanley quickly. "So, sunlight—does it hurt your skin?"

"No," said Grey. "My eyes."

"Ohh, your *eyes*," said Stanley. "Does it hurt them badly?"

Grey shrugged. "It's nothing I can't handle."

"But if you're uncomfortable—"

"*It's nothing I can't handle.*"

Stanley was silent for a moment, which seemed to suit Grey just fine. This might explain why Grey left lunch early yesterday and retreated to the hold: he'd had enough sunlight, and his eyes were hurting. An idea sprang into Stanley's mind.

"I'll be right back," he said to Grey, who didn't so much as flinch at the words. Retreating to the cabin, Stanley flung open the door and crept inside. As quietly as he could, he opened his suitcase and began to rummage around inside it. "Aha!" he said out loud, as he drew forth what he'd been looking for.

"Nurrph Murrph," murmured Alabaster from behind his bunk screen, before letting out a very loud fart.

Putting a hand over his mouth to keep from laughing, Stanley crept stealthily out of the room, closed the door behind him, and rejoined Grey by the wheel. "Here!" he said to Grey, holding up a small, black, oval-shaped case.

Grey glared at him. "What is it?" he asked sharply. Stanley popped open the case and brought out the contents.

"Sunglasses!" he said, displaying them as if he were in a commercial. "People wear them to protect their eyes from the sun—so they don't have to go around squinting all the time."

"Why are you giving them to me?"

"Well, I never really wear them. They were my Dad's, but he gave them to me when he bought a new pair. They're a bit too big for my head, but they'd probably fit you."

Grey glared at the sunglasses for a moment, then slowly reached out and took them daintily from Stanley's had.

"Dad said they're really good," said Stanley, as Grey examined the sunglasses closely. "Total U.V. protection, and they come with a lifetime warranty."

Grey paused in his examination, then put the sunglasses on. He peered around him, as if gauging the effect. It was anybody's guess how the glasses stayed put on his earless, noseless head, but stay put they did, and they didn't look half bad.

Stanley watched hopefully as Grey stared right at the rising sun. Turning back to him, Grey said,

"Not bad," and Stanley was convinced that had Grey's mouth been visible, he would have been smiling. Slightly.

"Do they help?" asked Stanley.

"Yes," said Grey, and then he did something quite unexpected: he said, "Thank you."

"No problem," said Stanley, grinning broadly.

Grey turned his gaze back to the horizon, and Stanley stayed beside him, watching the sunrise.

✷   ✷   ✷   ✷

Eventually, the rest of the Ogopogo's crew awoke and began to stir. Pericles was the first one up after Stanley, although he woke up a full hour after the sun had established its presence in the sky. The parrot fluttered down from the crow's nest and alighted on Stanley's shoulder, before bidding him a very good morning, and commending Grey on his nine-hour helm shift.

"That's exactly the kind of dedication we need," said Pericles pompously, as if he himself had asked Grey to join the crew. Grey glanced once at Pericles, but otherwise, didn't seem to be paying any attention as the parrot chattered away.

Uncle Jack, Alabaster, Nell, Benjamin, and Diego were up soon after, and all were duly impressed with Grey. Uncle Jack suggested that Grey take a break, and soon they were all seated in a circle on the deck, enjoying a hearty breakfast of moonfish and porridge. Stanley was sitting beside Grey, who was once again refusing to touch his food. So no one else could hear, Stanley lowered his voice and whispered,

"*Why aren't you eating anything?*"

"I don't need to eat," answered Grey, speaking at a normal volume, so that everyone took notice.

"You don't need to eat?" said Alabaster through a mouthful of porridge. "That's weird."

"Ahh, but *can* ya eat?" asked Uncle Jack, brandishing a spoon at Grey. "Can ya taste food, chew, swallow, digest it?"

"Yes," said Grey.

"Well then go ahead!" said Uncle Jack, "Ya might like it!"

"It doesn't matter if I like it," said Grey harshly, "it's a waste of resources."

"Now look here," said Uncle Jack reprovingly, "Benjamin, here went to a lot o' trouble to prepare this food, an' it's an insult to him, as a cook, if ya turn yer nose up at it."

Stanley looked at Grey's face, not doubting that behind the dark lenses of his sunglasses, he was scowling very fiercely, indeed.

"If I have to, I'll order ya to eat that food," said Uncle Jack evenly, "but I'd rather ya did it on yer own."

Grey glanced briefly at Stanley, who nodded encouragingly. With undisguised reluctance, Grey picked up his plate and bowl. As if by magic, a horizontal line appeared on his face an inch or two above his chin, and split apart to reveal his impressive set of jaws, fully equipped with their compliment of sharp, pointed teeth. Grey tipped his entire breakfast into his cavernous maw, chewed noisily, then swallowed. The mouth closed and vanished from his face, leaving it as flat and blank as ever.

The children were staring wide-eyed at Grey, as were Diego, Pericles, and Benjamin. Uncle Jack, however, had a benign expression on his face, as if this sort of thing happened all the time.

"Well?" he said, as Grey set down his dishes, "What'd ya think?"

Grey leaned his head back slightly, as if in thought, then said, "Very tasty."

"There ya go!" said Uncle Jack happily, "A compliment to the chef! Eatin' is an important part o' life, Mr. Grey, whether or not ya think ya have to. Yeh should really try it again sometime." Grey said nothing more, but Uncle Jack seemed satisfied.

"Okay, mates," he said, once everyone had finished their breakfasts, "I got somethin' to say." He stood up and clasped his hands behind his back. "Today, we embark on the last leg of our journey. It's a long leg, but it should be pretty easy—just a lot o' sailin'. We've all been through a lot on this mission, an' I gotta say that I ain't seen so brave an' stout-hearted a crew in many a year. Each an' every one o' ye have shown me that the true pirate spirit is still alive an' well in this world, an' that gives me great hope for the future.

"Now, ye all know what our ultimate goal is: to find the treasure 'fore anyone else does, an' for those o' ya who don't know yet, we got bigger problems than Chamberlain."

"Bigger than Chamberlain?" said Pericles, aghast. "Whatever do you mean?"

"I mean," said Uncle Jack gravely, "that we got a new enemy."

Alabaster and Nell glanced over at Stanley. He hadn't yet told them the full account of his adventures in the city.

"There's this new big shot on the scene," Uncle Jack continued, "an' he's runnin' the show, rulin' the Empire, usin' Chamberlain as his mouthpiece, his puppet."

"Well I never!" squawked Pericles. "Who is it?"

"Remember that mask-wearin' fellah who paid us a visit the other day?"

"Certainly, he ... one moment, you don't mean—"

"I *do* mean," said Uncle Jack. "That spooky sorcerer has made himself ruler o' the Empire, an' he's after the treasure, too."

"You mean that guy with the wings?" said Alabaster.

"Aye," said Uncle Jack. "Now Chamberlain, we can fight, but a powerful dark sorcerer ... well, let's just say we don't want him to catch up with us."

"This is terrible news!" wailed Pericles. "The entire Imperial Navy will be after us, with that mad magician leading the way!"

"Wait!" said Stanley, suddenly remembering something. "Maybe the masked man *won't* come after us."

"Eh?" said Pericles, "Why do you say that?"

"Well, it sounded to me like he doesn't want people to know he exists. Everyone thinks Chamberlain is in charge, even the marines. It's like he's been very careful not to reveal himself."

"What about when he landed on the deck in broad daylight?" said Nell.

"That might have been a huge risk," said Stanley, thinking quickly about all the things he'd heard the masked man say. "He thinks I'm important somehow, like I'm ... I dunno, dangerous or something. He'd planned to get rid of me that day, but something happened, and he didn't, and now he's confused ... I think."

"So you think that getting rid of you was so important to him, that he'd risk exposing himself?" asked Diego.

"Yeah," said Stanley. "I mean, it's not like there was anyone else around."

"We were on the outskirts of Ethelia," Uncle Jack mused. "Maybe he saw that as 'is last chance."

"Uh-oh!" said Alabaster, making them all jump. "We're out in the middle of nowhere right now! He could come swooping down at any moment and ... and ..." he looked fearfully at Stanley.

"He doesn't want to kill me *anymore*," said Stanley, as if it made everything alright.

"Aye, he coulda done yeh in back in the throne room," said Uncle Jack. "Nah, I don't think he'll be flyin' out to meet us. It's the treasure he wants, and he'll need ships if he hopes to cart it away."

"And if he needs ships, he'll need Chamberlain," said Diego.

"Yeah!" said Stanley, "He kept making fun of Chamberlain, and saying what a bad servant he was, but he's still got him doing jobs for him, and stuff. Uh, that's what it sounded like, anyway."

"Okay, this sounds like good news," said Uncle Jack. "Mr. Mask'll need the strength o' the navy, and for that, he'll need Chamberlain. With any luck, he'll send Chamberlain after us, an' stay nice an' comfy on his cushy throne."

Everyone seemed to feel that this sounded just about right.

"Okay then," said Uncle Jack, "the plan, then, is to get to the treasure as fast as we can, which, I think, is not gonna be too tough. But first," he said, "Diego, I think it's time."

Diego nodded solemnly and stood up. "I hid my half where no one would think to look for it—right on this very ship."

Wondering what Diego was talking about, Stanley watched him as he knelt down on the deck, apparently searching for something.

"Diego!" said Uncle Jack, "Ya don't mean—"

He was interrupted by Diego saying "Aha!" and tugging on one of the deck planks. Beneath the plank was a bundle of rags, which Diego carefully removed from its hiding place. "I told you, amigo," he said to Uncle Jack, "that as long as you had your ship, we'd be able to reach the spot where I hid my half." He unwrapped the bundle and held up what looked like a letter 'C' carved out of stone, with strange symbols etched into it.

"Diego, as I live an' breathe!" exclaimed Uncle Jack, "Ya hid it on the Ogopogo! It was right here all the time!"

"In the one place I knew it would be safe, amigo," said Diego, smiling. "With *you.*"

"An' here I was thinkin' we'd have to sail the seven seas to find the ruddy thing!" said Uncle Jack happily.

"I *told* you we wouldn't have to go far," said Diego.

"Well, ye were right about that," said Uncle Jack. "I'll be back in a sec." He made his way down to the hold, and returned promptly with a stone letter 'C' exactly like the one Diego held.

"Quite brilliant, really," commented Pericles.

"What is it, Pericles?" Stanley asked the parrot.

"Why, the Memory Mirror, of course!"

Stanley watched as Diego gave Uncle Jack his stone 'C'. The old man turned the two pieces towards eachother, then brought them together to form a stone circle. Instantly a bright white light flared from the circle, and when it faded seconds later, the halves were united as one, as if they'd been cemented together.

"This's the Memory Mirror," said Uncle Jack, holding the artifact up for all to see. There was much oo-ing and ahh-ing, particularly from the children, who got up and came forward for a closer look.

"How beautiful," said Nell, as she gazed, bright-eyed at the mirror. It was indeed beautiful. The markings etched into the stone were now glowing with a soft, blue light, and it looked as though a sheet of glass had appeared between the two halves. Nell reached out and touched the glass, and let out a surprised "Oh!" as the surface rippled as if made of water, letting out a pleasant humming sound. Images flashed across the watery glass, images of people, places, books …

"That's my Mom and Dad!" Nell squealed excitedly, pointing at the mirror.

"Neat, huh?" said Uncle Jack. "Remember when Pericles n' I told ya 'bout the Memory Mirror?"

Stanley watched as a new image swam into view in the mirror: an image of a dark room with a fireplace, filled with comfy arm chairs, and people sitting on them.

"That's us!" said Alabaster, "That's when Uncle Jack told us his story!"

"Aye," said Uncle Jack. "Anyone who looks into the mirror sees their own memories. If yeh were patient enough, yeh could prob'ly watch yer whole life on this thing."

"Why did it hum when I touched it?" asked Nell, still staring raptly at the images flashing by in the mirror.

"That means you activated it," said Diego. "You touch it to get it to show you your memories."

"And if *you* touch the mirror," said Stanley, "it'll show you the map to the treasure?"

"Pretty much," said Uncle Jack. "Speakin' o' which, I guess we'd better do just that. Diego, ya ready?"

"Ready, amigo."

Uncle Jack held the mirror up between himself and Diego, and touched the magical glass, making it hum in a much deeper tone than it had for Nell. Diego touched the mirror, too, and as the rippling effect died down, an image swam into view on the glassy surface.

"There's the map!" said Alabaster. The children crowded closer still around Diego and Uncle Jack, peering intently into the mirror. Sure enough, a map of the world had appeared on the glass. It was very thorough, with land masses drawn in great detail, and the names of towns and cities clearly printed in tiny black letters. A compass at the bottom right hand side indicated that the top of the map was north. A large black star at the westernmost edge of the northern land mass was labeled *Ethelia*, and a thin, dotted line ran west of the star for about an inch, leading out to sea.

"That line is the path to the treasure!" said Diego excitedly.

"But that can't be right," said Pericles, "It can't be that close to Ethelia."

"It ain't," said Uncle Jack. "There's no 'X'. 'X' marks the spot, remember?"

The group suddenly let out a collective gasp, as the tiny dotted line grew another half inch and turned at an acute angle towards the southwestern part of the map. A tiny '30' appeared just above the angle.

"The map draws itself *as we go!*" said Diego. "It draws itself so no one can see where the treasure is, till we get to it!"

"An' it tells us what course adjustments we have to make," said Uncle Jack. "Look, we gotta head thirty degrees southwest."

"So you made the map," said Stanley, "but you don't remember anything about it?"

"Right on, laddie," said Uncle Jack. "We stored our memories of it in the mirror, an' took 'em out of our brains, so to speak."

"Is it dangerous?" asked Nell. "I remember you told us about someone who used it to brainwash people."

"Aye, very dangerous in the wrong hands," said Uncle Jack, "but no problem if ya know what yer doin'. You kids can look at it, an' hold it if ya want, but just don't go pokin' at these glowin' runes." He indicated the glowing blue symbols etched into the stone. "They're like control buttons, ya see."

"Uh, maybe we'll just leave it alone," said Stanley, feeling that it would be safest to leave the magical artifacts to those who knew how to use them.

"That's prob'ly for the best," said Uncle Jack, seeing the wisdom of Stanley's words. "I'll put this on the compass box, so's whoever's at the helm can keep an eye on it." He walked over to the compass box and placed the Memory Mirror on top of it, then stepped behind the wheel. "I'll take the helm for now. Adjustin' course, thirty degrees southwest. Pericles, full power to the wind crystal, if you please."

The ship turned smoothly, and before long, was slicing swiftly through the waves on her new course, her crew in very high spirits.

Memories ...

That night, on his way back to bed after getting a drink from the water barrel, Stanley noticed Uncle Jack standing over by the compass box. The old man was holding the Memory Mirror, gazing at it intently. After some time, he sighed heavily and put the Mirror back on the compass box. Not wanting Uncle Jack to think he was spying, Stanley crept quietly back down to the hold and hid under the stairs until his uncle had passed by and retired to his cabin, at which point he deemed it safe to return to the main deck. He was passing by the compass box, wondering who was going to take over helm duty tonight, when a small flash of light from the Memory Mirror caught his eye.

Curious, Stanley crept over to the compass box and picked up the Mirror. What had Uncle Jack been looking at, anyway? He held the mirror up to his face, trying to make sense of the dark images swirling on the magical glass. Suddenly, a bright orange-gold light flared up from the depths of the mirror. Stanley started with surprise, and his hand clenched involuntarily, causing him to accidentally press one of the mirror's glowing runes with his thumb.

There was a sudden rush of air, and he closed his eyes. There came a deep *thwum* sound from somewhere, and he felt as if he were being pulled forward. The feeling quickly passed, and the orange-gold light flared up again, far brighter than before. Opening his eyes, Stanley saw that he was now standing just inside an ornate iron gate, on a wide stone path which led up to a grand mansion.

The mansion was in flames.

It was late night, for the three moons of Terra were high in the sky, but the light cast by the fire seemed almost as bright as day to Stanley. Even at the far end of the drive, he could feel the heat of the flames.

Where am I? He wondered to himself. *And how did I get here? What's going on?* There was something odd about the scene—he felt vaguely detached, as if he were watching it on television.

He turned at the sound of approaching footsteps, to see a young man running towards him. The man stopped at the gate, breathing heavily and looking through the bars, his eyes wide with horror and disbelief.

This is his house, Stanley thought sadly, though he didn't know how he knew. Perhaps it was because there was something oddly familiar about him.

The young man seemed to suddenly come to his senses.

"NOOOOOOO!" he cried, throwing open the gate and racing past Stanley towards the burning house. "MOM! MEGHAN! EMMA!"

At the sound of more approaching footsteps, Stanley turned round again, this time to see a pair of figures approaching. One was rather stocky, and the other tall and slim, and even in this light, Stanley recognized him.

It was Diego Montigo, which could only make the first man …

"JACK!" cried Diego, catching up with the first man, "You don't want to go in there, amigo."

"MY FAMILY'S IN THERE!" roared the first man, turning to face Diego, and Stanley could see that yes, it *was* Uncle Jack, though an Uncle Jack of many years ago. His hair and beard were short and dark; he didn't look a day over thirty. Without another word, the young Uncle Jack took off towards the house.

"JACK, WAIT!" shouted the stocky man, but Uncle Jack paid him no heed. He reached the house, kicked in the door, and disappeared inside.

"Damn," Diego swore, "Come on, Bart, he may need our help."

"No, wait!" said the young Bartholomew Crane, "It's too dangerous!"

Just as he finished speaking, there came a loud sound of cracking wood, and part of the mansion's east wing caved in, heaving ash and cinders into the air.

"We've got to do something," said Diego, squaring his shoulders. "I'm going in."

Just at that moment, another tearing crack rang out, as the mansion's entry way fell in on itself in an avalanche of burning timbers. The upper floors were all ablaze, and sections of the roof began to collapse. Stanley felt ridiculously useless.

"*Go get the fire department!*" he shouted at Diego and Bart, but they couldn't seem to hear him.

There was a sudden crash of breaking glass as a chair came flying through one of the ground floor windows. The young Uncle Jack leapt through the breach carrying something on his shoulders, just as a gust of flame belched forth into the night air. He lay his burden on the ground some distance away, and Stanley could see that it was a person—a girl in her late twenties.

"Jack!" cried Bart, "Are you alright?" He and Diego ran to his side, followed closely by Stanley.

"I'm fine," said the young Uncle Jack, "but Meghan and my mother are still in there. I have to go back and find them!"

"You're not going anywhere, amigo," said Diego, "I'm sorry, but I can't let you go back in there."

If Uncle Jack had anything to say about this, it was drowned out by the thunderous sound of the house collapsing. The walls buckled briefly, with a horrid sound of straining wood, and then the entire roof simply fell down, crushing the floors beneath it. The house was reduced to nothing more than a fiery ruin.

The young Uncle Jack stared at the wreckage for a moment, and then fell to his knees and bellowed loud and long at the sky. Stanley could only stare with horrified fascination.

Presently there came a rustling in the nearby bushes, and several men appeared. They looked like Imperial Marines, but the man in the lead stood out.

It was Ezekiel Chamberlain. He looked a good deal younger than when Stanley had seen him last, and he wore no eye patch, but there was no mistaking his haughty gait, or the cold sneer on his face.

"Jackson," said Chamberlain, as Uncle Jack got to his feet, "just look at this horrible mess. I *told* you bad things happen to those who go against the Empire."

"Ezekiel," said Uncle Jack, his voice shaking with rage, "*you* did this?"

Chamberlain smirked. "Of course. I had to catch you somehow, and this was the only method I could think of. Frankly, I wasn't even sure it would work ... but here you are, just as I had hoped! I'm finally able to put an end to you, and your entire family line, to boot!"

The young Uncle Jack made a sound of depthless rage, and drew a pistol from his coat.

But Chamberlain had already drawn his own weapon. The report was loud, and it echoed hollowly in the night. The young Uncle Jack staggered backwards. Chamberlain turned to one of his marines and pointed to Diego and Bart. "If they move, kill them. I want to watch this."

His breath coming in short gasps, Uncle Jack struggled to stay on his feet. "Ezekiel," he growled, his voice shaking with pain and fury, "You.... you ... how could you ..." Tears were spilling from his eyes and running down his cheeks.

"Oh please," said Chamberlain, his men laughing in the background. "*How could I do such a thing*, is that what you're asking? Ha! I think we both know the answer to that."

"Y-yer a cold-blooded m-*murderer!*" gasped Uncle Jack.

Chamberlain grimaced hideously. "And *you* are an enemy of the Empire," he snarled, now pointing his pistol at Uncle Jack's head.

"THE EMPIRE IS EVIL!" roared Uncle Jack, dropping to his knees and clutching his chest.

Chamberlain laughed. "His Majesty the Emperor disagrees. Any last words, Lee?"

"Y-yeah," coughed Uncle Jack, before mumbling something under his breath.

"What was that?" said Chamberlain, sounding amused.

Uncle Jack looked up, his eyes blazing.

"You only got me in the shoulder, Zeke."

"What—" Chamberlain began, but was cut off by the report of Uncle Jack's pistol.

BANG!

Chamberlain turned his head slightly at the last possible second; the bullet merely grazed the bridge of his nose, but managed to remove most of his right eye before flying off into the night.

"EEEEEYAAAAAH!" Chamberlain screamed as he clapped a hand over his ruined eye and fell to his knees.

BANG! BANG!
BANG! BANG!

Four more shots suddenly rang out, and Chamberlain's men dropped to the ground like sacks of dirt. They had not been paying attention to Diego and Bart, who now had smoking guns in their hands.

Uncle Jack sprang immediately into action. He picked up his unconscious sister, took a final pained look at his ruined home, and ran for the gate, closely followed by Diego and Bart. Chamberlain managed to squeeze off three shots to see them on their way, but none found its mark. He shouted a very loud and very rude string of curses, then staggered to his feet, blood streaming down his face from behind his hand.

"*LEE!*" he roared, and he continued to fire at nothing until his pistol was empty.

The scene suddenly grew dark, the sounds faint and distant. Stanley strained to see and hear what was going on, but it was no use. A shimmering mist suddenly filled his field of vision, and he was once again aware of a strange rush of air, and the sensation of moving very quickly, backwards this time.

His eyes momentarily went out of focus, and when he was able to see again, he found that he was gazing at the glassy surface of the Memory Mirror.

"Stanley? Are ya back, laddie?"

"Huh?" Stanley blinked and shook his head. "Where ...?"

"Yer right here, on the Ogopogo."

Stanley turned round to see Uncle Jack—the Uncle Jack he knew—looking at him intently. "Uncle Jack," he said, looking from the Memory Mirror to his uncle, "I ... I just picked it up, and I saw ... I mean, I was ..."

"Yeh saw one o' me memories," Uncle Jack finished. "One o' the more ... *unpleasant* ones, if that's the right word."

"But I—I was—it's like I was actually there," said Stanley. He tried to recall the scene, but it seemed to be fading from his memory, like a dream.

"Aye, ya must've hit this rune," said Uncle Jack, pointing to the one that Stanley had accidentally pressed. "It lets you re-live memories, in a manner o' speakin'. Sort've puts you in 'em, and ... ah, well ... that's not exactly a memory I'd've wanted ya to see."

"I didn't mean to ... uh ..."

"No, no, yer not at fault, laddie," said Uncle Jack, raising his hands. "I shouldn'a left that memory right there fer all to see. That ain't a scene fer young eyes. D'you remember any of it?"

"Yeah, but ... it feels like a dream. I can't remember it all, but I saw you, as a young man, and a burning house ... and Chamberlain, too, and ... uh ..."

Uncle Jack nodded. "The house was my house, back in Rhedland. Burned to the ground that night, it did ... with me Ma an' me sis, Meghan still inside. It was a trap, ya see, set fer me by Chamberlain. I managed to save me younger sis, Emma—yer grandmother—but ..." He sighed. "Chamberlain's a ruthless man; it's because he's capable o' things like that, that I can't allow 'im to get hold of me treasure. He could do a lot worse than burn one house to the ground, if he got hold o' some o' the things we found."

Stanley stared sadly down at the deck boards. "I'm sorry, Uncle Jack."

The old man put an arm about his shoulders. "Bad things happen in this life, m'lad, no denyin' that. We just gotta go on livin' as best we can, an' try to make sure that the same stuff doesn't happen to others." He sighed again, then took the Memory Mirror from Stanley and placed it back on the compass box. "I'm sorry you had to see that, lad."

"It's okay," said Stanley, shrugging slightly.

Uncle Jack nodded. "Well, g'night, laddie."

"Goodnight, Uncle Jack," said Stanley. He stayed out on deck long into the night.

CHAPTER TWENTY-ONE: STORM AND SERPENT

A week went by, and the Ogopogo's crew began to get restless. Though there is often plenty to do on board a sailing ship, even one as easily run as the Ogopogo, filling the hours of inactivity can become a challenge. The ones having the most trouble coping with boredom were the children. It wasn't that they had nothing to do; the problem was finding something that the three of them could do as a group. The sport of exploration was severely limited on a ship the size of the Ogopogo, and poking around in every nook and cranny took all of forty minutes.

Stanley was more than content to while away the hours leaning on the forecastle railing, gazing off towards the horizon as if in a trance, but Alabaster and Nell couldn't do it for more than twenty minutes at a time.

Alabaster was always ready with his Monopoly game, but even Monopoly has a saturation point, as Stanley and Nell informed him after their hundredth game. Nell spent plenty of time working on the stove, which seemed to break down almost daily, but when she wasn't messing about with the machinery, she'd suggest that they spend a day reading quietly. The boys wouldn't have it, saying that they didn't want to spend their days cooped up in the cabin while the sun shone brightly outside. Nell fought back, saying that if they were going to make her stare at the ocean and play Monopoly till it lost all meaning, the least they could do was spend some time reading with her, a pastime which, she reminded them, could be enjoyed indoors or out. Stanley and Alabaster grudgingly accepted this rationale, and set to work reading the books Nell shoved in their faces: *The Hobbit* for Stanley, and *Watership Down* for Alabaster.

"When you're done, you can switch," Nell said brightly as she settled herself behind *Anne of Green Gables*.

One pastime upon which the three could agree, was listening to stories. Uncle Jack, Diego, and even Pericles were happy to regale the children with exciting tales of the sea, both true and fictional.

"… So we came upon this wee cargo ship, all alone, gettin' attacked by four or five o' these fish." Uncle Jack was telling the children about the time he saved Diego's ship, the *Tadpole*, from a school of armour fish. "They'd been rammin' the hull with those hard heads o' theirs, and the poor ol' girl was already half sunk! Well, we pulled our ship up alongside, hopin' to rescue as many hands as we could. That's when I noticed that a bunch o' the lads from the Tadpole were floatin' in the water—they'd fallen overboard, or somethin'.

"So what'd I do? I lowered one o' the life boats, grabbed a rifle, and went out to save those lads. I was lucky the fish didn't notice me 'till I had everyone on board. Imagine my surprise when I pulled the last man from the water, only to find that it was me good friend Diego! He was just as surprised as I was.

"Now, just as I was pullin' Diego on board, one o' the fish bumped the boat and sent me flyin'. I was under water for only a few seconds, and I felt somethin' tug at me leg. I looked down, and what'd I see but the fish, starin' right at me with his big ol' orange eyes. I got back into the boat easy enough, but when I tried to stand, I fell over, an' that's when I noticed that me leg was gone! That fiendish fish had bitten me leg clean off, right below the knee! I didn't have time to think about it, though, 'cause all of a sudden, the fish rears up outta the water, right in front o' me, roarin' like a hurricane. He was just about to have us all for lunch, when I levelled me rifle, and BLAM!"

He paused for effect. "It did the trick, that's for sure. The other fish fled, so we got back to our ship okay, an' we had fish for breakfast, lunch an' dinner for the next two days!"

"You *ate* it?" said Stanley.

"Oh, sure," said Uncle Jack. "Catchin' a big ol' sea monster usually meant a real treat for the crew."

"Did it … hurt when the fish bit your leg off?" asked Alabaster.

"Did it ever!" said Uncle Jack. "After I noticed it was gone, I howled, I can tell ya that. But I was in good hands. We had some fine surgeons on board the Nautilus, an' they patched me up. Gave me a wooden peg-leg—this very one, as a matter o' fact!" He reached down and tapped his wooden leg affectionately.

Stanley's favourite storyteller by far was Uncle Jack, but Diego was good, too, and Pericles, though a bit longwinded, kept a relentless pace and expertly conveyed mood and tone. Plus, he could do all of the characters' voices. Even Stanley was called upon to do some storytelling of his own; Alabaster and Nell wanted to know all about his adventure in the Palace, and insisted that he tell and re-tell every minute of it, until they could practically recite the whole thing themselves.

Stanley didn't mind; Alabaster and Nell were a good audience, and the tale came out easier with each telling. Even after the seventh time, Alabaster and Nell still gasped at all the appropriate places.

"That part in the sewers *still* freaks me out!" said Alabaster, who all but shook with horrified delight, as Stanley again described his encounter with the siren.

"Me too," said Stanley, smiling at Alabaster's reaction. He found that talking about the frightening experience over and over again was very therapeutic.

"It's so weird how the thing could change its voice," Alabaster went on, with fully disclosed interest. "I mean, how did it know to make itself sound like Nell?"

When Stanley had first mentioned that the voice calling to him in the sewers sounded just like Nell's, she had turned quite pink and become very quiet. Stanley still couldn't quite figure out why this was, but he suspected that she felt a bit odd about having a monster imitating her voice. He hoped she didn't feel that he was blaming her for the siren attack

"You know," Alabaster rambled on, "maybe sirens can read minds. Like, maybe it read *your* mind, Stanley, and thought that if it used the voice of someone you knew, you'd come right to it! I mean, it must've known you'd want to come to Nell's rescue if she was in trouble."

Nell's face went bright red at this, but her expression was difficult to read. Was she angry? Stanley thought back to the last day of school, when Mrs. Drabdale had chased him and Alabaster down into the ravine behind the school. *Her* face had certainly been red that day. Of course, Nell might have been blushing because she was embarrassed about something. Perhaps Alabaster's talk of Stanley coming to her rescue was the cause … but what was so embarrassing about that? Things wouldn't have gone any differently if it had been, say, Alabaster's voice calling to him in the sewers—or would they have?

"The masked man is what bothers me the most," Nell said abruptly, simultaneously interrupting Stanley's thoughts and Alabaster's babbling.

"Huh?" said Alabaster, "Oh, oh yeah, he's pretty scary, too."

"What does it mean if *he's* in charge of the Empire?" she went on, ignoring Alabaster.

"What do you mean, what does it mean?" said Stanley.

"I mean," said Nell, "what's keeping him from sending a hundred ships after us? He must know we're gone by now."

"He probably does," said Stanley, pondering the thought for a moment, "but he doesn't know where we are—it'd just be luck if he found us."

"He found us once before," said Nell.

"Yeah, but that was right near Ethelia," said Alabaster carelessly. "And he was waiting for us, remember? *All this has been foretold!*" he said, in a comically weak impersonation of the masked man's voice. Stanley smirked, but Nell didn't.

"If he knew where we were *then*," she said ominously, "he just might know where we are *now*."

Alabaster's face was instantly wiped of any trace of laughter. "You mean he might be watching us right now?" he said, taking a nervous glance over his shoulder as if the masked man might be standing right there.

"Hold on," said Stanley shaking his head, "He told me that he can't see my future anymore, and seeing my future is how he found us the first time. If he knew where we were, we'd probably be surrounded by warships right now."

"Maybe you're right," Nell sighed, "but I'd sure like to know what it is he wants from you, Stanley."

"Yeah, me too," said Stanley.

"Me three," said Alabaster. "First he wants to kill you, then he wants to put you in jail, then he doesn't want to hurt you. Why doesn't he make up his mind?"

"It's like he's got some sort of plan for you, Stanley," said Nell. "Maybe he—"

"*Look,*" Stanley said sharply, "whatever he's planning, whatever he thinks, he's wrong. He said himself that he made a mistake, and as far as I'm concerned, that's all there is to it. Whoever that ... *maniac* is looking for, it's not me, and that's that!"

He hadn't realized it, but at some point he'd gotten to his feet and began pacing about. "Uh," he said, once his brief spout of ire had burned itself out.

"I'm sorry, Stanley," said Nell, as Stanley sat back down, "Let's talk about something else."

*   *   *   *

The days wore on, and Stanley soon ran out of things to keep him occupied. He had plowed through *The Hobbit* and *Watership Down* (and enjoyed them thoroughly), and was even considering taking a peek at *Anne of Green Gables.*

This, however, was not something he wanted to do, because a few days after the short discussion about the masked man, he had had a row with Nell.

Alabaster had made a comment about how cool Grey was, and Nell had said something that Stanley did not like: she said that if the Masked Man was clever enough, he might have used Grey as a spy, making it look like he'd helped Stanley and the others escape, when in reality, Grey might have been working for the masked man this whole time.

Stanley had gotten very angry at these words, and shouted at Nell that she was being stupid and paranoid, and that just because someone looks scary, or isn't friendly, doesn't mean they're bad, and that he was sick and tired of the idiotic way she would always glance sideways at Grey with a fearful look on her face.

"I've talked to him, and I think he's a good guy deep down, so you can just shut up about what you think of him!"

The words had felt strangely good coming out, but now, remembering the angry, hurt look on Nell's face before she stomped off to the cabin, slamming the door behind her, Stanley felt terrible. Why had he yelled at her like that? She hadn't deserved that kind of treatment, and what was more, Nell was his friend, not some smarmy prissy-girl from school. She deserved better. At length, something began to prickle in the back of Stanley's mind, and he realized why he'd gotten so angry.

He knew what it was like. He knew the feeling of having someone regarding him as a possible threat. Back in the dungeon, after meeting Grey for the first time, Stanley had had a conversation with Rick and Bill through the cell door. He remembered Bill's reaction when he realized that Stanley had been put in with Grey.

Bill had thought that Stanley might be a monster, a monster that could change its form to look like a boy, a monster that could kill four Knights of the Silver Sword. Being a rather sensitive fellow, Stanley had been deeply hurt by the look of fear in Bill's eyes as he stared through the small window in the cell door.

And that had been an isolated incident. Imagine, then, what Grey must have had to go through on a daily basis. People talking about him in nervous whispers, rumours filtering from cell to cell. How long had Grey endured such treatment? Years? His whole life, perhaps? Stanley could only imagine how awful it must be, to be feared, to know that everywhere you go, you will be avoided, shunned. He had experienced a few seconds of that feeling; Grey had experienced it his whole life. No wonder he acted the way he did.

The pity and indignation Stanley was feeling on Grey's behalf did not, however, justify his outburst at Nell, and right now he was working up the courage to apologize. Pacing round and round the deck, he rehearsed and re-rehearsed what he was going to say, until at length he realized that the sun had gone down. Benjamin Stone, who had been at the helm all this time, was politely pretending not to notice his odd behavior. Finally deciding that he had rehearsed enough, Stanley squared his shoulders and prepared to confront Nell—just as soon as he went to the bathroom. As he approached the small cubicle at the Ogopogo's stern, he saw something strange: with a fluttering of wings, something small and birdlike detached itself from the bathroom's outer wall, and went flapping off into the night. A moment later, the door opened and Grey emerged.

"Grey!" said Stanley, "Did you see that?"

"See what?" said Grey, scowling.

"That little ... uh ... *thing* ... something was hanging from the wall, and it just flew off."

Grey's scowl darkened. "Where did it go?"

Stanley pointed astern. "That way."

Grey glared out over the ocean, towards the distant horizon. "What did it look like?" he asked sharply.

"A bird," said Stanley, "or maybe a bat, I don't know."

Grey turned around and took a few paces past Stanley, scratching his chin with a clawed finger. He stood in thought for a moment, then said, "It's gone now, whatever it is." For some reason, he seemed eager to dismiss the subject. "What are you doing back here, anyway?"

"Uh, just waiting for the bathroom," said Stanley.

"I was cleaning it," Grey said, before Stanley could reverse the question. Grey reached back into the cubicle and produced a spray bottle and an old rag. "I've been asked to clean it every night for the past week." This fact seemed significant to Grey, but Stanley couldn't imagine why. Grey started to walk away, but Stanley called after him, saying,

"What's the matter, Grey? What's wrong?"

Grey stopped and turned to face Stanley. He was acting very strangely, even by his standards. "Stanley," he said, his tone softer than usual, "I don't need you to defend me."

"What?" said Stanley, not having a clue as to what Grey was talking about.

"I overheard you talking to the girl earlier. I heard you shouting at her."

"Oh," said Stanley, still a bit confused, "you heard that, huh?"

"Don't do that again," said Grey, ignoring the question.

"Er, no, I won't," said Stanley.

"I don't need you to defend me from the opinions of others, to 'come to my rescue' when people start saying things about me. Don't start hurting your friends on my account."

Stanley's confusion thickened. Why was Grey saying this? "I was only—"

"I know what you think you were doing, but I didn't appreciate it. I think you'd better apologize to your friend." And with that, Grey stalked off towards the hold, leaving Stanley completely flabbergasted. What was with him? Why was he acting like this, and where did he get off telling Stanley that he ought to apologize to Nell? A person should be grateful when a friend defends them from the negative opinions of others.

"He's got some nerve," Stanley muttered to himself as he opened the door to the cabin minutes later.

"Who's got some nerve?" said Alabaster, looking up from *The Hobbit*.

"Huh?" said Stanley. "Oh, Grey. Just now he said that he … uh … er …" He trailed off as he glanced over at Nell's bunk. The folding screen was drawn across it, and the absence of deep, rhythmic breathing indicated that Nell was still awake, and probably listening intently. Deciding that saying anything more without including her would be less than polite, Stanley took a deep breath. At least one thing Grey had said made sense: Stanley shouldn't be hurting his friends' feelings.

"Er, Nell?" he said tentatively, "Are you awake?"

"Yes," Nell answered from behind the screen. She didn't sound angry, which was a good sign.

Stanley shuffled his feet. "I'm reallysorryIyelledatyou," he said speedily. "Uh, I mean," he said, slowing down a bit, "I'm sorry I hurt your feelings."

Nell pulled back the screen and peered at him from her bunk. "I know," she sighed. "You were just trying to defend Grey."

"Yeah, but I still shouldn't've gotten so mad at you," said Stanley, relieved that Nell was talking to him.

"It's okay," said Nell. "Maybe I was a little too sensitive."

"So you're not mad at me?" said Stanley.

"Not anymore," said Nell with a slight smile.

"She sure *was*, though," said Alabaster helpfully. "She called you a big fat stupid poop-head." Not noticing the sudden murderous look in Nell's eyes, Alabaster went on, "I knew you didn't really mean it, though, Nell, just like I knew Stanley didn't mean to yell at you. See, that's why friends are great—they never *really* mean the bad stuff they might say to eachother. By the way, you guys have to kiss now."

"*What?*" Stanley and Nell cried in unison.

"*By-the-way-you-guys-have-to-kiss-now,*" Alabaster repeated, not taking his eyes off his book. "It's a proven fact that when a guy and a girl fight, they have to kiss and make up. It's sort of like a peace treaty. I won't look—I'll even leave the room, if you want."

"Forget it!" said Stanley. "I'm not kissing anybody!"

"It's the only way to truly make peace," Alabaster said sagely.

"It's not gonna happen!" said Stanley. He looked to Nell for support. "Right, Nell?"

"Uh, right," said Nell, hesitating microscopically. "Right! Besides, *Alabaster*, since when did *you* become an expert in … in … conflict resolution?"

"I'm just telling it like it is," said Alabaster. He closed his book and sighed. "Okay, okay, if you're not gonna kiss, you have to *at least* shake hands. Otherwise we'll never hear the end of this."

"We'd have heard the end of it five minutes ago, if you'd let it alone," Nell pointed out.

Alabaster, though, would have none of it. "Shake," he commanded.

"Alright, fine," said Stanley. "Let's get this over with." He held out his right hand, which Nell accepted. They shook hands with exaggerated vigour, then turned to Alabaster.

"Okay, we shook hands," said Stanley.

"Hmm?" said Alabaster, who had gone back to his reading, and hadn't been paying attention.

"You weren't even watching!" said Nell, pointing at him accusingly.

"Oh, let's not dwell on the past," said Alabaster. "What's done is done … and stuff. How 'bout a game of Monopoly before bed?"

*   *   *   *

Stanley was glad to be back on good terms with Nell, but his good feelings were somewhat reduced as he awoke the next morning to the first sunless day since they'd left Port Silverburg. A chilly gust of wind greeted him as he stepped out of the cabin. He shivered, and gazed up apprehensively at the ominous dark clouds scudding across the sky.

"Looks like rain," commented Alabaster, as he and Nell followed Stanley out onto the deck.

"Mornin', mates," said Uncle Jack from over by the wheel, before resuming a seemingly important conversation with Diego and Pericles. The children made their way over to where the old man was standing. The ship was rolling notice-ably, mounting the impressive waves being supplied by the strong wind, and coming down every so often with a mighty splash that sent drops of water flying every which way.

"Perhaps the map is inaccurate," Pericles was saying.

"Inaccurate?" echoed Uncle Jack, "Are ye kiddin'? This map couldn't be any *more* accurate! I'm tellin' ya, we've maintained the correct course headings, but we're just not makin' good time."

"But we've got the wind crystal running at full capacity, twenty-four hours a day," protested Pericles. "How can we *not* be making good time?"

"Just look at the figures," said Uncle Jack, brandishing the ship's logbook. "Our cruisin' speed doesn't match up with the distance we've covered. It should never've taken us almost two weeks to get where we're at now, even *with* all the course changes."

"Jack's right," said Diego, staring gravely at the Memory Mirror. "At the speed we're going, we should be … *here* by now." He pointed at a blank section of ocean several inches southwest of the Ogopogo's marked position on the map. "Oops!" he said, as the tiny dotted line grew a half inch to the west, once again altering the Ogopogo's course.

"New headin', Benjamin," Uncle Jack called to Benjamin Stone, who was at the wheel. "Fifty degrees starboard."

Stanley peeked around Uncle Jack to take a look at the Memory Mirror. There was the map, looking much as it had the first time he'd seen it, except that the dotted line marking the Ogopogo's progress was now quite long. It zigged and zagged every so often, but maintained a south-westerly direction.

"Mr. Lee," said Nell, also peering down at the map, "why does the map keep telling you to change course?"

"Ah, good question, Nell," said Uncle Jack. "The course changes are to throw anybody off the trail. If some scurvy swine were to look at the map now, all he'd see is that we're now on a westerly heading, after all that ziggin' around we've been doin'. He'd be able to see where we're goin' as of now, but he'd prob'ly go sailin' off to the west somewhere, never knowin' 'bout the next course change, which'll take us off this westerly course, an' onto a new one. It's all about throwin' people off our trail."

"But what if someone stole the map?" Stanley inquired. "Then they'd be able to keep following it."

"You'd think so," said Diego wryly, "but the map only stays as long as Jack and I are both nearby."

"What I don't get," said Alabaster, "is why we have to go find the treasure at all. I mean, I'm having a great time and all, but if Diego and Uncle Jack are the only ones who can find it, why not just leave it where it is?"

"Well, Alabaster," said Uncle Jack, "when it comes to somethin' like this treasure of ours, there's only so much ya can do to protect it. We hid it as best we could, an' it's been safe so far, but to be honest, *anyone* can find it, not just Diego an' me."

"*Anyone?*" the children echoed as one.

"Yes," said Diego, "but anyone who doesn't have the memory mirror would have to find the treasure by luck. The only way you'd find it without us, would be to stumble upon it by accident."

"Which is a lot tougher than ya think," added Uncle Jack. "Chamberlain's been tryin' to do it for forty years."

"So there's not really any magic protecting the treasure?" said Stanley. "I remember the masked man was talking about powerful magic, which makes it so that you can't find the treasure unless you know where it is."

"That's a rumour we started," said Diego. "But there certainly is *some* kind of magic at work. What did you call it, Jack?"

"A turnabout field," said Uncle Jack. "The treasure, wherever it is, is surrounded by some kinda field—magic or not, I dunno—which sorta messes with a person's sense o' direction. It makes it real easy for someone to lose his way, an' by the time he gets out of it, he's usually turned right back around, goin' back the way he came, frustrated an' ready to head home."

"Does the Mirror keep you from getting lost?" asked Nell.

"Aye," said Uncle Jack. "Once yer inside the field, ya pass yer hand over the mirror, an' ya get a signal that leads ya to the treasure. 'Least, that's what the mirror's shown us so far—we don't really remember doin' any of it!"

"It sure sounds like magic to me," said Stanley.

"Oh my," Pericles suddenly exclaimed. "Look at that!"

"What is it? What is it?" Alabaster said excitedly.

"Me old eyes ain't what they used to be, I guess," said Uncle Jack, squinting mightily. "I can't see anythin' 'cept the broad ocean."

"Your eyes are fine, amigo," said Diego, "I can't see it, either. Pericles, what are we looking at?"

"I keep forgetting," said Pericles, "that you people all have pitiful eyesight."

"Fine, keep it to yerself," growled Uncle Jack. "We'll find out what it is when we get to it."

"I can't tell from this distance," said Pericles, ignoring Uncle Jack, "but I believe it's some kind of structure. A tower, perhaps?"

"A tower?" said Diego. "In the middle of the ocean?"

"As I said, I can't tell for sure."

"Is that where the treasure is?" Stanley asked.

"Narr," said Uncle Jack, still peering intently ahead. "We wouldn't've stashed it somewhere so easy to see. But our current course is takin' us right to it—look, it just appeared on the map."

Sure enough, something had appeared on the map a fraction of an inch west of the Ogopogo's position. It looked like a very thin triangle, or perhaps the minute hand of a clock. "Hmm, I think I've got a good idea of what that thing is," said Uncle Jack. "Steady as she goes, Benjamin, an' let's just hope this weather blows over."

*   *   *   *

A little over an hour later, Stanley caught sight of the mysterious structure, and by noon, they had sailed right up close to it. It did indeed look like some kind of tower, rising right up out of the ocean. It was massive, much wider than any sky scraper Stanley had ever seen, and also much taller. It was made of black stone, and had many strange symbols carved into it. Some of them matched those found carved into the Memory Mirror.

"What *is* it?" Nell asked wonderingly as she gazed up at the structure's pointed peak, hundreds of feet above.

"Looks like an obelisk," said Alabaster casually, earning him a look of surprise from Nell. "What? They're all over the place in Egypt. My Mom and Dad've shown me pictures."

"They're archaeologists, remember?" Stanley said to Nell.

"You're quite right, Mr. Lancaster," said Pericles in a mildly impressed tone, "It *is* an obelisk—a monument of an ancient civilization."

"There's a bunch of 'em in different places around the world," said Uncle Jack. "Folks say they're part o' some lost continent that sank to the bottom o' the sea thousands o' years ago."

"Sounds like Atlantis," said Alabaster. "My Dad thinks it really existed."

"Why is it on the map?" Nell asked. "Is it some kind of marker?"

"Aye," said Uncle Jack, "it tells us that we're on the right track. An' look, the wee line's growin' some more—looks like we got ourselves a new headin'. Ninety degrees to port ... *south*."

In this context, the word *south* seemed to hold some special significance. "*South?*" squawked Pericles.

"That's what the map says," said Uncle Jack firmly.

"Oh, no no no no no no," said Pericles, shaking his head vigorously.

"What?" said Stanley, desperately wanting to know what was causing so much anxiety.

"The obelisk is also a warning," said Diego quietly, while Pericles continued to repeat the word *no* over and over. "It warns people that south of here lies *Marre Tenebroso*—the Sea of Darkness." Thunder boomed menacingly overhead, as if it had been waiting for someone to say just those words.

"The Sea of Darkness?" said Nell. "You've got to be kidding."

"I'm not," said Diego. "That's what it's called."

Stanley certainly didn't like the sound of 'Sea of Darkness'. "Er, it's not as bad as it sounds, right?" He asked hopefully.

"It's worse," said Diego. "It's an enormous area of the ocean, and it reaches depths unheard of in other parts of the world."

"An' there's the Great Abyss," added Uncle Jack, "An underwater trench that runs right down the middle o' the sea bed. They say it's bottomless."

"I don't believe this!" screeched Pericles. "Only you two buffoons would choose The Sea of Darkness as a hiding place for treasure! I should have known, I really should have! Here I was, assuming that you'd chosen a nice, quiet, out-of-the-way place, when all this time the real answer was right up there with my other deepest, darkest fears!"

"Pericles," said Uncle Jack.

The parrot ignored him. "I imagine I must have put up quite a fuss all those years ago, when we sailed into that deathtrap! I suppose it's a good thing I had all knowledge of the treasure's location wiped from my memory—otherwise, I never would have come on this mad quest!"

"Pericles," said Uncle Jack.

"But then, I suppose it makes sense," the parrot ranted on. "After all, what sea voyage would be complete without a trip to the most dangerous place in the world? I must agree that there's no better place to hide treasure—anybody who tries to find it winds up dead!"

"PERICLES!" shouted Uncle Jack, making the parrot jump. "That'll do. I'm sure we had our reasons for hidin' the treasure in there."

"We may not be able to remember it, but we *know* what's in there," said Pericles desperately. "There are worse things than krakens and armour fish living in the Abyss."

"We went in there once an' came out alive," said Uncle Jack, "an' we can sure as heck do it again!"

"We have to," said Diego stoutly. "It's the only way."

Pericles gave a small whimper.

"Right, mates!" said Uncle Jack, "Look lively—we're in for the most dangerous part o' the voyage."

Stanley vaguely remembered Uncle Jack stating that this last leg of their journey would be easy. He sighed heavily.

"I'll secure the hold," said Diego, saluting smartly.

"Good man, Diego," said Uncle Jack. "Pericles, yer on lookout. I wanna know what's comin' an hour b'fore it gets to us, ya got me?"

"Yes, captain," Pericles answered, saluting feebly and flapping off to the crow's nest.

"Benjamin, yer on cannon duty," said Uncle Jack, "an' I'll take the helm for a bit. You three," he said to the children, "brace yerselves—it's gonna be a rough ride."

*   *   *   *

The Ogopogo sped south over the rolling sea, while the clouds in the sky above grew darker and darker. When the storm finally hit shortly after sunset, Stanley, Alabaster, and Nell were confined to the cabin.

"Best if you three stay in here where it's safe," said Uncle Jack, shooing the children inside as water cascaded off his heavy-duty raincoat. "If ya hafta come outside, get a lifeline 'round ya, so ya don't get swept overboard." He indicated three lengths of rope which were attached to the mast. "I'll hang 'em just outside the door, so tie 'em 'round yer waist b'fore venturin' outside."

The worst part of the storm was the rolling of the ship. At least, Stanley and Nell found it to be the worst. They clung to their bunks for dear life as the Ogopogo pitched and rolled on the mountainous waves amidst blinding flashes of lighting and deafening rolls of thunder. As Stanley clung to his bunk, arms and legs shaking, feeling sure that he was about to be ill, the thought crossed his mind (not for the first time) that perhaps coming along on this adventure had not been such a great idea, after all. He glanced over at Nell, whose complexion had turned a sickly shade of green. Her eyes were closed tightly.

As reassuring as it was to have his friends close by, Stanley couldn't help but feel terribly afraid. Storms are scary enough on dry land, without the floor pitching and tossing, trying to unseat the unwary. He felt a distinct jolt of jealousy for Alabaster, who cried "WHEEEE!" every time the Ogopogo went into a nose dive.

"*This is better than a roller coaster!*" Alabaster cried ecstatically over the roar of the thunder.

How long the storm lasted, Stanley couldn't say; he lost track of time, and his stomach threatened to heave upward every time he tried to look down at his watch. The rain lashed viciously at the cabin walls, and the wind howled like a banshee sitting on a tack. Presently there came the sound of someone fumbling with the cabin door, and moments later Uncle Jack lurched in, out of breath and thoroughly drenched. He closed the door behind him as a colossal wave washed over the deck.

"Whew!" he breathed, leaning back against the door. "Not long now, mates. This little squall is startin' to let up."

Stanley wanted to shout "*LITTLE SQUALL?*" but was afraid that he would throw up if he opened his mouth.

"You three doin' okay?" asked Uncle Jack, as the Ogopogo began to ascend yet another towering wave. Stanley and Nell nodded weakly, but Alabaster, who was feeling fine, said,

"We're great! This is the best ride ever!"

Glancing uncertainly at the looks of abject terror on Stanley's and Nell's faces, Uncle Jack said, "Well, there's no need to worry, mates. The Ogopogo's been through much worse than this. It'll take more than a twenty-foot wave to sink *this* ship, I can tell ya that!" Despite Uncle Jack's intentions, Stanley was not encouraged.

There came a loud THUD from somewhere below decks, and the Ogopogo gave an unsettling lurch, which, in this weather, was saying something.

"Leapin' lobsters," exclaimed Uncle Jack, "What was that?" He flung open the door and was greeted by a sizable wave which knocked him backwards and washed into the cabin, soaking everything. Spluttering and coughing, he picked himself up and went unsteadily to the door, yelling, "PERICLES, REPORT!"

"NO DAMAGE, CAPTAIN," squawked the parrot over the din of the storm.

"FELT LIKE WE HIT SOMETHIN' THOUGH," shouted Uncle Jack.

The cabin door swung shut, and the children were left alone again, with two inches of water on the floor. The ship continued to pitch and roll, but there were no more odd thuds. Just as Stanley began to relax slightly, there came from the deck outside an unintelligible shriek that could only have come from Pericles. An instant later, Uncle Jack could be heard barking orders, and a loud BOOM indicated that the cannon had been fired. Stanley leapt out of his severely dampened bunk and tottered towards the cabin door, his footsteps splish-splashing as he went.

"Stanley, where are you going?" Nell demanded in a tone that would have been sharper had she not been on the verge of bringing up all over the cabin.

"To see what's going on," said Stanley, his fear of the storm having miraculously vanished (or at least, diminished).

"Oh no you don't," said Nell with a bit more conviction.

"Oh yes I do," said Stanley, reaching for the doorknob. "They might be in trouble out there."

"Stanley, *no*," pleaded Nell. "Your uncle said to stay inside, and I think this is the one time when you should do as he asks. It's too dangerous to go out there—remember the kraken?"

Nell had a point, though Stanley was reluctant to admit it. He'd been out on deck during the kraken attack, and hadn't escaped unscathed.

"Don't worry about Stanley, Nell," said Alabaster cheerfully, jumping down from his bunk and joining Stanley by the door. "He's Wolverine, remember?"

Stanley was about to concede to Nell's advice, when there came a loud shout from outside, followed by a splintering crash as the cabin's roof suddenly caved in. Nell screamed as something like a long, white spike came crashing down through the ruined roof and embedded itself in her bunk, inches from where she was sitting. Without even thinking, Stanley leaped forward and grabbed Nell's arm, hauling her unceremoniously to the other side of the cabin, mere seconds before the entire starboard wall was ripped away.

"*Holy moley!*" shouted Alabaster as they were assaulted by the howling wind and driving rain. Stanley and Nell chose to remain silent, gaping at the wreckage of the wall as it was lifted into the air, clasped in the jaws of a gigantic sea serpent. Lightning flashed, illuminating the slick, scaly hide of the creature's head, which was at least twice as big as an armour fish's. The serpent regarded the children for a moment, before getting hit square in the face by a fireball preceded by another loud BOOM. The fireball exploded and the serpent reeled drunkenly, dropping the remains of the cabin wall.

"RESILIENT SUCKER, AIN'T 'E?" came Uncle Jack's voice. "BENJAMIN, ANOTHER VOLLEY!"

"CAPTAIN, WATCH OUT!" shrieked Pericles.

The serpent had recovered from its brief stunning, and was letting out a low, angry hiss. Unlike other sea monsters, this one was surprisingly quiet. The serpent suddenly lunged towards Uncle Jack and Benjamin, but then Diego was by their side, toting a long rifle. Stanley saw him pull something from a pocket of his raincoat and throw it into the air, before aiming his gun and firing repeatedly at the advancing reptile, which twitched and hissed more out of annoyance than anything else.

Suddenly, a great black shape appeared out of nowhere and bowled Diego over. It was Grey, of course, performing his trademark move, and the reason became clear an instant later. The serpent's tail, which ended in a long, curving, wicked-looking blade, came crashing down onto the deck where Diego had been standing, cleaving the solid wooden boards as if they'd been made of paper. The monster hissed furiously at being denied a kill, and lunged lighting-quick at Grey. Grey was quicker, and swung upwards at the approaching jaws with a long black sword, which he seemed to have drawn from nowhere. The serpent lurched back and let out a sharp hiss as lighting flashed again, revealing a wicked gash in its reptilian snout.

Grey ducked as the deadly tail swept the rolling deck. Though it missed him, the tail connected with the cannon, and Benjamin was forced to jump out of the way as the trusty piece of artillery was knocked overboard, taking part of the railing with it. The serpent hissed in a satisfied way, as the scene descended even deeper into total pandemonium. Pericles was squawking, thunder was rolling, Uncle Jack and Diego had guns drawn, Benjamin was trying to pull them both away from danger, and Grey was making ready to leap overboard onto the serpent, into the very jaws of death itself.

Stanley had never felt more useless. He wanted to help, but how? He wanted to run, but where? He wanted to do something, but what? The sea was heaving violently, the rain was coming down in torrents, the wind was blowing with all its might, and the sea serpent was about to devour them all. He closed his eyes and prayed silently that they would make it through this.

A blinding light stabbed through the darkness, and the entire scene seemed to freeze, as if the light had been the flash of a giant camera capturing the moment forever on film. Everyone aboard the Ogopogo stared like animals caught in a car's headlights, and it is worth mentioning that the serpent did the same. Suddenly, there came a great booming noise; it wasn't thunder, but it was very familiar. An unpleasant whooshing sound followed the boom, and seconds later a dozen more rang out, as if trying to surpass the storm in noise production. The serpent twitched as each boom sounded, and there came a series of loud, wet smacking sounds as something impacted the creature's skull. The great reptile straightened itself and stared down at the Ogopogo, eyes open in serpentine surprise. It let out a groggy hiss before collapsing into the churning sea.

Stanley gawked at the place where the serpent had been only moments before. What had happened? The question was answered almost immediately. As if issuing from the light itself, an amplified voice called out,

"AHOY THERE!"

The voice was dishearteningly familiar. Uncle Jack made his way astern and stood beside Stanley in front of the wreckage of the cabin, raising a hand to shield his eyes from the blinding light.

"By Poseidon's beard, this can't be real," Stanley heard the old man mutter.

"I SAY AGAIN, AHOY!" called the voice. It did not sound friendly.

Lighting flashed, and Stanley let out a "whoa!" as the electric charge illuminated something some twenty yards off the Ogopogo's stern. It was a ship, a monstrously huge ship which made the Ogopogo look like an inflatable dingy. Stanley had enough time to catch a glimpse of the name emblazoned on the vessel's bow:

MAELSTROM

The bright light was issuing from a large spotlight mounted on the ship's forecastle. A figure stepped in front of the light and stood there, legs apart, silhouetted against the brilliant white sphere.

"WELL WELL WELL," came the amplified voice once more, "AREN'T WE A BEDRAGGLED LOT. IT LOOKS AS IF I CAME ALONG JUST IN TIME, WOULDN'T YOU SAY?"

There was no mistaking that voice; it belonged to Ezekiel Chamberlain.

CHAPTER TWENTY-TWO:
ABOARD THE MAELSTROM

"Heave! Ho! Heave! I said HEAVE!" Chamberlain bellowed at the group of sailors who were hauling on a pair of thick ropes, which ran through pulleys attached to two stout wooden cranes (called davits), which were supporting the weight of the Ogopogo as it was hauled out of the water. A half hour had passed since the Maelstrom's unprecedented appearance, and the storm had by now just about blown itself out. By the time the Ogopogo was out of the water and hanging securely off the Maelstrom's port beam, moonlight was shining down through rents in the clouds, illuminating the damp, shiny deck of the huge vessel, and the shapes of hundreds of sailors as they went about their duties. A plank was lowered between the Maelstrom and the Ogopogo.

"Kindly disembark from your vessel," said Chamberlain, standing there at the end of the plank, flanked by a half dozen Knights of the Silver Sword. He wore an expression of triumph, and stepped back with a slight bow as his captives disembarked form the Ogopogo.

Stanley gazed about at the sheer enormity of the Maelstrom. It had to have been at least six hundred feet long, and well over sixty across the beam. Its five masts looked like trees in a forest, with sails, yards, and rigging for leaves, branches, and vines. The ship was like some kind of floating city, and he wondered how on earth it could have docked at Port Silverburg.

"Welcome aboard the Maelstrom," said Chamberlain with unbearable smugness, but before he could say anything more, Uncle Jack sprang forward and grabbed him by the lapels.

"*How?*" snarled Uncle Jack. "How'd ya find us? How could ya have—*oof!*" One of Chamberlain's knights reached out with an armoured hand and cuffed Uncle Jack sharply, sending him sprawling backwards on the deck.

"*Hey!*" said Stanley, taking a step towards the knight, and then thinking better of it, as the knight drew his sword and pointed it at his face.

"I'm all right, I'm all right," grumbled Uncle Jack, swatting at Benjamin Stone, who was trying to help him up. "An' you, Stanley," he said as he got to his feet, "keep quiet! Don't go gettin' yerself in trouble."

"*You* keep quiet, you old fool," said Pericles. "You just rushed a man who has goodness knows how many knights at his command!"

"Please, please, enough harsh words," said Chamberlain, a wicked smile on his face. "I can understand that you're all a bit upset, but let's try and act like human beings, shall we?" He turned to look at Grey. "Now as for *you*," he said, reaching into his coat and drawing forth a gold chain, "let's just make sure you don't pull any of your little tricks." Chamberlain suddenly threw the chain at Grey, whose eyes opened wide with disbelief as the chain seemed to come alive and wrap itself around him, binding him so tightly that he couldn't move. The chain began to glow with a bright yellow light, and Grey let out a bellow of pain as he toppled over onto the deck.

Stanley, who would never have expected anything to hurt Grey so badly, dove to his side and put a hand on his forehead. Grey's eyes were tightly closed, and his teeth were visible again, clenched against whatever pain he was feeling. He was breathing in short, sharp bursts, but made no other sound. "*What did you do to him?*" Stanley shouted at Chamberlain, who looked mildly amused. "*What is this chain?*"

"It's a gift form a friend," said Chamberlain, "and it is my assurance that *your* friend here will not try anything funny."

"But it's hurting him!" Stanley said fiercely.

"Of course it's hurting him!" snapped Chamberlain. "Pain is the only thing that a monster like him understands. It's the only thing that can keep him in check. It's not my fault I have to go to such drastic measures, he simply cannot be reasoned with." He gazed nastily down at Grey's prone form. "I must say, though, he's doing an admirable job of enduring the pain. I can assure you, that chain is hurting him far more than he's letting on."

Grey opened his eyes and glared furiously up at Chamberlain.

"Hm hm hm," chuckled the Regent, kneeling down beside him, "Quite the tough-man, aren't you? Hmph. You'll be begging for mercy before long, my nightmarish friend. I guarantee it."

"Stop it!" Stanley said angrily, getting to his feet and glaring defiantly up at Chamberlain. For the second time since their first meeting, he was feeling a powerful urge to injure the Regent in a very serious fashion. Chamberlain merely stood up and smirked, clearly amused by the look of boyish fury on Stanley's face.

But then something happened: Chamberlain's expression changed. The cocky smirk vanished from his face, replaced by a look of ... surprise? Disbelief? Fear? Yes, it was a look of fear, there was no mistaking it; for a split second, Chamberlain's ice-blue eye had widened, as if he were suddenly seeing something horrible. *He's afraid of me*, Stanley thought to himself, *but why?* The question remained unanswered, for Chamberlain promptly regained his composure.

"Mind your place, boy," he snarled, drawing his cutlass and brandishing it threateningly. The Regent's face was set in a fierce grimace, but his ice-blue eye still bore a trace of uncertainty. Stanley was the only one looking Chamberlain in the eye, and therefore was the only one who saw any of this. For one wild moment, he found himself wanting nothing more than to fight Chamberlain to the death. Before he could do anything monumentally foolish, however, he felt a hand on his shoulder, and heard Nell's voice in his ear.

"That's enough, Stanley," she said firmly, easing him away from Chamberlain, then pausing to whisper, "*What's wrong with you?*"

"Good girl," said Chamberlain shortly, returning his cutlass to its sheath. "At least *one* member of your little crew has some sense, eh, *Jack?*"

"Blow it out yer rear, *Zeke*," growled Uncle Jack. "Are ya gonna bore us to death with yer smart-mouthed chit-chat, or are ya gonna tell us how ya found us, an' why we're still alive?"

"All in good time," said Chamberlain, his expression darkening. "Truth be told, I'd have truly enjoyed watching that sea serpent devour you ... but business before pleasure, and all that." He turned to the closest knight and said, "Take them to the brig."

*　　　*　　　*　　　*

The knight shoved Stanley roughly, sending him stumbling into the cell, where he landed in a heap on top of Alabaster.

"Oof! Watch it, Stanley!"

"Sorry," Stanley said absently as he picked himself up. He peered around at their new surroundings. The brig was merely a section of the sternmost part of the Maelstrom's hold, separated from the rest of the deck by a grid of iron bars. Several ancient, mouldy mattresses occupied one corner, with a single bucket close by for a bathroom.

"There's no way I'm using that bucket," Nell said to no one in particular.

"Down't yew worry, dawlin'," croaked the jailer, a portly, filthy-looking fellow with several teeth missing and no shirt. "I promise not to peek!" He chuckled hackingly until Diego, who had been lurking nearby, reached through the bars and grabbed him by the ears, pulling him forward to bonk his round, sweaty head on the solid iron.

"Keep talking, funny man," said Diego savagely as the jailer cried "OY!" repeatedly. Diego released the disgusting fellow, allowing him to stumble backwards and fall humourously on his sizable bottom. The jailer grimaced furiously and pulled a stout cudgel from his belt.

"Big mistayke, ya ruddy mongrel," the fat man snarled as he picked himself up off the floor. He produced a key ring from his pocket and was about to open the cell door and introduce his cudgel to Diego's face, when he stopped short. Benjamin Stone had appeared at Diego's side, arms folded, face set, eyes glaring fiercely down at the stout jailer.

"Er," said the jailer.

"Ya might want to be keepin' that door closed, matey," said Uncle Jack, joining Diego and Benjamin. "For yer own protection." The jailer considered this for a moment, then withdrew the key from the lock.

"Wotevah," he said carelessly as he shrugged and thrust the keys back in his pocket. "I down't need ta bash yar bloody brains in, anyways," he said with a gap-toothed grin. "It's satisfaction enough to 'ave th' faymous Black Jack Lee roight 'ere in me own brig! Har har har!"

"Enjoy it while it lasts, mate," said Uncle Jack.

"Oh, thank yew, I will!" said the jailer.

"You should've let him open the door, Jack," said Diego. "We could have shut him up, *and* been on our way—"

"Haw!" interrupted the jailer. "An' wheah wouldja gow, eh, moy son? 'Ow fah d'ya think ya'd get 'fore the knoights found ya, eh? One deck? Two? Yar better off in 'ere, believe yew me!"

At that moment there came the sound of footsteps from the nearby stairway, and down came Chamberlain, followed by a dozen knights. "Having a pleasant conversation, Mr. Blund?" enquired the Regent.

"Oh, er, yore Lordship, sir!" said the jailer, bowing clumsily. "No, sir, I was—"

"I told you not to speak to them, Mr. Blund," said Chamberlain slowly, "and I told you specifically to leave the girl alone."

"B-b-but sir, I didn't—"

"I heard every word, you porcine lout," snapped Chamberlain. "I was waiting at the top of the stairs."

The jailer now had a fearful look on his fat, greasy face. "I-I was on'y jokin' with the young miss, yore Lordship! Jus' a bit of fun, ain't that right, miss? Jus' a wee joke?" He looked hopefully at Nell, who made a disgusted noise and folded her arms crossly.

"Revolting," snorted Chamberlain. "I should have known that a disgusting lump like you could not be trusted. If I could, I'd have this ship crewed solely by *knights*, but, as that cannot be ..." He regarded the jailer disdainfully for a moment, then said, "Take this man and flog him. No less than twenty."

"Yore Lordship, please!" squealed the jailer as one of the knights gripped him by the arm, "Mercy, yore Lordship, *mercy!*"

"Not today, Mr. Blund," said Chamberlain, as the spluttering jailer was hauled away. The Regent sighed and turned towards the prisoners. "Sailors," he said contemptuously, "I don't know what it is, but ever since I became an admiral, I just can't stand them."

"That's funny," said Uncle Jack, "I'd've thought that slime like you would fit in just fine with slime like them."

"A comedian to the last, eh, Jack?" said Chamberlain, pacing slowly in front of the bars. "You always see the humour in a situation, no matter how dire."

"*I'll* tell ya what's humourous," said Uncle Jack, leaning against the bars. "Yeh treat the men under yer command exactly the way *yer* boss treats *you*."

Chamberlain frowned at this.

"I mean, I'll agree that Mr. Blund, there, deserves a good floggin', but—"

"*Don't you criticize me, pirate,*" hissed Chamberlain, lunging at the bars, pointing squarely at Uncle Jack with an index finger.

"Fine," said Uncle Jack, stepping back from the bars. "Now, *Ezekiel,* are ya gonna tell me what I want to know? I mean, ya got me locked up in yer brig, so I figure ya might as well tell me how ya found us."

"He cannot give you the answers you seek," said a low, rumbling voice from somewhere behind Chamberlain. An unpleasant jolt shot through Stanley's stomach at the sound of this voice, and he very nearly groaned with dismay, as several knights moved to one side, revealing the only person in the world who could have made this situation worse: the masked man. Clad in his usual hood, cloak and gloves, and concealed behind his blank, white mask, he came slowly forward and stood beside Chamberlain.

"My lord," said Chamberlain, not looking directly at the mask's depthless eye holes, "you did not have to reveal yourself—"

"But I chose, to, Ezekiel," said the masked man as he peered through the iron bars.

"Well if it ain't Mr. Mask," said Uncle Jack insolently. "I guess I should've expected to find yeh here holdin' Chamberlain's leash."

"Quite so," rumbled the masked man as Chamberlain let out a low and angry growl.

From his perch on Uncle Jack's shoulder, Pericles *hmphed* loudly. "If *you're* here, then why, pray tell, did your errand boy have to come along?"

Chamberlain exploded immediately. "I WILL NOT SUFFER SUCH INSO-LENCE ABOARD MY OWN SHIP—ESPECIALLY NOT FROM *YOU*, PARROT!"

"Calm yourself, Ezekiel," boomed the masked man. "The bird's question is a valid one. Ezekiel is here, parrot, because I need a ship, and what's more, I need a large, powerful ship, and frankly, I haven't the patience for sailing. Also, as is my preference at this time, I am able to remain hidden, whilst Ezekiel gives the appearance of being in command."

Stanley kept glancing at Chamberlain, who was looking more and more unhappy the longer the masked man talked. Just as he had done back in the throne room of the Imperial Palace, the masked man was displaying his fondness for humiliating Chamberlain. In spite of himself, Stanley found that he felt a bit sorry for the Regent, who was now staring glumly at the floor.

"How 'bout *my* question, Mr. Mask?" said Uncle Jack. "Ya say that Zeke, here can't answer it, ain't that right?"

"That's right," said the masked man. "Ezekiel cannot tell you how he found you, because he doesn't know."

"He doesn't know?" echoed Uncle Jack. "The commander o' the ship, an' he doesn't know how 'e found us?"

"*I* am the commander of the ship," said the masked man, pointing at himself. "I give Ezekiel the orders, and he relays them to the rest of the crew. And, to his credit, I must say that he did an excellent job of keeping his mouth shut during this little voyage—didn't question me once, not even after all the random course changes. It seems that the Regent is finally learning what it means to serve me."

"Wait just a sec," said Uncle Jack, "What'ya mean, *course changes?*"

"I mean the changes you made in your navigation," said the masked man simply. "You changed your heading quite often."

"An' just how in the blue blazes do ya know *that?*" demanded Uncle Jack.

Instead of answering, the masked man reached into the folds of his robe and withdrew a small, black sphere the size of a tennis ball. "Do you know what this is?" he asked, holding up the sphere for all to see. "No? Well then let me enlighten you." He gave the sphere a quick shake, and an instant later a pair of leathery wings unfurled themselves from it. The wings belonged to a small, bat-like creature with clawed feet and a single yellow eye. "This is a shadowbat," said the masked man, as the creature in his hand stared about blankly, flexing its wings every few seconds. Stanley had the sneaking suspicion that he had seen it before, but he couldn't remember where or when.

"They act as messengers," the masked man continued. "You might equate them with homing pigeons."

"So ya had one o' these critters followin' us, then, is that it?" said Uncle Jack. "That little fellah's been keepin' tabs on us all this time?"

"Not quite," said the masked man, an unpleasant hint of relish in his voice. "You see, a shadowbat can't stand sunlight. It would have proven impossible to use one to track you night and day, which is why I saw fit to employ the services of one of your crew members."

"One o' me crew members?" said Uncle Jack warily. "What're ya talkin' about?"

Something suddenly clicked in Stanley's mind, and he remembered where he had seen the shadowbat before. He recalled walking towards the bathroom one night, and seeing something small and dark detach itself from the cubicle and fly off into the night. He also remembered running into Grey, who had been cleaning the bathroom at the time.

Grey.

"There're no spies among the crew o' the Ogopogo," said Uncle Jack stoutly. "Yer just tryin' to make us suspicious, turn us against eachother, an' it ain't gonna work!"

But Stanley found himself doubting Uncle Jack's words. *Could* Grey actually be a spy? Had he been sending messages to the masked man every night, via shadowbat, since they had left Ethelia? Stanley stared at Grey, who was huddled against the opposite wall, still wrapped up in the glowing chain. His black face was inscrutable, and there was no trace of guilt or nervousness in those angry yellow eyes. Stanley stood up and took a step towards him.

"Is it you?" he asked sharply. "Are you the spy?" Everyone looked at him, then at Grey, but right then, Stanley didn't care *who* they were looking at. All he cared about was hearing the truth. He had felt an inexplicable closeness to Grey ever since meeting him in the dungeons of the Imperial Palace, almost as if Grey were some long-lost relative who Stanley used to know, but had forgotten. He had felt sorry for Grey, and had harboured the suspicion that there was more to him than met the eye, that somewhere underneath the frightening exterior and rude demeanor, there lurked something that one might not expect to find: something good.

Had Stanley's attempts at befriending Grey been a waste of time? Had Diego and Nell been right to be distrustful of such a fearsome newcomer? Had Grey been betraying them all this time?

Grey glowered at Stanley, but said nothing; it was the masked man who spoke next.

"Heh heh heh heh heh," came the low, rumbling laugh. "Him? A spy?" He laughed again. "He does look the part, though, doesn't he? No, *Stanley*, that unfortunate fellow is not the spy. But I think Lord Montigo can tell us who *is*—"

"That's enough!" Diego said sharply, as all eyes instantly locked onto him. He was looking a bit ill; his ruggedly handsome face was bathed in sweat, and his breath was shallow and quick.

"Diego," said Uncle Jack, stepping towards his friend and putting a hand on his shoulder, "what's this lunatic talkin' about?"

Diego flinched at Uncle Jack's touch, and remained silent, staring at the floor.

"Diego, *no*," said Pericles quietly.

"It appears that Lord Montigo is suffering a bout of stage fright," rumbled the masked man. "Therefore, I will speak in his place. My friends, Lord Montigo—"

"*Silence!*" yelled Diego.

"—is the spy," the masked man finished.

A palpable silence descended on the scene. Uncle Jack removed his hand from Diego's shoulder. The old man's expression was unreadable, but then a small grin appeared on his face, and he began to chuckle.

"Heh heh heh heh heh heh heh ..."

Stanley gaped at Uncle Jack. How could anyone be laughing at a time like this? Even the masked man had gone silent, and Stanley guessed that behind that blank, white mask was an expression of puzzlement. Uncle Jack's laughter grew louder and louder, until he fell to his knees in a fit of mirth.

"Hoo-whee!" he exclaimed, once he had regained his ability to speak, "Mercy! I've heard some whoppers in my time, but that one takes the cake! Hee-*hee!*"

Stanley couldn't see the humour in all this, and from the looks on the others' faces, neither could they.

"Heh heh heh," continued Uncle Jack, clambering to his feet. "Well, sorry Mr. Mask, but the joke's on you. Ya can't pull anythin' over on me, that's for true. Go on, Diego, tell 'im he's lyin'."

Diego, who was looking very unhappy, glanced sideways at Uncle Jack, but said nothing. He hunched up his shoulders and put his hands in his pockets. Still smiling, Uncle Jack took a step to the right so as to get a clear view of Diego's profile.

"C'mon now!" he said cheerfully, "Look 'im in the eye an' call 'im a filthy, dirtyrotten liar."

Stanley wished Uncle Jack would stop smiling and acting cheerfully; it was strangely painful to look at.

"Captain," said Pericles quietly.

"Not now, Pericles," said Uncle Jack. "I wanna hear Diego give Mr. Mask what for!" When Diego still refused to speak, Uncle Jack's smile faltered. "C'mon, Diego, speak up."

Diego turned to face the old man, and in a grim voice, said, "He's not lying."

"TRAITOR!" shrieked Pericles.

Uncle Jack's expression was now one of disbelief. "Diego ... you sold us out to this scurvy swine?"

"That he did," said the masked man. "I hid a box full of shadowbats aboard your ship while you were moored in the Ethelia harbour, and every night since then, Lord Montigo, my newest servant, has sent one back to me, along with your ship's exact position, as well as any changes in heading. He also had the brilliant idea of reducing your sailing speed at night, so as to make it easier for us to catch up."

Grey made an angry noise and sat up, glaring hard at Diego. "So that's why you kept relieving me of my helm shifts," he snarled.

"Yes, YES!" said Diego, his voice rising, "That's *exactly* why. I took the night shifts so I could safely turn down the wind crystal and steer the Ogopogo at a fraction of her top speed! I even tried to frame *you*, Grey, by planting the bats near the bathroom while you were cleaning it!"

"There now," said the masked man, once Diego had finished his brief rant, "doesn't it feel good to have all that off your chest? Please, come out of that squalid cell." He pointed at the lock, and with a metallic *click*, the cell door swung open on its own. Diego left the cell without a backward glance, and had just closed the door behind him when Uncle Jack suddenly threw himself at the bars.

"YOU—MUTINOUS—DOG!" he roared, as tears began to flow down his wrinkled cheeks, "*Why?* ... HOW COULD YA DO SUCH A THING?" He fell to his knees, and placed his forehead against the bars, crying quietly. Diego looked down at the old man and sighed.

"I'm sorry you had to find out this way, amigo," he said, not sounding very sorry at all, "but I guess you had to, one way or another."

"Yer me first mate, Diego," croaked Uncle Jack. "We're best friends! We've been through so many adventures together ..."

"I won't deny that I valued our friendship, Jack," said Diego, "but times change. *People* change. Friends grow apart."

"Best friends ain't *s'posed* to *grow apart*," said Uncle Jack bitterly. "That's why they're best friends."

"A lot has changed these past forty years, amigo. I'm not the man I was—"

"You sure ain't."

"—And neither are you," Diego finished.

There was a pause, and then Uncle Jack looked up through puffy, swollen eyes, and said, "How long, Diego? How long've yeh been plannin' to sell me to Chamberlain?"

"Ever since my capture back in March. But it wasn't Chamberlain who orchestrated all of this—it was *this* man." He indicated the masked man, who nodded briefly.

"It didn't take Lord Montigo long to see things from my point of view," he rumbled. "And the best part is that he volunteered to help me. All I had to do was propose my plan—"

"An' yeh went *along* with it?" Uncle Jack asked of Diego. "Y'agreed to hand this ... this ... *villain* our treasure on a silver platter?"

"Yes, I did," said Diego impatiently, "and I'll tell you why: I was tired, Jack. Tired of being an outlaw, tired of living life on the run. The age of pirates is over, amigo. It ended when you left, when you ran away. Without you, the BlackJacks had nothing. We fell apart."

"But I left ya in charge," said Uncle Jack. "Yeh had 'em at yer command, ye were s'posed to carry on in me absence."

Diego gave a short and hollow laugh. "Me, in charge? Hah! Diego Montigo, the pirate king, captain of the BlackJacks, and the second most feared pirate of all time." He spat bitterly on the floor. "What a joke. You honestly thought we could get by without you, Jack? That we'd be able to 'keep it together'?" He shook his head. "And you've been thinking it all these years. You're even more a fool than I was."

"Fool?" said Uncle Jack. "How were yeh a fool?"

"I believed in you!" Diego said sharply. "I believed that everything would be alright, that you had good reasons for leaving, and that I could carry on where you left off. I was a fool for not seeing you for what you had become: a coward."

"Don't you call my uncle a coward!" shouted Stanley, no longer content to be part of a passive audience. "He's not! He's brave! He's the bravest person I've ever seen!"

"Brave?" said Diego disdainfully, "Hah. Your *brave* uncle left right when we, his crew, needed him most. He became so afraid of Chamberlain, that he had to run away. He didn't stand and fight! He could have stayed and died an honourable death in battle, but he chose to run, to dishonour himself, to grow old before his time ... to become a disgrace to the name of pirate!"

"How *dare* you!" squawked Pericles. "You, who called yourself Jack's friend! The only one here who disgraces the name of pirate is *you!*"

"*Of course* I'm a disgrace!" said Diego. "I've been a disgrace for forty years. I'm no leader, no captain. I wasn't able to keep the BlackJacks together. For forty years my life spiraled down into ruin, as did *all* our lives, Jack. We were no longer the champions of the people that we used to be. The people didn't care about us anymore, especially after the death of the last king fifteen years ago. We pirates were reduced to nothing but a few scattered bands of rag-tag outlaws, hated and hunted by everyone.

"I'd been on the run for too long, Jack, and that's why I gave up."

Uncle Jack was shaking his head. "But what about the letter, Diego? What about all the things yeh said? What about savin' the treasure, rescuin' you? What about our reasons for GOIN' ON THIS RUDDY ADVENTURE?"

"All part of an elaborate scheme, I'm afraid," said the masked man, "a scheme of my own devising, with the sole purpose of luring you back to Rhedland, and back to your precious treasure."

"So," said Uncle Jack listlessly, "the letter was a forgery. None o' the news in it was true."

"Well, Lord Montigo *did* write it himself," said the masked man, "but he was, of course, required to exaggerate on a few details."

"This ... this can't be true," muttered Uncle Jack. "It can't."

"Oh, please!" said the masked man, "Are you really so arrogant as to believe that you made it this far on your own strength? Do you seriously think I was powerless to stop your escape from Ethelia? I have a legion of knights at my command! Did you not find it strange that only *two* of them were escorting you to the dungeons? Did you not wonder why your puny ship was being guarded by a mere *pair* of idiotic marines? Did you not wonder why the entire Rheddish navy wasn't mobilizing to stop you?"

Stanley looked around at his friends, all of whom had looks of shock on their faces.

"If it had been my wish," continued the masked man, "none of you would have left the city that day. I could easily have thrown you all into the deepest, darkest dungeon and left you there to rot, while I burned your ship to cinders. But I had an agenda, and if I've learned one lesson in my time on this earth, it's that careful planning is always rewarded. And I have to say that seeing the looks of disbelief on your dull, simian faces, is almost reward enough."

"An' what about *you?*" Uncle Jack fired at Diego, "What d'*you* get out've all this? What's *yer* reward?"

"A full pardon," said Diego, "A position in the parliament, lands, estates, a generous percentage of the treasure as it stands now … and *this*," he said, gesturing at his own face.

"In other words, a new lease on life," said the masked man. "You no doubt noticed Lord Montigo's youthful glow? *My* doing, of course, the product of many years of painstaking research."

"So," said Uncle Jack, not sounding too surprised, "Ya sold yer honour for youth, wealth, an' power, eh, *Lord Montigo?*"

Diego didn't answer.

"Yes, *Lord Montigo* did," said the masked man. "Pirate turned nobleman. It's like something out of a fairy tale."

There came a shout from the deck above. "*Lord Chamberlain, sir!*"

"Ezekiel," said the masked man, when it became clear that the Regent was not paying attention.

"Hm?" said Chamberlain, "Oh, forgive me, my lord, I was just … your plan was … was sheer brilliance, and I—"

"Of course it was brilliant," said the masked man, "and that is why I did not share it with you. Now then, I believe one of your men is calling you."

Looking more than a bit put out, Chamberlain cleared his throat and headed for the stairs. He returned a moment later. "My lord," he said stiffly, "my men have searched their ship from top to bottom. There is no trace of it aboard." He turned his icy-blue gaze on Diego. "Where is the mirror?" he demanded.

"It … it *should* be on the compass box," said Diego, looking from Chamberlain to the masked man.

"It isn't," said Chamberlain. "Otherwise my men would certainly have found it."

Diego began to look worried. "Perhaps it was washed overboard during the storm?"

"I hope for your sake that that is not the case," rumbled the masked man.

Diego looked sharply at Uncle Jack. "Where is it?" he demanded. "What did you do with it?"

"Threw it overboard," said Uncle Jack tonelessly.

"*What?*" cried Diego, "You wouldn't dare!"

"Sure I would," said Uncle Jack. "Better'n lettin' Mr. Mask get 'is hands on it."

Diego glared venomously at him. "Never mind," he said to Chamberlain and the masked man, "we probably don't need it, anyway. We must be close enough now that we—"

"*Probably don't need it?*" interrupted the masked man. "The greater part of my plan involved the Memory Mirror, so do not tell me that we *probably don't need it.*" He turned and started up the stairs.

"My lord," said Chamberlain, "where are you going?"

"To retrieve the mirror." And with that, he was gone. Chamberlain put a hand to his stubbly chin and stood for a moment in thought.

"Montigo," he said musingly, "do you think we are close to this fabled treasure of yours?"

"Well, yes," said Diego, "but—"

"Excellent," said Chamberlain. "We will continue on our present course. I've a feeling our goal lies just over the horizon."

"But ... don't you think we should wait for *him* to get back?" said Diego.

"He puts far too much trust in magical trinkets," said Chamberlain loftily. "You and I both know that there is no substitute for a sharp eye and a good glass."

"But I don't—"

"*I* am master of this ship, pirate," said Chamberlain, "and *I* say we find the treasure ourselves." He paused to smirk at Uncle Jack, then marched out of the room and up the stairs, followed closely by a protesting Diego.

Stanley watched them go, unable to decide which one he loathed more.

CHAPTER TWENTY-THREE: THAT SINKING FEELING

It was a subdued group that occupied the Maelstrom's brig, as the massive ship sailed southward through the Sea of Darkness. Diego's betrayal had come as a great shock to everyone. Even Stanley, who had only known Diego for a short time, felt a great sense of pain and loss, and had been sitting sullenly for hours in the corner by the bathroom bucket, when Alabaster approached him.

"Hey Stanley," he said, sitting down on the other side of the bucket.

"Hey Alabaster," Stanley murmured.

"How're you doing?" said Alabaster.

Stanley shrugged. "Better than Uncle Jack, I guess," he said, looking over to where the old man was hunched over, forehead resting against the iron bars.

Alabaster nodded. "Yeah. Nell's pretty mad, too. She told me to leave her alone just now."

"Hmm," said Stanley, only half-listening. They were silent for a moment, and then Alabaster said, with uncharacteristic seriousness,

"I'll never betray you, Stanley. We'll stay best buddies forever."

Stanley looked up at his friend's pale face. "Thanks, Alabaster," he said weakly. "Best buddies forever."

Alabaster nodded once, then went off to sit by himself. Stanley stared unseeingly at the wall for several minutes, then started with surprise as Grey flopped down next to him. "Whoa, Grey!" he said. "You scared me!"

Grey ignored this, and said, "Have you made peace with the girl?"

"Huh?" said Stanley. "You mean Nell? Yeah, I apologized for—"

"Good," said Grey. "I'm sorry if I was too … harsh."

Stanley raised his eyebrows. An apology from Grey was like snow in July. "Er … when were you too harsh?"

"When I told you not to defend me," said Grey. "I think I may have … said some things I didn't mean."

"Oh," said Stanley. "That's okay. But why are you telling me this now?"

Grey seemed to hesitate for a moment. "Because I … felt bad about it. I haven't felt bad about anything for a long time." He gave Stanley a very sharp glare, as if to convey the notion that his doom would be assured, should he breathe a word of this to anyone. Stanley quickly tried to change the subject.

"So uh … are you okay?" He eyed the glowing chain wrapped about Grey's arms and torso.

"I'll be fine," said Grey.

"Does it still hurt?" asked Stanley.

"Yes."

"A lot?"

"Yes."

If nothing else, Stanley was impressed with Grey's fortitude. "I wish there was something I could do," he said earnestly. "Isn't there a way to get that thing off?"

"Not that I know of," said Grey, wincing minutely.

Stanley found the chain's glow rather irritating; it made his eyes water a bit, and gave him a funny feeling, like his brain was buzzing. He wanted to put out that annoying glow, or at least diminish it. He reached out tentatively and grasped the chain, feeling a warm, prickly sensation in his hand as he did so. Grey had closed his eyes, and was not paying attention. Stanley gripped the chain tightly, and felt the warm prickliness run slowly up his arm. Staring in wonder, he watched as the magic chain grew dimmer and dimmer, until its glow vanished completely, leaving it nothing more than a normal, everyday length of chain. He let go and looked down at his hand. His whole arm now felt very hot, with that prickly pins-and-needles feeling running up and down it. He grimaced at the unpleasant sensation, but relaxed moments later as it began to fade. Within the space of five minutes, his arm felt normal again, all traces of unnatural heat having vanished. He looked up at Grey, who was now peering searchingly at him.

"The pain is gone," Grey stated. "What did you do?"

"I just held the chain for a bit, and it stopped glowing."

Grey eyed Stanley skeptically, then flexed his arms, straining against the chain. "I could break out of this easily," he said, scowling down at the dull metal links. "You must have done *something*."

Stanley shrugged. "If I did, I don't know what it was. Maybe it wears off after a while."

"Maybe," said Grey, flexing his arms again, making the chain protest.

"Wait!" said Stanley. "Don't break out of it yet—Chamberlain will probably just put another one on you."

"What are you suggesting?" said Grey.

"I dunno," said Stanley. "Why don't you just leave it on till the last minute? You know, let everyone think you're helpless, and then, when they're not expecting it ... *wham!*" He looked around the cell. No one else seemed to have been paying attention to the hushed conversation, not even Alabaster, who was sitting three feet away.

"Alright," said Grey. "I'll wait."

Stanley couldn't help but grin. He could imagine the look on Chamberlain's face when Grey broke free of the formerly-magical chain. A thought suddenly crossed his mind, and he looked up at Grey's midnight-black face.

"Grey," he said, tapping Grey's forearm, "can I ask you something?"

"Not much I can do to stop you," said Grey.

"Uh," said Stanley, "Okay ... er, why did you choose to come along on this trip?"

Grey glowered at him, then looked away. Stanley waited two full minutes for an answer, and was just about to give up, when Grey, still looking away, said,

"Back in the dungeons, your uncle asked you a question."

Stanley couldn't see how this answered *his* question, but kept quiet, waiting for Grey to continue.

"He asked you if I was a friend or a foe," said Grey.

Stanley remembered that. "And?"

"And," said Grey, turning his head and meeting Stanley's gaze, "You said I was a friend."

Stanley nodded. "Yeah, I did."

"I don't think I've ever had a friend," said Grey. He turned away again and closed his eyes.

Stanley tried to think of a way to respond to this emotional outpouring, but was interrupted as Uncle Jack got to his feet and cleared his throat. His eyes were puffy and red, but his voice was as strong as ever as he said,

"Mates, I've got somethin' to say to the lot've ya."

The crew looked up from whatever gloomy thoughts they were entertaining, and gave him their full attention.

"I ... I just wanna say," said Uncle Jack, "that I'm sorry ..."

"Oh, don't start," said Pericles.

"'Ere, just let me finish!" said Uncle Jack crossly. "I'm sorry we ended up in this fix we're in. Ye can say 'it's not me fault' as much as ya want, but really, it *is* me fault. As cap'n, I've gotta accept responsibility for the actions of me crew, an' that includes mutiny."

"Oh, wake up, Jackson!" said Pericles. "Diego's treachery had nothing to do with you. No one could have predicted that a man who once called himself your best friend, would turn on you and sell you to your arch enemy. We had no reason *not* to trust Diego."

"Be that as it may," said Uncle Jack, "we're now in a terrible fix, an' I ain't surprised if each an' every one o' ya 're wantin' to keelhaul me right now."

"We don't want to keelhaul you, Uncle Jack," said Stanley, not having the foggiest idea of what 'keelhaul' meant.

"Yeah!" said Alabaster, jumping to his feet. "If anybody should be keelhauled, it's Diego!"

Even Nell stood up, and Stanley saw a gleam in her eyes. "Mr. Lee," she said stiffly, "you've brought us a long way, and it's been dangerous, but *you got us through it!* The armour fish, the kraken ..."

"The masked man," said Stanley, "the siren, Chamberlain!"

"I think Diego was wrong," said Nell. "The age of pirates isn't over—not as long as people like you are around, Mr. Lee."

Uncle Jack's mouth was open. "Ya mean yer not all ... ready to make me walk the plank?"

"Of course not!" Alabaster burst out. "You're the greatest pirate ever, Uncle Jack! I knew it the moment I saw you, and so did Stanley! Right, Stanley?"

"Right!" said Stanley.

"We may not have chosen to come along on this adventure," said Nell, "but even if we'd had a choice, if we could go back and do it differently, I'd still want to be a part of it."

"Even if ya knew it'd end here?" said Uncle Jack.

"But we're *not* at the end!" said Stanley.

"Not at the end ..." mused Uncle Jack.

"Don't you see?" said Pericles. "Miss Hawthorne is correct. The age of pirates is *not* over. Just look at these children, listen to what they're saying. They are courageous, and adventurous! They're unwilling to give up! The age of pirates *can't* be over—we've a whole new generation of them right here!"

Stanley was partially aware that Pericles had just called him, Alabaster, and Nell pirates, and that he had never received a more flattering compliment in his life. Uncle Jack had a stunned expression on his face, and was gaping at the children as if seeing them for the first time.

"Aye," he said. "O' course ... *we're pirates, all, by thunder, an' pirates don't give up so easy!*" He began to spin on the spot, and broke into a brief rendition of his favourite song:

> *Our guns we'll let fly*
> *An' we'll never say die!*
> *An' the greatest of pirates we'll be,*
> *Oh, the greatest of pirates we'll be!*

"Right!" he said stoutly after finishing the verse, "Yer all absolutely right, an' I've been a ruddy fool. I'm proud to have each an' every one o' ya as part o' me crew, an' ... well, we'll find a way outta this mess, or my name ain't—"

"*LAAAAANND HO!*"

The cry came from above decks, and was followed by a symphony of running feet and excited chatter.

"Land ho?" echoed Stanley. "Could they have ..." He trailed off as Uncle Jack's face fell.

"What?" said Alabaster. "They've found land? Are we—"

"We've reached the island," said Nell solemnly.

"Oh dear," said Pericles.

Benjamin punched his own palm and sat down heavily beside Grey, who looked angry, as usual. Uncle Jack pursed his lips, then took a deep breath.

"Well, mates," he said, "it's lookin' like our worst fears've come true. Chamberlain's found the island where our treasure's buried. Looks like luck's been with 'im all along."

"Luck be damned," squawked Pericles, "if it leads a tapeworm like *him* to our treasure!"

"Take it easy, Pericles," said Uncle Jack, "an' watch yer language. Yer forgettin' somethin' important."

"Oh yes?" said Pericles. "And what is that?"

"Mr. Mask ain't around," said Uncle Jack, with a thoughtful grin. "There's no one around to keep ol' Zeke in line. We might just be able to swing somethin', if only we could get outta this—"

He was interrupted by the all-too-familiar sound of clanking armour, and moments later, a huge Knight of the Silver Sword came marching down the stairs. The prisoners remained still and quiet as the knight unlocked the cell door with a hefty iron key, and beckoned them forward.

"You are wanted above," said the knight, as he opened the door. "Do not try to escape, or I will be forced to end your mortal existence."

Despite this dire warning, Uncle Jack looked as if Christmas had come early. He followed the knight out of the cell and up the stairs, with Stanley and the others close behind. They ascended eight flights of stairs, and then they were out in the open air, standing in a semi-circle on the main deck. As fresh as the air was after hours in the smelly brig, the joy of being outdoors was reduced significantly by the presence of a thick fog. At first, Stanley was alarmed by the fog's presence, but he soon decided that it was nothing like the kraken mist they had encountered. This fog carried no feeling of oppression or foreboding, and was not nearly as thick. The ocean waves were also lapping cheerfully at the Maelstrom's hull, and there was no smell of befouled bleach.

The knight motioned for the group to follow, and led them to the Maelstrom's forecastle, where Chamberlain and Diego were waiting. Diego stared down at the deck and said nothing, but Chamberlain couldn't keep his mouth shut.

"Well well well!" he said smugly as Uncle Jack and the others approached, "If it isn't my noble adversary, Jack Lee, and his ragtag crew of pirates! Welcome!"

"What're ya welcomin' us for, ya daft pratt?" said Uncle Jack. "We've been aboard yer ship for hours."

"Ah, Jackson," said Chamberlain, smiling nastily, "always trying to ruin my fun. Well, you'll not ruin it today, I'm afraid. Behold!"

With a flourish, he pointed past the bow to something far ahead in the mist. It looked like a rock, or perhaps an island. "Your treasure island, Jack!" Chamberlain sang gleefully. "It won't be long before we arrive."

Uncle Jack sighed. "I guess that's the shape of it. Zeke, yer one lucky son of a—"

"*Sir!*" A gangly, greasy-looking sailor came tottering towards them and saluted hastily.

"What is it?" barked Chamberlain.

"Beggin' yer pardon, sir," said the sailor, "but th' compass 'as gone 'aywire, an' so's the chronometer! There's no way o' knowin' where we are!"

"Stop sniveling!" spat Chamberlain. "Stay our present course, towards that island."

"Aye sir," said the sailor, saluting again and scurrying off to relay the orders.

"I don't suppose *you* can explain this?" Chamberlain said to Uncle Jack.

"It's a turnabout field," said Uncle Jack. "A magical force generated by the very rock o' the island. It messes up machinery an' causes this here fog that we're sailin' through."

Chamberlain rounded on Diego. "And when were *you* going to inform me of this, *Lord* Montigo?"

"It, uh ... slipped my mind," Diego said lamely.

Chamberlain chuckled wickedly. "Our dark master would not be pleased with you right now, would he?"

Diego said nothing, and went back to examining the deck boards.

"Oh," said Uncle Jack with mock surprise, "Is Mr. Mask not back yet?"

"No," said Chamberlain, "and I suppose I should thank you for that, Lee."

"Want the treasure for yerself, eh, Zeke?" said Uncle Jack. "I guess yer boss doesn't keep ya 'round for yer loyalty an' affection, eh?"

"Don't talk to me about loyalty, pirate," said Chamberlain. "My loyalty is to the Empire, as it has always been, and now that the wealth and power of the BlackJack Bonanza are within my reach, I'm prepared to reclaim my rightful position as Regent. That mad sorcerer's days on the throne are over."

"Ha!" said Uncle Jack. "So yeh've just been bidin' yer time, waitin' for the right chance to betray yer evil master. You'd've made a good pirate, Zeke."

Chamberlain grinned hideously. "You may be right, Jack, you may be right."

*   *   *   *

Within a quarter of an hour, the Maelstrom had closed the distance to the island. The anchor was dropped and Chamberlain ordered his men to form a landing party. Every man who volunteered to join the mission was promised a minute share of the treasure, so it was no surprise that every one of the Maelstrom's rowboats was crammed with greedy, foul-mouthed sailors before you could say 'yo ho ho and a bottle of rum'.

Chamberlain turned casually to Uncle Jack and said, "It looks as if we'll be taking *your* boat."

"What'ya mean, *we?*" said Uncle Jack.

"*We*, as in you, me, and your crew," said Chamberlain. "I want you all to be there when my men unearth your treasure."

And so it was that Stanley found himself back aboard the Ogopogo, staring sullenly at the huge lump of rock that was Uncle Jack's treasure island. Also aboard were Alabaster, Nell, Benjamin, Pericles, Grey, and Uncle Jack, not to mention a battalion of Knights of the Silver Sword, who were crammed into the hold, and a gaggle of sailors who were already fighting over their shares of the treasure.

Stanley looked up at Grey, who was standing stock still and glaring ahead at the approaching island. The fact that Grey could escape at any moment was no longer a comfort; as powerful as Grey seemed, Stanley doubted that he could fight off thirty-five knights and a hoard of treasure-crazed sailors. Alabaster nudged Stanley, and said, in a conversational tone,

"D'you think *we'll* get a share of the treasure?"

"I doubt it," said Stanley.

"Well that's not very fair," said Alabaster. "You mean to tell me that the members of Uncle Jack's crew don't get any treasure, but all these smelly sailors *do?*"

"Alabaster," said Nell, "Chamberlain is *stealing* the treasure. Thieves don't give things to the people they steal from."

"Oh yeah," said Alabaster.

Stanley sighed. Under different circumstances, the sight of that rocky island coming closer and closer might have been exhilarating. He had pictured this scene many times in his mind: a bright and sunny day, a joyful squawk from Pericles, a shout of triumph from Uncle Jack as he called the children to the bow and pointed to an island covered in palm trees, with a waterfall cascading down a tall mountain at its centre. He had imagined the happy feeling of a job well done, the feeling that their quest was almost over.

Now, though, Stanley was standing quietly with his friends, a captive of Uncle Jack's enemy. There was no sun shining down on the tiny fleet of boats as they sailed towards the island, which was devoid of palm trees and waterfalls.

"All hands, disembark!" shouted Chamberlain as the Ogopogo bumped roughly into the island's rocky shore.

"'Ere, watch how ya treat me ship!" said Uncle Jack.

"It's *my* ship now, Jack," Chamberlain sneered as he pushed by, Diego at his heels.

The gangplank was lowered, and soon all the knights and sailors were out of their boats and trudging across the island's moss-covered ground. Stanley and the others were encouraged to walk at a brisk pace, for a line of knights followed close behind, swords draw, ready to jab any stragglers. All around them, sailors were rushing about, spades and pickaxes grasped in their hands, looks of acute greed on their faces. Some carried wooden boxes, upon which were written the words

DANGER! EXPLOSIVE

"NO ONE DIGS 'TILL I SAY SO," bellowed Chamberlain, as he marched along at the head of the procession.

The island sloped steeply up from the ocean, and there was no flat ground to be seen. The climb to the summit was a tiring one, mostly for the children, who were notably shorter than everyone else. Stanley slipped more than once on the damp, slimy moss, which seemed to be the only vegetation growing on the island. Here and there, small patches of smooth, flat rock were visible, but the moss covered the island almost completely. At last they reached the crest of the island, from which they could look all about at the surrounding area. There was not much to see. All around them the moss-covered rock sloped down to the sea. There was nothing particularly interesting about the land mass; no land marks or suspicious areas to show the shrewd treasure-seeker exactly where the hoard might be buried.

Chamberlain formed a search party and ordered them to sweep the entire area, but they returned with no helpful information. The island was bleak, bare, and empty.

Chamberlain turned to Uncle Jack. "I don't suppose you have any information that could be of use to us?"

"Like what?" said Uncle Jack.

"LIKE WHERE YOU BURIED THE BLOODY TREASURE!" roared Chamberlain.

"Sorry, Zeke," said Uncle Jack with a shrug, "but any memory I had o' the treasure's location is now in the Memory Mirror. Pretty frustratin' for *you*, eh?"

"You have no idea," growled Chamberlain. "And what about *you?*" he said sharply, rounding on Diego. "You don't remember anything, either, *hm?*"

"I remember even less than Jack," said Diego. "I guess we *do* need the memory mirror ..."

"*We do not!*" snapped Chamberlain. "The treasure is here, and we will find it. It's just a matter of time."

"What're ya gonna do," said Uncle Jack, "dig up the entire island?"

"If necessary," said Chamberlain.

"Better get at it b'fore yer boss gets back, eh?"

Chamberlain went a bit pale, and glanced nervously up at the fog-enshrouded sky. He then looked around at his men. "*Well, what are you waiting for, you useless sea-swine?*" he shouted. "START DIGGING!"

Every sailor promptly rushed off to find himself a spot to dig. The first pickaxe was raised for its first assault on the ground, when someone yelled, "WAIT!"

All eyes turned towards the man, as Chamberlain stalked over to where he was crouching.

"What is it, seaman?" demanded the Regent.

"Er, beggin' yer pardon, sir," said the sailor, "but I jus' thought as ya might want to take a look at this."

Chamberlain took a look, then straightened up and started to laugh. He laughed and laughed, and one by one, his men joined in.

"SHUT UP!" shouted Chamberlain, his laughter ceasing immediately. The sailors obeyed. "Jack," said Chamberlain, "Montigo, all of you, come closer, please."

Stanley, Uncle Jack, Diego, and the rest came cautiously forward.

"What's got ya in such a state?" asked Uncle Jack.

Chamberlain merely smiled and pointed at the ground. In the midst of the thick, green moss, a large patch of the island's rock had been laid bare. The rock seemed to have been cracked, and the exposed part looked like this:

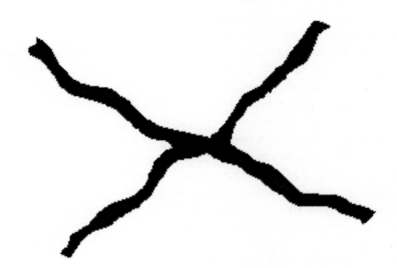

Stanley stared at the crack, then at Chamberlain, who was gleefully watching Uncle Jack's surprised expression.

"X marks the spot, Jack!" trilled Chamberlain. "X marks the spot!" and then he burst into another round of uninhibited mirth.

While Chamberlain doubled over with laughter, Stanley knelt down and examined the exposed patch of rock. The cracks certainly did look like an X, but there was something about them that just didn't look right. Looking at the rock and the cracks gave him a funny tickle in the back of his mind, as if he had seen them before.

"Get back, boy," said Chamberlain, shoving Stanley backwards. Having recomposed himself, the Regent spread his arms and shouted, "Alright men … LET'S DIG!"

With a collective cheer, the mob of sailors rushed forward and attacked the ground with spades and pickaxes. Chamberlain shooed Stanley and the others out of the way, and watched contentedly as the men worked frantically at the rock.

"Is it really buried here?" Nell asked of Uncle Jack.

"I dunno," he said. "I wish I could remember."

"I kinda thought it might be hidden a little better," said Alabaster. "I mean, not that it was easy to find or anything. I just thought it might be hidden, you know, magically."

A funny look came over Uncle Jack's face, but he said nothing.

Nell looked searchingly at Stanley, who was doing some very heavy thinking. "What's the matter, Stanley?" she asked.

Stanley was hesitant to answer; he wasn't really sure, himself. "I dunno," he said, tapping the side of his head. "Something about that rock with the X on it … like I've seen it somewhere before …"

"When could you have seen it before now?" said Nell, looking intently at the patch of rock, which was standing up well to the blows raining down upon it.

"Haargh!" growled a large, sweaty sailor. "This ain't goin' nowhere! Just look at me pickaxe!" The sweaty man held the mining tool up for all to see, and there was no questioning what was wrong with it. "All bent outta shape, it is!" cried the sailor, flinging aside the now useless implement.

The other diggers were faring little better; all around the dig site, men were cursing and complaining, and tossing their broken equipment away in fits of childish rage.

"Alright, alright, STOP!" roared Chamberlain, before the diggers could resort to hammering on the rock with their bare fists. "CEASE YOUR DIGGING!"

The men obeyed, and when Chamberlain was sure they were all paying attention, he said, in a much calmer tone, "How far down are we?"

None of the sailors answered.

"*HOW FAR?*" Chamberlain shouted, shoving two diggers out of the way to get a better view. Stanley couldn't see the Regent's face, but the deadly silence told him that he was not pleased.

"H-half an inch, m'lord," said the sweaty sailor.

"*Half an inch?*" hissed Chamberlain.

"Give or take a quarter-inch, m'lord ..."

"*We just ruined all that mining equipment for a bloody HALF-INCH?*"

"Give or take—"

"SHUT UP!" Chamberlain rounded on Uncle Jack, taking six menacing steps forward as he said, "*What-kind-of-rock-is-this?*"

"How should I know?" said Uncle Jack, herding the children behind him.

"Oh, that's right," said Chamberlain, "you don't remember. Convenient, that."

"Ain't nothin' convenient about it. It's the truth."

"*It's a lie!*" said Chamberlain, drawing his pistol and pointing it at Uncle Jack. "*Now you either start giving me some answers, or—*"

"*Stop!*" shouted Diego, placing a restraining hand on the Regent's arm. "He doesn't know!"

"Do not touch me again, Montigo!" said Chamberlain, shrugging off Diego's hand. "Or I may construe your current behavior as *treason.*"

"I tell you, Jack knows nothing without the Memory Mirror," Diego persisted.

"And I tell *you* that—"

Whatever Chamberlain had been about to tell Diego was forgotten as, with a deep, groaning rumble, the entire island began to shake.

"EARTHQUAKE!" cried several sailors, as the ground shook fiercely from side to side.

"STAND YOUR GROUND, YOU WORTHLESS CURS!" shouted Chamberlain, raising his pistol into the air and firing three times.

Stanley covered his ears and crouched down to keep himself from falling over. He had never experienced an earthquake before, but he found it rather tame compared to some of the dangers he had already been through. The tremor ceased, and a relieved sigh swept through the company.

"BACK TO WORK!" yelled Chamberlain.

"I'm not likin' this," said Uncle Jack in an undertone. "It don't feel right."

"I agree," said Pericles. "There's something about this island ..."

Stanley agreed, too. The thought that had been tickling at his mind was still there, and it had something to do with that big patch of rock with the X on it.

The sounds of digging could once again be heard as the sailors went back to work. Every so often, another tool was tossed aside, rendered useless by the unnaturally strong rock. Twice more, earthquakes shook the island, growing stronger each time. The third quake caught most of them off guard, sending people sprawling heavily on the ground. Stanley was knocked over by Nell, who had been knocked over by Alabaster, and the three of them tumbled down the slope. Instinctively, the children grabbed onto the moss, a great section of which tore away, revealing the smooth rock underneath.

"Something is very wrong with this island," said Nell, picking herself up of the ground.

"Maybe it's a volcano," said Alabaster, not sounding too worried by the idea. Nell, however, experienced a noteable lightening of complexion.

"A volcano!" she breathed. "You may be right, Alabaster."

"Ha!" said Alabaster. "You make it sound like a *bad* thing."

"It *is* a bad thing, *if we're standing on it when it erupts!*"

"Oh yeah," said Alabaster. "We should probably get off the island, then, eh?"

"Yes!" said Nell, "Of *course* we should get off the island! But we've got to tell—"

"'Ere, you kids, what're y'up to?" A grouchy-looking sailor had approached the children while they were talking, and was frowning at them. Alabaster and Nell both started talking at once.

"It's a volcano!"

"Well, it might be, we're not sure."

"It could erupt at any minute!"

"The island is definitely unstable."

"We've gotta get back to the boats!"

But the sailor wasn't paying any attention to their rambling. Instead, he was staring at the same thing Stanley had been staring at for the past minute or so.

"What the devil?" said the sailor, taking a closer look at the patch of exposed rock. He looked back up the hill to where his comrades were digging feverishly, then down at Stanley. "What's this?" he demanded, pointing at the rock, "Some kind of trick?"

Stanley didn't answer at first. He was starting to think that maybe the whole thing *was* a trick, after all, for there was an X marked on the rock, an X identical to the one at the top of the hill.

"Speak up!" barked the sailor.

"I don't know," said Stanley brusquely, "but there's another X right here."

"Aye, I can see that!" said the sailor. "What's it doin' 'ere?"

"Oh, how should we know?" said Nell, stepping in front of Stanley as if to shield him from an attack. "Do you think we go around drawing X's on the ground for fun?'

This seemed to bring the sailor to his senses. "Well, I s'pose not, but ..."

"Hey, look!" cried Alabaster. "I found another one!" Alabaster had pulled up another section of moss, revealing part of yet another X. Nell and Stanley looked at eachother, and attacked the moss themselves. The sailor joined in, and soon they had uncovered a thirty-foot-square section of bare rock.

"X's all over th' place!" exclaimed the sailor.

"Looks like a quilt," observed Alabaster.

"It's just the pattern on the stone," sighed Nell. "There *are* no actual X's."

The ground began to shake again, and when the tremor had subsided, Chamberlain's voice rang down from the top of the hill:

"WHAT ARE YOU DOING DOWN THERE?"

The sailor saluted and called back, "SOMETHIN' YEH SHOULD SEE DOWN 'ERE, SIR!"

Moments later, Chamberlain was staring furiously at the multitude of interconnected X's. "Very well," he said, turning around, "Come on."

The Regent led the way back to the dig site.

"You three alright?" said Uncle Jack as Chamberlain ordered the children to stand with the rest of the prisoners.

Stanley nodded. "Yeah, but there's—"

He was interrupted by a loud shout from Chamberlain.

"STOP DIGGING!"

Every man obeyed, stopping to look up at the Regent.

"*Clear the dig site!*" Chamberlain ordered. "*I want the explosives brought in!*"

"*Explosives?*" shrieked Nell. "You can't use explosives, the island is unstable!"

Chamberlain ignored her completely.

"'Ere!" said Uncle Jack, "Ya hear that, Ezekiel? Ya might not've been able to tell from the earthquakes, but—"

"Shut up," said Chamberlain. "Of *course* the island is unstable, but it was not *I* who chose to bury treasure here. I'll unearth that hoard, even if I have to blast this rock to pieces!"

"Now really!" said Pericles, "Are you saying that you're willing to kill us all, just for the sake of a bit of treasure?"

"It's a risk I'm willing to take," said Chamberlain. "Do you think I *like* serving that masked maniac? Do you think I enjoy the constant pain and humiliation? Do you think I *want* to be a puppet?"

There was a moment of silence as everyone stared wide-eyed at the Regent. The sailors were confused, and a bit shocked; having never seen the masked man before, they had no idea what their commander was talking about.

"That's right," said Chamberlain, "I'm nothing but a puppet, and have been for too long, but that will change *today*. I will use this treasure to re-take my place as true lord of the Empire, and cast down that demented sorcerer." He glared around at his men, then shouted, "SO GET THOSE EXPLOSIVES READY!"

*   *   *   *

In a matter of minutes, Chamberlain's men had packed a sizeable pile of explosives into the shallow hole they'd managed to dig. All were ordered to get away from the blast site, while the Knights of the Silver Sword formed a living barrier to keep everyone back. The ground rumbled, and more than a few faces wore looks of concern.

"I'm tellin' ya, Zeke," said Uncle Jack, as Chamberlain produced a box of matches from his pocket, "think about what yer doin'. If this island really is a volcano, we'll all be blown sky high!"

Chamberlain ignored him, but just as he was about to strike the match, Diego placed a hand on his shoulder.

"Chamberlain, wait—"

"Montigo, I warned you about what would happen if you ever touched me again."

"I know," said Diego, "but maybe we should rethink this."

"Getting cold feet, are you?" sneered Chamberlain.

"No," said Diego, "I just think that we're taking an unnecessary risk. Jack—er—*Lee* may be right. What if the island really *is* a volcano?"

"What if it *is?*" snarled Chamberlain. "What would you have me do, *hmm?* Waste lord knows how much time painstakingly excavating every inch of this accursed place? Wait for the dark man to come back and re-take control of the operation?"

"If we had the memory mirror—"

"But we don't. Which is why we're doing it my way."

"No," said Diego as the island gave another lurch. "It isn't safe, and I won't endanger these children just to—"

WHACK

Before Diego could finish speaking, Chamberlain dealt him a backhanded blow to the face, sending him staggering backwards. Stanley winced. Nell gasped. Alabaster cringed.

"Pathetic," hissed Chamberlain. "I knew you were not to be trusted, Montigo."

Stanley glanced over at Uncle Jack, who had taken a step forward as if to intervene, but was now holding himself back.

"A traitor to the crown is ever a traitor," said Chamberlain, as Diego nursed a bloody lip. "Your attempt to interfere is an act of treason." He struck the match and held it aloft. "For Rhedland."

"Well," said Alabaster, "if we're all about to get blown up, I guess things can't get much worse. Knock on wood," he added, rapping his knuckles on a nearby patch of bare rock. It made a hollow clunking sound.

Nell stared at Alabaster with mixed exasperation and disbelief. Stanley stared at the patch of rock, and as the sound of Alabaster's knocking vibrated across his eardrums, an electric chemical signal rippled through his brain. It was as if a piece of a puzzle had suddenly fallen into place. A memory leapt into his conscious thoughts, a memory from not so long ago: a memory from the first day at Uncle Jack's house:

Alabaster stepped closer and tapped the side of the head.
(The armour fish's head at the top of the second floor landing.)
"Hard as rock! Look at those armour plates!"
(Armour plates. Armour plates as hard as rock. Rock-hard armour plates. *Rock*.)

"This isn't rock!" Stanley suddenly cried, making Nell and Alabaster leap back in surprise.

"Steady, lad," said Uncle Jack, as Stanley began to babble incoherently. "Slow down."

"This-is-not-rock!" said Stanley. Why were they just staring at him? Didn't they understand? Couldn't they hear the urgency in his voice? Wasn't it all plainly, terribly obvious?

"If it's not rock, then what is it?" said Nell, trying helpfully to draw information out of him.

"Armour plates!" said Stanley, gesturing wildly. "Like on an armour fish!"

"Oh, no," said Uncle Jack.

"Well that's no reason to go nuts," said Alabaster.

"Actually, I think it may be," said Uncle Jack. "Dang, why didn't I see it b'fore now?"

"See *what?*" said Pericles.

"Armour plates," said Nell. "An *animal's* armour plates …"

"More like a shell," said Uncle Jack. "I … think we're standin' on the back of a Titanodon."

"What?" said Pericles. "*The mythical giant turtle-fish?* Now really—"

"Clamp it, Pericles," said Uncle Jack.

"Now wait a sec here," said Alabaster. "What's a giant turtle-fish doing on a volcanic island?"

"There *is* no island, you half-wit!" said Nell, grabbing Alabaster by the front of his shirt. "The turtle-fish *is* the island!"

"Neat!" said Alabaster.

"We can't let them blow up those explosives!" said Stanley.

"That we can't," said Uncle Jack. "Benjamin, c'mon!" He made his way towards Chamberlain, who had accidentally dropped his match, and was trying unsuccessfully to light a new one.

Stanley, meanwhile, had gone pale, and was feeling shaky all over. The idea of standing on the back of some gigantic sea creature was unsettling enough, but knowing that that same gigantic sea creature was about to become very angry added a whole new dimension to it all. Plus, he felt sorry for the poor beast, who was about to enter a world of hurt unless Chamberlain was stopped.

"*Ezekiel!*" shouted Uncle Jack. "*Stop! Yer makin' a big mistake!*"

"No," said Chamberlain, "*you* are making a big mistake. Detain him."

Two Knights of the Silver Sword stepped forward and drew their broadswords before advancing on Uncle Jack.

"This ain't the right island!" said Uncle Jack, trying to dodge around the knights. "It ain't even an *island*, it's a Titanodon! That's why we've been feelin' all these earthquakes—the beast's been movin' around! If we blow a hole in its shell, who knows *what'll* happen?"

A worried murmur swept through the crowd of sailors. They had all heard stories of the Titanodon, and standing here in this fog, with the ground shaking beneath them, those stories seemed plausible at the very least.

"What if it *is* the great turtle-fish?" said one sailor.

"Narr, 'tis just a story to scare kiddies," said another.

"It's th' beast itself, I'll warrant," said a third.

"Hogwash!" spat a fourth.

The discussion carried on for a time, but the sailors eventually agreed that returning to the boats for the time being was the best course of action.

"Nobody's going anywhere!" snarled Chamberlain, as the sailors began to make their way back to the boats. They all froze and stared at him uncertainly.

"But sir—" one of the sailors began, but was interrupted by a loud BANG as Chamberlain fired his pistol into the air. The men cowered as the Regent aimed the gun in their general direction.

Again the ground shook as Chamberlain said, "The next man who tries to make for the boats will be shot. We've come too far to be fooled by some stupid pirate's trick, and I will not leave until I've received my dues!"

The sailors looked at eachother uncertainly. Some looked angry, others looked afraid.

They're starting to see that he's a lunatic, thought Stanley.

"And," Chamberlain continued, "if any of you are entertaining thoughts of mutiny ..." He waved a hand at the Knights of the Silver Sword, who drew their weapons as if they'd been waiting for a cue. "Just remember who commands the knights."

The sailors grumbled at this, but none of them was fool enough to take on the knights; not at this juncture, at any rate.

Not quite understanding why, Stanley surprised everyone by shouting at the top of his lungs, "STOP HIM! DON'T LET HIM DO THIS! SAVE THE TITANODON, AND ALL OF US!"

Chamberlain rounded on him, a look of outrage and disbelief on his face. "*Insolent whelp!*" he raged, spit flying from his mouth as he pointed his pistol at Stanley.

"NO!" roared Uncle Jack, leaping to Stanley's rescue.

But he was too late.

BANG went the gun.

And the bullet flew forth to bury itself in Diego Montigo's chest. Diego Montigo, who had stepped in front of Stanley at the very last moment.

Diego staggered backwards while Chamberlain stood a short distance away with the smoking gun in his hand and a surprised look on his face. Diego turned, clutching his chest with both hands, and smiled at Stanley. A small trickle of blood issued from the corner of his mouth, and he swayed dangerously.

Stanley could only stare as Uncle Jack rushed to the stricken Diego's side. Diego coughed, and more blood came out of his mouth. He had gone very pale, and Uncle Jack helped him sit down.

"Diego," said Uncle Jack, his voice wavering only slightly as he propped up the wounded man in a sitting position.

"D-didn't want your … nephew to g-get … h-hurt," said Diego with some effort.

"Ya saved 'im," Uncle Jack said, gazing down at Diego's pale face.

"Good, good," Diego said, smiling weakly. "Jack," (his voice was almost a whisper now) "Jack …"

"I'm 'ere, Diego," said Uncle Jack, leaning closer. "I'm 'ere."

"I … I'm sorry," said Diego, pausing to take a shallow, rattling breath.

"Easy, easy," said Uncle Jack quietly.

Diego coughed weakly. "I'm sorry for betraying you … for tricking you."

"Shh-shh, quiet now," said Uncle Jack, "Don't you worry 'bout all that. I … I forgive ya."

Diego smiled. "I know now that I didn't … m-mean those things I said … back aboard the Maelstrom."

"I know, Diego, I know."

"The … the age of pirates isn't over, amigo … don't let it end yet … don't let him get the … treasure."

"Don't you worry 'bout that," said Uncle Jack.

Diego smiled again, his breathing now very short. He looked up at the fog-covered sky. "I … I long for the old days," he said, and then his body relaxed, his head lolling onto Uncle Jack's shoulder. All was quiet for a moment, and then Uncle Jack gently laid his friend down on the mossy ground.

Stanley could only stare in shock at the lifeless man before him. He had never even known anyone who had died, let alone seen it happen right in front of him. He felt numb, almost as if his brain didn't believe what his eyes were telling it.

Stanley looked to his left and saw that Nell was gripping Alabaster's shoulder very tightly. Her face was expressionless, but her skin was dead white, her eyes wide. Alabaster looked completely stunned, as if he wasn't sure what had just happened. And then the tears began to flow from Stanley's eyes, and he bowed his head, letting the salty drops of water fall to the ground like rain.

"Hmph," said Chamberlain. "A fitting end for a pitiful cur like him."

"CHAMBERLAIN, YOU RUDDY, LILY-LIVERED MURDERIN' SON OF A SEA SLUG!" Roared Uncle Jack, jumping up and drawing his cutlass, "I'M TAKIN' YOU DOWN RIGHT NOW!"

"I wouldn't try it if I were you," said Chamberlain, now pointing his pistol at Uncle Jack. "Not unless you want to end up like *Lord* Montigo, there."

Uncle Jack pointed his cutlass at the Regent, his eyes blazing. "Stop hidin' behind yer gun, Ezekiel, an' face me like a man, or else shoot me down an' prove once more that yer a stinkin' yellow-bellied coward."

Chamberlain's scowl was vicious, indeed, but after a moment, he lowered his pistol and tossed it on the ground. "Very well, Jackson. No more playing about. We will settle this here, on your treasure isle, once and for all." He drew his own blade and raised it above his head. "Have at you, pirate!"

Chamberlain rushed towards Uncle Jack and thrust his sword at his chest. Uncle Jack was far quicker than he looked, though, and easily side-stepped the attack, parried Chamberlain's blade aside, and elbowed him hard in the nose.

"Yer losin' yer touch, Zeke," said Uncle Jack as Chamberlain staggered backward, his hands held to his face. The ground gave an unsettling lurch just then, and from his perch on Benjamin's shoulder, Pericles squawked,

"Now really, that's enough, both of you! We *must* get off this island!"

Uncle Jack was standing before Chamberlain, the tip of his sword inches from the Regent's throat.

"Go ahead," hissed Chamberlain, as blood ran freely from his damaged nose, "finish me off. Take your revenge." He turned his head slightly and spat blood on the ground.

Stanley watched with horrified apprehension. Uncle Jack turned his head slightly, and met his gaze. A slight smile lit the wrinkled face for an instant, and then he turned back to Chamberlain and said,

"We're leavin'. Ya might want to do the same." And with that, he sheathed his sword and began to walk swiftly towards the boats. "C'mon mates," he called to his crew. "Back to the Ogopogo, an' be ready to make sail."

Stanley fell into line behind Alabaster, and took great satisfaction at the astonished look on Chamberlain's face as he passed by. The knights didn't move an inch, nor did the sailors, who looked almost as surprised as the Regent.

"Come back here!" shouted Chamberlain, getting shakily to his feet. "I don't want your mercy, *pirate!*"

"Too bad," Uncle Jack called over his shoulder, "ya got it."

"STOP THEM!" shrieked Chamberlain.

But none of the sailors moved to obey. Chamberlain rounded on them, his face taking on a monstrous look with the blood drying under his nose and the mad gleam in his ice-blue eye.

"I SAID STOP THEM!"

Still the sailors ignored him.

"YOU!" Chamberlain bellowed, pointing at the knights, "KNIGHTS OF THE SILVER SWORD! OBEY ME! STOP THEM!"

But the knights remained as still as statues.

"*OBEY ME!*" Chamberlain all but screamed.

Stanley, who had been looking over his shoulder at the ranting Regent, walked right into Alabaster, who had stopped suddenly. "*Oof!* Alabaster, what—"

But he didn't finish his question. The reason why Alabaster, and Nell, and Uncle Jack had stopped so suddenly was right there in front of them. A semi-transparent wall of darkness had sprung up out of nowhere, cutting off their path to the boats.

And beyond the wall stood the masked man. His hooded robe was soaked and dripping, and clung heavily to him, hinting at a sparse and skeletal frame beneath it. The white mask stared blankly out from the folds of the sodden hood, looking, if possible, more displeased than ever before.

But it's not the mask that's angry, thought Stanley as he felt the now familiar block of ice drop into his stomach, *It's what's* behind *the mask … and it's very angry.*

The dripping apparition came forward, stepping through the wall of darkness as if it were not even there. Stanley and the others backed away, but the mask only looked at them briefly as its wearer walked past. The masked man didn't stop until he was standing in front of Chamberlain, seeming to tower over him like some dark, dripping monument.

"So, you've returned," said Chamberlain, trying to sound defiant as he regained his feet. "And did you find what you were looking for?"

Wordlessly, the masked man reached into his robes and brought forth the Memory Mirror. Chamberlain grinned lopsidedly.

"You wasted your time, sorcerer," he said with bitter triumph, "Even now I am about to unearth the treasure, which I found without any of your enchanter's tricks."

The masked man raised a gloved hand, and Chamberlain cowered back involuntarily. A brief murmur issued from the mask, and then the hand passed over the Memory Mirror's mystical glass. Almost instantly, a beam of pure white light shot out from the mirror and blazed off through the fog in a southerly direction. The beam lasted for only a few seconds before flickering out, but its point had been made.

"The treasure lies at the end of that beam," rumbled the masked man. He didn't sound angry, but Stanley knew that he was; angrier than he'd been in a long time.

"N ... no ..." said Chamberlain, his face ashen.

"This is the end for you, Ezekiel Chamberlain," said the masked man. "Your part in this treasure hunt is over." He held up a gloved hand and made a slashing motion across Chamberlain's chest. There was a loud crack as the Regent was thrown backwards, his body engulfed in what looked like black fire. He writhed on the ground and seemed to be screaming, but no sound left his mouth. The masked man clapped his hands together. The sound was like a crash of thunder; the knights seemed to know what it meant. They snapped to attention, then turned as one and began marching towards the boats.

"*Hey!*" shouted one of the sailors, "What about us?"

The masked man turned to the group of filthy sea-farers and said, "You all die here." A dozen knights ceased their march and drew their swords. The sailors froze for a second or two, and then, with a cry of outrage, charged the advancing knights, waving shovels and pickaxes above their heads.

"We gotta get outta here," said Uncle Jack, pounding futilely on the wall of darkness.

Stanley glanced over at Nell. She looked afraid, but suddenly her eyes widened, and she shrieked,

"*Stanley, look out!*"

But it was too late. Before he knew what was happening, Stanley was yanked off his feet and dragged across the mossy ground.

"*Stanley!*" cried Alabaster, racing after his friend.

Stanley was lifted off the ground, and hung there, suspended in mid-air, staring into the deep, dark eye holes of the white mask.

"You will come with me," the masked man rumbled.

Stanley struggled feebly, but it was no use. Looking down at himself, he saw that he was surrounded by a black mist, which had obviously been conjured up by the masked man.

Suddenly, a mad cackling laugh rang out, causing everyone present to pause and look back towards the dig site. Chamberlain was standing there, his impeccable uniform hanging from his spindly frame in scorched tatters. His body didn't appear to have been burnt by the sorcerous black flame, but something ghastly had happened all the same. The Regent's skin had gone grey, and it looked as if he lost a great deal of weight. He had been reduced to little more than a skeleton with skin. An ice-blue eye bulged in its socket as another bout of insane laughter came forth from his wasted throat.

"IT ENDS HERE!" he shrieked, and then he struck a match, holding the tiny point of light above his ghoulish head.

"Neptune's beard!" breathed Uncle Jack.

"Oh no, no, no, no …" moaned Nell.

"FOR RHEDLAND!" shrieked Chamberlain.

And the match fell from his corpse's hand.

Everything froze. Only the match seemed to move, and its motion was slow indeed as it fell. Some faces were lit with anticipation as the tiny flame touched the ground and ignited the trail of powder. Others were lit with horror. Time itself seemed to pause and watch as the spark flickered and crackled its way towards the pile of explosives. It disappeared among the boxes, and then …

And then time went back to work.

KA-BOOM

The explosion was louder than loud, and the fireball that rose up blasted huge chunks of rock high into the air.

But it's not rock, Stanley thought to himself as he squinted from the brightness of the blast, *it's pieces of shell.*

The explosion picked up Chamberlain's wasted frame and tossed him into the crowd of sailors, who backed away with involuntary disgust. The island (*but it's not an island, it's a Titanodon*) gave its greatest lurch yet, and from somewhere deep below them, but not so far off, came a great, shuddering groan; the groan of a wounded animal. The ground shook back and forth almost rhythmically, and the sea churned and foamed.

Sailors were crying out in dismay. Nell and Alabaster were clinging to Uncle Jack, who was barely able to keep his feet as the ground rolled and shook. Knights and men were falling over one another, tumbling down the slope, only to be stopped by the impassable wall of darkness.

Throughout all this, the masked man stood there serenely, watching the pandemonium with what could only be mild interest. Stanley, still suspended in mid air, gaped at something huge rising from the ocean near the boats. A deluge of sea water cascaded off the thing, and there was no debating what it was.

It was a flipper; a colossal flipper, twice as long as the Maelstrom, and bearing every resemblance to that of a common sea turtle. The flipper came down with a tremendous splash, and the sea rose up and engulfed most of the boats as the massive Titanodon rocked on its side.

"BRING DOWN THIS WALL!" Uncle Jack yelled at the masked man, as the gigantic flipper rose once again into the air. The mournful bellow of the great turtle-fish rang out again, and the masked man peered blankly at Uncle Jack.

"I have no further use for you, pirate," came the dark, rumbling voice. "It pleases me to leave you here in the care of the Titanodon." He unfurled his great black wings, preparing to take flight, with Stanley in tow.

"*Oh no you don't!*" shouted Alabaster. He let go of Uncle Jack and charged the masked man, but he needn't have bothered.

With a squeal of protesting metal, Grey broke free of the no-longer-magical chain and dove upon the masked man. Stanley dropped to the ground, the spell broken as the sorcerer's concentration faltered.

"Stanley!" cried Alabaster, leaping at his friend and helping him to his feet. Nell was at their side an instant later.

"The wall's down!" she said breathlessly. "We have to go!"

"*C'mon, lads n' lassie!*" shouted Uncle Jack, as the ground gave a stomach-turning upward heave. "*We gotta move!*"

"Go, go, go!" cried Alabaster as they raced towards Uncle Jack, somehow enjoying himself, even in this hour most dire.

"Wait!" said Stanley, pulling back from his friends.

"What's the matter?" said Nell, her voice almost breaking with terror.

But Stanley didn't answer. He ran as best he could back across the heaving, shaking ground, until he was less than a dozen feet from Grey and the masked man.

They were fighting, raining blows upon eachother, rolling on the ground like animals. Grey's mouth was open, and he was snarling and slathering as the masked man tried in vain to fight him off. The two then locked together, hands around eachother's throats. A strange black mist began to encircle them, almost hiding them from view.

"*Grey!*" Stanley cried as the ground heaved upwards, threatening to send him flying.

Grey looked up, his eyes blazing. "*Go!*" he rasped.

"*Come on!*" said Stanley, "*We have to get out of here!*"

"GO!" Grey repeated. "I'LL KEEP HIM BUSY!"

"*You have to come, too!*"

"NO! I CAN'T! GET OUT OF HERE!"

"*But you'll die!*"

"IF YOU DON'T GO, YOU'LL DIE, TOO! GET OUT OF HERE!"

Horrible noises were coming from the masked man, noises that sounded like nightmares given voices.

"GET OUT OF HERE!" roared Grey, yellow fire now burning in his eyes.

"What do we do?" Alabaster asked frantically.

"We've got to go!" said Nell, trying to drag the two boys towards the boats.

"Let go of me!" said Stanley sharply, jerking his arm out of Nell's grasp. "We've got to help Grey!"

The ground pitched at an alarming angle, and suddenly Uncle Jack was there, with Benjamin Stone close behind. All around them, knights and sailors were milling about, tumbling over one another as they tried desperately to make it to the boats.

"YOU THREE, TO THE BOATS!" ordered Uncle Jack. "NOW!"

"NOT WITHOUT GREY!" shouted Stanley. Later, he would feel ashamed for yelling at his uncle, but right now, that didn't matter.

Uncle Jack frowned at the grappling forms of Grey and the masked man. "GREY!" he called.

"GET-THEM-OUT-OF-HERE!" Grey bellowed, as strange purple sparks began to emanate from his body and the masked man's.

"YOU SURE?" shouted Uncle Jack.

"VERY!"

"*C'mon!*" Uncle Jack said to the children, "*You heard 'im!*"

Stanley remained rooted to the spot, and Alabaster and Nell didn't want to leave him.

"Benjamin," said Uncle Jack, "get Nell an' Alabaster outta here!"

Quick as a flash, Benjamin swooped down and scooped up Nell and Alabaster, one under each arm, and bounded off down the slope towards the boats.

"Stanley," said Uncle Jack gravely, "it's time to go." When Stanley still refused to budge, the old man put a hand on his shoulder and said, "He knows what he's doin', lad. Let 'im be."

Stanley looked up at Uncle Jack with a pained expression on his face. The ground shook and pitched and heaved beneath his feet. It was amazing any of them were standing at all. He took one last look at Grey as he grappled with the masked man.

And then he ran.

He ran harder than he had ever run before, his feet hardly seeming to touch the ground. He ran past sailors, some of whom were running, some of whom were fighting with the knights, none of whom he saw. His eyes were full of tears, and it felt like his blood was on fire. He didn't know how long he ran, or how far, but before he knew it, he was standing in front of the Ogopogo, and he felt himself being whisked upwards. Opening his eyes, he found himself sitting on the main deck. The tiny ship was doing its best to sail away from the island that was not an island.

The island!

Stanley got to his feet and stood agape as the island heaved itself up out of the ocean. There, opening its mouth to emit an almost deafening roar, was the head of the vast turtle-fish. The Titanodon roared again, and raised its right flipper out of the water, bringing it down with a thunderous splash. The Maelstrom was unfortunate enough to find itself underneath the flipper as if came down. The ship was instantly pulverised.

Stanley watched all this with horrified detachment. He saw the sailors and knights still trapped on the beast's back. They raced here and there, looking very small now, and the island no longer looked like an island, as the turtle-fish dove beneath the surface, carrying more than a hundred men down with it, down into the briny deep, down to black, crushing oblivion.

CHAPTER TWENTY-FOUR:
SAINT ELMO'S FIRE

The last thing Stanley remembered before blacking out, was a mountain of water rushing towards the Ogopogo. When he opened his eyes, he was surprised to feel not the solid planks of the ship's deck beneath his head, but warm, white sand. He squinted in the bright sunlight and sat up, brushing sand from his hair and wondering where he was. A loud snort close beside him made him jump slightly, but he already knew what had made the noise. Alabaster was lying there on the sand, sleeping peacefully, and on his other side, also asleep, was Nell. Stanley peered around at their surroundings. They were on a small beach encircled by a great white cliff. Directly behind them, the cliff split into a wide pass which led to a jungle beyond. How had they arrived here? There was no sign of the Ogopogo, or, for that matter, of Uncle Jack, Benjamin, Pericles, Diego, or Grey.

An icicle stabbed at his heart as he remembered that Diego and Grey had been lost with the Titanodon, along with the masked man, Chamberlain, The Knights of the Silver Sword, and most, if not all of the Maelstrom's crew. Stanley sighed and hunched forward, hugging his knees as he stared morosely out to sea.

"Grey," he murmured to himself. To his left, Alabaster suddenly sat bolt upright and looked about with wide eyes. Noticing Stanley, his face lit up.

"Are we dead?" he asked brightly.

"Huh?" said Stanley, partially forgetting his glumness and smiling a little, "Uh, I don't think so."

"Hum," said Alabaster, getting up and brushing sand off himself. "I thought this might be Heaven." He peered behind him at the nearby jungle, then up at the clear blue sky. "The weather's nice enough!"

Stanley grinned, then stood up himself, and stretched, while Alabaster knelt down and poked Nell in the head.

"Mmf, oppit," she murmured as her eyes fluttered open. "Quit poking me!" She sat up and shook her head groggily, then looked around for a moment and said, "Where are we?"

Stanley shrugged.

"We might be in Heaven," Alabaster said bracingly, as if he expected Nell to suddenly burst into hysterics at the idea.

"Don't be silly," she said, clambering to her feet. "We're not dead."

"Really?" said Alabaster. "How do you know?"

"Do you think we'd look like *this* if we were dead?"

Nell had a point; the three of them definitely looked the worse for wear. Nell's chestnut hair, somewhat bleached by the sun, was out of its plait, and hung about her face in matted clumps. Alabaster had lost both his shoes, as had Stanley, and all three of them wore clothes that were filthy and stiff with salt.

Nell looked over at Stanley and said, "Are you okay, Stanley?"

"Huh?" said Stanley. "Yeah, I guess so."

And then, to his surprise, she came towards him, reached out with both hands, and pulled him into a warm embrace.

"I'm sorry about Grey," she said to his shoulder.

Stanley closed his eyes, ignoring the strands of Nell's hair that had gotten in his mouth. The hug felt good. It helped.

With a contented sigh, Alabaster draped his arms around the both of them, and the three children stood there together on the beach, while the waves lapped serenely at the shore.

Presently, there came a frantic fluttering sound from somewhere above, and Stanley looked up just in time to see a large green bird land clumsily on the sand. It was Pericles, of course, and he looked as if he'd been through a rough time. He had lost a good many feathers, and those that remained were sticking out at odd angles, making him look wild and unkempt.

"Pericles!" cried Alabaster, breaking out of the group hug and kneeling beside the dishevelled bird. "Are you okay?"

"Oh yes, thank you," gasped Pericles. "I'm just having a bit of trouble flying— lost some feathers, don't you know."

"What happened?" Nell asked. "How did we get here?"

"And where *is* here?" added Alabaster.

"And what about Uncle Jack?" said Stanley, "And Benjamin?"

"Half a moment!" squawked Pericles, "One question at a time! Jack and Benjamin are in perfect health. They sent me to look for you three whilst they went off to do some exploring. We are currently situated on a small island, Mr. Lancaster, which does not appear on any navigational charts. And to answer *your* question, Miss Hawthorne, when the Ogopogo was overtaken by the wave and our doom seemed assured, we were rescued at the last possible moment by ... er, this might be a bit difficult to accept, but—"

Pericles was suddenly interrupted as a familiar voice cried, "Ah, there y'are!"

Stanley looked up and was overjoyed to see Uncle Jack emerge from the nearby foliage, followed by a smiling Benjamin Stone.

"Uncle Jack!" cried Alabaster. "Benjamin! You're alright!"

"Well of *course* they're alright," said Pericles snippily, "I just finished telling you that they—"

"Well done, Pericles!" said Uncle Jack heartily, scooping up the parrot and placing him on his shoulder. "Despite major feather loss, yeh accomplished yer mission. I oughta promote ya to head scout officer!"

"I *am* head scout officer," said Pericles. "I'm the *only* scout officer!"

"Well then I hereby grant ya an extra ration o' crackers at suppertime," said Uncle Jack, a huge grin on his face.

"*Some* parrots would find that somewhat insulting," said Pericles.

"But not you, eh?" said Uncle Jack, tousling the parrot's head feathers.

"No, I find it *extremely* insulting. What's got you in such a good mood, pray tell?"

Uncle Jack grinned. "We found it."

"Found it?" echoed Pericles. "Found *what?* You don't mean ..."

"The treasure?" said Stanley, Nell and Alabaster in unison.

"Aye," said Uncle Jack serenely, "the treasure."

"Oh my, good show!" said Pericles, flapping his wings excitedly.

"Then this is it!" said Stanley, "This is your treasure island. This is the end."

He felt relief as he said these words, but also regret, and he didn't understand why.

"Almost, laddie," said Uncle Jack, "almost. C'mon, mates, time's a-wastin'!"

Uncle Jack led the way into the jungle, which turned out to be nothing but a small belt of forest less than thirty yards across. They emerged from the foliage on the other side, and found themselves on an ancient stone pathway, cracked and half-overrun with weeds. The path wound its way up a gentle slope, to a building of noteable elegance, despite its age and advanced state of disrepair.

The building was made of pearly-white stone, possibly marble. It was box-like, with a peaked roof, and seemed to be built right into the side of a rocky hill. The roof jutted out over the stone path, where it was supported by white pillars, forming a kind of porch, beyond which stood a solid rectangular door, five feet tall and three wide.

"Looks Greek," commented Alabaster, dipping into the archaeological knowledge bestowed upon him by his parents, and garnering him a rare look of surprise from Nell.

"Does, doesn't it?" said Uncle Jack thoughtfully. "Don't think it is, though. No Greeks 'round here, nor were there ever, far as I know."

"But there *might* have been," said Alabaster.

Stanley noticed two odd stones to the left and right of the door. In stark contrast with the pure, pearl-white stone that prevailed here, these two were jet-black, like onyx. They had been cut into tall, narrow forms with pointed tips, and strange symbols were carved vertically on their still-smooth surfaces. "Look," he said, pointing at the stones, "those look like that obelisk thing we saw sticking up out of the ocean, remember?"

"There *is* a rather striking resemblance," said Pericles.

"Did the people who made the obelisk make *this*, too?" asked Stanley, indicating the stone building.

"I'd say that's a safe bet, lad," said Uncle Jack. "An' what's more," he said, reaching into his coat pocket, "I think they made *this*, too." In his hand, Uncle Jack held the Memory Mirror. "It was beside me on the beach when I woke up," he said, contemplating the ancient artefact. "I thought I'd lost it when … ah …"

The small group was silent for a time, as each of them thought back to the most recent part of their adventure.

"Well, er, let's get to it, shall we?" said Uncle Jack, anxious to dispel any glum thoughts his crew might be entertaining. "C'mon," he said, and led the way right up to the big stone door. It looked very solid, and the old man knocked experimentally on the smooth surface. "Hmm," he said, scratching his head, "I wonder what we're supposed to—"

But he was interrupted by a loud, clear, toneful hum that seemed to come from the door itself. As if by magic, sixteen strange symbols appeared on the door and began to glow with a soft, silvery light. Uncle Jack consulted the Memory Mirror briefly, then approached the door and touched five of the symbols in sequence, as if they were buttons on a keypad. The door gave another musical hum, and with a sound of stone scraping on stone, sank down into the ground, revealing an opening which led into a dark tunnel.

Uncle Jack gave his crew a backward glance, his eyes a-twinkle, and started off into the tunnel, Pericles on his shoulder and Benjamin close behind.

"Wooo! This is it!" said Alabaster, almost shaking with excitement as he made for the door, tripping over a rock on the way.

Stanley was ready to go barrelling forward himself, when he looked around for Nell and saw her hanging back. She noticed him looking at her, and her face went pink.

"I'm not sure I'll be able to go in there," she said.

Stanley turned his head and peered into the dark tunnel. There was no telling how far underground it ran, but it didn't seem scary to him. Of course, he wasn't the one who suffered from claustrophobia.

"Maybe I'll just stay out here," said Nell. "You go ahead."

"But don't you want to see the treasure?" said Stanley. "We've come all this way, it'd be sort of weird not to …"

Nell sighed and stared at the ground, looking more than a little unhappy.

Anxious to cheer her up, Stanley said, "Er … it can't be half as long as the stairway back at Uncle Jack's place." He was relieved to see Nell considering this theory.

"You think so?" she said after a moment.

"Uh, probably … but even if it is, I'll stick with you so you don't … you know …"

"Freak out?" she offered, but she was smiling now.

"Yeah, freak out," he said with a short involuntary laugh.

Nell took a deep breath. "Okay," she said stoutly, "let's get it over with." She joined Stanley by the tunnel mouth, and the two of them went inside.

Half a dozen paces in, Stanley felt Nell's hand slip into his own and squeeze almost painfully. It gave him a funny feeling in his stomach, and for some reason he couldn't think of anything else, until suddenly he found himself standing in a large, brightly-lit chamber filled with

Gold.

Jewels.

Treasure.

The treasure.

Bright light shone from globes placed in brackets on the chamber's walls. The globes produced neither heat, nor fire, nor smoke as their light shone on a great mound of gold coins and colourful jewels. Stanley gawped at the vast richness of the hoard, dimly aware that his heart had begun to beat rapidly inside his ribcage. He stared in wonder at the gold, at the jewels, at the light glinting off suits of armour, at swords with huge gems set into their handles, at treasure chests, some of which were wide open, spilling their contents all over the floor, others of which were closed, their contents a mystery.

Uncle Jack was already there, of course, staring at the treasure pile with misty eyes. Pericles sat solemnly on his shoulder, and Alabaster and Benjamin stood to his left and right, patiently waiting to see what would happen next.

The mist swimming in Uncle Jack's eyes turned to tears which ran quietly down into his beard as he raised his hands to the ceiling, clenched them into fists, and cried, "WAAAAA-HOOOOO!", making everyone jump in surprise. "We've done it, mates!" he said happily, turning to face his crew. "This is it, the treasure, the BlackJack Bonanza! We found it! We found it ..." The old man put a hand over his eyes and cried quietly for a while.

Seeing his uncle cry made Stanley feel bad. Why was Uncle Jack crying now, at the end of the quest, which had turned out to be a success?

"Sorry, mates," said Uncle Jack, after a particularly loud sniff, "It's just a mite overwhelmin'. Seein' the treasure just reminds me of me old glory days, an' the other folks who were part o' me crew ... Bart, Jenny ... Albert, Sally ... so many others ... an' Diego. Diego shoulda been here to see the treasure again. We're the last o' the BlackJacks, mates, an' whether ya been part o' the crew fer years, like you, Pericles an' Benjamin, or if ya just joined up recently, like Alabaster, Nell an' Stanley ... well ... I wanna thank ya, an' salute ya as the true pirates that y'are."

He held his right hand over his heart, raised his head, and continued, "An' now, as tradition dictates, I salute the members o' the BlackJacks who didn't make it to the end o' this quest. I salute Diego Montigo, a good man who, unfortunately, made some bad choices. He saw the error of 'is ways in the end.

"I salute Mr. Grey." (Stanley felt Nell's hand tighten around his) "A strange fellow who was part o' the crew only briefly, but who more than proved his worth as a pirate. He laid down 'is life to save us, an' for that I salute 'im with the highest regard. It's me prayer that wherever our departed friends are now, they're happy." Uncle Jack finished his saluting, then turned back to the treasure. "Well, c'mon mates," he said after a moment of silence, "dive in an' look around!" And with that, he all but pounced upon the treasure.

"Alright!" said Alabaster.

Stanley and Nell raced towards the pile.

*   *   *   *

They spent a long time admiring the treasure, rooting through chests, digging through piles of coins, holding huge, fat jewels up so that the light shone through them. At first, Stanley wanted to fill his pockets with gold and jewels, but then Nell had taken him and Alabaster aside and explained that, since the treasure really belonged to Uncle Jack, Benjamin, and Pericles, it was only right that they should simply look for now. This made sense to Stanley, and he let the coins slip through his fingers where they fell back onto the pile with an enticing clink.

Even without the prospect of taking home a huge pile of treasure, Stanley found the examination of the hoard to be a fascinating experience. Aside from the gold and jewels, there were many other weird and wonderful things to see.

Alabaster found a sword made from what looked like blue crystal, and when he picked it up, it began to glow and hum softly. Stanley discovered a chest filled with colourful crystal orbs, each about the size of a grapefruit. He picked up a blue one and took a closer look. It appeared that there was something inside it, something which looked like a black mist. He held the ball right up to his nose, and almost dropped it when a pair of vividly red eyes appeared in the mist and stared at him insolently from the depths of the blue sphere. The black mist swirled about, and it seemed to Stanley that the thing in the sphere, whatever it was, was trying to communicate with him. He jumped as Pericles landed on his shoulder.

"You might want to leave those alone," said the parrot, sounding a bit uneasy.

"What are they?" asked Stanley, placing the blue orb back in the box and closing the lid.

"Prisons," replied Pericles. "They're one of the more … ah … unpleasant additions to the BlackJack Bonanza."

"I think there's something in that blue one," said Stanley.

"I think there's something in *all* of them," said Pericles.

Many of the treasure chests were locked, and from what Pericles told Stanley, it was better that they *stay* locked.

"We told you before that a great percentage of the treasure is not gold or jewels, but *weapons*," said the parrot. "We found them over the years and brought them here, where (it's to be hoped) no one would be able to get their hands on them."

"But what *kind* of weapons?" Stanley had asked, "Like guns and bombs?"

Pericles only shook his head and insisted that he did not want to know.

At length, Uncle Jack called for their attention. "Right mates," he said, but that was as for as he got, for he was interrupted by the sound of footsteps echoing hollowly down the tunnel. The footsteps grew louder, and it sounded as if an army were marching towards the treasure room, although there was something oddly insubstantial about the noise, almost as if it were coming from an old tape recorder.

Stanley stared at the tunnel entrance, wondering who could possibly have followed them all this way. There was only one person he could think of who could accomplish that feat.

Suddenly, every light in the room went out, leaving them in almost complete darkness. No one said anything, although Stanley could hear Nell breathing heavily as she fumbled blindly for his hand. He felt her fingers wrap around his, and he gave what he hoped was a reassuring squeeze.

The strange footsteps drew nearer, and Stanley noticed that the darkness into which they had been plunged was not complete. A pale blue light had sprung up from somewhere, and it grew brighter as the sound of footsteps drew nearer. With a sharp *fwoomp*, several jets of blue-white flame sprang up throughout the chamber, bathing everything in an eldritch glow. Stanley had a pretty good idea of what was going on.

"What is it?" Nell whispered in his ear.

"Saint Elmo's Fire," said Stanley. The flames were identical to those he had seen that first night aboard the Ogopogo. Uncle Jack had told him that the flames marked the territory of spirits.

The air grew cold, and the footsteps grew louder than ever, sounding as if whoever was making them had walked right into the treasure room, but there was nobody to be seen. The footsteps stopped, the flames grew brighter, and something began to materialise in the doorway.

It was a man, or seemed to be. He was tall and handsome, with dark hair and a goatee, but his features were strangely hazy and blurred, hiding his identity. He was dressed in a naval uniform much like Chamberlain's. He stood there with his hands clasped behind his back, and Stanley could see the hands, because the man was transparent. He glowed with the same blue light as the fires, and took a step forward as a score of other transparent men appeared behind him.

Stanley had heard his share of ghost stories, but he had never really believed any of them ... until *now*, for standing not twenty feet away from him was an entire group of transparent, glowing men. They were all dressed like men of the sea, some in naval uniforms, some with bandannas, eye patches, and peg legs. One of them even had a ghostly parrot on his shoulder.

"Back up now, mates," said Uncle Jack, getting in front of the children. He didn't sound worried, but he didn't sound happy, either. Stanley was glad to obey, though, and took a few steps back. Nell looped her arm through his and shivered, but she kept a brave face. Alabaster was staring at the ghosts with wide-eyed wonder, too much in awe to be afraid. Stanley felt his knees begin to shake, and hoped that Nell wouldn't notice.

Uncle Jack took a step towards the lead ghost and said, "Ahoy."

"Ahoy," replied the phantom, in a voice that sounded like it was coming from the bottom of a well.

"I am Jackson Warrington Lee," Uncle Jack stiffly.

"I know," said the ghost.

"Right," said Uncle Jack. "Yer the ones who rescued us, ain't yeh?"

The ghost nodded.

"So tell me," said Uncle Jack. "Who are yeh?"

"Step closer," said the ghost, "and know me better."

Stanley briefly considered telling Uncle Jack to get well away from the ghosts, but lost his chance as the old man did as the phantom asked.

"Do you know me?" asked the lead ghost as Uncle Jack peered intently at him.

"You ... are yeh ..." said Uncle Jack, and then he took a step back, as the ghost's features seemed to suddenly come into focus. "*Diego?*"

Stanley heard Nell gasp.

"Diego?" repeated Uncle Jack. "Is it ... really you?"

The ghost answered, "It is. Or at least, what's left of me. It's been a long time, Jack."

Uncle Jack stared. "But ... Diego, mate, yeh only just ... died ... a few hours ago ..."

"Hmm," said the ghost, "A few hours? It seems like much longer." He sounded sad. Slowly, he looked around at Stanley and the others, but he didn't seem to recognise anyone but Uncle Jack.

"But why are ya here?" asked Uncle Jack, "Why'd ya come back? What's keepin' yeh in this world?"

"I have unfinished business," said the ghost, "as do we all." He motioned towards the other phantom pirates. "We still walk the earth because there is much to be done. Dark times are ahead, my friend, and we who, in life, fought for the safety of this world, are bound to complete our duties, even in death."

Stanley noticed that Diego's way of speaking seemed to have changed slightly; it sounded more formal, and he didn't refer to Uncle Jack as 'amigo' anymore.

"But what duties could keep ya here after death?" said Uncle Jack. "Why do ya appear now, and here, of all places?"

"Dark times are ahead," repeated the ghost. "And we are here to help rectify our mistake."

"Mistake?" echoed Uncle Jack. "What—"

"We made a bad decision. This treasure is no longer safe, not even on this secluded island. We hid the treasure, instead of simply disposing of it, even though that action could have prevented trouble in the future."

"Aye, o' course we hid it. It's what pirates do!"

The ghost smiled. "I know. But we should have remembered that there is a law of piracy which states that no matter how well you hide your booty, somehow, someone will eventually find it. It's just a matter of time."

"An' that's why we're here," said Uncle Jack, "to save the treasure from those villains who—"

"You can't save the treasure," said the ghost. "No one can. It is dangerous, my friend, more dangerous than you, I, or anyone could have known. And because it can never be truly safe, it is necessary that this accursed hoard be placed beyond the reach of the darkness … if only for a while."

"But how?" said Uncle Jack. "What can I do to keep it safe?"

"You can do nothing," said the ghost. "You don't see it yet, but we are dealing with destiny, my friend, and no human can meddle with such a power."

"We hid it once," said Uncle Jack, "we can do it again."

The ghost shook his head. "The darkness grows strong. Its agents will find the treasure, just as they almost found it this time. Now, it is up to me and my brethren to deal with this matter."

"How?"

"I cannot explain. I can tell you, though, that we spirits are the only ones who can truly hide the treasure, and even then, it will not be for long. As for you my friend, you and your crew must leave this place at once."

Uncle Jack stared. "Leave? Now?"

The ghost nodded.

"But … no, I can't, I gotta take some o' this treasure with me … at least the stuff that ain't dangerous, I—"

"It all stays," said the ghost. "You may take those few items that you have already acquired, if you promise to keep them safe."

"Ya don't understand!" Uncle Jack persisted, "Let us take the gold, at least!"

"Our time is too short. Leave now, or stay forever. The choice is yours."

Uncle Jack looked back at his crew. The pale blue light of the spectral flames lit his face, revealing the pained look upon it. He didn't want to leave his treasure, not after coming so far and through so much to find it, especially on the orders of his best friend. The spirits, however, were not leaving him much choice.

"Choose," said the ghost of Diego Montigo.

Uncle Jack sighed. "C'mon, mates," he said. "I ain't ready to join this motley crew yet, an' neither are you. Let's move." He motioned for Stanley and the others to go on ahead of him. Stanley took a few steps towards the ghosts, then stopped. The ghost of Diego Montigo signalled for his phantom crew to move out of the way, and they silently obeyed, moving to either side of the tunnel mouth. Stanley, Nell, and Alabaster headed quickly for the exit. Stanley glanced up at the ghosts as he passed by. They looked back with sad expressions on their faces.

"You ain't the man ya once were," Uncle Jack said to Diego's ghost.

"That I am not," the ghost replied. "Farewell, my friend."

"Bye, Diego," Uncle Jack said shakily, and then he too made his way out into the tunnel.

They left the stone vault in silence, and the door closed behind them. The warm sun felt heavenly after being in the frigid presence of the ghosts.

"Ghosts!" said Pericles with exasperation, "As if krakens, sea serpents and armour fish weren't enough, we had to run into a crew of phantom pirates!"

Uncle Jack sighed. "I'll say this much—that was about the last ghost I'd expect to ever see."

"Was that really Diego?" said Alabaster.

Uncle Jack nodded. "Aye, 'twas him, no doubt about it … though a ghost is never quite the same as the person they were in life. Er, we'd best get goin'—I dunno what those spooks have in store for this place, but I don't wanna be here when it happens. Let's move."

They made their way through the small belt of forest and emerged on a beach, this one considerably larger than the one upon which Stanley, Nell, and Alabaster had awakened.

"Hey, look!" said Alabaster, pointing excitedly.

There, moored less than ten feet away from shore, was the familiar (if somewhat battered) form of the Ogopogo.

"The ghosts," said Stanley, "they were the ones who saved us, right?"

Uncle Jack nodded. "They did indeed."

"And they brought the Ogopogo here?"

Uncle Jack nodded again.

"That was sure nice of them," said Alabaster.

"It seems to me that we owe a great deal to the spirits," Pericles said solemnly. "One might say that the treasure was a fair exchange for our lives."

Uncle Jack pursed his lips. "C'mon," he said tersely, "everyone on board. Let's get outta here."

✳   ✳   ✳   ✳

They all clambered up the Ogopogo's rope ladder, and soon the sturdy little ship had pulled away from the island. Stanley wanted to know what would happen to the tiny land mass, and Pericles suggested that they stay and watch from a safe distance. Soon after, a mighty earthquake gripped the island, and blue lighting lanced down out of the clear afternoon sky. The island sank slowly beneath the waves, leaving not a single trace. The Ogopogo now sat on a section of ocean just like any other. The churning sea calmed, and the tiny ship sped off towards the northeast.

✳   ✳   ✳   ✳

Not long after, Stanley, Alabaster, and Nell were back in what was left of the cabin. Stanley was relieved to discover that his luggage, as well as Alabaster's and Nell's, was still on board, although all three suitcases had received thorough soakings. He wondered briefly how the luggage had stayed in the cabin, but decided that if ghost pirates could save an entire ship, they could no doubt save a few suitcases, as well.

Nell spent some time assessing the damage to the cabin, and kept muttering to herself about measurements and where they were going to get enough extra wood for the repairs.

Alabaster was pleased to discover that his Monopoly game was still intact (he kept the money and cards in plastic bags, and the board had stood up well to the seawater), and after having hung all their clothes and bedding out to dry, the three children were just about to sit down to a game, when Uncle Jack knocked on the door.

"Ahoy, mates," he said pleasantly as he opened the door, "Everythin' alright? Er, considerin', I mean."

The children nodded, and confirmed that everything was, indeed, alright. Stanley had to make a conscious effort not to glance at the ragged hole in the cabin's starboard wall.

"Sufferin' scallops, that slimy serpent sure did a number on this poor vessel ol' mine," said Uncle Jack, marvelling at the damage to the room.

"Don't we know it!" Alabaster said heartily.

Uncle Jack looked at the children and sighed heavily. "Look, mates," he said, taking a seat on the floor, "I hope yer not too disappointed with the way this whole thing wound up."

"What do you mean?" said Nell.

Uncle Jack sighed again. "Well, when we were first startin' out, ya prob'ly had visions in yer heads, of cartin' home huge piles o' gold an' jewels. I know *I* did, even though, on some level, I guess I kinda suspected we might have to do somethin' like what we … what *they* did … get rid o' the treasure for good, I mean."

Stanley wasn't quite sure where Uncle Jack was going with this, but he kept quiet.

"Anyway, what I'm tryin' to say, is that I hope ya don't come away from this adventure feelin' that it was a waste o' time … y'know, 'cause we didn't get any treasure out of it."

"A waste of time?" said Alabaster, aghast. "No way! This was the best trip I've ever been on! Right, Stanley? Right, Nell?"

"It certainly was exciting," said Nell thoughtfully, "and a lot happened. There were some pretty scary parts, but … well, we got a free cruise!"

Uncle Jack laughed at that, and Alabaster said,

"Nice one, Nell, you actually made a joke!" to which she responded by punching him playfully on the arm.

Stanley didn't say anything at first, though, because he was thinking. He was thinking about that day that seemed so long ago, when he had first met Uncle Jack.

So much had happened since then and now.

He thought about the rush of the waves and the smell of the sea breeze.

He thought of the sun sparkling on the ocean, and the power of a storm at sea.

He thought of the beauty of the night sky with the three moons hanging there like jewels.

He thought of Port Silverburg, and Ethelia.

He thought of the kraken, the siren, of One-Eye, the armour fish, and the masked man, of the pirate ghosts, of Mr. and Mrs. Crane, and Diego, and Grey …

All the memories of this voyage ran through his mind, and some of it was scary, and some of it was sad, but there were also parts that were wonderful, and powerful, and beautiful, and he suddenly thought that in its own scary, sad, powerful, beautiful, wonderful way ...

The adventure, itself was the treasure.

And when Stanley said so, Uncle Jack's eyes filled up with tears and he hugged his great nephew in a warm and grandfatherly way, and Alabaster and Nell joined in, both finding themselves agreeing with Stanley one hundred percent.

"Yer right, laddie, yer absolutely right," said Uncle Jack, wiping his eyes moments later. "I ain't heard words so deep or so wise in a long time. How often we forget that gold an' jewels are nice to have, but adventure is the true pirate's treasure." He sighed a third time, this time with contentment. As he got up to leave, he snapped his fingers, saying, "Oh, I almost forgot ..." He rummaged in his coat pocket and drew forth a small rectangular wooden box. "I found these while I was pokin' around back in the treasure room, an' they made me think o' you three, so ... well, I'd like ya each to have one."

He opened the box, and the children each gave a small gasp of wonder. Inside were three stones, each formed into a perfect sphere. One was blue, one was green, one was red, and each glowed with a soft, soothing light.

"Moonstones," said Uncle Jack, smiling at their reactions. "Very rare, very valuable. No one knows for sure where they come from, but they always form in groups o' three ... one stone for each moon. These're the only ones I've ever seen outside a museum, an', well, I think they make a nice bit o' symbolism, meself!"

Eyes wide, the children reached out at the same time, each taking a different stone from the box. There was no discussion, no talk of who would have which stone.

Nell reached across Alabaster to pick up the red stone. Alabaster took the green stone from the centre. And Stanley took the blue stone.

They sat in silence, admiring the soft glow of the stones, almost entranced by their beauty. At length, Stanley tore his eyes away from the small, blue sphere in his hand, and looked at Uncle Jack, who had just given him one of the most precious pieces of his fabled hoard, the BlackJack Bonanza.

Uncle Jack was smiling. "I can give ya each a separate box to put 'em in," he said, putting the empty rectangular box back in his pocket.

"Thank you, Uncle Jack," said Stanley quietly.

"Thanks, Uncle Jack," said Alabaster breathlessly.

"Thank you, Mr. Lee," said Nell reverently.

"Yer welcome, all three," said the old man with a quiet smile. "Keep 'em safe, an' may ye remember this adventure whenever ye take time to admire 'em."

Stanley promised himself that he would.

CHAPTER TWENTY-FIVE:
HOLIDAY'S END

The journey home was completely uneventful, and that suited Stanley just fine.

"I'm impressed," Nell said to him after five full days of monotonous sailing. "You haven't once complained about being bored."

"Right now, being bored is just what I need," he answered, and went back to staring at the ocean.

Actually, Stanley wasn't bored the entire time. He had decided to make a record of their adventure, so that he would always remember every detail of his days as a pirate. He got some paper from Uncle Jack, and set to work chronicling the voyage from start to finish, with illustrations throughout. He devoted two full pages to Grey.

*   *   *   *

This final part of the voyage really did feel like a holiday, and like all holidays, it had to come to an end. On the morning of the tenth day of north-easterly travel, the Ogopogo sailed into a familiar archipelago. Uncle Jack turned the wheel sharply, and there, right in front of them, was a large cave opening onto a dark tunnel which led into the largest island in the area.

Alabaster, who had been standing at the forecastle with Stanley and Nell, rushed to the Ogopogo's stern. "Goodbye!" he called to the tiny islands, "Goodbye, Ocean! Goodbye!"

And then they were in the tunnel, the point of light that was the exit growing smaller and smaller behind them until it vanished completely. Benjamin lit the lamp, and soon a warm, golden glow appeared ahead: the glow of the hanging lanterns that lit Uncle Jack's underground harbour. The anchor fell with a splash, the gangplank was lowered, and soon Stanley, Alabaster, and Nell were following Uncle Jack, Benjamin, and Pericles up the winding stairway (Nell hadn't hesitated in entering the smallish tunnel, but she grasped Stanley's hand just the same), and then they were emerging from the secret passage beneath the staircase, blinking their eyes in the brightness of the grand entrance hall, with its paintings, statues, red carpet, chandelier, and stuffed armour fish head, which, to Stanley, just didn't seem so scary anymore.

"Well, we're back!" said Uncle Jack, as the secret door closed behind them. "Arr, mercy, would ya look at this mess!"

Not surprisingly, the condition of Uncle Jack's grand mansion had not improved since they had last seen it. The front doorway was now little more than a huge, ragged hole in the wall, with the great oak double doors lying before it among chunks of rubble and plaster. The door to the dining room had also been torn off its hinges, and the dining room itself was a catastrophe of smashed plates and splintered furniture, with another huge hole in the west wall.

"My word!" exclaimed Pericles, "I'd forgotten all about this unfortunate state of affairs—was this *all* the work of those horrid vandals?"

Stanley, too, had at some point during the adventure forgotten about the mysterious attack, which had been the reason for their hasty departure in the first place. It all seemed so long ago.

"I'd say that's a safe bet, Pericles," said Uncle Jack, ruefully surveying his ruined entrance hall. "C'mon," he said after a moment, "let's assess the damage, an' all that."

The mansion's main floor had certainly taken a beating: much of the furniture had been overturned, thrown about, smashed, or a combination of all three, and a good number of windows were broken. Several more holes had been made in the east wing, two of which were large enough for three people to walk through. It was as if something very large had crashed through the walls.

Despite the ground floor looking like a war zone, the rest of the mansion seemed untouched, and this lifted Uncle Jack's spirits considerably.

"Well," he said, as they all came clambering back over the rubble and into the entrance hall, "it ain't as bad as it coulda been. Looks like those scurvy dogs only decided to mess up the front part o' the house."

Pericles snorted. "It could certainly have been *better!*"

"Who were they, anyway?" said Stanley, recalling the dark giant and his minions, who had broken through the front doors and attacked the mansion.

"I still don't have a clue," said Uncle Jack, scratching his head. "I'll make some inquiries 'round town, I think ... see if anyone knows anything."

"Hey!" said Alabaster, sounding excited, "What if they come back?"

They all fell silent at the ominous question, but Nell, who had found something of interest among the rubble, piped up,

"I don't think they'll be back. Listen—" She held up a rumpled-looking piece of parchment, and read:

To Jackson Warrington Lee and crew, welcome back! Very sorry about the damage to your house. Rest assured that the ones responsible have been taken care of, and will not trouble you again.

—Signed, *a Friend*

"Er ... well, that's good to know," said Uncle Jack after a brief pause. He took the note from Nell and inspected it closely. "I wonder who wrote this?"

"A *friend*," said Alabaster patiently, pointing at the signature.

There came a frightened squeak, and everyone looked up to see a small boy peeking in through the ruined front doorway.

"Timmy!" said Uncle Jack (Stanley noted that his 'pirate accent' vanished instantly), "Good morning to you! What brings you up here?"

"Er," said Timmy, "just ... uh ... delivering your ... er ... uh ..."

"The morning newspaper!" said Uncle Jack, snatching the rolled-up paper from Timmy's hand, "Thank you very much. Say hello to Mr. Whipple for me."

"Uh," said Timmy, gawping at the wreckage. He stood there for a minute or so, and then seemed to come back to himself. He said 'uh' one more time, then jumped on his bike and sped down the hill into town.

Within twenty minutes, Uncle Jack's front yard was swarming with people. Everyone in Westport wanted to know exactly what had happened. Everyone was talking at once, and Uncle Jack stood there on the doorstep, patiently trying to answer questions. Stanley and the others stayed out of sight in the entrance hall.

"We heard such a ruckus last night!" said an elderly man without a hair on his head. "So much crashing and smashing!"

"And screaming!" said an old woman who was assuredly the bald man's wife. "There was the most horrible screaming, and it just went on and on!"

There were sounds of assent from the crowd, accompanied by several shouts of "*WHAT WAS IT?*"

"Where's constable Smith?" someone inquired. "Didn't anyone call him to come and check things out?"

"He *did* come and check things out," answered somebody else. "He was up here on the hill for no more than five minutes, when he came a-running back home like a dog with his tail between his legs!"

"What? What did he see?"

"Dunno—he locked himself in the bedroom and won't come out! His poor wife is still at home, trying to talk some sense into him. Whatever he saw, it gave him an awful fright!"

As if one cue, several more people shouted "*WHAT WAS IT?*"

A portly man came forward and said, "Jack, surely you must know what happened to your own house!"

"I *don't* know!" said Uncle Jack. "I was away last night, as I've told you three or four times now! Please, everyone, listen for a moment!" The crowd quieted down. "Friends, I don't know what happened here last night, but I have reason to believe that the situation has been resolved. So please, try not to worry! You can all go back home now!"

"We're not going anywhere!" said the portly man.

"Eh?" said Uncle Jack, "Why not?"

The portly man smiled a portly smile. "We've got to get this house of yours fixed up!"

*   *   *   *

"C'mon, folks!" said the portly man, who seemed to have appointed himself project foreman, "Let's get this mess cleaned up, and then we can start bringing in the lumber!"

"Boy, look at everybody helping out," said Alabaster. "At first I thought they were going to lynch Uncle Jack, but now they're all fixing his house!"

"Lynch him?" said Pericles, who was perched on Stanley's shoulder, "I should hope not. Jack is very well-liked around town. Although, truth be told, I didn't expect anything like this!"

"Er, sorry to change the subject," said Nell, as Pericles took off in search of Uncle Jack, "but am I the only one who's noticed this?"

"Noticed what?" said Stanley.

"Everyone's saying that the attack happened last night," said Nell.

"Yeah ... wait a minute—*last night?*"

"What about last night?" said Alabaster. "C'mon, tell me!"

"It's impossible!" said Nell. "We *left* the night of the attack. We've been gone for ... for weeks, maybe even a month!"

"A month!" said Stanley, jumping up suddenly, "My Mom and Dad were only supposed to be gone for two weeks!"

"So?" said Alabaster.

"They would have got here and found an empty house!" said Stanley, almost on the verge of panic. "They're probably wondering where we are! They would have seen the house trashed ... they've probably gone home by now! They probably think we're dead!"

Just then, Uncle Jack came back into the entrance hall with the morning newspaper in his hand. "No need to worry, mates," he said, a calm smile on his face. "Take a look at today's date."

Stanley did. "June the twenty-seventh," he read aloud. "Wait a minute—"

"The twenty-seventh?" said Nell, "But ... but we left on the twenty-sixth!"

"The twenty-sixth?" said Alabaster.

"Yes!" said Nell.

"So that means," said Stanley, "today is ... the day after we left? How is that possible?"

"It's not," said Nell, shaking her head.

"Take it easy there, mates," said Uncle Jack as he rolled up the paper. "Now, I don't know a lot about *time*, per se, but I've learned that it can be a funny thing ... especially when yer travelin' between worlds. I wouldn't worry about it too much if I were you." He winked, and left the room.

"Well, okay," said Stanley, "if it's the twenty-seventh, then I guess it's the twenty-seventh."

"Whether it makes sense or not," said Nell. "Ooh, it almost hurts to think about it!"

"So don't think about it!" said Alabaster. "*I'm* not thinking about anything!"

*   *   *   *

The repairs to Uncle Jack's house took just under six days, and by the end, it was almost hard to believe that a gang of mysterious ruffians had laid waste to the place less than a week before. Stanley and Alabaster stayed out of the way for the most part, but Nell dove right in, helping with the carpentry, and even showing some of the grownups a thing or two about electrical wiring.

"This young lady should go into business for herself!" said Mr. Plumber, the local carpenter.

"If she did, she'd probably put us *out* of business!" said Mr. Tailor, the electrician.

Nell pretended not to hear, but her face was beet red for at least an hour.

Finally, the repairs were finished, the furniture was replaced, and all was back to normal, as far as anyone could see. It was the last day of Stanley's and Alabaster's visit, and the members of the Ogopogo's crew were eating a late breakfast in the dining room.

"It certainly is good to see the dining room restored," observed Pericles.

"Aye, I'd have to agree," said Uncle Jack. "Quite nice to have the old place back in working order! ... Hmm, better finish up, mates, Stanley's folks'll be here soon."

After breakfast, the children packed up their bags and hauled them down to the entrance hall, awaiting the arrival of Stanley's parents.

"Well, all in all," Alabaster was saying, "I'd have to say that this was definitely the best holiday I've ever had."

"Really!" said Uncle Jack.

"Absolutely!" said Alabaster. "I've never been on such an awesome adventure! I want to tell my Mom and Dad all about it! 'Course, I think I'll leave out the more life-threatening parts."

"Uh ... maybe we should keep quiet about the whole thing," Nell suggested. "No one would believe us, anyway."

"Ah!" said Alabaster, "Then I can tell them anything I want!" to which Nell responded by rolling her eyes and sighing.

"Well," said Stanley, "I don't think it matters whether or not anyone believes us. Either way it'll make a great story!"

"Hey, yeah!" said Alabaster, "When we're all wrinkled old coots, we can tell it to our grand kids! All grandpas tell great stories to their grand kids! I can't wait!"

Uncle Jack grinned. "Seems that the pirate spirit is alive and well, wouldn't ye say, Pericles?"

"I was just thinking the same thing, captain," said the parrot.

Stanley jumped as a deep, rolling voice suddenly began to recite:

> *"If sailor tales and sailor tunes,*
> *Storm and adventure, heat and cold,*
> *If schooners, islands, and maroons,*

And Buccaneers and buried gold,
And all the old romance, retold,
Exactly in the ancient way,
Can please, as me they pleased of old,
The wiser youngsters of today:

So be it, and fall on! If not,
If studious youth no longer crave,
His ancient appetites forgot,
Kingston, or Ballantyne the brave,
Or Cooper of the wood and wave,
So be it also! And may I
And all my pirates share the grave
Where these and their creators lie."

Stanley, Nell, and Alabaster stared agape at the speaker, who was Mr. Benjamin Stone.

"Why Benjamin!" said Uncle Jack, clapping his hands, "That was lovely! Stevenson, isn't it? From *Treasure Island?*"

"The same," said Benjamin.

"Very appropriate, my friend, very appropriate, indeed!"

Benjamin grinned at Uncle Jack, then looked down at the children. "Stanley, Alabaster, Nell," he said, shaking each of their hands in turn, "I would just like to take a moment to say that it's been a pleasure."

"Th-thanks!" said Stanley.

"Yeah, thanks!" said Alabaster.

"The pleasure was ours," said Nell, elbowing them both.

"Y'know," said Uncle Jack, turning to the children, "Countin' today, I've heard Benjamin, here, speak three times in his entire career." He laughed. "But when he does say somethin', you can bet it's gonna be good!"

Benjamin beamed.

*　　　*　　　*　　　*

"So what are you going to be doing for the rest of the summer?" Nell asked of Stanley and Alabaster.

They were sitting on their suitcases at the foot of the stairs, awaiting the arrival of Stanley's parents, who were a tad overdue.

"Hanging around East Stodgerton, I guess," said Stanley.

"I'm staying over at Stanley's," said Alabaster. "Till my parents get back, anyway."

Nell looked a bit put out by this. She was going back to stay with her aunt and uncle at the Shark's Head Inn. "I wish I could come with you guys," she said, "but I guess I should really just stay ..."

"Well why don't you come visit?" said Alabaster.

"Yeah, maybe I will," said Nell, her face lighting up.

"And when you move to East Stodgerton, we can hang out all the time!" said Stanley, and Nell smiled even wider.

Pericles suddenly fluttered to the floor in front of them, cleared his throat, and said, "Stanley, Alabaster, Prunella, I would just like to take this opportunity to articulate what an honour and a pleasure it was to—"

DING-DONG

"Oops, that'll be them," said Uncle Jack, limping towards the big double doors. He had replaced his trusty old wooden leg with his fancy new metal one.

"Oh, now really!" said Pericles, and then he said, very quickly, "It'sbeenan honourandIwishyoutheverybest,youarethreeofthetruestpiratesIhaveevermet." He took a deep breath and fluttered over to Uncle Jack, alighting on his shoulder.

"Rose! Robert!" cried Uncle Jack, as he opened the doors, "Come in, come in! So nice to see you again! We've been looking forward to your return!"

"Hello, Uncle Jack," said Mrs. Brambles, giving Uncle Jack a hug and a kiss.

"H'lo, Jack," said Mr. Brambles, shaking the old man's hand.

"Oh, Stanley!" squealed Mrs. Brambles, rushing forward and sweeping Stanley up in her arms. "Oh, how are you? We've missed you so much, my little Stanny!"

"Mmph, mmph," said Stanley, feeling his ears burning.

Mrs. Brambles transferred Stanley to Mr. Brambles, and proceeded to fuss over Alabaster.

"How are you?" said Mr. Brambles, hugging Stanley warmly. "Have a good time?"

"Oh yeah," said Stanley, catching a wink from Uncle Jack.

"And who's this?" said Mrs. Brambles, noticing Nell. "Are you a friend of Stanley's?"

"Yes ma'am," said Nell, "My name's Nell. I live here in Westport."

"How nice," said Mrs. Brambles. "I'm Rose, Stanley's mother. It's lovely to meet you, dear."

Nell smiled shyly and shook Mrs. Brambles's hand.

"Way to go, son!" said Mr. Brambles, elbowing Stanley obnoxiously.

"Well, Uncle Jack," said Mrs. Brambles, "Thank you so much for look after the boys."

"Yes indeed," said Mr. Brambles, "Thanks for putting up with them!"

"Not at all, not at all!" said Uncle Jack. "It was a pleasure having them, and they're welcome back any time."

"Even later on in the summer?" said Alabaster hopefully.

"Oops, sorry, Alabaster, *almost* any time," said Uncle Jack. "I'll actually be leaving on a trip tomorrow, with Benjamin Stone."

"Oh," said Mrs. Brambles. "What for?"

"Well," said Uncle Jack, "one of my boats is in rather bad shape, so I'll be taking it in for repairs, and staying with friends for a while."

"How nice," said Mrs. Brambles.

The children exchanged a knowing look.

"But I'll keep in touch," said Uncle Jack, leading his guests towards the big oak double doors.

"Well, have a lovely time," said Mrs. Brambles.

"Thanks!" said Uncle Jack.

They all went outside to where the Brambleses' car was waiting. Mr. Brambles loaded the boys' suitcases into the back, started the engine, and came back to say goodbye.

"Goodbye, Jack!" he said. "Goodbye, Benjamin!" And he patted Pericles on the head, saying, "Goodbye, Polly!"

"It's *Pericles*," said the parrot.

Mr. Brambles did a double-take.

"Awk," said Pericles.

"Goodbye, Uncle Jack," said Mrs. Brambles, "Goodbye, Benjamin! Goodbye!"

Stanley and Alabaster turned to Nell.

"Well," said Stanley, "I guess we'll see you later in East Stodgerton."

At which point Nell grabbed him by the shoulders and pulled him towards her. Before Stanley knew what was happening, Nell had kissed him on the cheek and hugged him, saying,

"Goodbye, Stanley."

She did the same for Alabaster, and told them both not to forget to write.

"We won't," said Stanley, a bit dazed. "Uh, forget to write, I mean."

Nell laughed, and watched them as they made their way towards Uncle Jack.

"Bye, Uncle Jack," said Alabaster, shaking the old man's hand. "Thanks for having us over—I'll say it again: this was the best holiday ever!"

"Alabaster, my friend!" said Uncle Jack, beaming. "It
: same without you."

"'re Pericles, 'bye Nell," said Alabaster, and he waited for
n door.

Stanley stood before Uncle Jack and tried to say goodbye, but the words
wouldn't come out. Instead, he reached out and hugged the old man as tears
escaped from his eyes.

"Oh, there, there," said Uncle Jack, hugging Stanley and patting him on the
back. "Don't worry, I'll still be here next time you want to come for a visit. I'm
only a car-ride away!"

He leant down and lowered his voice so only Stanley could hear. "There now,
laddie, don't be sad, we'll stay in touch, an' don't worry—we'll be seein'
eachother again. I can feel it in me bones. Yer a good lad, m'boy. Bless you."

Stanley drew back from his uncle. "Goodbye, Uncle Jack," he said quietly. "I
love you."

"I love ya, too, laddie," said Uncle Jack, his eyes twinkling. "Off ya go now."

Stanley headed over to the car, and before he got in, turned and waved. Uncle
Jack, Benjamin, and Nell waved back, and even Pericles raised a wing.

With a sigh, Stanley climbed into the car. The windows were rolled down,
and as the car began to pull away from the great house, Pericles suddenly burst
into song:

> *All we need is our friends*
> *Till we reach the world's end*
> *And the greatest of pirates we'll be*
> *Oh, the greatest of pirates we'll be!*

Stanley couldn't help but grin. He noticed that Alabaster couldn't help it,
either.

"Well," said Mrs. Brambles as the car descended the hill and began to wind its
way through the sleepy seaside town of Westport, "You boys seem to have had a
fine visit."

"We sure did," said Alabaster.

"The best," said Stanley.

"And you made a friend, too," continued Mrs. Brambles. "Nell certainly
seems nice."

"Er," said Stanley.

"Quite the parrot Uncle Jack has, eh?" said Mr. Brambles enthusiastically.
"Amazing birds, those parrots."

"And of course he's got it singing *pirate* songs," said Mrs. Brambles, shaking her head.

"Well, it certainly makes sense, considering—" Mr. Brambles paused as Mrs. Brambles shot him a withering look. "Er … considering the strong Maritime tradition that keeps such ancient works of music alive!"

Mrs. Brambles looked annoyed for a moment, then shoved Mr. Brambles playfully, as Stanley and Alabaster winked at eachother.

*   *   *   *

"Here we are," said Mr. Brambles as the car pulled into the driveway of the big red brick house on Bubbletree lane, "Home at last."

Stanley unbuckled his seatbelt and opened the car door, listening to Bruno's deep, booming barks from inside the house.

"Bruno will certainly be happy to see you," Mrs. Brambles told Stanley as she got out of the car. "We just picked him up at the kennel yesterday, and I think he was getting lonely."

"Well, my lads," said Mr. Brambles as he unloaded the car, "I'm afraid that after two weeks of fun and excitement at Uncle Jack's, home is going to seem terribly boring!"

"That's okay," said Stanley. "After a visit with Uncle Jack, a nice, quiet holiday sounds pretty good."

"Pretty great!" said Alabaster.

And they all went inside to have lunch.

THE END

978-0-595-43792-4
0-595-43792-3

Lightning Source UK Ltd.
Milton Keynes UK
UKOW042316200613

212588UK00001B/29/A